Praise for

LISA JACKSON

"When it comes to providing gritty and sexy stories, Ms. Jackson certainly knows how to deliver."
—*Romantic Times BOOKreviews* on *Unspoken*

"Provocative prose, an irresistible plot and finely crafted characters make up Jackson's latest contemporary sizzler."
—*Publishers Weekly* on *Wishes*

"Lisa Jackson takes my breath away."
—*New York Times* bestselling author Linda Lael Miller

COLD BLOODED

"*Cold Blooded* grabs you by the throat from page one and does not let you off the edge of your seat for a moment after that."
—*Romance At Its Best*

"Taking up where last year's phenomenal *Hot Blooded* left off, *Cold Blooded* is a tight, romantic, edge-of-your-seat thriller."
—*Romantic Times BOOKreviews*

"*Cold Blooded* is an exciting serial killer thriller...an entertaining tale."
—*BookBrowser*

"Crisp dialogue, a multilayered plot and a carefully measured pace build suspense in this chilling read that earns the WordWeaving Award for Excellence."
—*WordWeaving.com*

THE NIGHT BEFORE

"*The Night Before* is a page-turner that will have you racing toward the finish."

—*Reader to Reader*

"A typical thriller is a meander through a dust bowl compared to *The Night Before*'s tumult down a rocky mountainside."

—*Affaire de Coeur*

"Lisa Jackson sets her own standards [in] women's fiction today, weaving her magic and providing us with literary works of art."

—*The Road to Romance*

"An exciting romantic psychological suspense filled with plenty of twists."

—*Allreaders.com*

WHISPERS

"Author Lisa Jackson delivers a tour de force performance with this dynamic and complicated tale of love, greed and murder. This is Ms. Jackson at her very best."

—*Romantic Times BOOKreviews*

"What a story! This is a perfectly put together, complex story with more than one relationship and mystery going on...a perfect meld of past and present. I loved it!"

—*Rendezvous*

"Author Lisa Jackson has delivered another must-read romantic suspense novel."

—*Gothic Journal*

LISA JACKSON

SECRETS

HQN™

ISBN-13: 978-0-373-77282-7
ISBN-10: 0-373-77282-3

SECRETS

This edition published by arrangement with Harlequin Books S.A.

www.HQNBooks.com

Printed in U.S.A.

CONTENTS

Dear Reader,

Talk about a walk back in time! When Harlequin suggested repackaging *Pirate's Gold* and *Dark Side of the Moon* for a 2-in-1 novel, I was propelled to the early eighties when I first started writing. Actually, I think these two books were penned in the era of MTV, big hair and leg warmers! My two boys were preschoolers and I spent my days entertaining them and writing around naps, play dates and my exercise class. I wrote on an electric typewriter at the time with my sister, author Natalie Bishop (aka Nancy Bush), in her basement. It seems we drank a lot of diet cola, ate peanut M&Ms and wondered how in the world we were ever going to afford computers. (This was secondary to worry about how in the world we would ever run one if we got one.) I remember our first real book signing with two young up-and-coming authors who lived in Washington, Debbie Macomber and Linda Lael Miller, who have become great friends as well as incredible, famous authors.

It was an exciting time in my life, as my career was just starting. I remember plotting out *Pirate's Gold* and throwing a little mystery into the plot. In *Dark Side of the Moon,* my concern was to make the book a little broader in scope, as it was part of a new, more sophisticated line for Silhouette Books.

I think the books stand the test of time and hope you think so, too.

For more information on *Secrets* and my upcoming releases, please log on to www.lisajackson.com and see what's new.

Enjoy!

Lisa Jackson

PIRATE'S GOLD

CHAPTER ONE

REVENGE.

Just the sound of the word appealed to him. It hadn't always been so. Once Kyle Sterling had considered it a pointless waste of time and effort. But that seemed a lifetime ago, long before the accident, and now he savored the bittersweet flavor of revenge.

The antique clock on the hand-hewn mantel ticked off the endless seconds of the long afternoon. With each sweep of the second hand, Kyle vowed to get even with his ex-wife for the needless pain she had unwittingly inflicted upon his child. He sat at his desk and stared at the phone, as if by watching the black instrument he could make it ring. It didn't.

Impatiently he strode across the airy room. At the bar he paused and then poured himself a stiff shot of bourbon. One hand rubbed his neck to loosen the tension in his shoulder muscles as he paced restlessly before the wide bay window and the view of the serene Pacific Ocean. He frowned into his glass and absently swirled the amber liquid. Deep lines of worry surrounded his piercing gray eyes when he examined his life. He didn't like what he saw. For thirty-seven years he had been kidding himself, caught in the reckless struggle for success.

The last ten years had taught him much: the shallow

value of wealth, the folly of quick friendships and the brutal reality that a man had to stand alone, trust his own instincts and survey the rest of the world as the enemy. Kyle's thin lips twisted into a grim line of self-contempt that hardened the rugged angles of his famous features. Some people might call his ideology paranoid, or at the very least jaded. Kyle Sterling saw it as the simple truth, taught him by the mistress of deceit, his ex-wife, Rose Sterling. Or Sterling Rose, as she preferred to be known. Because of Rose, Kyle had learned a seething passion for revenge.

He seriously doubted that he would be foolish enough to trust a woman again, and he found that he really didn't give a damn one way or the other. The less he had to do with the opposite sex, the better. This whole wretched week had only reinforced his opinions, and he realized that his daughter was the only thing that really mattered to him.

He drained his drink, set the empty glass on the window ledge and loosened his tie. Though he expected a visitor later in the day, he didn't care that he looked as dog-tired as he felt. Ryan Woods was coming over later in the day to talk about business. Kyle had long awaited Ryan's report. He should have been anticipating the afternoon with relish, but he wasn't. No matter how he tried, Kyle couldn't take his mind off his child and his fear for her.

After contemplating another drink, Kyle rejected the idea and drummed his fingers restlessly on the polished surface of the cool window frame. His stormy gray gaze moved over the craggy cliffs on which his Spanish-style manor stood. He had to squint against the ever lowering sun. In the distance, brightly colored sailboats skimmed elegantly on the horizon, breaking the expanse of aquamarine sky and sea.

"Ring, damn you!" he muttered through clenched teeth as he glanced malevolently at the phone. Beads of sweat collected on the back of his neck, and his nerves were stretched to the breaking point. Yesterday's visit to the hospital and the gut-wrenching scene with his daughter still haunted him.

He remembered Holly's strained face, flushed and wet with hot tears. Her dark eyes were filled with anger, and her voice echoed down the hospital hallways when she screamed at him. "Go away. I hate you, Daddy...I don't want you here. I don't. Just go away and leave me alone, like you always have. I don't need you anymore!" The white bed sheet had been twisted in her fingers, and the nurses had had to subdue her. The last picture in his mind was of Holly holding her face in her hands and sobbing hysterically, her slim shoulders shaking from the ordeal. She looked young and pale in the sterile white room. At the doctor's request, Kyle had left the hospital, but Holly's words had continued to reverberate dully in his mind.

He raked his fingers through his coarse hair and glanced once again at the clock. How long could the operation take? Two hours? Four? It had been nearly five hours and still he had no idea as to her condition. All of his wealth couldn't buy him peace of mind or assure him that his daughter would ever be the same as she had been before the accident that had nearly taken her life six months ago. Holly had recovered, though slowly, and this last operation, a delicate one, was designed to repair her damaged uterus. Her life was no longer in jeopardy, but the center of her womanhood was.

Kyle considered calling the hospital again, but pushed the thought out of his mind. It had been less than an hour since his last call, when he had been politely but firmly told that Miss Sterling was still in surgery. Wasn't a father allowed any rights? Or had he given them up ten years ago when he and Rose were divorced?

The twinge of doubt he felt when he thought about Holly and the agony she had suffered at her mother's hand forced him to turn away from the window. He crossed the room, grabbed the opened bottle of bourbon and, despite his earlier abstention, splashed another drink into his glass. It was gone in one swallow.

Once again he tried to blame Rose for his daughter's hatred of him, but a nagging thought that he was partially at fault refused to leave. Even the pain that Holly was enduring, wasn't it in some indirect manner his fault? Though two parents were divorced, didn't a father have some responsibility to protect his child?

His thin patience snapped and he found that he couldn't wait another minute in the den. The appointment with Ryan Woods was still a couple of hours away and the damn phone refused to ring. Kyle felt as if the brushed plaster walls were closing in on him. He could feel a muscle working the corner of his jaw as he stalked down the tiled corridor toward the far end of the rambling hacienda.

His voice interrupted the stillness as he approached the kitchen. "Lydia?"

The elderly Mexican woman he employed was hard of hearing and didn't respond to his initial greeting. He entered the immense room filled with hanging brass pots and trailing vines. Lydia was working industriously on the countertop. The soft Mexican ballad she was humming was familiar to him; he remembered it from his childhood. She was kneading dough for home-baked bread. It was the same routine Kyle had witnessed for many of his thirty-seven years. "Lydia?"

The plump woman turned around to face him as she wiped the flour from her hands on her worn apron. A slow, warm smile spread over her round features. "I thought you were in the den."

He returned her grin with an uneasy imitation. "I was, but I couldn't stand it any longer." She nodded as if she understood him perfectly. "I'm going out for a while."

"But you haven't heard from the hospital?"

The corners of Kyle's mouth turned downward. "No."

"Are you going there?"

Kyle hesitated, but shook his head. "I don't think so. Ryan Woods will be here shortly."

The older woman didn't budge. "But certainly you can change your plans. Mr. Woods will understand; he has a family of his own. What is business when you have a daughter in the hospital?"

"Rose is there," Kyle responded, hoping to satisfy the kindly old woman.

Lydia's dark eyes snapped. "Humph!" She repinned her graying hair before making a quick sign of the cross over her ample bosom. "That woman is no mother," she muttered under her breath. "*You* should be with Miss Holly!"

"Apparently the divorce courts didn't think so, nor does Dr. Seivers."

Lydia turned her attention back to the dough and attacked it with a vengeance. "What does he know about families?" She continued to talk to herself in Spanish, and Kyle suspected that Rose was getting the verbal abuse she deserved.

"Holly doesn't want to see me."

"*That woman,* that Rose, she poisoned Miss Holly's mind against you!" Lydia waved her hands frantically in the air, dusting the room with white flour. "Miss Holly, she's too young to know what to think!" This time the stream of Spanish was too rapid for Kyle to understand at all.

The telephone shrilled and Lydia's voice quieted as Kyle reached for the receiver. Lydia watched his movements with worried brown eyes. She had cared for Holly as an infant and loved her still. Rose had never approved of Lydia, even though the Mexican woman had helped raise Kyle. Though Lydia had suffered the insult of being pushed aside once the divorce was final, she had never stopped caring for Kyle Sterling's only child.

Kyle's greeting was an impatient hello.

"Mr. Sterling? This is Dr. Seivers." The voice on the other end of the line sounded weary.

"How is my daughter?"

"She's fine. Came through the operation like a trouper. She's down in Recovery now."

Despite the optimistic words, Kyle detected a hint of hesitancy. "Then you were able to correct the problem?"

There was a slight pause. "That remains to be seen. I'll have to be honest with you, Mr. Sterling. Right now I'd give Holly a fifty-fifty chance of a full recovery.... You have to understand that her uterus was badly scarred from the accident. Though her fallopian tubes weren't damaged, the uterine wall was ruptured. It will take time to determine the success of the surgery."

"What happens if the operation doesn't work?"

"There is no reason to borrow trouble, Mr. Sterling."

"It's a simple question, Doctor."

There was an audible sigh as Dr. Seivers decided how much he could tell Holly's father. "We'll have to see," he replied evasively. "But if she doesn't heal properly and continues to hemorrhage, I'll probably advise additional surgery."

Kyle's hand clenched around the receiver until his knuckles whitened. "What kind of surgery?"

Dr. Seiver's response was patient but grim. "I would most likely recommend a hysterectomy."

The weight of the doctor's words settled on Kyle's shoulders like lead. His tone was emotionless, but his face was stern. "Dr. Seivers, my daughter is only fifteen."

"And lucky to be alive. Six months ago, she was fighting for her life. Today she's nearly recovered."

"But she's a child..."

"You asked me a hypothetical question—I answered. I'm only giving you my professional opinion. With any luck at all, we won't be faced with the possibility of another operation. Holly's very strong. A fighter. She's had to be for the last six months. There's a good chance that she'll be fine."

Kyle wasn't reassured. "I'd like to see her."

Once again there was a weighty pause in the conversation. "I think you might wait a few days, Mr. Sterling. It will be several hours before she's out of the recovery room and after that I'll keep her sedated. Any emotional outbursts or trauma at this time couldn't help her condition."

"She's my daughter, damn it!"

"And she's my patient. I saw her reaction to you yesterday. Are you willing to risk the chances of her recovery?"

"Of course not!"

"Then take my advice and give Holly some time to get well before she faces the emotional strain of seeing you again. Her mother is with her at the moment."

Kyle withheld the hot remark forming on his tongue. He had no choice but to listen to Dr. Seivers. He was the best gynecologist in California, perhaps the western

United States. Ben Seivers was calling the shots. "All right, Doctor. I trust that you'll keep me informed of Holly's condition. If there's any change, you'll call?"

"Of course."

"Thank you."

Kyle replaced the receiver slowly into the cradle. Lydia's warm brown eyes widened and her round face had paled. "Miss Holly?"

"She's going to be fine. The doctor assured me that she came through the operation with flying colors." Kyle was grateful that his voice sounded more convincing than he felt.

Lydia studied the strain on Kyle's face above his cheekbones. She knew him as well as anyone and couldn't be put off easily. "But you are still worried about her."

His face softened. "Yes." There was no reason to lie to Lydia. "The doctor thinks her chances for a full recovery are very good, but at this point, he can't be certain."

"Dios," Lydia whispered to herself.

"I'm going out for a while—just to walk around and clear my head. If Ryan gets here, show him into the den and fix him a drink, okay?"

Lydia nodded quickly. She was fingering the cross suspended from her neck and quietly praying for Kyle's child. When Kyle closed the door behind him, she began working the bread dough feverishly. It wasn't fair. Miss Holly's pain and suffering, all because *that woman* got drunk and lost control of the wheel. *"Dios."*

THE OCEAN ALWAYS HAD a way of calming him. Whenever the problems in L.A. became too much for him, he would drive down the coast to the old Spanish house overlooking the sea. On the uncrowded beach, with the endless miles of the Pacific stretching before him, Kyle Sterling always found a way to work out his problems. Today was an exception. No amount of walking against the salty breeze could quiet the voice of anger within him whenever he thought about Holly and the fact that Rose had nearly killed her. He grabbed a fistful of sand and tried to hurl it out to sea. The dusty granules spread in the wind and filtered back onto the beach.

He climbed the wooden stairs along the cliff and tried to turn his mind away from his child and back to the record company. Over the last few months he had grown careless as his concern for his daughter had overridden his interest in his business. For the first time in his life, he found it difficult to concentrate on record sales. For once, something was much more important than any business problem, and yet, he couldn't ignore the fact that things weren't going well for him businesswise. For several years record sales had been slumping and Sterling Recording Company had posted losses rather than earnings until recently. Just when things had appeared bleakest, the introduction of videotapes on cable television had boosted sales. Now the problem was the cost of producing quality video images. For the past couple of years Sterling Recording Company had used freelance artists and production companies for the video recordings, but the trend was toward in-house work. There would be more control if the videotapes were produced by Sterling Records and thereby several problems would be controlled: cost, quality and pirating, a phenomenon that had only recently come to light.

Right now, Kyle had no interest in his business, but he realized that he couldn't let his company crumble along with his personal life.

When he reached the top of the sea-weathered stairs, Kyle took one last searching look at the sea. Not finding an answer to his worries, he retreated into the house and noticed through the foyer window that Ryan Woods's car was parked near the garage. Kyle hurried to the den and forced a severe smile as he opened the door. "Sorry I'm late," he apologized as he entered the room. Ryan was seated in a high-backed chair near the desk.

"No problem." Ryan was a man of about thirty; slim, with receding black hair and a keen mind. He stood and accepted Kyle's handshake, noticing Kyle's uneasy smile. It was the same restless smile that had accompanied large deep-set brooding gray eyes and graced the jackets of several country albums ten years earlier. Kyle Sterling's music hadn't been hurt by the fact that the man was ruggedly handsome. Ryan Woods doubted that the platinum albums adorning the walls of the den would be there today if Kyle Sterling hadn't been so damnably earthy and sensual. Sterling's voice had been classified as mediocre and his ballads were too complex for most of his audience, but Kyle Sterling was a shrewd man who had used his striking looks to his advantage. He had turned his songs into money that he had invested in an ailing recording company. Within five years, Sterling Records had become one of the most prominent recording companies in the country.

Kyle poured himself a drink, offered Ryan another and took a seat near his guest. His eyes seemed haunted. Something was eating at Kyle Sterling and Ryan suspected that it was more than the pressures of running the company. He kept his suspicions to himself. If Kyle wanted to talk about his personal problems, the man would have to initiate the conversation himself. If not, so be it. Ryan Woods hadn't earned his reputation as a crackerjack troubleshooter by sticking his nose where it didn't belong….unless he was paid for it.

Kyle took an experimental sip of his drink, rested his head on the back of the chair and came straight to the point. "I assume that you've come here with some sort of proposal."

Woods inclined his balding head and nodded. "Finally."

"Good! I owe you for this one, Ryan. I just haven't had the time to put all the information together. This is a major decision."

"That's what you pay me for."

Kyle mutely agreed. "Let me guess what you found out: You think I should handle all the videos at the studio—produce them at Sterling Records."

Ryan shifted uneasily in the chair. He was seated near a large bay window and noticed that dusk was beginning to paint the sky in uneven streaks of magenta and carmine. The warm Pacific sun had settled behind the calm sea and only a few dark sailboats were silhouetted against the horizon. Outside, the view was spectacular. Inside, the wealth of Kyle Sterling surrounded him. It was evident in the thick weave of the imported carpet, the immaculate shine on the tiled floor, the expensive grain of the modern furniture and the original surreal paintings on the thick plaster walls. But with all his fortune, still Kyle Sterling seemed…disenchanted.

Ryan snapped open his briefcase after finishing his drink and declining another. He pulled out a sheaf of neatly typed papers and handed them to Sterling. "You're not going to like what I found," he warned.

"Let me be the judge of that. The way we've been handling production of videos has been a thorn in my side for the last two years. We need more control." He studied the pages thoughtfully. Ryan Woods had done his homework and proved in dollars and cents exactly why in-house production was imperative.

He leaned back in his chair and pushed the reports onto his desk. "All right, you've convinced me. We'll hire a crew, the best we can find, and give them a suite of offices on the third floor." He noticed the look of hesitancy in Ryan's eyes. "Is there a problem with that?"

Ryan shook his head. "Not really. I suppose it will make things easier—for everyone."

"What are you getting at?"

Ryan reluctantly handed Kyle one final report. "You asked me to check into the pirating problem we had a few months ago…"

"You're not telling me that it still exists?" Kyle asked, astounded. Had he neglected his business that badly?

"See for yourself." Ryan nodded toward the report.

Kyle's dark eyes scanned the black print and his frown deepened into a scowl of anger. His gaze was even when it was raised to meet the pale blue eyes of Ryan Woods. "You're certain of all this?" Kyle asked, skeptically running his fingers over the pages.

"I'd stake my reputation on it."

"You just have." Kyle rubbed his thumb over the edges of his straight white teeth and his eyes narrowed in thought. "Damn!" he cursed, mainly at himself.

"What is it?" Woods inquired. He'd known Kyle for eight years and had seen the dangerous look of anger in the recording company's executive more than once in the past.

"It's just hard to swallow, that's all. We've been dealing with Festival Productions for over three years. Everything we've gotten from them has been the best—top quality recordings." He shook his head as if trying to dislodge a wayward thought. "Why would Maren McClure try and rob me blind?"

"She only owns the company. It doesn't necessarily mean that she's involved. Anyway, the problem will be solved once you stop dealing with Festival, and as far as I can tell only three of the tapes have been copied and sold on the black market."

Lydia knocked on the door, refreshed the drinks and provided a tray of sandwiches. Kyle managed a quick smile for her and then turned his attention back to the problem at hand.

"All right, Ryan, so you think we should just ignore the problem and maybe it will just go away?"

Ryan smiled and set his partially eaten sandwich aside. "Unfortunately, it's not going to be that simple."

"That much I already know."

"Then you realize that you have some long-term contracts with Festival?"

Kyle tented his fingers under his chin and nodded. Ryan finished his sandwich, withdrew a cigar from his pocket and rolled it between his fingers. Thoughtfully he studied the tip of his cigar before lighting it and puffing a blue cloud of smoke that circled lazily to the raised ceiling. Theatrics were part of the game, the rules of which he had learned while studying law at Yale. "As I see it, you have several options."

Kyle raised his eyebrows, encouraging the other man to continue. "You can buy out the contracts and quit using Festival completely, or you can confront the owner with your suspicions and hope that she'll back out of the contracts because of fear of bad publicity and a possible lawsuit."

"Too easy."

"What do you mean?"

"I can't do either one."

"Why not?"

"First of all, I don't have the time. I've just signed several big names to Sterling Records, paid top money for them, and I can't take the chance that the video cuts of their top hits will be stolen or reprinted. I'd not only lose the artists, they'd sue me for every cent I've got based on any grounds their agents or their lawyers might dream up."

Ryan puffed on the cigar and shrugged. "So have the tapes produced by someone else until you get your crew together. There must be a hundred production companies that can make a four or five minute minifilm. Those videos aren't much more than advertisements for a song…easier, really. There's no dialogue involved."

Kyle downed the rest of his drink and his clear gray eyes looked suddenly stormy. "That's where you're wrong. The videotape of a current song is the single most important piece of artistry put together. In some cases it's more valuable than the recording. It sells the song. A good video can beef up a mediocre record, and unfortunately, the reverse is true. Even the most marketable hits don't make it without the right video packaging. It really is an art, and Festival Productions has an uncanny way of molding music to story and coming up with an incredible finished product. They're slick. Three years ago no one had even heard of Festival Productions. Today I've got rock stars *demanding* to work with that company, to the point that it's written into their contracts. I've had entire recording deals balanced in Festival's gifted hands."

Woods was skeptical. "What makes Festival so much better than the rest?"

"Haven't you been listening to a word I've said? It's their artistry, their interpretation of the song, their ability to give the audience a brilliant, unforgettable visual story to identify with the song."

"I can't believe they are *that* good."

Kyle nodded curtly. "Have you ever heard of the rock group Mirage?"

Ryan drew on his cigar and squinted. "Vaguely," he admitted in a stream of smoke. "I'm not up on all this new-wave nonsense."

Kyle waved off his ignorance with a quick rotation of his wrist. "It doesn't matter. The point is, two years ago, no one had heard of them, not in the U.S. They were just one in a thousand obscure English rock groups that had never caught on, not here. They released a single and it bombed. Never broke Billboard's top one hundred."

"So?"

"So the lead singer, a kid by the name of J. D. Price, was smart enough to figure that with all-day cable video music, videotapes would be the next growth phase for rock and roll. He took all the group's money, invested in an expensive video for that same song that bombed, released the tape and presto—" Kyle's fist pounded on the corner of the desk "—Mirage was an overnight success." He paused for dramatic effect, but Ryan could feel what was coming. "Do you want to take a guess at the name of the firm that produced that videotape?"

Woods smiled as he stubbed out his cigar. "All right, you've convinced me. Festival Productions can walk on water as far as hard rock is concerned. Now, let me convince you of something. Regardless of the pirating scheme, you're better off producing your own videos. If Festival is so talented, hire the talent away from this Maren McClure."

Kyle considered the idea. "If I can," he thought aloud. "From what I understand, she's the one with the talent." His lips pursed together. "It irritates the hell out of me to think that someone would steal those tapes. It just doesn't make any sense. Festival needs me as badly as I need it."

"People will stoop to almost anything for a quick buck. I shouldn't have to remind *you* of that." Ryan had intended to say more but quickly decided to hold his tongue. He hadn't meant for his remark to have been so personal and the look in Kyle's eyes was deadly. He tried to apologize. "Don't get me wrong."

Kyle ignored his friend's attempt at amends. They'd known each other far too long to take offense at careless remarks. Besides which, Ryan was right. Kyle had been burned before, and badly. Rose had capitalized on the publicity surrounding their divorce to pad her career. He didn't intend to make the same error twice. No one was going to profit from his mistakes! He had ignored his company, but he was determined to change that, right now. The slow smile that spread across his features didn't quite reach his eyes. "You're right, Ryan." He settled back into the chair and reached for a ham and cheese sandwich while watching his friend. "Why don't you tell me exactly how you think I should handle this situation."

Ryan was pleased. At least he'd gotten through to Kyle. He considered that a major accomplishment, because in the last few months, Kyle hadn't shown much concern for his business—probably because of his kid's accident. "I think you should buy this McClure woman out. If Festival's got the reputation you claim, you buy out the company lock, stock and barrel. Then clean house—find out if anyone there really is duplicating the tapes and get rid of him… or her."

"What if she doesn't want to sell?"

"Everyone has a price."

Kyle didn't seem convinced. "All right, I've told you all I know about Festival, why don't you tell me what you've dug up. If I know you, you've poked around a bit."

Ryan grinned uneasily and scanned his notes. "The most interesting thing is that Festival is run by a woman, but you already know that. Have you ever worked with her?"

Kyle nodded. He looked calm but vengeful. His expression made Ryan uncomfortable. "I've met her a few times...parties, social gatherings, but she's kept her distance. Most of the day-to-day office work is done between our secretaries."

"She's something novel in the recording industry—a woman making a go of it in a predominantly man's world." Kyle agreed with Ryan's assessment. When he'd met Maren, Kyle had been surprised by her cool dignity and grace. He's noticed that she was more than beautiful; she had a sophisticated manner that intrigued him. He'd been interested, but wary.

"There aren't many female executives in this business..." Kyle commented absently.

"From what I understand, Maren McClure is not just any woman. This lady is a mixture of beauty, brains and artistic talent. The kind that makes men like me very uncomfortable."

"Why?" Kyle asked sternly.

The question was unexpected. "Because she's different, I guess. She can't be pigeonholed."

Kyle's laughter held no mirth. "And that's how you like your women—stereotyped?"

"I didn't say I liked them that way, I said it made me feel more comfortable."

"And you think she might sell the company?"

"It's a good guess. She's always in need of money."

Kyle's eyes darkened. "How do you know that?"

"I talked with one of her employees. According to this guy, she runs that office on a shoestring."

"I wonder why?"

Ryan shrugged. "Who knows?"

"I guess I'll have to talk to Ms. McClure and see if she's interested…." A wicked smile of satisfaction stole silently over the features of Kyle Sterling's famous face. He didn't understand it, but the thought of meeting with Maren McClure was pleasant…very pleasant.

CHAPTER TWO

MAREN CLOSED HER EYES and removed the clasp restraining her hair. As it fell around her shoulders she pushed her fingers through the thick auburn curls, hoping to release the tension of the afternoon. Slowly she leaned her head against the padded back of the overstuffed couch that adorned her office. Out of habit she rewound the tape for the fifth time and tried to concentrate on the mood of the song. It was difficult. Though the tempo was a light reggae, the lyrics were downbeat, a real bluesy type of song; one of those country western crossovers that always seemed to give Maren fits.

The phone rang and interrupted her thoughts. She snapped off the tape player, walked across the room and leaned over the desk to answer the call from her secretary. "Yes?"

"Kyle Sterling is on line one. Can you take the call? He says it's important," Jan explained.

Maren's elegant black brows pinched together. "I always have time for the head of Sterling Records," Maren replied. "Thanks." She sat on the edge of the desk, removed her earring and pushed the flashing button on the phone. Using her most professional voice, she spoke. "Good afternoon, Mr. Sterling. This is Maren McClure. How can I help you?" If she was nervous, it wasn't audible in the even tone of her voice.

"I'd like to meet with you, Ms. McClure."

Maren frowned to herself. His request was out of the ordinary, and from what she knew about Mr. Sterling, he usually didn't do the legwork himself. He preferred the privacy he could well afford. The one time he had been in the office concerning one of his artists had been brief and to the point. From that one experience Maren realized that Kyle Sterling was a determined man who didn't waste his time. "Is there any particular reason or problem?" she asked, remembering the as yet unfulfilled contracts on several of Sterling's top artists. Maybe that was why he was calling. He wanted to cancel. Maren nervously tapped her fingers on the desk.

Kyle didn't hesitate. He knew that discretion was in his favor. "Nothing serious, Ms. McClure," he assured her. Maren's jaw tensed and the headache that had been threatening all afternoon began to pound in the back of her head. "When would be a convenient time for you? Sometime this afternoon?"

Maren quickly scanned her appointment book. It was filled for the rest of the week. "I'm sorry, Mr. Sterling. Today is impossible and I'm afraid the rest of the week is hectic as well. If you can give me a few minutes, I'll try to make some calls and rearrange my schedule so we could meet on Monday of next week." Kyle Sterling was one of the most important names in the recording industry and a valuable client to Festival Productions. Whatever it was he wanted to discuss, it was certain to be a matter of priority. The head of one of the fastest-rising recording companies in L.A. didn't call to pass the time of day.

"Are you free this evening?" he asked, taking Maren completely by surprise.

She didn't immediately respond. She dealt with pushy

people every day, and she didn't really like it. Kyle Sterling was definitely pushy—but he had to be, didn't he? One didn't rise to the heights he had reached by being Mr. Nice Guy. "I don't have any plans," she admitted.

"Then let's discuss business over dinner at Rinaldi's. I'll pick you up at the office...around seven. We can go to the restaurant from there." It almost sounded like a command and involuntarily Maren's lips tightened. She'd been in this business five years and still hadn't gotten used to the way big shots threw their weight around. Trying to ignore Sterling's demanding tone, she once again checked her calendar.

"Could you make it seven-thirty? I have a late appointment that might run over."

"Fine."

Maren didn't replace the receiver until she had heard the sound of Kyle Sterling ringing off. She reflected on the telephone conversation. It was strange. She'd been working with recording companies for nearly five years and she could count the number of times on a single hand that Kyle Sterling had called her for what sounded like an imperative meeting. Usually any business was concluded over the phone by one of his underlings. She wanted to think that her luck was finally changing, and that the reason for the call was an offer of exclusive business, but she couldn't. Instead she was overcome by a disturbing sense of restlessness.

What could he want? She gazed out the window, past the flowering cherry trees to the hazy Hollywood hills in the distance. The soft blue slopes rose quietly out of the suburbs of Los Angeles, seeming to guard the sprawling city.

Still sitting on the desk, she rang for her secretary. Jan's voice responded quickly. In the background Maren could hear the rapid clatter of typewriter keys as Jan didn't bother to break stride in her work. The woman was amazing.

"Could you bring in all of the unsigned contracts we have with Sterling Records?"

"In a flash," the pert secretary responded.

True to her word, Jan appeared in Maren's doorway within a few minutes' time. Her purse was slung over one of her slim shoulders and she was balancing a thick stack of papers in her hands. "You're sure you want all of these?" she asked dubiously as she placed the heavy pile of legal documents in the middle of Maren's desk.

Maren's blue eyes widened in amazement. "None of these have been signed?" she inquired as she shook her head and began to shuffle through the stack.

"None."

"But aren't some of these already on the production schedule?" She picked up one of the documents. "Here, this contract with Mirage, I'm sure I told Ted we'd be ready to shoot in a couple of weeks..." She spotted another contract. "And what about Joey Righteous? That kid wanted to get his tape out before he started his tour of Japan, which, I think, is slated for sometime in late June."

"And it's already April."

"Precisely! What the devil's been going on, Jan?"

"I wish I knew," the thin secretary admitted. "For the last two and a half weeks, I haven't been able to get any signed contracts *or* information out of Sterling Records. I've called Angie Douglass—she's in charge of the contract department—at least twice a day since last Friday, and I haven't been able to get a straight answer out of her." Jan dropped into a side chair near the desk as Maren studied the terms of a particular contract.

"Hasn't she given you a reason?"

Jan nodded her blond head. "Oh, sure she has. The usual. You know, 'Mr. Sterling is out of town for the week,' or, 'the artist is balking over a certain clause in the agreement,' or some other lame excuse." Jan's mouth turned into a disgusted grimace and she fished in her purse for a cigarette. She looked tired and drawn, probably from too much work.

Maren pursed her lips together as she thought. "Then I take it you don't believe that Ms. Douglass is telling you the truth?"

"Not all of it." Jan lit her cigarette, tilted her head back and blew a thin stream of smoke toward the ceiling. "She's always been very efficient, and now, out of the blue, she can't seem to get her act together."

"So, you've surmised that someone is deliberately telling her to stall."

Jan shrugged thoughtfully. "I really don't know. But something isn't kosher. I'd planned to let you know about it later today, after I'd given Angie one last chance."

"You should have told me about it earlier."

Jan smiled ruefully. "I didn't think you needed any more headaches."

Maren returned the smile. "On that count, I'd agree with you. But maybe I could have gotten to the bottom of this mess."

"Is that why Sterling called?"

"I wish I knew," Maren replied. "He didn't say why he wanted to see me, just that it was important. When I couldn't see him this afternoon, he insisted upon tonight. I guess I'll find out soon enough." Her light tone couldn't hide the worry in her eyes.

'So, you're having a hot date with the infamous Kyle

Sterling," Jan teased with a nervous smile and a twinkle in her dark eyes.

"More like being called on the carpet, I'd guess."

"You can handle him," Jan predicted as she stubbed out her cigarette and rose to leave.

"What makes you so sure?"

Jan pretended confusion and touched the tip of her finger to her forehead as she winked. "What is it they say? Something about the bigger they are, the harder they fall?"

"Yeah, something like that," Maren agreed with an uneasy laugh. Jan chuckled as she went back to the reception area and Maren continued to look over the contracts with Sterling Records. What was the hitch? Was Kyle Sterling considering pulling his account from Festival Productions?

Her stomach knotted as she thought about the last time she had seen Kyle Sterling. It had been her first and only glimpse into the personal side of the man. All other contact she had with him had been strictly business.

Nearly a year ago, feeling the pressures of social commitments for the sake of making a name for Festival Productions, Maren had accepted an invitation to a gala event celebrating Mitzi Danner's recently signed multirecord deal with Sterling Recording Company. In a much publicized event held at the attractive young singer's Beverly Hills address, Maren had quietly sipped her champagne and watched Kyle Sterling from a distance.

The man had style. Whether natural or acquired, genuine or fake, the man had style. Begrudgingly Maren noted that he always seemed to be the center of attention in a crowd of the Hollywood elite. He wasn't loud, quite the opposite. It was his understated manner, brooding gray eyes and flash of a rakish smile that made him stand out.

The festivities were held in the center courtyard surrounding an oval-shaped pool. The house was a rambling, two-storied nineteen twenties home built for a silent-screen star. It was as eccentric as the gaudy young singer who now occupied it.

Kyle had seemed at home beneath the colored Japanese lanterns that were strung from the fragrant lemon trees surrounding the pool, and yet, as Maren watched him, she noticed that there was something about him…a restlessness that added to his aloof charm. Through part of the celebration, he had somehow seemed detached, as if he would rather be anywhere else than in the throng of Hollywood faces who were milling around the oval pool. In the crowd of the most famous people in Hollywood, Kyle Sterling alone had held Maren's interest. She had tried to blame it on the fact that he was a powerful man in the recording industry, but she had the disturbing feeling that she was deceiving herself.

And now, at the memory of that warm summer night, Maren was apprehensive. She searched through the large stack of legal papers on the desk for some clue as to why Kyle Sterling wanted to see her. What was happening? Festival Productions needed Sterling Recording Company and, until earlier this afternoon, Maren had suspected the reverse to be true. If Sterling decided to pull his account, it would be difficult to keep Festival Productions operational. It was true that recording stars finally had discovered Festival and business was beginning to increase, but by the same token, the costs of expansion were staggering. On top of all the ordinary costs was the large outstanding debt to Jacob Green, the original owner of Festival. The escalating payments in the contract took an ever larger bite out of an already tight budget. All of which didn't begin to touch Maren's personal expenses, which were monumental. But that was her fault, she reminded herself grimly. Her fault and her responsibility. Unfortunately there was no end in sight.

It would be no less than a disaster if Sterling Records decided to pull out. Maren couldn't let it happen. She'd worked too hard to make Festival Productions profitable, and she wouldn't let it slip. She couldn't. If not for herself, she had to at least think of Brandon. He was depending on her.

Quickly she pressed the intercom button on the phone. "Jan, could you please cancel all of my appointments for the rest of the afternoon? Reschedule them for later in the week."

"I'll give it a try.... What about Joey Righteous?"

Maren had to think swiftly. Joey was hot on the charts and a real pain in the neck. "Reschedule him for sometime...make that *any*time tomorrow and explain that I'm working with Mr. Sterling on Joey's latest solo album... what's the name?" Maren quickly retrieved Joey's contract from the stack. "Here it is...*Restless and Righteous,* can you believe that? Anyway, that should put him off for a while."

"Put him off or tick him off?"

"Probably both." Jan had a good point, but Maren persisted. "I know you can do it, Jan. You have a way of pouring oil on troubled waters."

"And you have a way of conning me into anything."

"You love it."

"Sure. Sure I do," Jan replied sarcastically. "Okay, I'll give it a try, but if Mr. Righteous comes blasting in here with one of his usual tirades, don't blame me."

"Consider yourself absolved."

Maren picked up the intricate pages of legal work,

carried them over to the couch and flopped down in her favorite spot on the couch. She put on her reading glasses to survey the top document, which was a contract for five songs from the soon-to-be-released Mirage album. Maren began to pore over the complicated legal contract, hoping for just a glimmer as to why Kyle Sterling wasn't satisfied. Intuition told her he wanted something more from her, but she didn't understand what it was. Why had he been so insistent about meeting with her tonight? It didn't make any sense.

JAN HAD LONG SINCE LEFT the office and Maren was finishing reading the final contract. Other than a few typographical flaws, she found nothing out of the ordinary in the documents. The small ache in the back of her head had magnified as the hours had passed and there was still no answer to the puzzling question regarding Sterling Records.

She pulled herself out of the cramped position on the couch and stretched, letting her fingers work out the tension in her shoulders. She rotated her head as she opened her eyes and stared out the window that overlooked the parking lot. From her position on the second floor she could see that the long shadows against the concrete promised an early dusk. A slight breeze moved through the palm trees near the entrance of the building and a brilliant orange sun slipped lower on the horizon.

Though it was only a few minutes after seven, a sporty silver Mercedes rolled to a stop near the building. Maren's fingers stopped massaging her shoulders as she watched the owner of the car with unguarded interest. When he stretched out of the car, Maren's throat constricted with the recognition of Kyle Sterling. As president of Sterling Records, he held all of the cards concerning the fate of

Festival Productions in his hands. That wasn't true, she argued with herself. Festival relied on Sterling Records, but surely it wouldn't crumble if the contracts weren't signed. Or was she kidding herself?

Apparently Mr. Sterling had ignored her request to change the time of the meeting. Though he had agreed to a time of seven-thirty, he was nearly a half hour early. Convenient, she thought sarcastically to herself as a slow burn crept steadily up her neck.

He didn't bother to lock his car, but Maren wasn't surprised. What had come as somewhat of a shock to her was that he drove at all. She'd expected a man of such celebrated reputation as Mr. Sterling only to suffer the indignities and snarls of L.A. traffic behind the protective tinted glass of a chauffeured limousine. So the infamous Kyle Sterling was human after all. But she'd guessed that much, hadn't she, at the party in Beverly Hills. The woman in her had intuitively known about his nature as a man.

Kyle strode toward the building as if he were a man with a mission. He was taller than Maren remembered. Though his shoulders were broad, his torso was lean, and he moved with the purpose and grace of a hunter stalking his prey. His dress was sophisticated, but casual: tan corduroy slacks, an ivory sweater and a brown tweed jacket. The tabs of a pale blue collar showed against the neckline of his sweater, but there was no evidence of a tie.

For some strange reason she couldn't completely understand, Maren smiled. It was comforting to think that Kyle Sterling rebelled against the formal convention of a tight silk tie knotted at his throat. It made him seem more real—less of a legend. As he approached the building he made no effort to straighten his jacket or comb his slightly unruly dark hair. It was as if he really didn't care much about his appearance.

When he passed out of view, Maren hurriedly ran her fingers through her hair, put her glasses in her purse and snapped the contracts into her briefcase. She heard the sound of his footsteps on the stairs. Was that how he kept himself slim—by avoiding elevators? The door to her office opened after a brief knock. She had just tossed her jacket over her arm.

It was when she lifted her eyes to meet the uncompromising gaze of Kyle Sterling that the full impact of the man and what he represented hit her. From a distance his eyes had been interesting, a bold gray set deep into his head and guarded by thick black lashes and brooding ebony brows. Within the proximity of the small room, they were more than commanding or masculine, they held a controlled power that threatened to become unleashed at the slightest provocation.

"Mr. Sterling," Maren managed to say, meeting his severe gaze squarely and ignoring the challenge in his eyes. "You're early."

His gaze swept the room. "And you're alone…Miss…excuse me, *Ms.* McClure. Sometimes I forget that we live in liberated times."

"Intentionally?"

The hint of a smile tugged at the corners of his mouth. "If it serves my purpose," he admitted.

Maren inclined her head and smiled stiffly. She extended her hand. "Please call me Maren. It makes things simpler." Her smile softened and seemed sincere. It allowed Kyle the tantalizing glimpse of straight white teeth and a small dimple. For an uncertain moment he had the feeling that hers was the most honest smile he had ever seen. Her handshake was firm, her fingers warm. He released her palm reluctantly.

She was more beautiful than he had remembered. He'd met her twice. There had been once in this office for only a few minutes and he'd noticed that she was good-looking. He hadn't really thought much about it because he met many good-looking women on a daily basis. But there had been the party at Mitzi Danner's. He'd sensed at that time that she had been staring at him, but by the time he'd had the opportunity to confront her, she was gone. He had never pursued her, knowing instinctively that it could prove dangerous.

But now, as he stared into Maren's mysterious blue eyes, he could imagine himself drowning in their intense indigo depths. The blue color was cool, but Kyle suspected it warmed easily for the right man. Delicate black brows and a slightly upturned nose gave her an innocent look that contrasted suggestively with her elegantly sculpted cheekbones and full lips. Maren McClure was an enigma…a provocative enigma.

Kyle shifted his weight and pushed his hands deeply into his pockets, never once releasing her from the power of his gaze. "I thought you had a late appointment."

"I did. I managed to cancel." Once again he was rewarded with the trace of a smile.

"Even though you thought I'd be here later?" he asked skeptically.

"I wanted to be prepared."

"For what?"

A fire sparked in her icy blue eyes. "For whatever it is you think is so important."

His brows rose slightly. "And are you?"

Was it her imagination, or was he toying with her? "I hope so, Mr. Sterling."

"Kyle," he interjected.

"Kyle." The word seemed to stick in her throat, but she

managed to ignore the familiarity his first name engendered. "I assume you want to talk to me about the unsigned contracts between Festival Productions and your firm."

His jaw tightened and he walked across the room. After a quick glance out the window, he balanced his weight on the ledge, supporting himself with his hands, his long legs extended on the floor. He seemed entirely at ease, as if he owned the place, and yet he avoided her question. "That's part of the reason I'm here," he finally allowed. "We should clear up a few of the problems with the contracts."

"I wasn't aware there were any."

"No?" He was dubious; mocking. It made Maren uneasy, but she contained her case of nerves under a thin, tight smile.

"No." She crossed her arms under her chest. "You keep hinting that we have a problem. Let's quit beating around the bush. What exactly is wrong? I read all of the contracts this afternoon and they seem in perfect order. Is there any particular clause to which you object?"

"Several. We'll discuss them later."

"Along with the other part of the reason you're here," she pressed.

"Of course." His gaze dropped from her eyes and slid past the gentle slope of her shoulders to the swell of her breasts hidden annoyingly by the tie of her blouse. Abruptly his eyes returned to meet her gaze. "There's something more important to talk about."

"More important than the contracts?" she repeated, as a puzzled expression crossed her finely sculpted features. "Such as…?"

"For one thing, the relationship of Festival Productions with Sterling Records."

"Is it in jeopardy?" she asked calmly.

"Not really, but there are a few things I'd like to change."

"Major things, I take it."

His smile was sincere and there was a gleam of satisfaction in his eyes. "You don't miss much, do you?"

"I hope not."

"But you did have a bit of trouble here," he prodded, and for a strange reason Maren felt as if her back were against the wall.

"What do you mean?"

"A couple of our videos were duplicated and put on the black market."

This was a subject she had hoped to avoid. Kyle Sterling didn't seem to miss a trick. "That's true," she agreed hesitantly. "We had a dishonest employee—he's no longer with us."

He watched her intently. Was it his imagination, or was there just a trace of doubt in her clear eyes? He pushed himself away from the window and walked toward the door. "Are you ready?" he asked, positioning his body against the door in order to allow her to pass.

"As ready as I'll ever be," she whispered, picking up her briefcase and puzzling over his cryptic comments concerning the relationship between her company and his. Apprehension knotted her stomach. They walked down the stairs and out of the building into the emerging evening. In the dusky twilight, Maren slid a secretive glance in Kyle's direction.

His was a hard face. A face that had once been in the nation's eye. A face that had been posed perfectly onto the record jackets of more than a few albums. A face that represented the American dream: A poor boy from the back hills of the Blue Ridge Mountains makes good. Perhaps it was the shadowy twilight that made his features appear more rugged than they had earlier, or maybe it was the years of living on the road that made his face seem strained. Whatever the reason, Kyle Sterling was still an attractive man and despite the webbing of crow's-feet near his eyes or the hint of gray at his temples, he conveyed a raw masculinity that was lacking in most of the men Maren had met in her lifetime.

He opened the car door for her, but she paused before taking a seat. He stood on one side of the silver door, she the other. She met his gaze levelly, but her brow was furrowed, as if she were reading an unfathomable passage. "My curiosity has the better of me," she confided, noting his uplifted brows. "Just what is it that you want to change? It's not every day that the president of Sterling Records comes begging for my company."

"Maybe tonight will change all that," he replied cryptically.

"Oh?"

"We'll see. I've got a proposition for you, if you're interested."

"Is it related to that enigmatic statement in the office—you know, about the duplicating of the tapes?"

"Only slightly. That's not why I had to see you personally. The black market will always be there, no matter who Sterling Records does business with."

She slipped into the soft leather seat of the expensive car and waited while Kyle got into the Mercedes and maneuvered it speedily down the freeway. Though she worried over his mysterious remarks, she held her tongue, deciding it was better to bide her time and let the cryptic man sitting next to her make the next move. She was conscious of every movement he made as he drove.

Without looking in her direction, Kyle slipped a tape into the cassette recorder on the dash. The interior of the car was filled instantly with soft-rock music. "Do you like it?" he asked, referring, of course, to the driving beat and sultry lyrics of the song.

She concentrated for a moment, knitting her dark brows. "It's all right," she said a few moments later. The last thing she wanted to do was offend this man. She knew that he was playing some obscure game with her, but she wanted to understand the rules before she committed herself to what was apparently a test.

"Ever heard it before?" The question seemed innocent enough. Kyle's eyes never moved from the darkened freeway and the endless taillights of the cars speeding west through the sprawling city of Los Angeles.

Maren's nerves were stretched more tightly than piano strings. It had been a long day and she wasn't up to guessing games with a man who could very well decide her future. She tried to focus all of her attention on the recording. The beat was unfamiliar. "No."

She shook her thick copper-colored hair and cocked her head thoughtfully. The blend of voices and musical instruments was distinctive. "I don't think I've heard it, but the group sounds like Mirage."

"It is. The song is the title track from their next album."

Maren nodded noncommittally. It was the album for which Festival didn't have a signed contract. Was Kyle toying with her? Why? She sensed that he expected something more from her, but she didn't understand what. The entire situation added to her unease. She shifted uncomfortably in the seat and turned her attention to the view from the window of the car.

The city was alive. Motorists and pedestrians crowded

the concrete streets. Several popular restaurants sat on the edge of the boulevard and traffic snarled as cars attempted to squeeze into parking spaces.

The people were as diverse as the city itself. Maren smiled to herself as she saw punk rockers dressed in outrageous leather outfits walking next to couples conventionally attired in silk dresses and conservative business suits. Only in L.A., she thought. It was a city of glitter and serene beauty, home for the very rich or the incredibly poor, a city caught between the sea and the mountains in an incongruous collection of communities joined together in four hundred and sixty-five square miles. Where else could you drive from the Pacific Ocean to the Mojave Desert, or tour through Beverly Hills and Hollywood in the beautiful Santa Monica Mountains? Maren had lived in southern California all her life and had never grown tired of the warm climate or the ever-changing city of Los Angeles.

As they continued to travel west on Wilshire Boulevard, Maren eyed the bold skyscrapers of the business district of L.A. Lights from the man-made towers illuminated the night. Grand hotels built in the flourish and style of the twenties stood next to the more austerely constructed office buildings of the seventies.

Elegant palms swayed in the wind moving inland from the ocean. The air was clear and warm, adding to the feeling of electricity in the air. It was the kind of California evening that Maren had learned to love. If not for the tension within the confines of the car, she could envision herself enjoying this evening.

When the song ended, Kyle ejected the tape. The silence in the car became oppressive. His fingers rubbed over the smooth plastic surface of the cassette, as if he were rolling a weighty decision over in his mind. "Here," he finally stated. "This is your copy of the music." He placed the black rectangle in her hand. "Five of the thirteen cuts on the album are on that tape. We plan to release them as singles about every four to six weeks, depending on how they do on the charts. The first song is scheduled for the end of May."

"Next month?" she inquired, accepting the cassette and wondering why it felt so cold.

"That's right."

"Not much time," she thought aloud. "I don't know if we'll be able to produce a video that would be ready for release in six weeks."

"You'll have to," he retorted sharply.

"Then I guess you intend to sign the contract."

"Of course."

Maren pinched her lower lip between her teeth. Finally she shook her head and turned it toward him, in order that she could watch his reaction. "You're cutting it too close."

His voice softened. "I'm sure you can work it in," he suggested, knowing full well how dependent she was on his company's business.

Carefully turning the black cartridge over, Maren ran her fingers along the smooth plastic casing. It was as if the fragile relationship between Festival Productions and Sterling Recording Company rested between her palms. "Is there something significant about these songs?"

"Yes."

"I thought so."

Kyle turned off Wilshire and headed south on the Coast Highway. Night had deepened the color of the ocean to a purple hue and only a faint ribbon of magenta colored the horizon where the sun had settled into the serene waters of the Pacific. A few dark images of distant boats sailed on the quiet sea.

They traveled the rest of the distance in silence, each consumed with private thoughts and vague speculations of what the night would bring.

Rinaldi's was located in Manhattan Beach. The stucco two-storied building sat on the edge of the white sand and had an impressive view of the ocean. The walls were painted a soft apricot color, and a balcony off the second story was supported by columns of marble imported from a rock quarry near Naples.

A parking attendant opened the door for Maren. She got out of the car and dropped the cassette into her purse, knowing that Kyle's dark eyes missed nothing of her actions. He was scrutinizing her; watching her every movement.

Several minutes later they were seated at a private table on the balcony. The waiter had poured them each a glass of Cabernet Sauvignon before disappearing into the restaurant for their orders. One small candle stood in the center of the table, its flame flickering dangerously in the slight breeze.

Kyle took a sip of wine and set the glass on the table. He rested his elbows near his plate and supported his chin on his clasped hands. His eyes never left Maren's face. "First of all," he said quietly, "everything I'm about to tell you is very confidential and I expect you to keep it that way."

Her blue eyes didn't waver. The candlelight was trapped in their mystic depths. "Of course."

"I can't afford to take the chance that the competition might find out what we're doing because we're working on an entirely new concept." It sounded like a warning. His eyes had deepened to a threatening gray in the gathering dusk.

"I understand." She took a sip from the wine to clear her

throat. A warm breeze lifted her hair away from her face and the candlelight caught on the burnished strands. "What is this *new concept?*" She couldn't mask the interest in her voice.

He watched her carefully. "What we want from you is a thread of continuity in all of the cuts from that one album. For example, the first song, the one you just heard in the car, is about a young man who finds out that his live-in lover has been unfaithful and that she's leaving him for the other guy. All in all the lyrics are pretty basic, melancholy rock and roll."

Maren nodded. Nothing he had told her was out of the ordinary. Not yet. But apparently he thought he was offering her the opportunity of a lifetime. She could read it in his intense gaze.

"Okay. In the following song, this same man is out on the streets, looking for another woman. He's still alone, but instead of hoping his lover will see her mistake and come back to him, he's relieved that their affair is over."

"So much for love everlasting," Maren noted cuttingly.

The corners of Kyle's mouth quirked as if he might smile, but he seemed to think better of it. "The point is that I want to see some part of the original tape cut into the second and quite possibly the third. I want a visual image that carries through the entire five-song story. For example, the actress who plays the lover on the first tape should also appear in the following sequences. I don't care if she's just an elusive memory, or if he actually sees her again. I'll leave that part of it up to you. But I want the visual story to flow smoothly and be not only a story in itself, but also to contain a vital part of the five-chapter song."

"And the reason you're doing this is so that one side of a video disk will display a twenty-five-minute movie that you can sell."

Kyle smiled and the lines of his face seemed less harsh. "One reason," he agreed slowly. Ryan had tried to tell Kyle about Maren McClure's intelligence, and the man had been right. The lady was definitely not easy to pigeonhole. Kyle wondered why a man would even want to try and stereotype Maren. Her air of mystique intrigued him; her keen mind beckoned him...Maren broke into his dangerous thoughts.

"So you're looking for a record of something like a television miniseries."

"You could look at it that way," he acquiesced. The woman with the icy blue eyes and flaming hair was quick, there was no doubt about it. "The principal characters of the plot would, of course, be members of Mirage."

Maren held back the sigh in her throat. Teaching rock stars to act was one of the largest stumbling blocks in the making of videotapes. The musicians were great when called upon to lip-synch the words to a studio recording while playing their instruments, but when called upon to act, very few could perform without a considerable amount of coaching. Fortunately J. D. Price, the lead singer for Mirage, was handsome and had some acting experience—two big plusses. It made Maren's job considerably easier.

"So you expect me to outline all of the action on storyboards for all five cuts and have the first tape ready to be released by the end of May?" Kyle nodded as the tuxedoed waiter brought steaming platters of Italian scampi to the table. After refilling their glasses, the waiter once again left them alone on the balcony. Maren thought about the work ahead of her, should she accept Kyle's offer. " That's a tall order."

"I'd pay you for your trouble."

She considered his proposal as she ate the tangy

seafood. Though the meal was excellently prepared, Maren had little appetite. She remembered the cassette in her purse. It represented a fortune, and she needed money badly. It was a tempting offer, one that she hated to turn down. Though she tried desperately to mentally allot the time needed for the project into her schedule, it was impossible. The next six weeks were already crammed with appointments and deadlines.

All the while she was lost in thought, Kyle watched her. He witnessed the silent play of emotions clouding the elegant lines of her face. Something was bothering her, he was sure of it. But *what?* He hadn't even broached the subject of buying out Festival Productions, and he was sure that she was being honest when she stated that the pirating of videotapes was a problem that no longer existed.

Shadowy light from the candle played upon her hair, streaking the rich auburn color with bursts of fiery red. The silken strands framed her face in thick curls that were cut in several fashionable layers and finally rested just below her shoulders. Though she was dressed in a smartly tailored business suit of cream-colored linen and the collar of her turquoise blouse tied over her throat, Kyle knew that she was the most seductive woman in the restaurant. It wasn't what she was wearing that added to her attraction, it was the sophisticated manner in which she carried herself.

"It's a tempting offer, Kyle, and I really do wish that I could take you up on it, but I just don't see where I'll be able to find the time to do everything you want by the end of May. I'm already behind in the production of several tapes—some of which are Sterling Recording Company's releases."

"You're turning me down?" His jaw tightened and he

couldn't hide the sarcastic bite to his words. After reading the financial statements of Festival Productions, he had been sure that she would gladly accept his offer…along with any others he might make concerning the business at hand.

"I'm not turning you down, Kyle, I'm being honest with you." She smiled slightly, displaying just the hint of white teeth. "My first instinct is to say yes and agree to anything you want, but that would be unfair, not only to Sterling Recording Company, but also to some of your artists who are expecting my services."

Kyle rubbed his thumb under his chin and his dark brows drew together in a deep scowl. "Whom?"

"There are several," Maren admitted. "The first one who comes to mind is Joey Righteous. I'd hoped, in fact I'd almost promised him that his videotape would be completed before he started his tour of Japan. I don't think I can just push him aside for a special project, and I'm not sure that I'd want to."

Kyle felt the muscles in the back of his neck begin to tighten. "Have you already started working on his tape?"

Maren let out a long breath. "I've got the idea on paper, pending Joey's and Sterling Recording Company's approval." She pushed her plate aside and ignored the rest of the meal. "We could start shooting as early as next week, except for one major hang-up."

"And what's that?"

She was suddenly dead serious, her blue eyes arctic. "The fact that I can't get anyone at Sterling Recording Company to help me. Joey's contract, along with about seven others, hasn't been signed by anyone of authority at your firm."

Kyle's mouth tightened into a firm hard line. "I'm prepared to correct that."

"Fine. I happen to have to the contracts with me." His eyebrows arched in interest and she forced herself to continue. "But that doesn't help my production schedule, does it?"

"You're asking for more time?"

Maren shook her head. "I'm trying to explain that you're asking the impossible."

Kyle felt his teeth grinding together in frustration. So this was what Ryan Woods had attempted to warn him about: Maren McClure's clever way of turning the game around to suit her needs. Just when he had expected her to jump at the juicy morsel of bait he had offered her, she had turned him down flat, not accepting it until some other business had been accomplished. He would have staked his life on the fact that Ms. McClure would do practically *anything* for the contract he was offering her. He had been wrong; seriously wrong.

"All right, Maren, I think we can stop playing games."

She managed a thin smile over the rim of her wineglass. "Good. It's getting a little cumbersome, isn't it?" Had she pushed him too far? She couldn't afford to offend the head of Sterling Records; too much was at stake. Her heart began to pound, but her gaze remained outwardly calm.

Kyle twisted the stem of his glass in his fingers. "I know that J. D. Price of Mirage thinks that you're single-handedly responsible for the group's success. And, for whatever it's worth, I'm sure he's at least partially correct. Without that first videotape of 'Danger Signs,' the song might never have hit the charts."

Maren disagreed. "It was a good release."

"It was a bomb. No one bothered to listen to the record until your video hit cable TV."

Maren smiled at the memory of making that tape. The

dusty on-location shooting of the videotape for "Danger Signs" had run over budget, had several lighting flaws in scenes that had to be reshot and everything that could have gone wrong did. But it had been the beginning of Festival Production's fame. "We were lucky."

"Maybe. But the point is that J. D. Price will have no one but you and your company produce this series of videotapes for Mirage's album."

"Is that right?" she asked with a satisfied smile.

"What do you think?"

"I think I need more time to come up with what you want."

Kyle Sterling smiled despite the uncomfortable feeling that he was being manipulated. "And I think you drive a hard bargain."

"Just wait," she volunteered. "We haven't begun to talk money."

"I was just coming to that."

She inclined her head as she took a swallow of wine, encouraging him to continue.

"Actually, it's not the money that's the problem," he allowed. She waited, sure that he was finally coming to the point of this intimate business meeting. "You see, I think it would be better if Sterling Recording Company had more control in the making of the videos."

Her eyes narrowed as she put her empty glass on the table. "More control?" she repeated. "How?"

"We're considering producing the tapes in-house."

Maren somehow managed to smile faintly. "I don't understand. You just offered me a very specific and expensive piece of business."

"That's because I was trying to make my offer attractive to you."

"What offer?" Her pulse was racing and she had trouble keeping her voice even. The bottom was falling out of her world and Kyle Sterling was the man responsible.

"I want to buy out Festival…." He read the look of disbelief and dismay in her cool eyes.

"Why?" She swallowed back the apprehension rising in her throat.

"Because I want you to work for me. You would still have complete discretion concerning the making of the videos, and you would be paid very well."

"But I would only be able to work with your artists."

"That's true," he agreed. "But you would be able to work with *all* of them, and from what I understand Sterling Recording Company is your major source of income."

His last statement was the final nail in the coffin. He knew how desperately she needed his business. He knew it was a matter of life and death for her small company. If she could only hang on a few more months, business was beginning to turn around and come from other sources than Sterling Records. But right now, she needed the contracts from Sterling desperately.

"I'll be honest with you, Kyle, I've never really considered selling Festival Productions, and I'm not sure I'm comfortable with the idea. I like working for myself and being my own boss."

"Do you like the headaches of keeping Festival afloat?"

She smiled distantly. "It's all part of the game, I guess. A challenge. I don't know if I'm willing to give it up."

"You don't have to…. We can even use the location of your offices until your lease is up and we've made room for you downtown."

"What about my staff?" she asked, her blue eyes trying to read the gray depths of his.

"The staff is up to you...within a reasonable budget."

"And you're the one who decides what is 'reasonable.'"

He settled back in the chair and returned her inquiring gaze. "Ultimately, yes."

"If I decide against this...what happens to the unsigned contracts?" she asked.

"They'll probably remain unsigned. This is important to me, and if we can't get your cooperation, then I'll have to find someone else. I'm giving you first opportunity."

"Because J. D. Price and a few other artists will insist upon it."

"Right."

"I'm not crazy about the idea," she conceded.

"And you feel forced into it?"

"I think 'coerced' is the term I would use," she replied thoughtfully. "I suppose you want an answer tonight."

"It would make things easier for me."

Maren felt as if her world were falling apart. Festival Productions was little security, but it was all she had in the world. It would be hard to give up. "I'll have to think about it," she whispered. "And of course I'd want to see a firm offer with an employment agreement attached to it in writing." He waited, expecting other demands, but there was only the one. She stared at him evenly, without the slightest evidence of anxiety. "The only way I would consider your offer is if in the purchase price you included shares of Sterling Recording Company stock."

His eyebrows raised in surprise and the corners of his mouth pulled into a tight frown.

"It's not unrealistic," she pointed out. "I want to make sure that I have some say in what goes on."

"And you think by owning stock in my company, you will?"

"We'll find out, won't we?" she countered, hoping that her bluff would remain uncovered. What did she have to bargain with?

He noticed the deadly gleam in her eye and couldn't help but smile. After running his fingers through his sun-streaked hair, he shook his head and smiled. His laughter was low, rich and infectious. It seemed to relieve the tension in the air. "Lady," he said with his amused grin familiarly in place, "I have the distinct feeling that I've been had." He refilled his glass and chuckled.

"That makes two of us," she confided with less enthusiasm. If the situation weren't so serious, she, too, might be inclined to laugh. As it was, she could barely manage a smile.

The cool wine slid down her throat and Kyle winked at her. "Lighten up," he instructed with a sly smile. "Things can only get better. You may as well enjoy yourself."

"I suppose you're right," she replied and a spark of interest danced in her clear blue eyes.

Kyle Sterling was certainly an interesting man, she thought to herself...a very interesting man.

CHAPTER THREE

THE REMAINDER OF THE EVENING passed quickly. The uncomfortable tension had eroded and though Maren wondered how she was going to handle Kyle's proposition, she felt herself relax in Kyle's company. Though the conversation centered around business, the intimate restaurant provided a warm, quiet atmosphere that created a sense of familiarity. All too soon the waiter had served the final cups of cappuccino and the conversation lagged.

Moonglow shimmered on the dark sea and the soft waves broke into white foam as the tide caressed the opalescent sand. Maren wondered at the feeling within her; she felt almost as if she had known the enigmatic man with her for most of her life. And she had, really. During Maren's early twenties, Kyle Sterling was a household word, his life an open book, edited carefully by his press agent. What Maren had known of him then was only what she and the rest of the record-purchasing American public were supposed to see.

There had been glimpses of the private Kyle Sterling that even his smooth-talking agent hadn't been able to hide. Rumors of a stormy marriage to a beautiful country singer, a child born, the marriage crumbling, and more recently, a near-fatal accident had continually headlined the scandal sheets. Conjecture ran high as far as Kyle

Sterling was concerned. Maren had discounted the stories, knowing from personal experience how easily the press could misrepresent the facts.

As she stared across the small table into the bold eyes of the famous man, she felt as if she could trust him with her life. It was strange. She could sense that he didn't completely trust her, but she chalked it up to the fact that it had been only hours since they had really met on a personal level.

"Where can I take you?" Kyle asked as he rose from the table and tugged at the lapels of his jacket. His eyes never left hers and for a heart-stopping moment, Maren imagined a seductive glint of passion in their mysterious depths. What would he say if she responded that he could take her anywhere he pleased? A tinge of scarlet touched her cheeks at the wayward thought—what was happening to her? In one evening she was willing to push aside all of her morals just to feel the touch of this one man. It was a disturbing thought, completely out of character, and she wondered if she was turning into one of those brash, lost souls called groupies.

With obvious embarrassment she regained her fragile poise and managed to smile. "My car is at the office."

He helped her with her jacket and the warm tips of his fingers brushed the back of her neck. For a dizzying second they seemed to linger and leave a heated impression on her skin.

They walked to his car in silence, listening to the sounds of the night: the quiet lapping of sea against sand, the muted chatter of guests in the restaurant and the hum of cars moving about the city. Maren noticed the lovers walking on the moonlit beach and she felt an urge to reach for Kyle's hand and lead him to the water's edge. It had been so long since she had felt this way about a man. It was a dangerous, yet exhilarating sensation.

While driving toward the office, Kyle had become pensive, lost in thoughts that seemed miles distant. Maren was aware of nothing other than Kyle. She could smell the scent of his cologne lingering in the air, see his hard profile as he squinted into the night and feel the unleashed tension building within him. She knew now how he had been so successful as a country singer: There was a raw magnetism about him that contrasted to the quietly aloof image he attempted to project, a fire burning beneath the ice that enticed Maren. Kyle Sterling was captivating, and just being with him was risky.

Soon they were back at the office. He made no move to help her out of the car. Instead he continued to grip the steering wheel and stare into the black night.

Maren reached for the door handle.

"Don't go," he commanded. "Not yet." His voice was hushed and raw. It forced Maren's heart to her throat.

"I wasn't looking forward to this meeting," Maren admitted cautiously. She felt the urgent need to explain herself.

"Neither was I."

"But I guess I should thank you for your offer to purchase Festival. I realize that *you* think it would not only be in your best interests, but mine as well."

"Oh, Maren, haven't we talked enough business for one night?" His hand moved from the steering wheel to touch her cheek. It was a gentle caress and quickly withdrawn, leaving Maren suddenly cold.

"Are you asking me to leave?" she asked haltingly.

"What do you think?"

Maren signed. "Truthfully, Kyle, I don't know what to think."

"You're the most interesting woman I've ever met." It

was a flat, emotionless statement and it almost sounded as if the admission disgusted him.

"I guess I should consider that a compliment."

Kyle's eyes found hers in the darkness. They drove deeply into her soul. "You should, lady, because I meant it to be one. I find you incredibly alluring. You're beautiful, I suppose you know that much. But…it's not your looks that make you so damned captivating…it's more than that. A lot more."

"And you don't like it," she finished for him.

Kyle's smile was grim. "I don't know how to handle it."

"I find that hard to believe."

"I suppose you do, but then you don't know me very well, do you?"

Honesty flashed in her clear blue eyes. "Not as well as I'd like to."

"Now that's the problem, isn't it?" he whispered. "Because I want to know you better as well…a whole lot better. You know it and it scares you." His voice had lowered to the point where it was barely audible. His eyes searched her face and she knew in that instant that he was going to kiss her.

His hand reached under her hair and gently pulled her head toward his. She offered no resistance. She could feel the warmth of his breath fanning her face, heating her cheeks. He groaned when his lips first touched hers and conveyed the depth of his need. Liquid sparks of passion raced through her blood as his arms tightened over her body, crushing her to him with a savagery that bespoke hours of restraint. She closed her eyes and let him part her lips with his tongue. Hungrily he tasted the sweetness of her mouth and felt her soft, teasing body pressed against his.

His lips moved over hers, gently coaxing the warmth within her to flood her senses. She felt devastatingly feminine, and the womanly ache within her began to grow as it spread upward through her body.

"Oh, Maren," he moaned, kissing her eyelids and letting his fingers twine through the thick fiery strands of her hair. "Let me be with you tonight. Come home with me." His breath was ragged against her ear. It softly beckoned her to respond. Her throat became dry, her emotions torn.

Against the persuasive touch of his fingers on her skin, she slowly pulled herself out of his tender embrace. A thousand reasons to go with him filled her mind, but she ignored them. "I can't," she whispered. He heard the regret in her words.

"Why not?" He attempted to take her into his arms again, but she held his hands away from her body. Her hair was tousled, her breathing ragged, her heart pounding.

"This…this has nothing to do with desire or want," she attempted to explain. "I just need some time to sort out my feelings about you." Her blue eyes, darkened by the night and her passion, pleaded with him to understand. "Until a few hours ago, I hardly knew you, and now I want to fall into your arms without so much as a thought to the future. I can't do that, Kyle. Not yet. Now that we may become business partners…or maybe not…I don't think it would be wise to become…involved."

"I'm not asking for a lifelong commitment."

"And I'm not ready for a relationship."

"Is that what you think I want?" The question, like a silver blade, cut through the silent emotions stretching between them.

She shook her head. "I don't know what you want, Kyle, but I know that neither one of us would be satisfied with a one-night stand." She watched him cautiously, her head tilted upward to meet his impassioned gaze. Without a word she dared him to deny the truth.

A lazy smile stole over his rugged features. "How do you know so much about me?" he asked, as he gently pushed an errant copper lock out of her eyes.

"I don't. Not yet. But I hope to God that any man I'm attracted to isn't interested in one lonely night of passion just to fulfill basic sexual needs."

His dark brows raised. "You really lay it on the line, don't you?"

"It comes with the territory," she sighed, trying to calm her racing pulse. Why did she feel compelled to explain herself to him? Why did she *care?* "I've worked hard to get where I am, and it hasn't been easy in a predominantly man's world. If I had become sexually involved with any of the men I've worked with, I'm sure the business would have suffered. And to me, it's just not worth the price." She could see his eyes narrowing in disbelief.

"Are you trying to convince me that you're a hard-nosed business woman who puts her company before everything, including her own pleasure?" he asked dubiously.

"Considering the circumstances, I think you should be pleased."

"What I am is unconvinced." Just what kind of a woman was he dealing with?

The hint of a smile teased her lips. "Good. Because I'm trying to point out that to me, sex is more than just pleasure."

"A commitment?"

"Yes."

He paused and the silence in the car weighed heavily on Maren's shoulders. How much of her soul could she afford to bare? "Is that what you expect from me—*a commitment?*"

Maren grinned at his obvious discomfort. "No. What I'm trying to tell you is that *I'm* not ready to give one," she explained.

Kyle let out a gust of air and ran his fingers through his hair. He chuckled despite the uneasy feeling in the atmosphere. "I'm afraid that meeting you might turn out to be the biggest mistake of my life."

"And why is that?" Her heart seemed to miss a beat. She knew that he was joking, but there was an undercurrent of truth beneath his words.

"Because not only are you going to cost me a fortune in videotape production, but you're also going to frustrate the hell out of me!"

"You're breaking my heart," she teased with a wicked gleam lighting her eyes.

"If only I could," he muttered, almost to himself.

The smile on her face faded. "Then why don't you try being honest with me—*completely* honest."

"I have been."

She pursed her lips and shook her head, dismissing his statement as a careless lie. "I don't think so. It doesn't take a genius to figure out that something's up—something big.

"Such as?"

"I wish I knew, Kyle," she replied, a sad smile resurfacing. "I've been in this business for nearly five years and I can sense when someone's not leveling with me."

"I don't know what you're talking about."

"Then let me take a guess…"

"All right."

"Does this have anything to do with the pirating of your recordings?" she asked.

"I thought you explained all that."

"So did I. But for some reason, I feel that there's still an element of trust missing in our conversation. If it doesn't hinge on the tape duplication, I'm at a total loss as to what it might be."

She looked at him and the moonglow seemed entrapped in her eyes. Kyle hadn't counted on the depth of Maren's perception. Ryan Woods had warned him about her, but Kyle had been convinced that he could handle any woman, including Maren McClure. But, once again, he'd been proven wrong...dead wrong. The thought was an irritating thorn in his side, and the worst part of the situation was that Kyle was attracted to her—more attracted than he had been to any other woman in his life. The situation was rapidly getting out of hand and he had no one to blame but himself.

"If there is a problem," he replied as he pulled on his lower lip, "I think it's that I had no intention of becoming attracted to you."

"Then you're not concerned about the pirating?" she asked dubiously.

"Of course I'm concerned. I have to be. Someone is duplicating our recordings, and the videotapes as well. They're being distributed on the black market several weeks before the albums are released." He had her full attention and to his relief her eyes remained clear, unclouded by fear.

"And you think that someone at Festival might be involved?"

"You said the problem was corrected."

"But I'm not sure that you believe me."

Kyle weighed his words carefully. "I'm convinced that you're not involved." In one short evening his opinion about Maren McClure had changed and taken a hundred-

and-eighty-degree turn. Kyle would be hard-pressed to believe that Maren knew anything about the duplicated tapes, other than what she had told him. It was the honesty in her eyes that arrested him, and he found it impossible to think her a consummate liar. He frowned at the irony of it. Maybe he was more of a fool than he knew. The last thing he would have expected this evening was to be taken in by a woman.

"But you still think that someone at Festival Productions might be on the take. That's it, isn't it? That's why you want me to come to work for you—to tighten your security! And I was gullible to think that it was my talent, but it's only because the *artists* are insisting on working with me! This way you can kill two birds with one stone!" Her small fist clenched and pounded against the pliant leather seat. "Damn!"

"I haven't accused anyone at Festival of anything..."

"Yet!"

"And you think I might?" he asked warily.

"You don't have to!" She sank back against the cushioned upholstery. "I didn't mean to react so violently," she apologized. No matter how angry she became, she couldn't forget who this man was and what he represented. She had to keep her pride in perspective. "Maybe I did jump to the wrong conclusion. I hope so."

"You act as if you *expect* me to accuse Festival Productions of having a part in the pirating," he said evenly. "Do you?" Dark gray eyes held her transfixed.

The lie slid easily over her lips. "Of course not." It was impossible to explain her unfounded suspicions about her own company. If Kyle Sterling lost faith in Festival, he could take away his offer and start his own in-house production company, robbing Festival of the business it so desperately needed. If he found out about the internal problems at Festival, Kyle would never sign a contract with Festival again. It would be a crippling blow, considering Festival's poor cash flow position. The last risk Maren could take was to lose this man's trust, and for all she knew, everything at Festival *was* aboveboard, and the missing cassettes had been found. The entire incident had been cleared up in a matter of two hours, and yet it still made Maren uneasy.

"I guess I'm a little sensitive," she amended, "because of the trouble we had a few months ago."

Was it his imagination, or had she paled? "But you're sure it no longer exists."

"Positive." Maren placed her hand on his arm. She felt his muscles tense. "I think it's only fair," she began nervously, "since you've offered me such a unique opportunity, that I be straight with you. I know that you still have some suspicions about Festival, and I don't know how to convince you otherwise. The only thing I can do is promise you that if we have any more trouble, to let you know immediately. That's the best I can do."

"Am I to assume that you're declining my offer?"

"I'm just going to need a little time..."

She felt the warmth of his fingers over hers. "All right, Maren, but I'm not a patient man."

Her breath caught in her throat. "Should I take that as some kind of warning?"

A wicked smile twisted the thin line of his lips. "I would never threaten you, Maren...but you might be able to convince me to make promises..."

"That you wouldn't keep," she supplied, reading his impassioned thoughts.

His face was so close to hers that she could feel the

warmth of his skin. His eyes roved restlessly over her face and his voice became a hoarse whisper. "All I know at this moment is that the only thing I can think about is you and what I would like to do to you."

The night seemed to close in on her and she swallowed with difficulty. "Those kinds of promises can be dangerous."

"Only if you let them." He squinted into the darkness as he surveyed the seductive curve of her lips. He traced the pout with the top of a finger. "Besides, unless I miss my guess, you're the kind of woman who loves to flirt with danger."

"You're wrong," she denied, aware only of the raw masculinity of his strong features and the power of the hand that held her bound to him. Strong but gentle, coarse but kind…if only she could let him touch her…. She refused. "You're wrong about me," she repeated.

"Prove it." Before she could protest further, he lowered his head and his lips touched hers softly. She gasped and his mouth pressed against hers, hard and demanding, claiming her lips in a kiss that warmed her body and promised to find her spirit. Though she tried to fight it, she felt her body melting against his, becoming alive beneath his persuasive touch. The heat of desire in his body flowed into hers and she yearned for more of the sweetness his touch inspired.

"This is crazy," she whispered, when finally their lips parted. Her dusky blue eyes were glazed with a hunger, deep and anxious.

"It's not crazy, it's right." He kissed her again, letting her know of the throbbing passion buried within him.

His fingers found the tie of her blouse and tugged slowly on it until it loosened and fell open. Maren's heart hammered loudly within the confines of her rib cage, her blood pounding incessantly in her eardrums. The silky fabric parted, exposing the soft white skin of her throat and shoulders. Kyle's lips touched her neck, and his tongue left a dewy impression near her shoulder. Maren felt the warm moisture cool in the night air and she sighed with the consuming need beginning to awaken within her. His lips lowered to her neck and he kissed the delicate hollow of her throat, leaving his moist imprint on her delicate bone structure.

Maren tilted her head, exposing more of her throat to him. Her dark curls touched his neck in an intimate caress known only to lovers. His lips touched her skin and dipped lower, closer to her breasts. Maren swallowed against the bittersweet yearnings and her senses became confused in the once-forgotten passion rising within the deepest core of her. "Don't," she managed to whisper when his finger slid a button through the hole. His hand flattened against her chest, feeling the warm skin rising and falling with each shallow breath she managed to take. The only sound in the darkness was the desperate beat of her racing heart.

"You want me," he whispered as he felt the fluttering irregular cadence.

"Yes," she admitted.

He groaned and moved closer to her, pressing her into the soft leather cushions. His shaking hand gingerly cupped her breast, rubbing the silky texture of her blouse against her skin, until she thought she would go insane with frustrated longing. She swallowed to moisten her throat and had to force her hand to restrain his wrist. "Please...don't."

"You can't deny it...you want me as much as I want you."

"I...I haven't denied anything. But it's not enough."

"What is, Maren?" he asked, his lips brushing the silk over her breast. He felt the tautness of her nipple straining against the flimsy fabric and found that he was unable to cope with the frustration burning within him. "What is enough?"

His hot breath against her breast encouraged a thin layer of perspiration to collect between Maren's shoulder blades. "I don't know," she conceded with a sigh.

He clenched his teeth together to stem the tide of desire rising in his body. Reluctantly he pulled his head away from her swollen breast. Without considering her actions, she placed a protective hand over her heart.

Regarding her through half-closed but penetrating eyes, he spoke. His words were punctuated with his uneven breathing. "Sure you do," he accused, "You're just not willing to admit it. You said you weren't ready for a commitment, and I believed you. Hell, we had barely met!" He clenched his fists to fight against the emotional and contradictory feelings battling within his mind. "But you still want something from me, don't you? You want to hear words of love, whether they have meaning or not."

Maren bristled. "You're wrong, Kyle. I'm thirty-three years old, and I've learned not to confuse sexual attraction and physical desire with love."

"Then what is it you want?" he asked raggedly, hoping to understand just a little part of her.

"Time." She pulled out of his embrace and reached for the handle of the door. "I don't think it's an unreasonable request considering the circumstances." She opened the car door and slid outside. He followed.

A gentle breeze blew through the two stately palm trees that stood near a lone lamppost, forcing the leaves to dance in the air and cast moving shadows in the ethereal gray light. That same soft wind lifted the parted fabric of

Maren's blouse and made it difficult to rebutton. Caught in the moving air, the silk tie and the copper strands of her hair fell away from her neck and throat. Her eyes shimmered in the lamplight, changing from deep indigo to an intriguing shade of silver-blue. She seemed strong and yet vulnerable, innocent and wise; a bewitching creature who turned his head around.

She was still fumbling with the tie when Kyle reached her. He lifted her face with his hands and gently kissed her trembling lips. "Promise me that you'll see me again," he coaxed. His fingers slid against her throat and rested upon her shoulders. She wondered what it would be like to be controlled by those persuasive hands.

"I will," she hesitantly agreed, aware only of his fingers softly tracing her jawline. "We have business—"

"Shh..." He placed his finger against her lips. "Not business. I want to see you again."

"I don't know." Once again her heart was racing. What was it that scared her so?

He wouldn't be put off. "I want you to come to my home in La Jolla for the weekend. I want to walk on the beach with you. I want to show you where I live. I want to get to know you...all of you."

"You live alone?" she asked breathlessly. She was afraid of the answer and she prayed for any excuse to avoid the intimacy they had shared this evening. It was much too perilous. She couldn't afford to fall in love with Kyle Sterling and she realized that it would be easy...too easy.

"My housekeeper is gone on the weekends."

"But...I thought...don't you have a daughter?"

His silvery eyes darkened in pain. "My ex-wife has custody."

"Even on the weekends?"

His jaw tensed and his eyes hardened against the bitter memories. "I don't see my daughter very often. Holly prefers it that way."

"I'm sorry…"

"Don't be. It's not your fault."

For the first time that evening Maren had some insight into another, more private side of Kyle Sterling. It was a part of his life that was shielded from the press and definitely brought him torment. Maren was surprised to understand that he, too, had suffered at another's hand. She saw it in the set of his jaw and the shadows under his eyes. All of his money and fame hadn't bought him happiness. "I…I didn't mean to pry," she said, avoiding his gaze.

He dismissed the subject with a frown. "It's all right." His fingers pressed more warmly against her shoulders. "Will you see me again?"

She forced back the lump that had swollen in her constricted throat. "I don't know…if I want to get…involved with you," she replied, attempting to control her ravaged emotions. "There's a part of you that seems so remote…so untouchable. Not only are you wealthy, but you're famous…really famous…and you own the company that is the single largest account of Festival Productions. It's all so overwhelming…" Her voice faded into the night. It wasn't like her to be indecisive. Kyle was disturbing her equilibrium. She wasn't thinking rationally.

"I'm a man who just wants to spend some time with a very interesting woman. Can't you understand that?"

She smiled wistfully. "I suppose so. I just don't know what to do about it."

"Trust me." The words echoed dully in her brain. She'd heard them in the past and they had betrayed her.

"I want to," she allowed.

"But you can't?"

She smiled despite the unwanted tears burning in her throat. Had she really come to the point where she could trust no man? "I guess I'm just not a trusting soul."

His hands slid down her arms and she felt the pressure of his fingers gently holding her wrists. "Because you were hurt by someone else?" His features contorted with anger. Despite the threatening tears, she looked upward at him defiantly. The silvery glow of the streetlamp reflected in the unshed teardrops. She brushed them away with the back of her hand, refusing to cry because of painful memories.

"I don't think I know you well enough to discuss what has happened to me—anyway, it's not all that interesting."

He looked down at her hopelessly. "You're hiding something from me. What is it?"

"It has nothing to do with you…or your company."

"To hell with the company. Something's bothering you." If only she would open up to him, perhaps he could help. He had the urge to protect her.

"It's none of your affair," she replied, her eyes once again dry. "And none of your concern."

She shook her head against the insistence of his furrowed brow, but the fingers over her wrists tightened. "Tell me," he demanded.

"I can't."

"Why not?" His voice was rough.

"Because…because…"

"Because you're ashamed?"

Blue eyes blazed and she jerked her arms free of his possessive grip. "Because I don't want you to know everything about me. I don't want my personal life to become entangled with my business—"

"Another man hurt you!" he accused, refusing to believe her lie. His body had become rigid, his eyes accusing. "A man whom you loved very much!"

"It's over," she snapped back. Her entire body was shaking from the ordeal. Why, tonight, was she reminded of Brandon?

"You still love him." He waited for her denial, silently counting the condemning seconds as they passed. When the silence remained unbroken, he turned on his heel and walked to the car.

Her hands came up to cross over her breasts as if to ward off a sudden chill, but her head remained regally high. She watched him leave and ignored the urge to call out to him and tell him her deepest secrets. Those silent thoughts were better left unspoken.

CHAPTER FOUR

SLEEP WAS ELUSIVE and the night stretched endlessly before her. As she lay in the darkness on her bed, she tried to rest, but painful memories made her restless. Kyle's image with its dark brooding gray eyes couldn't be erased. Nor could she forget the warm feel of his fingers when they caressed her skin. Her response to him had surprised her; she had thought her desire had been buried so deeply it would never resurface.

Haunting memories of another man destroyed her warm thoughts of Kyle. Trapped in her mind were painful thoughts of Brandon, a man to whom she was hopelessly bound. She wondered if she would ever be free of him. She doubted it.

The nightmares of Brandon disturbed what little sleep she managed to find. It had been three years since the divorce was final, but she still bore the scars from her passionate but brief marriage. It had ended because Brandon was a man who couldn't abide the restrictions of a monogamous relationship, and Maren couldn't bear the torment of wondering who was warming her husband's bed. She had hoped that the divorce would release her from him. It hadn't. Theirs was a relationship that couldn't be broken easily, and even though they both knew it to be a mistake, they had once considered reconciliation.

It had been that weekend at Heavenly Valley that had altered the course of Maren's life. Brandon was a natural athlete and had been showing off on the slopes, attempting to race down the most dangerous runs at breakneck speeds. Maren's insides had twisted as she watched him put tougher demands upon his body. He ignored the fact that he was obviously tired and pushed himself to the limit. His last chilling run had ended in tragedy. The fall should have killed him, but it didn't. Maren had witnessed his loss of control of the skis and the jump that had ended in a body-wrenching dive against the packed snow and ice. Her strangled screams had brought the rescue team to Brandon's side within minutes. Somehow he had managed to survive, though he only recovered partial use of his legs.

Maren shuddered at the memory and pulled the blankets more tightly around her neck. She could remember the emergency room of the stark hospital and the fear that had gripped her in its cold grasp when she had first understood that Brandon might never walk again. The doctors had been grim, but persistent. If it hadn't been for a succession of expensive operations, Brandon would still be confined to a wheelchair. As it was, he could now walk painfully with the aid of a brace. In time, the orthopedists were predicting, he could recover, if he could somehow manage to get over the emotional trauma of the accident. Brandon had not only lost his ability to walk in that terrifying leap, he had also lost his career as a tennis pro and his self-esteem as a man.

As the first golden streaks of dawn began to lighten her room, she thought about Kyle's vicious accusation. Could he have possibly been right? Did some small part of her still love Brandon? Could she still love a man who had thought so little of her while they had been married? She had quit asking herself that question after the divorce had become final, and she had vowed to forget both him and his endless affairs with younger women. But that had been before the skiing accident at Heavenly Valley, and before Brandon had become financially dependent upon her.

She shook her head, turning it slowly against the pillow, hoping to dislodge her unpleasant thoughts. The past was dead and gone. Her love for Brandon had withered years ago, but regardless of the fact that she no longer loved him, she couldn't turn her back on him; not yet, not while he still needed her. She was the only scrap of family he had, and if she had to imprison herself to give him the emotional security he needed, so be it.

Though it was barely six in the morning, Maren dragged herself out of bed and headed for the shower. Rather than concentrating on problems she couldn't begin to solve, she would push herself ever deeper into her work. She had to make things work for her, and she had to seriously consider all the ramifications of Kyle Sterling's offer. Just at the thought of him, she felt a blush rise to her cheeks.

She let the bathrobe slide to the floor and stepped into the hot shower, lounging under the soothing spray. She tried to think of anything other than Brandon and the guilt she carried because of him. How many times had she attempted to convince herself that his accident wasn't her fault? And how many times was she left with the same condemning conclusion: If it hadn't been for Maren, Brandon would never have gone to Heavenly Valley. It had been her suggestion that they spend the day on the snow-laden slopes; he had only complied, and in so doing, ruined the rest of his life.

"Stop it!" she told herself fiercely. "You can't blame

yourself!" She plunged her head under the spray and let the water run over her. Her wayward thoughts turned to Kyle Sterling and without realizing it, Maren began to smile. Kyle was such a puzzling man; so unique.

While lathering her shoulders, she reflected on the events of the previous evening. Despite the fact that it had turned sour, last night had been the single most inspiring evening she had spent in years, and the man she had shared it with was more fascinating than she could have ever guessed. His intrigue was more than the fact that he was a wealthy man with a colorful and famous past. It was his energy, his sensuality, his gentle touch, that had captured her. The quiet sound of his low laughter had entrapped her in its honesty. She knew intuitively that he was a man who didn't laugh often, and that knowledge made the short time she had spent with him all the more endearing.

She had just reached for a towel when her thoughts turned dark. Kyle had sought her out only because he wanted Festival Productions, and very badly. His primary motive in seeing her was to try and force her into a position to sell Festival to him. There was also the pirating scheme to consider. Kyle had been trying to ferret out information from her, and though he said he was satisfied, he seemed a little uneasy about it. Could he really suspect someone, at Festival, or was he merely being cautious because of the fact that he intended to purchase the company at whatever the cost? She shook her head and water from her hair beaded against the sides of the shower stall. No, if he had really been suspicious, he would never have made the offer. Then again, he hadn't signed the contracts, had he?

The full impact of her thoughts hit her with the force of a slap in the face. She slumped against the wet tile when she realized that she had left her briefcase, with the contracts, in Kyle's car. In her fumbling efforts to dissolve the growing intimacy between them, Maren had hurried out of the car with her purse, forgetting the briefcase and the valuable contracts therein. Maren rolled her eyes skyward. This wasn't like her, not at all. She usually wasn't a bundle of nerves with a man, nor was she forgetful. But Kyle Sterling wasn't just any man, and his image continued to play havoc with her reason. If she had indeed left the contracts with him, it wasn't the end of the world, but it would certainly make her seem irresponsible, and that was the last impression she wanted to leave with Kyle Sterling.

Disgusted with herself, Maren scrambled into her bathrobe and raced through the small apartment, leaving a wet trail on the carpet as she confirmed with her eyes what she had mentally discovered. Her briefcase was missing. It wasn't in the closet, nor under the hall tree, nor near the foot of the bed, nor tossed recklessly on the kitchen table. After checking the usual spots, she began to search the obscure ones. It was gone. Muttering an oath at her own carelessness, she dialed the offices of Sterling Recording Company and was politely informed by a prerecorded message that the normal business hours for the company did not begin until eight o'clock.

She began to dry her hair, going through the motions without bothering to check her reflection in the steamy mirror. Several minutes later, when the condensation from the shower had disappeared and she looked directly into the blue eyes of her mirror image, she questioned her motives. Had she left the briefcase in Kyle's car with a purpose? Subliminally, she might have created a convenient excuse to see him again. But she didn't need an excuse, she argued with herself. Kyle had made it crystal clear that he wanted to see her again. All she had to do was summon the courage to call him. If she wasn't able to do that much, she would certainly see him soon regarding the buyout…if there was going to be one.

She considered calling him in the time it took to dress and drive from the apartment to the office, but she decided to wait until Sterling Recording Company had opened its doors. She didn't want to appear too anxious by tracking him down. She needed to find out that he had the contracts, but certainly it could wait until he had made it in to his office.

As was usual, Maren was the first employee of Festival Productions to arrive. It was the bookkeeper's day off, and the production crew was on location. For the past few weeks Jan had been arriving at the office late in the morning. Jan was always apologetic and managed to get her work done, so Maren didn't force the issue. Maren had come to suspect that Jan was having trouble with Jacob again.

It was well after nine when Jan finally got to the office. Maren had already begun working on the layout for the first song on the Mirage album. She had listened to the song "Yesterday's Heart" until she could sing the lyrics along with the band. Over the sound of the sultry music, Maren heard Jan arrive.

For a moment she tried to continue working, but couldn't. She sighed as she took off her reading glasses and got up from the drafting table in the corner of her office. After she switched off the tape player, she walked slowly into the reception area.

Jan was already at her desk and the meticulous mask of makeup couldn't hide the dark circles under her eyes or the pallor of her skin. Maren poured Jan a cup of black coffee, which the blond woman accepted gratefully. Jan took an experimental sip, grimaced and blanched.

"Bad night last night?" Maren asked cautiously as Jan lit a cigarette with unsteady hands.

The secretary managed a weak smile and set the coffee aside. "Not the best," she admitted. "But I did manage to finish all of this correspondence." She blew out a thin stream of blue smoke before handing Maren a sheaf of typewritten pages. Maren could see in one quick glance that the papers were letter-perfect.

"You don't have to work after hours," Maren offered, sitting on a corner of Jan's cluttered desk.

"I know. But I've been getting in later and later... and...well, I feel guilty about it."

"You shouldn't."

"It's not your fault that I can't seem to get my act together." She avoided Maren's probing gaze and picked up the steaming coffee. Uncomfortably she stared into the black brew.

"Jan, is something wrong?" Maren asked gently.

Jan froze before stubbing out her cigarette and quickly lighting a replacement. She had to blink back her tears as she inhaled deeply on the cigarette. "Nothing really," she replied.

Maren didn't move. "You're sure?"

Jan nodded, afraid to trust her voice.

Knowing she was getting nowhere, Maren patiently waited. She cared too much about Jan to see her become a shell of her former self because of a contemptible man like Jacob Green. "Would you like to take your vacation early this year?"

"Look, I'm all right. *Really!*" Jan snapped angrily.

"I'm sorry. I didn't mean to pry." Maren got up from the corner of the desk, straightened her skirt and started toward the door leading to her office.

"Maren...wait," Jan called. Maren turned to face her

friend. Jan looked miserable. "I'm sorry," the secretary whispered. "I don't know what's gotten into me…no, that's a lie. I do know."

"You don't have to talk about it."

"Maybe I should," Jan murmured. "At least I owe you an explanation as to why I've been getting in late…" Maren leaned against the doorjamb. She didn't really want to hear about Jan's personal problems, but she needed to help her friend, if she could.

"I trust you, Jan. If you get in late, I know you've got a good reason."

Jan seemed to wince under Maren's kind words. Tears threatened to spill from her large brown eyes. "Look, I'm a little upset, that's all." She breathed deeply. "We had another fight last night."

"You and Jacob?"

"Right." Jan nodded and pursed her white lips together. For a moment Maren thought she would break down, but Jan squared her shoulders and bravely fought against the tears.

"I take it that it was bad."

"Are there any good ones?"

Maren frowned into her empty coffee cup. "No, I guess not. But some are worse than others."

"It sounds like you've been there."

A wistful smile formed on Maren's full lips. "I've got a few scars," she conceded. "Anyone who's managed to reach the age of thirty-three has seen her share of battles."

"So, are you here offering advice?" Jan asked with just a hint of sarcasm.

"I don't know if I'm qualified to give it. Do you want to hear my opinion?"

"I don't know what I want…not anymore," Jan sighed.

"You see, there's more to it than just a simple fight." Maren waited, watching grimly as she witnessed the tortured play of emotions distorting Jan's usually cheery features. Her admission came slowly. "I think I'm pregnant."

Maren swallowed and closed her eyes for a moment. "How do you feel about it?" she asked.

For the first time that morning, Jan's smile was genuine and illuminated her pale face. "I'm happy, I think. Can you believe that, the girl who said she'd never have any kids?"

"I think it's wonderful," Maren said with heartfelt enthusiasm. "Congratulations!"

Jan seemed partially relieved. "That's one of the reasons I've been getting in later.... I haven't felt all that sharp in the mornings."

"Don't worry about it. It's all right. You certainly have a good reason, and from what I understand, morning sickness doesn't last forever."

"Thank God," Jan murmured fervently.

"How did Jacob take the news?" Maren asked and immediately regretted her question when Jan's face sobered.

"I haven't told him yet," Jan replied, warding off Maren's surprised stare with a wave of her hand. "I told you that we haven't been getting along very well, and that's an understatement. We fight all the time. I'm afraid he'll think I'm using the baby to trap him into marriage."

Maren silently agreed, but decided it was best not to voice her fears. "Give the guy some credit, will you? We're talking about a child—*his* child. I bet he'll be thrilled by the news."

"I doubt it."

"Jan, you've got to tell him sometime."

"I know and I will, once I go to the doctor and find out that I really am pregnant. I have an appointment scheduled for next week." Jan lowered her eyes and fidgeted at the desk.

"You're sure you're happy about this?" Maren prodded.

A shadow of doubt clouded Jan's dark eyes. "Yes, I'm sure. About the baby, that is. But I'm worried about Jake…he's changed, Maren…a lot. I…I don't know how he's going to take the news."

Maren understood Jan's concern, but forced herself to smile. "Don't borrow trouble. You don't know, the man might be ecstatic at the prospect of becoming a father."

"He has grown children and never sees them," Jan replied tonelessly.

Maren winked with feigned enthusiasm. "Maybe *this* one will make the difference."

"I hope so."

Maren turned toward her office, but Jan's whispered voice kept her in the room. "Maren?"

Maren looked over her shoulder, but Jan was no longer facing her. Apparently she had changed her mind. When Jan did meet Maren's inquisitive eyes, the secretary's face was pulled into a tight knot of confusion. "Forget it," she said, reaching for another cigarette. Maren noticed that the second one was still burning unattended in the ashtray near the typewriter. "I'll…I'll talk to you later," the secretary said dismissively.

"All right…and you'd better check with your doctor soon. I'm afraid he's going to suggest you stop smoking."

"Great. That's just what I need," Jan muttered to herself.

After casting a worried look in Jan's direction, Maren went back into her office and closed the door. Finally she understood the young secretary's behavior. For the last few weeks Jan had been edgy and forgetful, and Maren had suspected it had something to do with her on-again, off-again romance with Jacob Green. Now that her suspicions were confirmed, Maren could at least understand Jan's actions and her reticence to discuss her problems.

Jan and Maren had always been friends, but over the past year, during the time in which Jan had become involved with their former employer, Jacob Green, the relationship between the two women had suffered and sometimes been strained. Maren knew that she was more than partially to blame because she had never liked Jacob, and that fact was transparently clear to Jan. Both Maren and Jan had worked for Green before Maren had purchased Festival Productions from him. Now that he was no longer in the business, Maren tried her best to avoid him.

There was something about the man that had always bothered her. Maybe it was because he had made a pass at Maren years ago when she had still been married to Brandon. Since that time, she had never completely trusted Jacob Green. The man was shifty. If it hadn't been for the contract on the business and the fact that she still owed him nearly eighty thousand dollars, Maren would have made it a point never to see him.

And now, to complicate things, Jan was carrying Jacob's child. Maybe a baby would change him; make him realize what was important in life. Maren seriously doubted it, but for Jan and the baby's sake, she pushed her forebodings aside and hoped for the best.

The intercom beckoned her and Maren answered the call. Jan's voice, once again cool and professional, greeted her. "Kyle Sterling is on line two, returning your call."

Maren's pulse jumped. "Thanks, Jan." She sat in the desk chair for a moment to steady her nerves. Why was she so jittery? No man had ever affected her like this, and it was damned unsettling. Resting her forehead in her palm, she cradled the receiver between her shoulder and her ear and pressed the flashing light on the telephone. "Hello."

"Maren? My secretary said you wanted to get in touch with me." His voice was cold and distant. Gone was the intimacy of the night.

"Not an easy thing to do," she allowed.

"I instruct my staff not to give out my telephone number."

"Not even to business associates?"

"To no one."

"I'm sorry to bother you," she replied evenly, though her heart was pounding an irregular cadence in her chest, "but I think I left my briefcase in your car last night."

There was a weighty pause on the other end of the line. "You're sure about that?"

"Yes." Maren couldn't hide the strain in her voice. "Didn't you find it?" Her dark brows drew together. What was he trying to do—scare the devil out of her? The briefcase had to be in his car.

"Wait a minute. I'll check."

"Kyle—" But he was gone. Her mind revolved backward in time, recalling the events of the evening. She remembered putting the briefcase in the backseat. It had to be there. Certainly Kyle had noticed it when he'd driven to work—unless of course he took another car. Maren tapped her fingernail nervously on the desk. The only other alternatives were dismal: Either her briefcase had been stolen, lost, or Kyle was deliberately withholding it from her, though for what purpose, Maren couldn't begin to guess.

"Got it." Kyle's voice broke into her thoughts. "You were right. It was in the backseat."

Maren felt a wave of relief wash over her. "Good. I'll send someone over to pick it up early this afternoon."

There was a deep-throated chuckle on the other end of the fragile cord linking her to him. "Oh, you will, will you?" Why did he sound so amused? Maren's tight nerves got the better of her.

"Is there a problem with that?"

"Not for me. I plan to be here the rest of the week."

"The rest of the week? But it's Friday…" Suddenly a dim light dawned in her worried mind. "Kyle, where are you?"

"San Diego…I drove down last night after…our discussion. I didn't think about your briefcase."

"Neither did I," Maren admitted. "So you're at your home in La Jolla?"

"Uh-huh." Maren could imagine the seductive twinkle in his silvery eyes.

"Great." She glanced at her watch. Though it was still before noon, the drive to San Diego would take over four hours round-trip. It was pointless and a waste of time, except for the fact that she had planned to work over the weekend. She needed her case. Damn!

"Do you need the contracts immediately?"

"It would help—especially considering your proposal."

There was an awkward silence. "I can't bring them to you, Maren."

"I didn't expect you to."

His voice became low and all too familiar. "Why don't you come down for the weekend? You can get the contracts and we can work out a few ideas for the Mirage album… besides which, I could talk you into selling Festival to me."

"You think so?"

"Sure of it."

The sound of determination in his voice made a chill skitter up her spine. "I'd love to Kyle, but…"

"You're afraid." He was angry. She could hear it in his sharp accusation.

"I didn't say that."

"You didn't have to. What is it, Maren? Are you committed to another man? Was last night just an idle flirtation? All that talk about one-night stands and commitments, was that just sophisticated hype?"

"Of course not." Her voice had begun to shake. She had to sink her teeth into her lower lip.

"Talk is cheap."

"What do you mean?"

"Prove yourself. Come down here tonight."

Despite her anger, she forced herself to remain calm. "I don't have to prove anything to you other than that I can produce the best, most artistic and marketable videotapes on the market today."

"You're right, if what you want from me is strictly business. Last night I was left with a different impression."

"I wish I knew what I wanted from you," she admitted.

His tone softened, and when she closed her eyes, Maren could imagine the look of frustration on his rugged face. "Let's find out," he suggested, "We're two adults, and I won't force you into anything you don't want."

"I know that much," she conceded. It wasn't his needs that frightened her; it was her own.

"Then what d'ya say?"

She couldn't help but smile. "All right—why not?" she asked, laughing at the folly of it all. This whole idea bordered on insanity. "I'll need your address and telephone number, just in case I get lost."

"Or have second thoughts."

Her lips pursed into a provoked frown as she scribbled his hasty instructions on a memo pad. After hanging up the telephone, Maren wondered if she had the courage to take him up on his offer, or would she, as he had intimated, back down?

A thousand excuses for avoiding the trip filled her mind, and just as many reasons for going refuted them. It was foolish to get involved with Kyle Sterling. She knew it as well as her own name. And yet, she was enticed by him, drawn to him as a moth to flame.

CHAPTER FIVE

THE PHRASE THAT CAME to Maren's mind when she first drove through the gates and caught a glimpse of Kyle Sterling's home was "la casa grande." The house was magnificent. Wrought iron gates and a stucco fence guarded the estate, keeping the curious sightseers at bay. Softly arched palm trees and fragrant hibiscus lined the circular drive leading to the two-storied Spanish home. The exterior of ivory plaster gleamed in the sunlight and contrasted to the angular red-tile roof. Long narrow windows had taken on the hue of the lowering sun.

The house stood proudly on a cliff overlooking the calm blue-green waters of the Pacific Ocean. Maren parked her car near a sprawling garage and tried to ignore the fact that the house and well-tended grounds reflected the image of the man living on the estate—private, wealthy and powerful. She hesitated before getting out of the car and wondered if this weekend might become the single largest mistake of her life.

It wasn't that she hadn't been around wealth. In the recording industry, it was impossible not to run across a young overnight success story who ran through money as if it were water. But dealing with Kyle Sterling was entirely different. Though Maren had often rubbed elbows with the Hollywood elite, she had meticulously avoided being swept up in the Hollywood social tide. It was too fast moving and dangerous for her. She had refused to get involved with any man since Brandon, and now that she was becoming emotionally entangled with Kyle Sterling, she felt twinges of doubt. What did she really know about the man? Business with a man as powerful as Kyle Sterling was one thing, but a one-on-one relationship was quite another.

Calling herself a fool, she walked up the flagstones leading to the courtyard and tried to bolster her wavering confidence. Don't let all of this overwhelm you, she cautioned herself. Remember that he's only a man. Ah, yes, her worried mind tossed back at her, but a man who wants the one thing you have: Festival Productions!

Maren couldn't ignore the fact that Kyle wanted very much to own Festival Productions and, for that matter, herself as well. He knew that she was the artistic force behind Festival, and there was no doubt that he would do just about anything in his power to entice Maren into selling him her production company. More than anything, she had to keep a level head while in his company. She couldn't allow herself the luxury of trusting him completely, because she understood his motives. How much of his affection for her was sincere and how much was just a part of the game? Was his interest in her merely a well-rehearsed act carefully planned to seduce her into selling Festival? She wanted desperately to believe that he really did care for her, but her common sense instructed her to tread warily.

After stiffening her backbone, she pressed the doorbell and braced herself for another meeting with him. Poise and control were the order of the day. Why then was her pulse racing in anticipation?

Lydia was gone for the weekend and Kyle had awaited Maren's arrival impatiently, watching the clock as the slow hours passed and cursing himself for his own impetuosity. Right now, the last thing he needed cluttering his life was an entanglement with Maren McClure. Why then was he so anxious to see her again?

There was something damnably seductive about that woman. It had captivated him last night and ruined his sleep. He had lain awake for hours, frustrated by urges he hadn't felt in years. It was as if he were compelled to see her again, forced to confront her. He only hoped that the frustration would soon end; that they would become lovers and his lust for her would be satisfied. It would be better for everyone involved if his fascination for her would die a quick death. A quick affair would serve his purpose. He could convince Maren to sell out Festival to Sterling Recording Company, satisfy his physical needs and then be back on track. It had been a long time since he had been with a woman. Maybe that was his problem.

The chimes alerted him of Maren's arrival. Without realizing it, he smiled and the deep furrows of concentration that had lined his brow softened. He opened the door and stared into Maren's incredible blue eyes. Sunlight filtered through the fronds of the palm tree and caught in the dark strands of her hair, streaking the rich auburn color with fiery bursts of burnished gold.

Kyle's smile broadened to touch his eyes as he wedged himself between the heavy door and the wall. "So you made it," he greeted.

"Were you afraid I wouldn't find the place, it being so small and all?" she returned, showing off just the hint of a seductive dimple.

He cocked an appreciative dark brow. "I try to keep

things simple," he responded with a hearty laugh. Moving out of the doorway, he pushed the door open and silently invited her inside. "I'm glad you're here," he admitted, with only a trace of reluctance. His knowing gray eyes were warm and tempting. "I assume you're planning to stay..."

"I don't think that would be wise."

"Why not?"

It was difficult dissuading him. He noticed the hesitation in her eyes. "You *are* having second thoughts."

"Maybe. I'd prefer to think of it as considering all of the alternatives and carefully deciding what's the best course of action."

"Boardroom double-talk," he muttered as he motioned her inside the house. "Are you always so...poised and careful, Ms. McClure?" he asked as he followed her inside the hacienda and closed the door behind him. That single action seemed to cut the two of them off from the rest of the world.

Maren managed to hide her unease with a composed smile. "I'd like to think that I am," she replied, ignoring the sarcastic bite to his words. "And I would think that you, above all people, would understand my caution, and appreciate it."

"That's the problem. I don't understand, not at all."

She paused for a moment, waiting until her eyes had adjusted to the dim light of the interior, and hoping that she could somehow convey her feelings to him. It seemed important that he understand her.

Once inside the plushly carpeted sunken living room, Maren turned to face the solitary man who made this estate his home. "I don't know you very well," Maren conceded, cocking her head and letting her hair fall away from her face. “In fact, I wasn’t sure that you would be here, alone…or that you would meet me at the door. I really didn’t know what to expect.” The expression on Kyle’s face was still puzzled, and Maren realized that she wasn’t making much sense. She started over.

“Look, Kyle, I know that you run with a pretty fast crowd.” His thick brow quirked, indicating that he had heard her. The rest of his face was set in an intent expression as he regarded her silently, patiently waiting for her to continue with her explanation. Fascinating slate-colored eyes held her stare.

“And you don’t…run with a fast crowd?”

“Right. I’m a little…no, make that *very* uneasy with the idea of spending a weekend with a man whom I barely know, and a business associate to boot. I’m not like Mitzi Danner or any of those other glamorous Hollywood types who change lovers as easily as they change shampoos.” She shook her head and held her palms skyward in a supplicating gesture. “I’m not apologizing for my sense of values, but I thought you should know that this sort of thing is just too casual for me—not my style…”

“Thank God,” he murmured, obviously relieved and slightly amused. The laughter in his eyes fueled her unexpected anger.

“I don’t even really know what I’m doing here,” she admitted. “I shouldn’t have agreed to come and should have told you to put the briefcase in the mail!”

“What is it that you’re afraid of? Is it me—or men in general?” he asked.

“Fear has nothing to do with this—”

“I think it has everything to do with it,” he argued, his eyes darkening dangerously. “The conflicting signals I get from you lead me to believe that something about me scares you—more than just a little. Now it could be that I intimidate you because I own Sterling Records and Festival strongly depends on its relationship with my company," he suggested calmly. "Or, it might be that you're *afraid* of any kind of relationship with a man, because you let yourself get involved in a bad relationship in the past."

"Or it could be," she said loftily, "that all my instincts tell me that spending a weekend with you might end up to be one monumental mistake!" Unwanted scarlet crept up her neck. "I'm not afraid of you...but I'm not...easy, either, and I'm not comfortable with the idea of spending a weekend with a man I don't know. Is that so hard to understand?"

Impatience flashed in his eyes. "Damn it, woman," he whispered as he shook his head in disbelief. "How many times do I have to tell you that I like your 'style'?" After crossing the room, he reached for her and traced the ridges between her wrist and fingers with his strong hand. He captured her gaze in the warmth of his stormy gray eyes.

She was still wary. "Does my 'style' include my production company?" she whispered. "Isn't that what you really like about me?"

A muscle near the back of his jaw began to tighten and his eyes bored into hers. "I admit that I'm interested in Festival Productions. You know it, and I haven't tried to hide the fact. I thought I put my cards on the table last night. I'm very interested in your production company." She was about to interrupt but he held a finger to her lips. "But that is *not* the reason that I invited you down here."

"But on the phone you said—"

"It doesn't matter what ploy I used to get you here." He saw the argument forming in her eyes and warded it off.

"It won't change things to accuse me of being underhanded," he warned with a rakish grin. "I've heard it before." He took both of her hands in his, forcing her to face him squarely. "I don't want to get involved with you any more than do you with me, but it seems to be in the cards, wouldn't you say?"

Gently he kissed her palm. Her teeth sunk into her lower lip at the intimacy of the gesture and her heart began to beat in a syncopated rhythm. "I just hope the deck isn't stacked against me."

Again his eyes drilled into hers. "Would I do that?"

"I don't know. Why don't you tell me?" she replied, her voice becoming ragged. He was getting to her, just as surely as if she had willingly let him in to her heart.

"Let's not argue," Kyle suggested, releasing her hand. "I've had enough of that for one day."

Maren was perplexed. "From me?" The sudden tensing of his body warned her that she was prying into forbidden territory.

His gaze clouded. "No." He didn't elaborate and Maren didn't press him. The private battles he was fighting were none of her business and she knew intuitively that the less she became entwined in the personal aspects of Kyle Sterling's life the better. "Can I offer you a drink?" he asked abruptly, effectively changing the subject. When she nodded, he strode over to an ornately carved wooden sideboard that had been converted into a bar.

While Kyle was mixing the drinks, Maren took the time to examine the living room. It was expansive, with an open-beamed ceiling rising a full two floors. A polished tile floor was covered with a tightly woven cream-colored carpet. The furnishings were modern pieces in variegated hues of brown and rust with clean, strong lines. A bank of tall windows facing west opened to a commanding view of the restless azure Pacific Ocean. A few potted plants were casually arranged near the heavier pieces of furniture and watercolors of dusky mountain ridges adorned the walls.

When Kyle turned his attention back to Maren, she was struck by his overwhelming masculinity. She suspected that it wasn't an image he attempted to cultivate, but the power surrounding him couldn't be disguised. He was dressed in faded blue jeans and an open-throated shirt. His arms were bare and bronzed, and when he handed her a glass of amber liquor, his arms flexed to display lean, corded muscles that moved smoothly under his dark skin. He was more ruggedly sensual than any man Maren had ever met, and he wore his masculinity with a pride and near arrogance that fascinated the woman deep within her. Though she tried to think of him as the opposition and not as a man, she found it impossible.

"Is brandy all right?"

"Fine," she responded, taking the glass. "I try to keep things simple, just like you." She was rewarded with his amused smile. His eyes were warm and seemed to caress her skin. For an awkward moment there was silence. She sipped the drink before motioning toward the watercolors. "Did you do those?"

His smile broadened. "'Fraid not. My artistic ability is limited to a twelve-string guitar."

"And sheet music."

"Some people would beg to differ on that point."

She smiled and relaxed a little. "But they couldn't argue with your success."

He seemed about to say something, but thought better of it. His eyes became guarded. "That was a long time ago," he whispered.

Realizing that she had touched a sensitive nerve, Maren changed the subject and forced her attention back to the watercolors. The brandy slid easily down her throat as she concentrated on the varied hues of purple and blue. She inclined her head in the direction of the most distinctive work of art. "Do you know the artist?"

Kyle shrugged. "Not really. I met him once and liked his work. He was working on a series of watercolors of the Blue Ridge near the town where I was born. I bought the entire series."

"So this is where you grew up?" Maren asked, eyeing the pictures with new interest.

Kyle corrected her. "You might think so if you listened to my agent for very long. He seemed to like to perpetuate the old rags-to-riches story about a good ol' boy from the Blue Ridge."

Maren focused her attention back on the man. "Isn't that the way it happened?"

"Not exactly…you see, my parents moved out here when I was pretty young. I've been a Californian ever since. My agent and my manager didn't think having a client from southern California was nearly as interesting as a genuine country boy from the South. My agent thought it would add to my…image. I went along with him."

"And it worked. You convinced the record-buying public that you were the real thing."

"I was. What did it matter where I grew up? They wanted country songs—and that's what I gave them. That's the business we're in, Ms. McClure, or have you forgotten?" He drained his drink and set the glass on a nearby table. "There are a lot of things about me that you don't know—or maybe even have misconstrued. Why don't you take a chance and get to know me better? Stay with me."

He was standing only inches from her. The warmth of his body seemed to touch her skin. "I try not to make a practice of taking chances," she said softly, never letting her gaze waver from his. "They could become dangerous."

"And you're trying to convince me that you aren't attracted by risk?" he asked dubiously. Before she could respond, he continued. "Don't bother to waste your breath. No woman could have achieved what you have without taking a few gambles along the way."

"And the chances I have taken didn't include sleeping with someone to get what I wanted." She tilted her head upward, daring him to pursue the subject.

"I know that. Neither have I."

She smiled in spite of herself. "No female executive ever got you in a compromising position?" she asked.

"Not until now."

Maren's heart seemed to skip a beat. When she raised her glass to her lips, her hands were trembling. There was something disturbing in his quiet gaze and in an instant she realized just how desperately he wanted her. "This is very difficult for me," she admitted, her voice suddenly rough.

"That makes two of us."

The air between them was tense. Maren knew that if Kyle were to touch her, she would fall willingly into his arms. She wanted to believe that his desire for her was more than just physical; she needed to know that there was more involved than lust. The idea of spending the night with a man she barely knew made her uneasy. Things were moving much too rapidly, and it was difficult to keep her feelings for Kyle in perspective.

"I think there are a few things we should get straight,"

Maren volunteered as Kyle shifted and walked toward the fireplace. He rubbed the back of his neck as if to erase the tension developing between his shoulder blades.

"Ground rules?" He captured her with his questioning gray eyes.

Her smile was frail. "I suppose you might call them that," Maren allowed.

"Okay, shoot." He leaned against the rough stones of the fireplace and crossed his arms over his chest. The fabric of his shirt strained against the muscles of his shoulders and back. One foot was poised on the raised hearth. Maren noticed that his thigh muscle was tightening. Kyle's pose was obviously seductive, and Maren wondered if it were spontaneous or contrived.

"I talked to my lawyer today," Maren began.

His gaze never faltered. No trace of emotion threatened to distort the even features of his face "And?"

"She advised me—"

"She?" he interrupted. His jaw tightened and his eyes seemed to darken dangerously.

"Elise Conrad. My attorney." Maren could read the suddenly wary look crossing his eyes. "This *is* the nineteen eighties, Kyle. There are such things as female lawyers." For a reason she couldn't define, Maren felt defensive.

"Don't I know," Kyle returned evasively. He lowered his hand to his knee, still keeping his gaze fixed on Maren. "What did this woman, pardon me, *your attorney,* suggest?"

"Nothing out of the ordinary. Elise said that you should give me a firm offer for Festival in writing, and that I shouldn't sign *anything* until she has had the chance to go over it."

'Sounds like an attorney," Kyle muttered angrily.

"It sounds fair."

"Then I guess you'd better tell me exactly what you want for your business," he decided aloud. "And I'll want a full financial report on Festival. Then you'd better determine whatever other terms you want: cash outright or contract? Employment agreement? Anything else. I think *my* attorney will insist upon them." His face had hardened menacingly and in a fraction of an instant Maren witnessed a transformation in Kyle. One minute he was a sensitive man intent on seducing a woman, the next he was a ruthless executive bent on only one thing: getting what he wanted for his company.

"You act as if this transaction might get a little vicious."

He shook his head and frowned. "You're the one who brought in an attorney," he reminded her.

"You expected me not to?" She was incredulous. "What kind of an idiot do you take me for?"

His frown disappeared as he gazed into her eyes. "I think of you as a lot of things," he admitted. "But an idiot? Never! I hope that we can accomplish the purchase of Festival without shedding too much blood, but it doesn't hurt to be prepared."

"Are you always so calculating?"

'Only when I have to be, and I'd say that with you, as far as business is concerned, I'm going to have to be careful—damn careful."

"And that bothers you?" she guessed.

He lifted his shoulders and shook his head. "Not really. I just don't want to spend the rest of the weekend arguing about dollars, cents and Festival Productions."

"No?" Cocking her head to the side, she smiled, showing the flash of even white teeth. "Why don't you tell me exactly what it is you want to do?" There was an alluring invitation in her seductive indigo gaze.

Though Kyle was several feet from her, she felt as it they were nearly touching. His eyes caressed her and held her gaze in an intimate and familiar embrace. As he rose and crossed the room, Maren felt her heart begin to pound mercilessly in her chest. His masculinity unnerved her; his self-assured power disturbed her equilibrium. "I just want the chance to get to know you..." he replied, reaching her and touching her shoulders lightly. The warmth of his fingers permeated the light fabric of her linen jacket, leaving a torrid imprint on her skin. "Why can't you understand that?"

"I do," she admitted.

"But?" His dark eyes coaxed her.

"But I can't help but think that the owner of Sterling Recording Company might have ulterior motives for seeing me."

"You expect me to seduce you into selling Festival?"

"I expect you to *try*."

"Then what's to worry—since you're onto my game plan?" he mocked, with a twinkle of expectation lighting his eyes. He lowered his head and his lips hovered over hers for a breathtaking instant. "What I wouldn't do for just one chance," he sighed as his lips touched hers in a kiss as warm as it was sensual. Maren didn't move, but felt as if every muscle and bone within her body were melting. Strong lean arms wrapped possessively around her, and Kyle's hand slipped under the hem of her jacket to touch the bare skin exposed by her backless sundress. At the touch of his fingers against the sensitive skin, she shuddered, and she felt his muscles tense. He groaned in frustration as his tongue traced the soft flesh of her lips before probing the warm recesses of her mouth.

A soft sigh escaped her as she hungrily returned the

fervor of his kiss. Her heart was beating mercilessly in her eardrums, and a warm ache was uncoiling deep within the most secret part of her. Never had she felt desire so molten; never had she so boldly responded to a man.

"Stay with me," Kyle encouraged as he dragged his lips from hers and kissed the column of her neck. Shivers of anticipation raced down her spine.

With all the effort she could muster, she gently pushed him away, placing her palms on the hard muscles of his chest. "I'll think about it," she agreed.

"What are you trying to do to me?" he demanded, his breath as ragged as her own. "One minute you say no, the next yes. What do you expect from me?"

"Time—"

"I'm not made of stone," he replied. "And neither are you. Do you get a kick out of teasing me?"

"That's unfair, Kyle. Teasing is for children and teenage flirts. I'm only trying to be sensible and go slowly. I don't want to do anything either of us might regret."

His hands fell to his sides. Frustration darkened his eyes. "You don't have to play games with me, Maren. I thought we understood at least that much from our conversation last night. I don't expect you to pretend to be a born-again virgin, for God's sake."

Maren's lips pursed. "Virginity isn't the issue—and really, neither is sex."

"Forgive me, I'm missing the point."

"Casual sex is what I'm worried about."

"You could have fooled me."

She ran her fingers through her hair. How could she make him understand? "You're a very famous man, Kyle. You're used to fan adulation, and groupies—"

"And casual sex," he finished for her.

"Yes!"

"You've been reading too many trashy movie magazines," he accused, "and you haven't listened to a word I've said in the last forty-eight hours." He stalked away from her angrily, only to turn and face her with accusing, omniscient eyes. Every muscle in his face had hardened. "But this really isn't about me, is it? This cat-and-mouse game and talk about commitment has to do with the man who hurt you." She didn't respond and his fist clenched angrily at his side. "If I ever have the misfortune to meet the bastard, I'll personally destroy him," Kyle promised.

The telephone rang impatiently, and Kyle answered it gruffly. The anger seething within him continued to rage. It was a one-sided conversation, punctuated only by Kyle's pointed remarks. "Just who do you think you are?" he asked. "Don't you think you ought to consider Holly's feelings.... I wish I could talk you out of this.... Take this as a warning; I'm not about to bail you out, not this time, not ever..."

Rather than eavesdrop on the personal conversation, Maren decided to leave Kyle and whoever was on the other end of the line in privacy. Earlier she had noticed a door leading from the living room to a covered deck, and when she tried the handle, she found the door unlocked.

Kyle's anger continued to rage, and the last statement Maren heard before the sound of the sea drowned out the remainder of the conversation was "...you know that I'm never too busy for Holly," Kyle conceded, disgust audible in his voice. "...You'd better believe that you're in for the battle of your life..." The rest of his warning was lost to Maren as she quietly closed the door behind her and stood near the wrought iron railing surrounding the porch. Far below the rugged cliffs was the sea. Maren breathed deeply of the salty air and listened to the roar of the surf as it crashed against the buffer of dark rocks protecting the lonely stretch of sand.

The sun had lowered into the sea, coloring the aquamarine water with streaks of gold. Maren was leaning on the railing, staring at the distant horizon and the dark silhouettes of sailboats when she heard Kyle approach. "I didn't mean to listen in," she apologized, still staring out to sea.

"You didn't." He stood next to her and focused his attention on a craggy jetty to the north. "Rose always has had an incredible sense of timing," he muttered. At the mention of Kyle's famous ex-wife's name, Maren's stomach knotted. Of course—why hadn't she guessed that he was talking to the petite blond country singer? As if to dismiss his ex-wife completely, Kyle touched Maren on the cheek. "Come on, let's go inside and I'll show you where I work."

Kyle led Maren to the far end of the deck. Opening the door, he escorted her into a room that appeared to be his office. "This is the den," he explained as they entered the oversize room. "When I'm not in L.A., this is where I spend most of my time."

The desk was cluttered with papers. The walls were covered with gold records and pictures of a girl with dark hair and intense green eyes. Maren suspected the portraits were of Kyle's child. The furniture was expensive but slightly worn, and Maren could picture Kyle very much at home in the comfortable, eclectic room with its expansive view of the sea.

Maren's briefcase stood near the desk. She was surprised to note that it seemed to belong in this private room. Dismissing the thought, she picked it up and turned to face Kyle. "I think I should go now," she stated, clutching the briefcase in a death grip.

"You have what you came after?"

She hesitated slightly. "Yes…"

"The least I could do is offer you dinner." His voice was low and seductive. The shadowed room began to close in on her.

"You did that last night, and I appreciated it."

"I have reservations at a nearby restaurant, and I'd much rather dine with you than spend the evening alone. It's your choice…" He smiled engagingly and Maren knew she'd lost the battle. More than anything else, she wanted to stay with this enigmatic man with the mysterious gray eyes.

A small smile graced her face. "You've convinced me," she agreed. "I'd like nothing better."

THE RESTAURANT WASN'T FAR from Kyle's house. The ancient structure had originally housed an order of monks but had fallen into disuse until recently, when it had been renovated into a secluded restaurant and hotel. The original gardens had been restored to lush grandeur, and the ancient woodwork had been polished to a warm luster. The smooth stones of the floor were only partially covered by new carpets, and electricity illuminated the rooms where only candles had burned in the past. Waiters dressed in somber brown robes brought the dishes to the table, and Maren felt as if she had been thrust backward in time.

"Do you come here often?" she asked, taking a final sip of burgundy.

"When I can," Kyle replied. "I like it here, maybe because it's so quiet."

"A strange statement from a man in your profession," Maren observed.

"Not so strange. Everyone needs a little solitude in his

life. Especially a person who is a public figure." Candlelight flickered in his eyes, and Maren noticed a deep pain lingering in his gaze. She had the uncanny sensation that she should comfort him, but refrained from putting her hand on his by telling herself to wait and try to remain objective. The feelings beginning to well within her would only complicate her life. She couldn't afford to feel obligated to another man; not now, when she was still tied to Brandon. The fact that she wasn't married to him wasn't the issue: Brandon still depended upon her financially.

Kyle drove back to the house without speaking, and Maren was content to stare into the black night. The silence gave her time to think and consider the situation. She was tempted to stay with Kyle, to spend a weekend of pleasure with this captivating man—and yet, she was wary.

When Kyle parked the car, he withdrew the keys from the ignition before turning to face her in the darkness. His eyes were as dark as the night. "Would you like a cup of coffee?" The question was simple, but another, deeper, unasked question lingered between them. Gently his fingers touched her chin, and her eyes closed.

"Yes," she whispered, accepting anything he could offer and knowing it to be an incredible mistake.

She felt his nearness as he helped her from the car. Though he didn't touch her as they walked toward the house, she could feel his eyes caressing her, and she found herself wanting to know what it was like to be touched by Kyle Sterling.

Upon entering the kitchen, Maren relaxed slightly. In the blaze of the electric lights, the seductive spell woven in the ancient monastery was broken. The kitchen was airy and light. Maren glanced appreciatively at the warm clay-colored tiles and the contrasting hand-painted tiles glazed in rich hues of blue and gold. Green plants were clustered near the windows, and shining brass pots hung from the ceiling.

"A gourmet's delight," Maren commented, running her fingers against the cool tiles.

Kyle smiled as if amused at the thought. "I don't know how gourmet she is, but Lydia seems to like it in here," Kyle observed as he heated the coffee.

"Lydia?" Maren's tongue nearly tripped over the unfamiliar woman's name.

"My housekeeper." Kyle poured the coffee into cups and added a little brandy to the steaming brew. "Actually, she's more than just a housekeeper." Maren swallowed with difficulty. "She helped raise me when my parents moved here from North Carolina. She's a Mexican-American who's lived with me off and on from the time I was nine."

"So much for your country image."

"Just don't let on to my agent."

"You still have one?"

Kyle shook his head. "No. Thank God those days are gone." He frowned into his coffee cup, as if calculating how much of his life story he should divulge to Maren. "Lydia came to work for me after Holly was born…but Rose never cared much for Lydia. When Rose and I were divorced, Rose got custody and refused to let Lydia stay on. So Lydia came here to take care of the place."

Rather than dwell on the personal aspects of his story that seemed to make him uncomfortable, Maren changed the subject. "One woman looks after all of this?"

"I let her hire the help she needs."

"Isn't this house a little overpowering for one man?" Maren asked. "Especially when it's your second home?"

Kyle frowned and looked out the window into the darkness. "I guess you could say that," he acquiesced. "I certainly didn't buy it with the intention of letting it sit idle." He set his cup on the table and concentrated on the night. "But, at the time, I didn't know any better. I always thought I would fill it with a lot of kids..." He shrugged. "It just didn't turn out that way." His voice and eyes seemed distant, as if he were locked in a past he couldn't accept.

Maren shifted uneasily and set her empty cup next to his. His brooding silence was as uncomfortable as a tight-fitting shroud, and just as bleak. "I didn't mean to pry," she offered, wondering at the pain he silently bore.

"You didn't."

"It's none of my business."

Without hesitation, Kyle crossed the room to wrap his arms possessively around her waist. He was standing behind her and his warm breath fanned the back of her neck. Without thinking about the consequences of her actions, she folded her arms over his, tightening the embrace. His voice was low and persuasive. "I asked you to come and stay with me. I expected you to inquire about personal aspects of my life. It's only natural."

"For some teenage groupie maybe—"

"Shh.... For anyone." He kissed the back of her neck and felt the air rush out in a sigh from her lungs. "There are things I'd like to know about you," he admitted, gently tugging on her jacket and removing it.

"Such as?"

"Everything." He tossed the jacket over the back of a chair and guided her toward the door leading to the porch. "Let's take a walk."

"Now?"

He flashed a charming smile—the same smile she had seen in numerous promotional posters when he was still the nation's most-photographed country singer. Slowly he released her waist and took one of her hands in his. "Come on."

He helped her down the worn steps running along the face of the cliff, and when they finally reached the bottom of the stairs, he kicked off his shoes and encouraged her to do the same. "This is the best time of day," he announced with a wicked smile.

"It's night."

"Yes, but the sand is still warm even though the sky is dark."

He coiled his fingers over hers and gently forced her hand into the pocket of his pants. Through the soft lining of the pocket, Maren could feel the movement of his thigh muscles with each of his strides. "So I take it you're a night person," she observed, trying to concentrate on the conversation and ignore the warm flesh straining beneath her fingertips.

He frowned pensively into the incipient night. "I don't sleep much," he admitted. "When I was on the road, late nights were common. I guess I never got out of the habit."

They walked near the ocean's edge. The sand was wet but firm, and their feet left soft impressions near the frothy waves. Occasionally the sea would rush over Maren's bare feet, splashing against her legs and threatening to dampen the hem of her sundress. The first stars began to wink above the fading streaks of light from the sunset.

"I think I owe you an explanation," Kyle decided aloud.

"About what?" Maren noticed the change in his voice. He seemed to be tossing something around in his mind. She slid a glance in his direction and noticed that his frown had deepened into a black scowl. In the darkness his features appeared more severe—as if he had suffered wounds too deep to bear.

"I know that you overheard part of my conversation with Rose."

Maren braced herself. "Not intentionally."

"I know." Kyle smiled sadly. "It doesn't matter. The point is that now that you're here with me, you're entitled to know what's going on."

Maren stopped dead in her tracks, forcing Kyle to do the same. How much did she want to know of this man? She didn't want to hear anything that might endear him to her further. Her blue eyes held his. "You don't have to tell me anything you don't want to," she whispered. "You're not obligated to say a word about that conversation or any part of your private life. I didn't come here to intrude—"

"Why *did* you come?" he demanded, surveying her with renewed interest. "And don't give me that garbage about Festival Productions, there's more to it than that!"

He took his hand from his pocket and drew her to him. The sea breeze ruffled his thick near-black hair. Danger sparked his intense gray eyes. His fingers coiled tightly over her bare arms, his jaw clenched threateningly. "Why can't you admit that you came here to be with me? Is that so difficult?"

"Of course I came to see you—"

"Because you want me!" All of the pent-up frustration was tearing at him. He had been patient with Rose, with Holly and now with Maren. But the strain of the last six months was tearing him apart, and he couldn't deal with another woman who wouldn't face the truth.

Anger sparked in her cool blue eyes. "I'll admit that I want you, Kyle, if that's what you want to hear. But I loathe the idea of being compared to one of those starry-eyed teenagers who see you as a God. Country Singer, Record Mogul, Songwriter, *God.*"

"I'm only asking that you look at me as a man." His voice was as low as the softly rushing tide. "And that frightens you."

Her lips trembled before she steadied herself. She leveled her gaze upward, giving no hint of the quivering emotions erupting within her. "It would be easy to say that I'm not afraid of you or what you represent, but that would be a lie, Kyle. I am afraid. I'm not used to dealing with men who are so pushy and forward. And I don't know how to react to you!"

"Reactions should be automatic," he replied, pushing his body against hers, fitting his legs around hers, pressing against her, muscle to muscle. The thin fabric of her sundress was a frail barrier against the hard power of his muscular frame.

"When reactions are automatic, and no logical thought controls actions, one person is lost to another." She tried to still the hammering of her heart; attempted to ignore the warm pressure of his hands against the small of her back.

"I wish I understood you," he moaned.

"Try, damn it, just try! Can't you see? I'm trying desperately not to confuse physical lust with mental attraction."

"Is there a difference?" he growled as his lips touched the crook of her neck and a shiver of anticipation skittered up her spine.

"I hope so," she answered. "Dear God, I hope so…"

His fingers splayed against the bare skin of her back. The rose-colored halter dress was little defense against the warmth of his palms. His lips touched her eyelids and slid over her cheeks. In a voice that was raw with tortured emotions, he whispered against her ear: "What is it you want from me?"

A lump rose in her throat. "I need to know that this is not just physical need.... I...I have to know that some of the attraction is mental."

"Oh, God," he swore as if the breath were torn from his lungs. "Can't you see what you do to me? Don't you know that the agony, the frustration, is as much in the mind as the body? Contrary to what you might think, Maren, I'm not a horny teenager chasing anything that moves. I haven't wanted a woman for some time now." His broad shoulders slumped with the weight of this admission. "But with you, it's different. I haven't been able to think of anything but you since I left you last night." With one hand he pulled her head away from him, twining his fingers in the long dark strands of her hair and compelling her to look into his passion-glazed eyes. *"Last night was the loneliest night of my life."*

If only she could believe him. She wanted with all of her heart to think that she alone would make such a lasting impression on him, but she was realistic enough to understand that his words were gentle words of seduction. Their meaning was lost in the warm, enticing mystique of night.

"Let me make love to you," he coaxed. His head lowered, and his lips brushed tantalizingly against hers. "Let me make you feel like the woman you are."

In silent invitation her lips parted and she felt his moist tongue slide between her teeth. The tongue invaded her mouth, arousing within her feelings she had thought dead. She could taste his need; sense the urgency with which he held her. Warm damp pressure was placed against her back. His hands kneaded the soft muscles and traced the length of her spine. A warm flood of prickling desire ran in her veins, and she sighed against him.

"I want you so badly," she conceded, the ache within her beginning to burn.

"Don't fight it…" His tongue rimmed her lips, teasing her until she groaned in frustration. Her heart pounded as loudly as the restless surf, the emotions grinding within her making her pulse race erratically, the arguments in her mind slowly dimming. She wanted this man. With more desire than she had ever before experienced, she wanted Kyle Sterling. Nothing else seemed important. If she were to fall in love with him, so be it. Let fate cast her what it would. It had been so long since she had been with a man…so long.

His lips warmed a path from her cheek to her neck. She rolled her head to the side, exposing more of her throat to his tantalizing exploration. Her heart threatened to explode within her and a film of perspiration clung to her skin. His hands moved slowly up her back, tracing the muscles until he reached under her hair, to her neck, to the single ribbon that held the bodice of her dress in place. "Let me undress you," he pleaded hoarsely as his fingers freed the ribbon. The soft fabric dropped, and the cold breath of the sea embraced her naked breasts.

"Oh, God," Kyle groaned as he stepped backward and watched the silvery moonglow caress each of the supple white mounds. Maren's nipples hardened under his intense stare. Goose bumps rose on her flesh as the sultry wind rushed over her naked torso and caught her hair, ruffling it away from her face.

Standing alone, one hand clasping the dress as it draped over her lower body, her eyes turning silver with the moonlight, Maren didn't move, but returned Kyle's unguarded stare. Surely he could see the hint of love lingering in her gaze; surely he knew that she would willingly give him what she had denied so many.

Kyle raked his fingers through his hair and pondered whether she was the most regally beautiful woman he had ever met. He closed his eyes for a second, hoping that with that one gesture he could stem the rising passion taking hold of his entire body. Desire throbbed in his eardrums and heated his loins.

When he opened his eyes, Maren took a step nearer to him and let go of her dress. It fell limply to the sand, leaving her naked except for her lacy underwear.

Kyle tried to hold back the passion threatening to take him over, body and soul. "If I didn't know better, I might think you were seducing me," he whispered, just as she reached him and stood on her toes to press her mouth against his lips. Her arms encircled his neck, and her fingers caught in his hair.

"Isn't this what you wanted?" she asked, trying desperately to understand him.

His throat was dry. "Yes," he whispered, "Oh, yes, but Maren, don't do this to *please* me." The blood was rushing through his body, his fingers sinking into the soft skin around her waist.

"The only person I'm pleasing is myself," she lied, hopelessly lost to the fires he ignited within her.

He groaned against her ear. A deep savage noise erupted from his throat and pierced her soul. His thumbs moved upward, tracing each of her ribs until his hands found the weight of her breasts. She sighed as he fondled her and the aching in her breasts was soothed as his hands traced their shape as if he were sculpting her.

"Undress me," he commanded, taking her hand and pushing it beneath the fabric of his shirt. "I want to be closer to you." Her fingers pulled the shirt over his head, feeling the strength of each of his rippling muscles.

The hard flat wall of his chest crushed against her breasts, and his lips kissed hers heatedly. Gently he lowered her to the sand and managed to kick off his pants. The cold sand pressed against her buttocks and shoulders while the warmth of his body heated her chest and abdomen. "You're more beautiful than any woman has the right to be," he confided. He traced the hollow of her throat with his fingers before letting his tongue rim the delicate bones. The heat in her veins sparked when his tongue flattened between her collarbones and then licked downward to rest between her breasts. His hot breath warmed her skin, the smell of the sea permeating her senses, and his hands, God, his loving hands, stroked her skin, softly kneading it until she thought she would go mad with longing.

Fires raged deep within her; aches demanded to be satisfied. His tongue encircled first one nipple and then the other, teasing the dark points until they were rock hard and bursting to be soothed. He pressed his mouth over the brown circle and took the entire nipple in his mouth, suckling her with the bittersweet pleasure of his moist affection. Unconsciously she arched upward to meet his body, and her fingers dug into the hard muscles of his back. She wanted more from him—all of him.

In a deft movement he removed her underpants, and she lay naked against the sand. She moaned her need, but he pulled away, taking one last look at her slim nude body on the sand. Moonlight mingled with passion and tinged her eyes an insatiable shade of blue. Her hair was tousled away from her face, and two points of color pervaded her cheeks.

"You do things to me that I can't explain, love," he admitted, moving over her and poising his body atop hers.

"I feel as if I've waited all my life for this moment." He lowered his head and bestowed urgent kisses upon her mouth. His body hovered over hers until his weight began to press her down into the cool sand. His legs parted hers slowly, as if by his restraint he could stretch the magic out a little longer; prolong the anticipation until just the right second.

"Make love to me," she pleaded, unable to restrain herself any longer. "Make love to me, Kyle, and never stop."

With a moan of surrender, he claimed her, and her sigh of contentment was lost against the sound of the relentless sea. She felt the heat of his passion, his explosion of desire and her answering shudder of surrender. The weight of his body fell against hers, and she knew the supreme ecstasy of resplendent love. Her body melted against his, and she became aware of his uneven breathing against the shell of her ear. Dear God, Maren thought to herself, how easy it is to love this man!

CHAPTER SIX

THE QUARTER MOON CAST a thin shifting ribbon of silver on the purple ocean. Stars winked conspiratorially in the blackened sky. Slowly Maren's rapid heartbeat became normal, and she sighed with contentment as she lay in the protective cradle of Kyle's strong arms. His features were shadowed with the night, but the soft moon glow caught in the slate-colored depths of his eyes, making them appear a ghostly silver.

Maren reached upward with her hand and lazily traced the line of his jaw. It was a tender gesture that silently expressed the feelings of love growing within her. He captured her hand with his fingers and kissed her soft fingertips.

"I could get used to this," he admitted roughly.

"So could I."

He pulled on his pants before reaching for her dress and gently easing the rose-colored garment up her legs. It was a natural feeling to have him dress her. As natural as it had been for him to remove her clothes. She lowered her head and lifted her hair off her shoulders, allowing him to retie the ribbon. Her skin tingled where his fingers brushed against the back of her neck. It was a strange seductive feeling—one she had never previously experienced. The few times Brandon had helped her dress had been from necessity only. It had never been an erotic experience. But with Kyle, anything he did with her became sensual. Maybe I've been too long without a man, she worried, but managed to push the unlikely thought aside. Long ago she had learned to live without a man, and although many men had been eager to help her forget Brandon's betrayal, Maren hadn't been interested in anything they had to offer. Until she had met Kyle. Whether she wanted to admit it to herself or not, she was beginning to fall desperately in love with Kyle Sterling; and love was the one emotion she had vowed to avoid. Falling in love with Kyle could only end in disaster, not only personally but professionally as well.

"I said earlier that I owed you an explanation," Kyle said softly as they walked back toward the worn staircase.

"It's not necessary," she replied. She paused to pick up her sandals and slip them onto her feet before taking the hand he offered and climbing the stairs.

"I usually don't talk about my marriage, not to anyone."

"I'm not asking any questions," Maren pointed out. "Just because we made love doesn't mean that I need any explanations or confessions from you. You don't have to tell me anything about your life. What happened between us doesn't change that."

"There are things I would like you to know."

"Not now," she sighed as the cool wind touched her back and the full force of her actions taunted her. Why had she let the intimacy growing between Kyle and herself get so far out of hand? Why had she so willingly offered herself to him? "I don't think we should discuss what happened between you and Rose—at least not for a while."

He hesitated on the steps, and she felt the warmth of his hands on her waist. Rotating to face him, she looked into his eyes. "What are you running from, Maren? What is it about me that scares you?"

"I'm not scared," she asserted, her chin lifting defiantly, "but I'd be a liar if I didn't admit to being overwhelmed..." A look of genuine confusion darkened her clear indigo eyes. "I don't know if I'm ready for all of this..." she gestured with her upturned palm toward the rambling hacienda and the sea far below.

"Because of your ex-husband?" His voice was low and deadly.

She wanted to lie and tell Kyle that Brandon had no control over her. She needed to explain that her love for her ex-husband had died before ever really blossoming, but the words wouldn't come to her. "I don't love Brandon, if that's what you're inferring.'

Leaning insolently against the worn railing, Kyle's gray eyes accused her of the lie. "Then what is it with you? One minute I get the feeling you want me and the next I sense that you're pulling away. It's as if you won't let me get too close."

"I'm just not sure how involved I can be right now," she sighed. The words were difficult to say. "Maybe it would be better if I just left...now."

His eyes darkened dangerously as he climbed the two steps separating their bodies. "I want you to stay..." Gathering her into his arms, he pressed his lips urgently against hers. His reawakening hunger, savage and raw, was imprinted upon her skin. Her flesh quivered expectantly under his fingertips. "Don't go," he whispered roughly against her ear. "Stay with me." Once again his lips found hers in an urgent kiss that silently conveyed the depth of his passion. Warm fingers splayed against her back, and the reasons for leaving him faded into the night.

She dragged her head away from his, hoping that she

could find the strength to deny what she so desperately wanted. "I think it would be better if I returned to L.A. tonight. I need time to think things through."

"I'm not asking for a commitment for the rest of your life," he reminded her gently.

"I know." She pulled out of his embrace and felt a pang of regret when he didn't attempt to stop her.

"I'm not a man to beg," he stated, dark brows drawing over his eyes.

"Good. That will make it easier, won't it?" she managed to reply, hoping to hide the reluctance in her voice. "I'll get the briefcase—" She hurried up the remainder of the steps and raced into the den. By the time he caught up with her, she had the briefcase tucked safely under her arm. "I'll let you know about my decision concerning the sale of the production company after I talk to my attorney."

He nodded curtly, responding as if he were in a boardroom, with no hint of emotion registering on his rugged features. Handing the jacket to her, he let his fingers touch hers for a moment, but still his face showed no sign of feeling.

His jaw was tight. "And I suppose that you'll do your best work on the series of videos for Mirage."

"You can count on it," she responded, her clear blue eyes holding his gaze evenly.

"So that's the way it is—all business with you."

"When it has to be."

A shadow of frustration blackened his eyes, but was quickly disguised as she turned toward the door. "Good night, Kyle," she called over her shoulder, not expecting or receiving a response. He began to follow her, but stopped at the front door and frowned to himself as he watched her leave.

Maren slipped into her car and hesitated only slightly

before pushing the key into the ignition and putting the car in gear. Caught in the reflection of her side-view mirror, the well-lit Spanish house stood proudly in the night, silently watching her leave. A sadness settled into her heart as Maren realized that she had just abandoned the most interesting man she had ever met. The darkness of the night seemed to taunt her as she remembered Kyle's warm, inviting embrace.

THE REMAINDER of the weekend passed uneventfully for Maren, and though she hoped that Kyle would call, she was disappointed. She tried to keep herself busy and concentrated on ideas for the Mirage videos, but she couldn't put thoughts of Kyle or their short time of lovemaking out of her mind.

When Monday morning finally came, Maren was up at the crack of dawn. As Maren walked through the doors of Festival Productions, the real world came crashing back to her and the distant thoughts of Kyle were replaced by her concern for the production company. When she sat down at her desk, she realized that time had stopped for Festival Productions and the same nagging problems she had left behind her on Friday were still waiting to be solved. Added to her already weighty workload were her concerns about the company. Kyle had insinuated that Festival might still have a problem with pirated videotapes. Though Kyle's manner had been unsuspicious and casual, Maren had been left with the impression that he was concerned about the problem and had brought up the bootlegged tapes as an obscure warning.

As she considered the conversation about the piracy, Maren took the cassette from her purse and placed it in the tape player. Rather than dwell on Kyle's cryptic remarks, she decided to tackle the work ahead of her. Slowly an idea for the Mirage videos was beginning to form in her mind. She pressed the play button on the tape deck and within a split second the inflamed lyrics of "Yesterday's Heart" filled the small office. Maren leaned against the back of her chair, closed her eyes and tried to study the words of the song, but she was unable to block out Kyle's strong image. Would he be like the unfaithful lover in the song? Dear God, she hoped not. Despite her brave words, Maren prayed that Kyle's lovemaking was a form of commitment.

Would it be possible for a man of Kyle Sterling's wealth and reputation to love her with even a fraction of the emotion she harbored for him? She shook her head and pressed her eyelids tightly closed, trying vainly to dispel her love. If she sold the production company to Kyle, she would have to work for him and see him frequently. Was it possible to be an employee by day and lover at night? What would happen if she sold her equity in Festival Productions and Kyle decided that he wasn't interested in her? Could Maren, like the hero in "Yesterday's Heart," pull herself back together?

The disturbing questions rattled around in her mind, nagging at her until the final strains of the song faded. Without thinking, Maren quickly rewound the tape and listened to the song again. The idea for the video began to expand and she envisioned an action sequence during the final refrain. Absently she started jotting notes to herself as she heard someone arrive in the outer office. Just as the throb of the music disappeared, Jan entered Maren's office with two cups of steaming coffee.

"Mirage?" Jan inquired, placing a cup on Maren's desk. Maren smiled gratefully at the blond secretary. There were deep circles under Jan's brown eyes, evidence of more than one poor night's sleep.

"Yes." She took a sip of the coffee. "Thanks," she murmured, as she set down her pencil and leaned back in the chair. "It's a song called 'Yesterday's Heart': the first single to be released from Mirage's next album."

Jan held up her palm. "Slow down," she suggested. "The last I heard, Festival didn't have a signed contract on that album." Before Maren could respond, the secretary caught on. "Don't tell me—let me guess. The infamous Kyle Sterling, as I predicted, fell at your feet like a penitent lover."

Maren was forced to smile at Jan's graphic image. "Not quite," she replied, "but I did manage to get him to sign a few of the contracts."

"The gentle art of persuasion," Jan surmised.

"I think we're back in business, at least for the time being," Maren admitted with obvious relief.

Jan withdrew a cigarette from her purse. "I just hope that one of the contracts belongs to Joey Righteous. That kid's been driving me crazy…" She inhaled deeply on the cigarette and blew a thin stream of smoke toward the ceiling. Some of the tension left her wan features.

"Unfortunately for Joey, we're going to have to concentrate on the Mirage videos first," Maren asserted, regarding her friend with worried eyes. Jan looked as if she hadn't been able to rest for over a week.

"Joey's going to be fit to be tied," Jan predicted.

"Isn't he always?"

The secretary chuckled and nodded her blond head in agreement. "Yeah, I suppose he is."

Maren took another sip from her cup and tapped her pencil nervously on the desktop. She was concerned about

Jan and hoped the secretary would open up to her. Even though Maren considered Jan a friend, she hated to pry into her personal life. "Has anyone from production managed to make it in today?"

Shaking her head and blowing out a cloud of blue smoke, Jan frowned. "Not yet, but Ted thought he'd be in around eleven. He's helping edit the final takes of the Mitzi Danner release—"

"*Going for Broke?*" Maren guessed.

"That's it."

"Is there a problem with it?" Maren asked, her dark brows pinching together in worry. The last thing she needed was a problem with Mitzi Danner, whose hot temper was as well-known as her sensual songs. "I thought that tape was supposed to be finished last week."

"It was."

"So there was a problem." Maren experienced a sinking sensation.

"What do you think?"

Smiling at the private joke, Maren looked questioningly at Jan. "Okay, so fill me in—what happened?"

"Don't panic—it wasn't anything *too* serious," Jan said with an amused laugh. "There were a couple of outdoor shots that came out too dark—probably because the sun had already set by the time Mitzi managed to get herself ready. The final scene of the song was supposed to be backdropped by a setting sun—"

"I remember."

"Anyway, when Ted realized that the scene was too dark, he convinced Mitzi to reshoot over the weekend."

"I bet she loved that," Maren observed sarcastically.

"Well, according to Ted, Mitzi managed to pout throughout the filming." Jan laughed aloud at the image.

"Actually, Ted was pleased. Mitzi's petulant look was perfect for the take."

"Thank God for small favors." Maren leaned her head against the back of the chair and ran her fingers through her hair thoughtfully. "Let's hope the final takes were okay. I'd hate to be the one to have to call Mitzi and explain that we had to do it all over again."

"Amen," Jan agreed, with a frown. "You've never been too crazy about her, have you?"

A fleeting image of Mitzi draped over Kyle's arm near a swimming pool flashed through Maren's mind. "Are you kidding?" Maren replied lightly. "I've got every record she ever released."

"You're hedging," Jan accused.

"And you're right. I really don't have any problem with Mitzi. She's a good client, and she has a tremendous talent for picking the right songs to complement her style."

"But," Jan coaxed.

"I could do without the prima donna routine."

"You and me both." Jan stubbed out her cigarette and slowly pulled herself out of the chair. The color drained from her face as she straightened.

"Are you all right?" Maren asked with genuine concern. She noticed the expression of pain on Jan's tired features.

Jan offered her boss a tentative smile, hoping to ease Maren's mind. "As well as can be expected."

"I assume that means you've seen a doctor."

Jan's nervous smile broadened, but there was a catch in her throat when she tried to speak. "I went this morning. It's official: I'm going to have a baby early in November."

"Jan! That's wonderful!" Maren exclaimed, expressing her heartfelt enthusiasm. "Have you told Jacob yet?"

Jan took in a deep breath. "No," she admitted reluctantly, "but I will, tonight or later in the week. He's been pretty moody lately, so I think I'd better wait until just the right moment before I spring it on him."

"You might be surprised by his reaction."

"I doubt it," Jan confided, pursing her lips together in order to hold back the tears burning behind her eyes. Visibly straightening her shoulders, she managed to slip her poise back into place by turning the conversation away from Jake and the baby. "So tell me, how did you manage to get Mr. Sterling to sign those contracts?"

"Careful negotiation," Maren joked, hoping to lighten the somber mood that had settled on Jan's slim shoulders.

"Negotiation?"

"That's right. It seems that Sterling Recording Company is very interested in buying out Festival Productions. Kyle wants me to sell my interest to him and continue to run the operation from the recording company. It would be an easy way for Sterling Records to start producing their videos in-house."

Jan looked as if she'd been struck. "But surely you're not considering his offer—"

"It might be the answer to our problems," Maren stated. Why was Jan so distressed? The poor girl actually looked as if she were frightened of something. Maren noticed the trembling of Jan's lower lip and the widening of her dark eyes.

"But you've worked so hard to make it on your own!" Jan protested vehemently. "Are you going to give up all your freedom, your artistic license, all this..." With her arm she made a sweeping gesture to encompass the furnishings of the office.

"I'm considering it," Maren stated evenly, trying to understand Jan's uncharacteristic paranoia.

"Why?"

"First of all, I wouldn't be giving up that much; I'll have everything I want written into the contract of sale, and secondly, Festival needs a more secure future. How much longer can we survive living from contract to contract?"

"But things have just started to turn around! I know for a fact that J. D. Price will have no one but you handle his videos. Even Joey Righteous thinks you're divine, and that's a mighty big compliment from someone who considers himself a deity."

Maren tried to placate the anxious secretary "Jan, what's wrong? Nothing is going to change—at least, not significantly. Everyone in production will still work under me. It's just that Sterling Records will be my employer. We'll all be a lot more secure, and that includes the record company. Kyle feels that he needs tighter control on the videos."

Jan's entire body tensed. "Why?" she whispered, looking as if she expected the roof to collapse.

"Videos are big business. They've turned the recording industry slump around. Sterling Records wants to cash in on them now, while they're hot. No matter what *I* do, Kyle Sterling is determined to produce the videos in-house. I'm just lucky that he wants to work with me instead of edge me out of the business."

Jan leaned against the wall, and her brown eyes narrowed suspiciously. "Don't you think that's exactly what he's doing?"

Maren smiled, trying to hide the doubts forming in her own mind. "No, I think he's sincere."

"Then why didn't he sign *all* the contracts?"

"I didn't press him, I guess."

Jan's expression hardened. "That doesn't sound like

you. What's happened to you, Maren? You've never let a man push you around before."

"I don't think I'm being pushed, Jan." It was Jan's tone of voice more than her accusation that made Maren uneasy.

"Don't tell me that you've started to fall for the guy..." When Maren didn't immediately respond, Jan rolled her eyes expressively toward the ceiling. "Don't do it, Maren. Don't let that guy get to you. He has a reputation as long as my arm for using women. Don't you remember what a field day the press had covering his divorce from Sterling Rose? And then, what about all the women and men he stepped on to get where he is today! Even Mitzi Danner didn't get away from him unscathed."

"Look, Jan," Maren interjected, hoping to quell the tide of anger welling within the secretary. "I told you I was considering his proposal to buy out my interest in Festival. Until I see a firm offer in writing, I won't make up my mind."

"It sounds as if you already have," Jan stated weakly.

"For the time being, nothing's changed," Maren assured the young woman. "And I just wanted to let you know what was going on. I didn't mean to upset you. You don't have to worry about your job."

"How can you be so sure of that?" Jan charged. "What do you know about Sterling Recording Company and the way it handles its employees. Kyle Sterling has a reputation for being a very shrewd and ruthless businessman. He'll step on anyone who gets in his way. There're just no two ways about it, the man's an A1 bastard!"

Maren stood her ground. Her blue eyes were determined; her soft voice was calm. "I've heard about his reputation, Jan. I haven't gotten where I have by hiding my head in the sand. But I've also met the man, and I think he's going to play fair with me."

"How do you know that? You're talking about everyone who's involved with Festival. All of our futures are at stake!"

"And I won't let anyone, including Kyle Sterling, pull a fast one on me. If you don't trust me, certainly you can rely on Elise Conrad, Festival's attorney. Everything will be reviewed by her office before I make a final decision. Don't worry," Maren urged with an indulgent smile. "Everything's going to work out very well."

"Since when did you become an optimist? Since meeting Kyle Sterling?" Jan asked, still visibly shaken. "What exactly happened between the two of you?"

"Not much," Maren evaded. "We met and talked business and got to know a little more about each other."

"Oh, Maren," Jan sighed, seeing through Maren's words. Jan hesitated in the doorway and stared at the floor before raising her dark eyes to meet Maren's questioning gaze. "What you do with your personal life is none of my business," she began uneasily, "but I just hope you're careful. I'd hate to see you become another one of Kyle Sterling's conquests. From what I understand, he'll destroy anyone or anything he considers a threat." The secretary attempted a smile and failed miserably. "Don't get into anything you might regret later," she advised.

"Such as enter a relationship with Kyle Sterling?"

"Such as getting involved with the wrong man." Without another word, Jan left Maren's office, leaving her employer to wonder if Jan was offering advice from her own experience. But why the absolute hatred of Kyle? From the look on Jan's face, Maren could tell that Jan's relationship with Jacob Green hadn't improved. Perhaps that was the cause of Jan's distress. If her situation with Green was insecure, the pressure of the pregnancy coupled with a change in job status might account for the young woman's concern about the sale of Festival. But it didn't explain Jan's angry remarks about Kyle.

Maren tried to shake the uncomfortable feeling enveloping her and concentrate on the storyboards for the Mirage videos. The theme tying the separate cuts of the album together was taking shape in her mind, and she worked furiously on her sketches for the rest of the day, pausing only during lunch to discuss her idea with Ted Bensen, who was in charge of the production crew.

It was nearly five when she received the call from Kyle.

"Kyle Sterling's on line one," Jan announced with audible reluctance.

"Thanks," Maren replied before pressing the lighted button on the telephone.

"Maren?" Kyle's rich voice called to her before she had a chance to answer. The sound of her name reminded her of the night she had lain in his arms. The moon had cast its silvery glow over the sea before resting in Kyle's gaze. He had lain over her, whispering words of love into her ears. Her heart hammered mercilessly in her rib cage.

"I was beginning to think I wouldn't hear from you." Her tone was light and carefree and disguised the misgivings that had plagued her. Jan's warning echoed in her ears: *"He'll destroy anyone he considers a threat."*

"I've been busy," was the abrupt reply. "But I did manage to call my attorney. He promises that you'll have an offer for Festival within the week."

"And I assume that you want an immediate response."

"As quickly as possible." There was a moment of hesitation. "You can get hold of me here. I doubt that I'll be in the office for a couple of weeks."

"What about the other contracts—there were a few you didn't bother to sign."

"You can bring them with you, with the sales agreement."

"You expect me to bring them to La Jolla?" she asked incredulously.

"If you want them signed. I won't be back in L.A. for a while."

"I'll have to have my attorney look over the sales contract," Maren stated, slightly unnerved by his totally businesslike tone.

"I realize that. Call me when you've made your decision."

With his final words, he hung up the phone, and Maren was left with the disturbing feeling that Jan's warnings were about to come true.

CHAPTER SEVEN

ONE WEEK STRETCHED into two and Maren had had barely a moment to herself. The days at the office were a whirlwind of paperwork, meetings and production schedules. Maren drove herself at a furious pace until late each night. Somehow she managed to keep up with the bookkeeping, correspondence and client relationships, along with creating a complete set of storyboards for each of the five cuts on the Mirage album. J. D. Price had tentatively approved her story lines and had only offered a few bits of advice about changing a couple of action sequences. The next man to tackle was Kyle. As far as Maren knew he was still in La Jolla.

The short nights crept by at a snail's pace. Though Maren felt dead on her feet by the end of each day, she was unable to fall asleep promptly when she finally crawled under the covers and collapsed in a weary heap. Thoughts of Kyle crowded her tired mind, and her body ached for his gentle touch. Memories flooded her senses when she thought of the one night she had spent with him, and she wondered if she would ever feel the warmth and power of his arms around her again. Or had that one solitary night meant nothing to him?

Thursday morning the ringing of the phone jarred her out of her restless sleep. Muttering angrily to herself, she reached for the telephone and knocked the receiver on the floor before summoning enough dexterity to grasp the slippery instrument. "Hello?" she mumbled ungraciously into the phone.

"Maren?" Kyle asked. "I realize that it's early—"

"I guess." Maren smiled and yawned. It felt good to wake up to the sound of his voice. "What time is it?" She forced her gaze to focus on the digital display of the clock radio near the phone. "Six o'clock!" She rubbed her hand over her eyes before raking her fingers through the tangled strands of her hair. "No one in his right mind calls at this hour," she accused with a sigh.

"It was now or never. I doubt that I'll be near a phone for the rest of the day and I wanted you to know that I'll be in L.A. late this afternoon." There was a weighty pause in the conversation. "I was hoping that we could meet to discuss the Mirage videos and my offer on Festival. You have made a decision, I assume."

"Not until Elise Conrad approves," Maren hedged.

"Has she seen the offer?" Kyle's voice had become strained. Maren could hear it in the sharpness of his words.

"I sent it to her on Monday."

"Good. Then maybe we can tie all the ends together tomorrow before I have to return to La Jolla."

"I doubt if it will be that easy," Maren replied.

"I don't have much time."

Maren's lips pulled into a frown. Why was he pushing so hard? Was he afraid she might back out of the sale? Was it *that* important to Sterling Records? "This is a big decision for me, you know."

There was an exasperated sigh on the other end of the connection. "I understand that, Maren, but I'm caught between a rock and a hard spot. The sooner this sale is complete, the better for everyone involved, including you. Right now, I can't afford not to produce the videos at Sterling Records. If you're not going to accept my offer, or at the very least negotiate a deal, then I'll have to hire someone else to establish Sterling videos on the market. As I said before, I don't have a hell of a lot of time to waste while your attorney nitpicks through each clause of the contract."

"You don't like the idea of attorneys being involved in this, do you?" Maren charged.

"I've dealt with quite a few in my time—"

"And obviously been burned," Maren interjected angrily before managing to regain control of her temper. Kyle Sterling was too important a client to infuriate, and regardless of her conflicting emotions toward the man, she had to remain rational and calm. "Look, Kyle," she said more calmly, "I'll see what I can do. I'll call Elise this morning and find out what she thinks about the offer."

"I'd appreciate it, "he responded curtly. "Can you meet me at my office?"

Maren mentally reviewed her schedule. "I think so. What time?"

"How about four?"

"I think that will work out. I want to bring along the storyboards for the Mirage videos: It's time we put 'Yesterday's Heart' into production."

"I'll see you then." He paused for a moment, as if he might have something more to add. Maren waited while her heart pounded in anticipation. If only he could let her know that what they shared together was more than just a night of passion.... "Goodbye."

"Goodbye," Maren whispered as she heard him sever the fragile connection. A dull pain twisted in her heart. She set down the phone and leaned back into the pillow. What had she expected, anyway? Maren knew that Kyle's primary interest in her was Festival Productions; he'd admitted as much. She also realized that he was attracted to her and probably, in his own sophisticated way, cared for her. But the love she felt for him could never possibly be returned. It just wasn't possible, no matter how desperately she wanted to believe that he loved her. "No sense in deluding yourself," she mumbled miserably as she tossed back the covers and compressed her lips into a line of disgust. Knowing that falling back to sleep was completely out of the question, Maren reached for her robe and decided to go into the office early. There were still a few details she had to straighten out on the first Mirage video, and she wanted everything in perfect order when she met with Kyle later in the day.

THE PARKING LOT was usually empty. This morning was an exception. The warm morning sunlight reflected brightly off the sleek imported sports car parked in front of the building housing Festival Productions.

Maren parked her car and approached the building. As she neared the silver import, Jacob Green extracted himself from the vehicle. He was a slim man of medium build with perfectly combed sandy-colored hair and an equally manicured smile. Maren knew that Jake had to be pushing fifty, but he managed to keep himself fit and looked a good ten years younger than his age.

"Hi Maren," Jacob greeted, falling into stride with her as she headed up the concrete steps.

Maren forced an uneasy smile onto her face. "Good morning." After unlocking the glass door, Maren stepped inside the building. Jacob Green was quick to follow her, and Maren felt an uneasy sensation take hold of her.

"If you're looking for Jan," Maren said, picking up the newspaper that had been forced through the mail slot near the door, "she's not here yet." Certainly Jacob knew of Jan's whereabouts, Maren thought; Jan was living with him.

"Actually," Jacob replied smoothly, "I wanted to see you."

"Oh?" Maren lifted her eyes from the front page of the *Los Angeles Times,* and started up the stairs. "What's up?"

"I thought you and I could discuss our contract on Festival," Jake suggested.

Maren was instantly wary, and her back stiffened. "Is there a problem?"

"Not yet." His words were cryptic, and they made her uneasy. It took every ounce of civility within her to hang on to her poise.

"Good. Why don't you wait for me in my office," Maren suggested as she mounted the stairs. Jacob was only a couple of steps behind her, and she had the uncanny feeling that he was eyeing her hips as she climbed the stairs. "I'll get us each a cup of coffee."

"Great!" They reached the second floor and Jake started toward Maren's office. "Don't forget the sugar." He disappeared into the other room.

"Wouldn't dream of it," Maren mumbled to herself. There was just something about the man that made her anxious and unnerved. It didn't help matters to know how unhappy Jan had been recently. Jan had never mentioned telling Jacob about the baby, and Maren had never pried. It was evident that something was eating at the poor girl, but the one time Maren had commented on that fact, Jan had told her nicely but firmly that it was really none of her concern. Rebuffed and slightly embarrassed, Maren hadn't mentioned the situation again.

"Here you go," Maren announced, setting a cup of coffee along with several sugar cubes next to Jake's chair. "Now tell me, what is it you want to discuss?"

Maren took a seat behind the desk, feeling more comfortable with the large piece of furniture separating her from Jacob. The barrier, however frail, gave her some sense of strength. Jacob stirred his sugar into his coffee and took a long swallow. When he looked up at Maren he hoped his smile seemed sincere.

"You always could make a great cup of coffee," he stated with a slippery grin.

"And you've been known to beat around the bush. I'm really very busy today, Jake. In fact, I've got a nine-o'clock appointment. So why don't you tell me what it is that's bothering you about the contract?"

"It's no big deal, really," he said, shrugging his shoulders. Maren could tell by the way he avoided meeting her gaze that he was lying. Whatever it was, it was very important to Jacob Green. Something was up. Something big. "I was hoping that you could make the May *and June* payments on the fifteenth."

Maren regarded him silently for a moment. She would like nothing better than to pay him his money and send him packing. Dealing with him had always been difficult. Her blue eyes narrowed as she considered the possibilities. Finally she shook her head. "I'm sorry, Jake, but I just can't swing it. If I remember correctly, the June payment escalates by another thousand dollars. There's just no way I can stretch my budget right now, at least not until I get some cash from the April billings, and they just went out."

Jacob's friendly smile faded, and he set his cup on the table. "Can't you work something out, Maren? I'm really strapped right now." He stood from the chair and pushed his hands into his back pockets as he faced her.

Maren managed to conceal her surprise. She had always assumed that Jacob was well-heeled. Not only had he received a large amount of cash when she had purchased Festival, but she paid him monthly on the contract. The last she had heard he was working at Sentinel Studios. Where could his money be going?

"I just can't handle a larger payment this month."

Jacob's eyes traveled around the room, noting the few but expensive pieces of furniture. From what he could discern, Maren's operation was doing well—very well—and the gossip in the industry indicated that her services as a producer of videotapes were in considerable demand. He changed his tactics.

"Jan tells me you might be selling the business."

The hackles on Maren's neck rose. She had expected her secretary to hold her tongue. But that might not have been possible, considering Jacob's link to Festival. "That's right," Maren conceded unwillingly. "I'm considering the possibility. Nothing more."

"Jan seemed to think it was all wrapped up." Once again Jacob took a seat. He felt as if he had unwittingly gained the advantage in the discussion. Lines of worry creased Maren's normally smooth forehead.

"I'm still thinking about it," Maren hedged. As far as she was concerned, what she did with Festival Productions was none of Jacob Green's concern as long as she paid him off.

"You still owe me about eighty thousand dollars," Green pointed out with a bitter smile.

"I realize that."

"I just wanted to remind you that the contract is non-transferable. I want my share in cold hard cash."

"And that's what you'll get," Maren assured him. "If and when I decide to sell."

"Damn it all, I never thought that videos would take off the way they did," Green admitted with a trace of disgust. "If I had, you can bet I never would have sold this operation to you!"

"When I bought Festival, you were concentrating mainly on commercials," Maren observed. "I don't think you had even thought of doing videos."

"Yeah, well, maybe that's true. But you can bet that I would have changed course once I'd figured out how hot those videos would become. They're a goddamn gold mine!"

"I told you that before you sold the business to me," Maren pointed out. "You didn't listen."

Jacob waved off her words with the back of his hand. "How was I to know they weren't going to be some overnight flash-in-the-pan fad that was here today and gone tomorrow. Son of a bitch!"

Jan entered Maren's office, and her dark brown eyes took in the scene before her. Maren was surprised and grateful for Jan's arrival. "Jacob?" Jan asked uneasily, her thin lips pulling into a tight smile. "What're you doing here?" Her liquid brown eyes accused Jacob of something Maren couldn't understand. It was probably another lovers' quarrel and none of Maren's business, she decided, trying to find an excuse to leave the two of them alone.

Jacob was immediately defensive. "I was just havin' a chat with Maren, babe," Jake replied with an uncomfortable grin. He rubbed the back of his neck after setting his coffee cup aside. "You know," he cajoled, seeing Jan's obvious distress, "it's about that time again. The rent's due, so to speak." A flush of scarlet crawled up Jan's neck, disguising her wan pallor.

Trying to pull herself together, Jan ignored Jacob for the moment and looked toward Maren. "Joey Righteous will be here at nine," she reminded her employer as she crossed the room and placed a stack of neatly typed letters on the corner of Maren's desk.

"Should I have my attorney present?" Maren joked, and Jan forced a laugh despite the disturbing situation. Jacob looked from one woman to the other, not completely understanding the private joke.

"I don't think it will be necessary today," Jan said, relaxing slightly.

"Good." In an effort to get rid of Jacob Green, Maren pulled the checkbook from her file cabinet and wrote a check for the May fifteenth contract payment. Jacob took the check and stuffed it into his wallet while Jan effectively ushered him out of Maren's office.

Angry portions of the argument between Jan and Jacob filtered through the closed door. Though Maren switched on the tape player and concentrated on the third song to be released from the Mirage album, she couldn't shake the feeling of concern overtaking her. Maren cared for Jan, and it was apparent that the secretary was very unhappy. Something wasn't right between Jan and Jacob, and Maren suspected it was more than just the pregnancy. Jan hadn't been herself lately. She was nervous and jittery. Perhaps it was because of the pregnancy, but Maren doubted it. Maren had never known Jan to attack anyone; she was a reserved girl who usually kept her opinions to herself. But the other day, without provocation, Jan had verbally assaulted Kyle. It was unusual. Obviously Jan was under a tremendous amount of pressure from Jake.

Maren's musings were cut short when Joey Righteous burst into the room. He was sporting a black leather jacket, dark sunglasses and tight-fitting red leather pants. He looked the part of an overnight R & B sensation. "Hey, Mama, what's happenin'?" he asked as he sprawled into one of the chairs. His charming smile spread evenly across his dark skin, exposing perfect white teeth.

Maren returned the smile. Despite his infamous hot temper, Joey Righteous boasted a certain charisma that couldn't be denied. "Save the 'bad, black and beautiful' routine for someone who'll buy it," she returned with a knowing laugh. "You might be able to convince the record-buying public that you're just a poor ghetto kid from the streets of Chicago, but I know for a fact that you graduated from Stanford."

Joey exaggerated his cringe and put his finger to his lips. "No more of that talk," he whispered. "You'll destroy the image."

"Impossible." She eyed the gaudy outfit and grinned in amusement. "No one would ever believe that you graduated with honors in math."

"Shame on you," Joey accosted, lifting his dark glasses and giving Maren a glimpse of his sparkling black eyes. "You been checkin' up on me."

"Just doing my homework—same as you."

Joey, anxious to get down to business, slapped his broad palm on the desk as if to change the subject. "So how's my video comin'?"

Maren leaned back in her chair. Her blue eyes never left Joey's dark gaze. "I'm afraid it's been put on hold for a little while."

"*What?*" he shrieked. "What you talkin' 'bout?" anger sparked in his dark eyes.

"Your contract with Festival hasn't been signed by Sterling Records."

"Why not?" he demanded.

"It's nothing serious," Maren said, holding up her palms as if physically attempting to soothe him.

"Oh, yeah? Tell me about it!"

"I'm taking your contract with me today. I have a meeting with Kyle Sterling. I'm sure he'll sign the contract, and we can proceed with the video. Then I expect there will be no further delay."

"Sounds like double-talk to me," Joey complained. "Or honkie bull…"

"Not from me, Joey. We've done business for a couple of years now, and we haven't had a problem, have we?" She didn't wait for his reply. "I promised you that the video would be completed before your tour of Japan. I'm sure Sterling Records will agree."

"You ain't jivin' me?" Joey asked, unconvinced.

Maren shook her head, keeping her warm smile intact. "No, but if I do have a problem with Sterling, which I don't anticipate, I'll let you know immediately. What do ya say?"

Joey frowned pensively, and his head bounced to an angry beat. "I don't know."

Maren pushed away from the desk, stood and walked over to her long cabinets. Bending on one knee, she pulled open a drawer and extracted her sketches. She handed them to Joey. "Here are the storyboards for 'Restless Feelin'.'" Joey balanced his sunglasses on the top of his head as he studied the drawings. "What do you think?" Maren asked when Joey raised his head.

"You sure know your business," he admitted with a low whistle.

"I try."

Plopping his shades back onto his nose, he rose from

the chair and towered over Maren. "What's this I hear about bootlegged videos?"

Maren's smile froze. "What do you mean?"

"Didn't Festival have trouble a while back?"

"There was a problem. It's been corrected."

"I hope so," Joey whispered. His dark face seemed suddenly threatening. "I wouldn't like it if my video was pirated."

"Neither would I."

Rubbing his chin, Joey smiled again. "No, I suppose you wouldn't. Hey, now, you'll call me if the record company gives you any trouble 'bout signin' that contract?"

"As soon as I find out," Maren assured him.

With his lower lip protruding speculatively, Joey seemed at least partially mollified. "Okay, Mama. I be expectin' your call." He sauntered out of the room with a disjointed stride that promised the rhythm and soul of his popular songs.

Maren walked with him to the door and accepted his palm along with his collusive wink. When Joey was gone, Jan turned from her typewriter, her worried eyes accosting Maren. "Trouble?" she guessed.

"Not much," Maren replied, hiding her concern over Joey's remarks about the video pirating. Within the last few weeks, the subject of pirated videos kept haunting her. Maren tried to shake off her unease and answer Jan's probing gaze. "Joey was pretty laid-back...for Joey, that is."

"Telling me that Joey is 'laid-back' is like saying a hurricane is a gentle breeze." Maren laughed and Jan released a troubled sigh. Her serious eyes clouded unhappily. "I should apologize for Jacob's behavior," she said, reaching for her cigarettes.

Maren waved off Jan's attempts at amends. "Don't worry about it, Jacob and I have business together. It wasn't a big deal"

As Jan lit the cigarette, Maren noticed that the blonde's hands were shaking. "I told you he's changed," Jan reaffirmed, inhaling deeply on the cigarette and leaning back in the chair to blow the smoke toward the ceiling. "I don't understand him sometimes."

"We all need a little extra cash now and again," Maren observed, not knowing how to console Jan. "I know that as well as anyone."

"I suppose," Jan agreed reluctantly and closed her eyes. "I finally told him about the baby." She turned to face Maren.

"And?"

"Nothing." Jan shook her head, as if to clear the cobwebs of mistrust. "He didn't say anything. He just stood there and looked at me as if I'd completely lost my mind. I know this sounds crazy, but I think it would have been better if he had gotten angry."

Maren disagreed but kept her thoughts to herself. She'd been on the receiving end of Jacob Green's vehement anger once in the past. It had happened when a take for a commercial had to be scrapped and reshot. Jacob had been so angry that he had thrown his paperweight through the glass door of the building. "Maybe the prospect of becoming a father again came as a shock," she suggested.

Jan leaned her chin into her hand. The cigarette was poised near her cheek, and smoke curled lazily up to the rafters as she considered Maren's words. "It was more than a shock, I'd say, but at least he didn't try and talk me into an abortion…not yet, anyway."

Maren was sickened at the thought. "Give him a while to get used to the idea of having a baby around," she suggested. "This might not be easy for him. His other kids are grown."

Jan sighed and looked away from Maren. "Yeah, well, we'll see, won't we?"

"Things have a way of turning out for the best," Maren predicted, knowing her words sounded lame.

"I hope so," Jan thought aloud. "God, I hope so."

CHAPTER EIGHT

LOCATED JUST FIVE BLOCKS north of the famous intersection of Hollywood and Vine stood the Sterling Records Building. The modern structure was smaller than the nearby circular Capitol Records Building, but distinct in its own manner. Rising from the ground like a silver wedge, the three-sided building was a unique architectural triumph constructed of gray concrete slabs and reflective glass.

Maren had visited the building many times but had never ceased to be awestruck by the magnificent edifice. As she walked through the carpeted hallways, she realized that soon, if Kyle had his way, she might have her own office somewhere in the building. She wondered how it would feel to work with Kyle on a day-to-day basis and how it would affect her relationship with him. If she were to agree to the sale, would she lose all the freedom and respect for which she had fought so diligently? And what was to prevent Kyle from tossing her out, should he become unhappy with her? A simple clause in a contract was little consolation. Sterling Recording Company had lawyers and capital at their disposal that Maren couldn't begin to match. Once Festival Productions was his, Kyle could do just about anything he pleased with it.

A disturbing sense of dread ran down her spine as she

followed a plump well-dressed woman to Kyle's office. After a quick rap on the door, the secretary pushed it open, allowing Maren to enter Kyle's domain. Taking her cue, Maren strode into the room, her eyes sweeping the cluttered interior of the office. Kyle was seated at a modern chrome and glass desk, the top of which was littered with papers. A quick glance at the rest of the spacious room indicated that it was in no better shape than the desk. Maren guessed that the room was lavishly furnished, though it was difficult to discern. Filled boxes, pictures, awards and various memorabilia were strewn haphazardly over the floor and furnishings. "Mr. Sterling," the complacent secretary announced just as Kyle looked up from the desk. "Ms. McClure is here."

"Thank you, Grace," he replied, dismissing the secretary.

Grace nodded curtly, seemingly oblivious of the disarray in her employer's office. She walked past an overflowing wastebasket, and with as much professionalism as she could muster, softly closed the door behind her.

"What's going on here?" Maren asked, eyeing Kyle suspiciously. "It looks like you're cleaning house, but I doubt that you made the trip to L.A. just for that."

"I came up here to see you," he said pointedly as he rose from behind the desk. "We have unfinished business." He was wearing slacks and an oxford cloth shirt. The sleeves had been rolled away from his wrists, and his tie was tossed carelessly over the back of a chair near his discarded sport coat. His arms were crossed over his chest, and his gray eyes held hers fast. His body was lean and tense, as if he had been waiting for her, anticipating what was to come.

"I'm moving," he stated as he circumvented the desk and walked over to her.

"What?" Her sea-blue eyes swept up to meet his determined gaze. "Moving? Where? To another office?" She stood as if rooted to the floor, the confusion on her face demanding answers.

"I'm moving the things I need back to La Jolla," he replied. Without further explanation, he dusted his hands on his slacks and then pressed his fingertips against his neck as if trying to alleviate muscle strain in his shoulders. Maren managed to hold on to her frail smile, but disappointment welled within her. *He was leaving*—leaving the position of running the company on a daily basis to one of his vice presidents. Inexplicably she felt betrayed, as if he had lured her into nearly selling Festival Productions to him, only to abandon her and the production company to some faceless underling. For the first time since the start of negotiations for the sale of Festival, Maren realized that if she did indeed sell, she might not end up working for Kyle at all. Perhaps he intended to remain only the figurehead of Sterling Recording Company, or, worse yet, maybe he intended to sell the entire operation, lock, stock and barrel. Included in the various holdings of Sterling Records would be Festival Productions. At the thought an uncomfortable knot formed in Maren's stomach.

"I'm glad you're here," Kyle admitted, a reluctant smile forming on his lips. He came across the room swiftly and folded Maren in his strong embrace. Powerful arms held her prisoner as his lips found hers. The kiss was bold and demanding. Maren sighed as she closed her eyes and felt a delicious swirl of excitement course through her veins. Her tormented doubts disappeared when he whispered her name softly against her ear, and her entire body felt as if it could melt into him.

His hands were warm where they splayed familiarly

against the small of her back. The soft fabric of her jersey dress was only a frail barrier between his hands and her body. His lips brushed against her neck, and she moaned at the warmth he inspired. His fingers reached for the buttons at her shoulder.

"Kyle, wait," she murmured, the taste of him still fresh on her lips. She attempted to extract herself from his commanding embrace.

"I have," he admitted, once again kissing the soft column of her throat and letting his tongue gently probe the sensitive skin near her ear. "Too long…"

Gathering in a breath of fresh air to clear her senses, Maren managed to press her palms against his chest and force his head away from her. His eyes, when he raised them to meet her confused gaze, had darkened to a smoky gray. She could read the torment of restrained passion in their smoldering depths.

"Listen," she whispered, trying to ignore the desire infecting her. "I need to know a few things…what is all this?" Her upturned hand made a sweeping gesture to include the scattered contents of his office." What do you mean you're moving to La Jolla? You're not resigning, are you?"

"Me? Resign? What are you talking about?" Pain lingered in his eyes, and his voice was edged with the frustration that had been building in him for nearly a week.

"I don't understand, Kyle. Who's going to run the company?"

"I am."

"From La Jolla?" she asked incredulously.

"Yes."

"Why?"

"There are a lot of things you don't know about me,"

Kyle replied. "I tried to explain some of them to you when you were in La Jolla, but you didn't want to hear them. I have personal reasons for staying near San Diego." Slowly Kyle released her, and it was evident that he was willing his desire to ebb. He raked impatient fingers through the sun-streaked strands of his dark hair.

Kyle knew that Maren was disturbed about something—something involving him. His throat went dry with dread. Just yesterday a bad copy of Mitzi Danner's as-yet-unreleased single had been discovered in a raunchy San Francisco nightclub. The pirated tape had to have come directly from Festival Productions—perhaps that was what Maren wanted to discuss. She had promised to let him know if the pirating problem resurfaced.

"I still don't understand. Who will be responsible for the day-to-day decisions of running the company?" Maren didn't ask about his personal reasons for staying in La Jolla. She suspected they might have something to do with his ex-wife, and she couldn't bear the thought of competing with Sterling Rose or sharing Kyle with any woman.

Kyle leaned against the edge of his desk, his long legs stretched in front of him, his fingers curling around the chrome frame of the desk to aid his balance. Thoughtful lines of worry creased his tanned forehead. "Several people will run the various departments, just as they do now. If a problem develops that a department head isn't able to handle, Ryan Woods will either make the appropriate decision or contact me in La Jolla…at least until I return."

"Then you do plan to move back here?" Maren's dark brows arched inquisitively.

Returning her direct stare, Kyle shrugged. "Circumstances permitting…"

"That's ducking the question."

"You were the one who didn't want to get involved in my personal life. Remember?" he charged, his temper flaring.

'That was before I realized that your 'personal life,' as you refer to it, influences what happens to me and everyone else associated with Festival Productions. You're asking me to make a decision about selling my company *and* my talent to Sterling Recording Company and you might not even be involved with Festival once the sale is final!"

"What does that have to do with anything?"

"I like to know where I stand before I sign on the dotted line," she snapped. "Whoever runs Sterling Records will be making the decisions regarding my future..."

"And you might not trust whoever I appoint?"

"Or sell Sterling to."

His smile was bitter, his gray eyes determined. "I have no intention of selling the record company." He crossed his arms over his chest, and his eyes bored into hers. "For once you're going to listen to me." Before she could voice the protest forming in her throat, he strode across the room. He touched her, and his fingers tightened over her forearms. His gaze was deadly from the tension holding his muscles taut. "I have to stay in La Jolla because of my daughter, Holly. There's a chance that I might gain custody of her. If I do, I won't be coming back to L.A., at least not until she graduates from high school. Her entire life is centered near La Jolla, and I'm not about to drag her to Los Angeles and disrupt her life any more than it has been already."

His daughter! The child Rose gave him. So that was why he was moving to La Jolla. Maren witnessed the pain in his eyes, and her heart bled for him. Her concerns for the business seemed insignificant when compared to his worries over his child.

"Listen, Kyle," Maren whispered, her throat suddenly rough with emotion. "You don't have to tell me anything about Holly. It's…it's really none of my business…"

The hands encircling her arms clenched more tightly and jerked her roughly against him. She could feel the muscles of his thighs touching her dress, pressing the soft fabric against her legs. Her breasts were crushed against the firm expanse of his chest. He shut his eyes so tightly that the webbing of crow's-feet at the corners disappeared. For one tense moment he held her, and then slowly released his grip. "Oh, Maren," he sighed, almost to himself. "What is it about me and my daughter that scares you so?"

She stood her ground and slowly let her gaze travel upward to meet his condemning stare. "I'm not afraid," she protested in a throaty whisper. "Just cautious. I don't want to get myself into something I can't get out of."

"What's that supposed to mean?"

Her thoughts returned to Brandon and the monetary bond that still shackled her to him. Would she ever be released—free to commit herself completely to another man? Her voice was hoarse, and the shadow of regret darkened her eyes. "It means that because of our negotiations over Festival, I can't afford to get too involved with you—"

"I think you already have, wouldn't you say? Or was our night on the beach just a solitary moment of weakness?"

"You know better than that."

"Do I? Why do you run so hot and cold with me? One minute I think I understand you, the next I'm not so sure."

"Maybe we've both got too much at stake because of the business," she lied, unwilling to bring her hopeless relationship with Brandon into the argument.

"You're evading the real issue," he charged, his eyes narrowing contemptuously.

"I don't think so. You know as well as I do that the production of videotapes pulled record sales out of the cellar. The entire recording industry was slumping pitifully until video came along and put it back on its feet. The point is, Sterling Recording Company needs Festival Productions as well as the reverse."

He lifted a finger and pointed it accusingly in her direction. "Stop it, Maren. Business isn't the issue here. Our relationship is. Are you trying to let me know that you don't want to see me except when we have to work together?" Every muscle in his body tensed for her reply. A small muscle in his jaw tightened until his teeth clenched together.

Her voice was low and unsteady. "I don't know what I want," she admitted. "At least not with you. And I'm not sure that what I want is what would be best for either of us." She laid bare her heart in an uncontrolled moment of weakness. "We've both been through bad marriages..."

"I'm not asking you to marry me, for God's sake. I'm only asking for a little of your time. Is that so hard to accept?" His anger was replaced by confusion, and when Maren stared into his perplexed eyes, she felt her heart melt. *He cared.* It was evident in the concern on his face. Jan and all the others who judged him by the scandal sheets or industry gossip were wrong! This man really cared.

"I guess not," she replied, forcing back the tears threatening to pool in her eyes.

The rigidity of his muscles relaxed. "Good. Then let's

get down to the business at hand and get it over with. We have more important things to do," he declared cryptically.

Ignoring his seductive remark, Maren reached down and picked up her briefcase. She was grateful for the change in mood in the office and relieved that their argument had subsided, at least for the present. It had been much too long since she had seen him, and she didn't want to spend her time with him doing verbal battle. She put the briefcase on the cluttered desk, opened it and extracted her preliminary sketches.

"These are still a little rough," Maren warned, clearing a space on the desk and laying the drawings faceup on the glass surface. "What I've decided to do is use the same principal characters in each video for the Mirage album, just as you suggested. But the interesting twist will be that each song will be set in a different time period. For the first cut, 'Yesterday's Heart,' I've started with the Depression. With each successive song, I've moved forward by fifteen to twenty years. The final cut will end in a futuristic world."

Kyle frowned as he sifted through the large sketches. His thick brows drew downward in concentration as he stared at the images. When he didn't comment on the drawings, Maren was forced to continue the one-sided conversation.

"I hope you approve of this idea, because I've already hired the dancers and a couple of bit-part actors for the action sequences on the first three cuts. The costumes are being designed, and the only problem so far is that the actress who agreed to do all five songs broke her leg while roller-skating in Venice last week."

Kyle raised his thoughtful eyes to meet hers. "Have you been able to find a replacement?"

Maren nodded, "I think so. I'm still waiting to hear from her agent. I doubt if it will be a problem." Maren waited anxiously as Kyle returned his gaze to the sketches. She was unable to decipher the dark frown on Kyle's features. "Well," she prodded, more than a little exasperated that he couldn't even make a comment. "What do you think?'

"They look fine to me," he conceded.

"Just fine?" She couldn't hide the frustration in her voice. "Those storyboards represent nearly two solid weeks of blood, sweat and tears."

His gaze hardened. "I expected the best from you, and I'm not disappointed. What more can I say? I'm not very good at visualizing the finished product until I see it on film. As a matter of fact, this is the first time I've every seen the artwork for a video. Someone else usually handles it." He pointed a long finger at the top sketch. "These drawings don't mean a hell of a lot to me until I can actually hear the music and watch the action. That's why I hired you and why I want to purchase Festival." He read the slightly rebuffed expression on her elegant features. "What did you expect from me? I'm not the kind of person who hands out effusive compliments for a job well done, at least until it's finished."

"I just thought you might show a little more enthusiasm," Maren replied with a widening grin.

"Look, Maren, I hired you because you're the artist." He slapped his palm on the first drawing. "If you tell me that this action sequence will work, then I'll believe you." He leaned over the desk, both arms supporting his weight as he looked up at her. "Now, tell me, do you foresee any problems with production?"

Maren shook her head, and the light from a lowering

sun caught in the coppery strands. "I don't think so. J. D. Price and the rest of Mirage have approved, the location sites have been selected, the choreographer has worked up two of the dance sequences..." She raised her shoulders elegantly. "Barring a strike from the musicians' union, we're right on schedule."

"*If* you can sign the actress."

"I don't think it's anything to worry about. The girl I want is relatively unknown, and she sees this as her chance at the big time. Ever since Cindy Rhodes—whom Sly Stallone reportedly first spotted on Toto's 'Rosanna' video and later cast opposite John Travolta in *Staying Alive*—made the transition into movies, videos have become relatively easy to cast. The girl I want is Janie Krypton." Maren hesitated, and Kyle shook his head, indicating that the actress's name meant nothing to him. "Janie's a big fan of Mirage, and I'm sure she'll work out well opposite J.D."

"Good." Kyle handed her back the sketches. "Then you think you can make the deadline?"

"I think so. The actual filming will take a couple of days for the first song, but the editing will require another week or so. Unless something unforeseen happens, we'll make the June first deadline." She searched her briefcase once again. "In fact, I think I can even squeeze Joey Righteous's video of 'Restless Feelin'' into production, if you'll be so good as to sign the contract." Placing the storyboards neatly into the briefcase, she waited for Kyle to sign and return Joey's contract.

He hesitated. If Ryan Woods had been correct, the latest Mitzi Danner video had already been duplicated. How could he take the same chance with Joey Righteous? The Mirage album was already a very costly gamble.

"Don't you think you should concentrate on Mirage first?" he suggested.

She could feel the undercurrents of tension quietly charging the air. Something was wrong. "We can handle all of it, and I promised Joey that the video would be ready when the single was released. Unless my information is faulty, 'Restless Feelin'' is scheduled about the time Joey takes off for his tour of Japan in June."

"That's right. But it's not until the end of the month. Let's wait until the first Mirage video is finished," he decided, handing her back the contract.

Maren had the uneasy suspicion that he wasn't telling her all of the story. Why did he want to wait? Was it because of the impending sale? "Is there something you're not telling me?" she asked, accepting the contract and leaving it on his desk. He didn't comment on the fact that she didn't put it back into her briefcase.

"Such as?"

"Why you're hedging on the Righteous contract? That's not like you," she charged.

"I suppose it isn't," he agreed, "but I think it would be best for both parties if we don't get too involved with unfulfilled contracts until we've come to terms on the sale of Festival."

"You mean that you're going to keep the unsigned contracts dangling like the proverbial carrot until I sign on the dotted line?"

"That's not what I meant."

"But it's true," she pointed out, her cheeks coloring with unwanted anger. "Are you just stringing me along, Kyle?"

"Why can't you trust me?" he asked, his temper flaring in his cold eyes.

"Because trust is a two-way street, and I'm smart enough to notice when someone's deliberately baiting me."

"You've got it all wrong."

"Prove it, Kyle." Maren picked up the contract and waved it angrily in his face. *"If I'm wrong, sign the contract."* Her voice was shaking, and her eyes had darkened warningly.

'I don't have to prove anything to you, Maren," Kyle defended himself. His voice was low and menacing. "You know me well enough to realize that I'm as good as my word."

"Are you saying that I'm not?" she asked, wondering at all the hidden innuendos in his words.

"No, but I'm asking you this much: If you were having any serious problems at Festival, you would tell me, wouldn't you?"

"Of course."

"Even if it threatened the sale?" he pressed.

"Kyle, what are you getting at? If there's something bothering you about my business, just spit it out."

"It's a purely hypothetical question," he lied, thinking of the Mitzi Danner video. He wasn't convinced that it had really been duplicated, but Ryan Woods had promised to bring it to him. Until he had his facts straight, he couldn't accuse her.

"Then you had better think about signing the Righteous contract. Joey is counting on both of us. I told him that I would talk to you, and if you agreed, we'd schedule his video into production."

"And if I said no?" Kyle asked, muscles rigid.

"I can't imagine why you would. But I told Joey that if I had problems getting the contract signed, I would call him and he could deal directly with you," Maren explained.

"Now *that's* a threat. I've been on the receiving end of Joey's hostility more than once."

"The choice is yours," Maren pointed out.

"Either I sign, or you sic Joey on me?"

"It's your decision."

Kyle smiled cynically. "I can handle Joey Righteous—I have before."

"Why do you insist on being so insufferably stubborn?" she asked in utter confusion. "Is this the kind of response I can expect from you if and when I sell the business to Sterling Records?" Her indigo eyes reflected her concern.

"I'm just being cautious right now," he reassured her. "We've had a few problems here, and I've got to get a handle on them before I take on any more." He took the contract from her hands and flipped it in the air. It fluttered downward to land in the middle of his chaotic desk. "It's after five," he noted, capturing her wrist with his hand. "Let's forget about business for the rest of the night."

Pulling her wrist gently forward, he enticed her to lean against him. "I can think of other things I'd rather concentrate on," he coaxed against her skin. His lips brushed lightly over hers, awakening her senses with their dewy promise. "Do you have any plans for tonight?" he asked, warm fingers lightly caressing her throat.

"I do now," she sighed, forgetting about Joey Righteous, unsigned contracts and Festival Productions, and letting her fingers run through his thick sable-colored hair.

He smiled cryptically, and his gray eyes sparkled. "Let's go upstairs," he suggested.

"Upstairs?"

"I have a place up there, a studio apartment of sorts, where I stay when I'm in town."

Maren tilted her head, lifted an eyebrow and viewed him through a thick fringe of dark lashes. "Are you attempting to seduce me, Mr. Sterling?" she teased.

"More than that," he promised with a rich laugh. "Oh, lady, what I intend to do to you." His smile was infectiously wicked as he swung his coat over his shoulder, picked up her briefcase in one hand and pulled on her wrist.

The apartment was located on the uppermost floor of the building. It was warmly decorated in tones of burgundy, navy and ecru with modern furniture clustered in small groupings near the windows overlooking the city.

"You call this a bachelor apartment?" Maren asked dubiously. It was true that all the living was concentrated in one large room, but it hardly qualified as the cramped quarters usually associated with a bachelor's apartment.

"I used the term loosely," he conceded.

"I guess. I think you could house three families in here."

He had released her hand, set down her briefcase and tossed his coat over the back of a plush chair. When he turned back to face her, his eyes drove deeply into hers, and she experienced a chill of excitement racing through her blood.

"Are you hungry?" he asked, taking both of her hands in his.

"Starved…"

"I ordered out…something very sophisticated and romantic," he whispered huskily.

A small smile, showing just the hint of a dimple and the flash of even white teeth spread across her pouty lips. "So you expected to entice me up here," she surmised.

"Hoped," he corrected. "I hoped to show you where I live when I'm in L.A." He crossed the room, walking past a heavy sectional sofa in muted shades of blue and gray. "Come here..."

She followed him to the tall windows on the far wall. From the apartment's vantage point high above the surrounding buildings, one had a panoramic view of the surrounding community of Hollywood. "I bet this is breathtaking at night," Maren commented, watching the flow of heavy traffic moving toward the freeways.

"If you stay long enough, you can see for yourself." He disappeared into an alcove, which Maren decided was the kitchen. Within a few minutes, he reentered the room and placed a large carton on the table.

"Pizza?" she asked, as he opened the box.

"Warm pizza and cold beer," he stated.

"This is your idea of 'something very sophisticated and romantic'?" she inquired, laughter dancing in her soft blue eyes. "Why was I expecting Veal Oscar and chilled champagne?"

"I don't know," he replied, motioning for her to take a seat at the small table, "because I wasn't talking about the meal; I was referring to the company."

Maren's gaze locked with Kyle's, and she smiled under the warmth of his compliment. "If you're trying to charm me into signing the sales contract," she said, "you're certainly on the right track.'

"This has nothing to do with your business or mine. This evening is just between you and me." He poured a glass of beer and handed it to her. "Is that all right with you?"

"Fine," she admitted, taking a sip of the cold liquid. "Just fine."

It was dusk when they had finished eating and had cleared the small table. The conversation had been light and carefree, and Maren had relaxed enough to kick off her shoes and feel the weave of the thick carpet through her hose.

Kyle opened one of the windows, and the sounds of the city reached upward to them. Muted voices, the rumble of car engines and an occasional shout or blast of music from a passing car filtered into the apartment.

Maren sat on the floor near the windows staring out at the looming night. She drew her bent legs to her chest, encircled her knees with her arms and rested her chin on her kneecaps." Do you enjoy living here?" she asked, as he sat next to her. "It's so different from the house in La Jolla."

He contemplated the curve of her jaw before replying. "It's been convenient." He reached forward and traced the soft column of her neck with his finger. The touch of his fingers against her throat made Maren's pulse begin to race. When she turned her head to look at him, she noticed that all traces of amusement had faded from his eyes. His voice became a throaty whisper, desperate with the heated yearnings of his body. "God, woman, you can't imagine what I've gone through these last two weeks, wanting you and not being able to touch you. It's nearly driven me mad."

All the lighthearted pretenses melted in the ever-lengthening shadows in the room. The light mood that had taken hold of Maren throughout the casual meal disappeared and was replaced by an aura of gravity. Kyle's eyes had darkened with restrained desire as he reached over and his forearms entrapped her in their intimate prison.

"Tell me you've wanted me," he commanded, holding her gaze with his smoldering eyes. "Tell me you've lain in bed alone and wished that I were there beside you, that I would appear and satisfy the ache within you."

His words enticed her heart to beat unsteadily. Her breath caught in her throat as she remembered the last lonely nights without him and the agonizing hours she had lain awake with only memories of his warm caress. "Oh, yes," she sighed, squeezing her eyes shut to emphasize her words. "I've wanted you, Kyle.... I've wanted you so hopelessly that there were times when I thought I couldn't stand being away from you a moment longer."

Groaning in satisfaction, he let his hands move upward to cup her chin. "You've got to be the most fascinating woman in the world," he proclaimed softly before pressing his anxious lips to hers. Tenderly, with as much restraint as his eager body could stand, he kissed her, and with an answering sigh, she parted her lips, quietly inviting him to explore and invade her, body and soul.

Their tongues met and entwined in an intimate dance of restless union that forced her blood to run in swirling rivulets of liquid fire. Her fingers caught in the heavy strands of his coarse hair as she pressed him closer to her. She felt his hand on her breast, kneading the aching mound through the soft fabric of the jersey dress. Her nipples were tight, her breasts swollen with need, ready for him and the wondrous feelings he could inspire. When he took his lips away from her mouth, she moaned in disappointment, but as his moist tongue lapped softly against her throat, Maren felt her body respond. The feminine ache within her burned as his tongue circled the hollow of her throat, leaving a wet impression on her skin and the soft neckline of her dress. Cool, moist fabric rubbed against her heated flesh, and a rosy blush of expectation colored her skin.

His lips moved to her shoulder and toyed with the buttons holding her dress together. Maren tilted her head to the side, letting her hair fall away from her neck and shoulders. His hands continued to hold the weight of her breasts, gently rubbing her taut nipples until they strained against the silky lace of her slip.

"Let me love you," he whispered hotly against her shoulder as he slowly unfastened one button.

"Dear God, Kyle, please," she murmured weakly. Another button was released from its bond. His tongue moistened her skin, and she shivered in anxious response. Her throat was dry from the short raspy breaths coming from her lungs.

The final button slid through its hole, allowing the soft muscle of her shoulder to part the powder blue dress. Warm night air massaged her skin as the fabric gaped off her shoulder, exposing the elegant swell of her swollen breast. A tiny droplet of perspiration ran from her neck down the dusky path between her breasts, and Kyle captured it with his waiting tongue. He lowered the strap of her slip down her arm, baring her breast to his eyes. His groan was a savage admission of lustful surrender.

Lowering his head, he let his lips tenderly seize the bold nipple, while his tongue rimmed the dark point. Her cry of bittersweet agony ripped him to the bone, and she gripped his hair more tightly, desperately holding him more closely against her bosom. Hot breath fanned the wetted breast, and the ache within her grew to a white-hot intensity.

Drops of perspiration beaded his brow, and it took all his thin patience to withhold the act of love and prolong the agony. The desire in his loins throbbed for release, but he repressed the urge to tear off her dress and savagely lose himself within her. Instead he let his fingers slowly touch her calf and with feather-soft strokes move upward, sensuously feeling the tantalizing seduction of her nyloned leg beneath his fingertips.

Maren released a shuddering sigh when his mouth released her nipple and the night air embraced her naked breast. Her breathing became erratic; her breasts heaved with the strain of taking in air. She felt liquid warmth engulf her as his hand traveled in painstaking hesitation up the length of her leg.

The dress gathered and pulled as his fingers found her inner thigh. Her small hands balled with frustrated longing as slowly—oh, lord, how slowly—he removed her undergarments before deftly tugging her dress over her head.

As she lay on the carpet in the near darkness, Kyle's eyes roved restlessly over her body. She shuddered at their intimate touch. He was kneeling beside her, and he slowly began to unbutton his shirt. Maren watched in anticipation as the oxford fabric parted to display the finely sculpted muscles of his chest and abdomen.

When he slid the shirt down his arms, she reached up and let her fingers trace the supple curve of his biceps before haltingly touching his neck and lowering her hands to the flat rock-hard ridges of his chest. She noticed the way his muscles contracted as he shifted positions to remove his shirt and slacks.

Finally he was naked beside her, kneeling over her, his bold gray eyes holding her gaze with promises of mysterious longing. She ran her fingers up the outer side of his thigh, letting the soft hair on his leg bend upward as she reached for him.

He leaned closer and her heart pounded out an erratic cadence of passion as her arms encircled his waist. He twined his fingers through the tangled waves of her fiery hair as he settled against her. She could hear his heartbeat, watch the anxious desire in his eyes, feel the rock-hard contour of solid muscles as they slid over her own. His weight was a welcome burden.

Elbows propped beside her head, lips pressed hotly against hers, he moved slowly, parting her legs with his knee and teasing her by rubbing his body over hers in intimate persuasion. The pounding in her ears began to explode and she arched more closely to him, assuring him that what she desired most in the world was the feel of his passion erupting with hers.

Her eyes were glazed in surrender, and when Kyle looked down upon her, seeing the way her damp hair framed her face, witnessing the ragged rise and fall of her breasts, feeling the heat of her body arching against his, he could no longer keep his primal urges at bay.

"I love you." he cried as he entered her, molding himself to her as man to woman. "I love you, Maren," he promised, straining against her flesh and filling her with all the love he could offer.

CHAPTER NINE

MAREN SLOWLY OPENED her eyes against an intrusive ray of sunlight piercing through the skylight. She stretched in leisure as she watched Kyle's sleeping form. His dark skin contrasted with the sky blue sheets, and his sun-streaked hair was tousled against the pillow. Smiling to herself, she reached forward and pushed the hair out of his eyes. Just as she did, his hand caught her wrist and his eyelids opened to reveal clear gray eyes.

"You weren't asleep, were you?" she asked with a knowing smile.

"I've been awake for nearly an hour." His eyes roved restlessly over her exposed shoulders.

"Why didn't you wake me?"

"Because I enjoyed watching you sleep." His eyes glittered seductively as he released her arm to drag the sheet slowly down her body. His eyes followed the bedsheets downward until the tops of her breasts were exposed. Light from the skylight warmed her naked skin, but she felt a sudden chill as his wet lips pressed against the swell of her breasts.

She moaned softly as a spreading liquid fire began to heat her blood. The sheet, now moist from the touch of his tongue, was pulled still lower, to drape across her abdomen and bare her dark nipples.

"Dear God, you're beautiful," Kyle groaned as he positioned himself over her. Gently his hand massaged one of her supple breasts, unhurriedly rubbing the soft mound until the nipple hardened in readiness.

Anxiously Maren arched against him, her body hungry for more of his enticing touch. He kissed her tenderly on the lips, teasing her until she twined her fingers in his hair and pressed her hot lips more urgently to his. His tongue rimmed the corners of her mouth, softly prodding her lips open. She felt the delicious warmth of his tongue touching the most intimate reaches of her mouth, and a small cry of desire formed in her throat.

His hands continued to knead her flesh, promising fulfillment as they touched and explored her body. Knowing fingers flattened against the small of her back, drawing her torso against his, letting her feel the urgency of his desire as he rubbed against her.

When his head descended to moisten a path down her neck, Maren felt her breath constrict. His lips pressed wet kisses against her collarbone, and she shuddered beneath his expert touch. I'm falling in love with him, she thought helplessly, and there's no way to prevent it.

Erotically he cupped a breast in the palm of his hand before easing his lips over the succulent nipple. She held on to his head, holding his body against hers, ignoring the doubts filling her mind and giving in to the pleasurable sensations welling within her. She felt the warmth of his tongue and the bittersweet pain of his teeth against her skin.

He kicked away the bothersome sheet separating their lower bodies and placed his legs between hers. The soft hairs on his thighs caressed her legs. When he lifted his head, his eyes had darkened to a smoldering hue of smoky gray and her wetted breast cooled in the early morning air.

"Darling Maren," Kyle murmured as he let his hands slide slowly down her rib cage, outlining each rib with his fingers. "How desperately I've wanted you." His admission came reluctantly, as if it were a sign of weakness.

"And I you," she replied, gazing dreamily into his eyes. She felt his muscles tighten, and he lowered his body over hers as he gently forced her knees apart.

A soft groan echoed deep in his throat when he at last gave in to the urges of his body and thrust himself into the invitation of her soft body. She sighed as they became one, and she held his body close to hers, content to feel the gentle rhythm of his love. He seemed to sense when her womanhood was fully aroused, and she felt his shuddering surrender at the moment of her fulfillment.

"Oh, Kyle," she moaned. "Please love me."

"I do," he promised. "Oh, lady, I do." His words were comforting and filled with conviction. Maren's eyes filled with unwanted tears and for one wondrous moment she let herself believe him.

"I want you to consider moving in with me in La Jolla." It was a simple statement and sincere. His heartbeat had quieted, and his dark gray eyes seemed to pierce Maren's soul.

Maren's voice caught in her throat, and she hesitated. The words of love he had whispered while making love to her had to be considered nothing more than vague endearments murmured in the heat of desire. They couldn't be construed as promises of a love everlasting. Maren knew that impassioned words of love deep in the night had a way of fading into forgotten vows with the coming of dawn.

"Did you hear me?" He pulled her more closely to him, molding her slim body to the contours of his. Maren's throat was rough with unwanted tears. She sighed deeply as she lay in the comfort and security of his arms.

"I heard you," she whispered, still facing away from him. "I just don't know what to say…"

"Say yes," he persuaded gently as he pressed his lips against the back of her neck and breathed in the scent of her hair.

Her supple body became rigid in his arms. "Kyle…I know that I laid it on a little thick when we first met."

"What do you mean?"

She sunk her teeth into her lower lip as she gathered her thoughts. "You were coming on pretty strong, and I didn't really know how to handle it. All that talk about commitment, it doesn't matter, not now. At the time I was afraid of an affair."

"But now you're not? Is that what you're trying to say?"

"Now I'm not," she agreed softly.

Broad hands gently pushed on her shoulders until she was forced to face him. As she stared into his brooding eyes she thought she would like to drown in his gaze. Her love for him was so great that she could sacrifice her principles and live with him without marriage. She would never selfishly bind him to a marriage he didn't want.

As if reading her thoughts, he frowned and his dark brows drew downward in confusion while he brushed a stray lock of auburn hair out of her eyes. "And you'd be satisfied with an affair?" Disbelieving gray eyes held her captive.

"Yes." Her voice trembled only slightly. "Don't get me wrong, I still don't believe in casual sex…"

"I know that."

"But I think…with us, it's more than that."

"Of course it is. That's why I want you to live with me." His hands were resting on her bare shoulders and his thumbs slid temptingly against her soft skin. How easily he could coax her into doing anything for him.

Her fingers clutched the sheet as she shook her head. “I can’t do that.”

“Why not?” He pushed himself up on one elbow to stare down at her.

She smiled despite the tears welling in her eyes. More than anything she wanted to live with Kyle and share his deepest secrets. She swallowed with difficulty. “For one thing,” she whispered hoarsely, “I’ve got a lot of work to do…”

“Can’t you do it as well in La Jolla?”

“Of course not! Kyle, be sensible! You know how tight my schedule is already. You’re the one who put a crimp in it!”

“And you thought you had a little extra time to work on Joey Righteous’s video.”

“That’s hardly the same thing.”

“I know that, but can’t you forget about work, just for a little while?” he asked.

“Hard to do, considering that I’m in bed with the boss.”

“Don’t think of me as the boss—just as your lover.”

She blushed at the thought. His hands took hold of her slender wrists and held them bound to her sides. Slowly he lowered his head and moistened the tip of one breast. The dark nipple hardened in response. “Come with me,” he suggested. When she laughed and tried to resist him, he only held her more tightly. “Come with me,” he pleaded again.

“I’d like to, but it’s impossible.”

“Maren, please…” He released her arms to touch her tenderly on the chin. “Come down to La Jolla, just for the weekend. We’ll talk about the future after that.” He saw the protests forming in her eyes and fended them off with logic. "There's a lot of work you can do from the beach house. You can use the library. It has a desk and a phone..." He sensed that she was wavering. "...and a breathtaking view of the ocean."

"You're twisting my arm." She sighed longingly.

"Then say you'll come."

She considered his request and the earnest look of concern in his eyes. "Okay," she agreed, "but it can't be until tomorrow."

"That's fine with me." He kissed her on the cheek before rolling over to the edge of the bed.

"Kyle?" Her voice halted his movements. "Why haven't you asked me about your offer on Festival?"

As he stood, he rotated to face her. She was huddled on her side of the bed, the sheet clutched tightly over her breasts and her eyes uplifted to penetrate his.

"I didn't think the timing was right."

"But I thought you wanted an answer."

"I do. I have an appointment scheduled later today with my attorney and Elise Conrad. Apparently she has some misgivings about the sales contract. Is that right?"

"There're a couple of things she wants cleared up."

"And if I satisfy her, will you be ready to sell?" he asked, regarding her carefully.

"I think so. Of course, I would have to talk to Elise first."

"Of course" was his clipped reply. He noticed the question forming in her eyes. Draped in the blue sheet, her tangled coppery hair framing her small face, she seemed more vulnerable than he had imagined.

"There's something I have to know," she said quietly.

He braced himself against the accusation he felt would surely come. "What?"

"You know that you're not obligated to me, don't you?" she asked.

"Obligation has nothing to do with the way I feel about you," he replied. He frowned darkly, his jaw jutting outward and his cold eyes drilling into hers in frustration. "I'm asking you to come live with me because I want to. Don't delude yourself into thinking it's out of any heroic sense of duty just because we slept together."

"Or because I haven't signed the contract of sale on Festival?" she prodded, witnessing the angry storm gathering in his eyes.

"You're incredible," he charged. "Sometimes that lingering sense of paranoia of yours surprises me, and that's hard to do. I'm used to dealing with all sorts of fears and phobias in this business, and I had the erroneous impression that you were a woman who really knew her own mind." He turned on his heel, angrily reached for his clothes and stalked furiously toward the bathroom. "I'm not about to dignify that question with an answer." With a final oath, he slammed the bathroom door and effectively cut off any further argument.

Maren pursed her lips together. "Coward," she whispered, pounding her fist into the pillow. Why did he get so furious? What was he hiding? She couldn't ignore the shadows of doubt that would cross his eyes. It was as if he distrusted her. Something wasn't right between them; Maren could feel it. There was something he wasn't telling her and it involved his purchase of her business. Why did he have to be so damned cryptic and manipulative? Again Jan's warning echoed in her mind.

Maren's anger slowly simmered while she dressed. By the time Kyle emerged from the bathroom dressed only in black slacks, Maren managed a remorseful smile. His dark hair was dripping as evidence of a recent shower, and he seemed surprised to note that Maren was completely dressed and quietly sipping a cup of coffee. She sat in a chair by the windows near where they had made love the evening before. Observing him over the rim of her cup, her dark brows arched expectantly as he came over to her.

"You can be a real bastard when you set your mind to it," she charged with a sweet smile and a devilish glint in her eye.

"Only when provoked by the right woman."

Maren's lips pursed into a petulant pout. "I poured you a cup of coffee—it's in the kitchen."

He bent down and touched her shoulders with his fingertips. "You mean you're not going to get it and serve it to me?" he cajoled, his secretive smile pleading.

"Not on your life."

Kyle returned with the cup and sat in a chair facing hers. He slipped his arms through his shirt and left it gaping open as he sipped the hot black liquid. "Tell me," he suggested with a self-satisfied smile. "Are you always so even tempered when you wake up?"

"Only when I'm provoked by the right man."

Kyle smiled. "Can I take you to breakfast?"

She shook her head and set her empty cup on the table. "Not today. Especially if I'm coming to La Jolla this weekend. I've got a million-and-one things to do." She checked her watch. "And I'm late as it is."

"Will you be at the meeting with Elise Conrad?"

"I plan to."

"Then we can have dinner afterward in La Jolla."

"Maybe," she replied.

"Other plans?" His eyes darkened.

"I just don't know when I'll finish with everything I

have to get done. If you remember, I've got to put 'Yesterday's Heart' into production immediately. Ted Bensen and I are going to run over the first scenes. They're a little tricky since the setting is the Depression. We have to be sure that the sites appear authentic and that there are no modern trappings to mar the effect."

"Then I'll call you at the office."

"Fine," she agreed, standing. "I'll try and wrap up everything by five, if I can, and I'll bring the paperwork to La Jolla."

She started toward the door, but his firm voice arrested her. "Maren?"

She turned inquisitively at the sound.

"Holly is living in La Jolla with me. I thought you'd want to know."

"Your daughter? But I thought Rose had custody..."

Kyle willed back the rage that overtook him every time he thought about his scheming ex-wife. "She does," he said. "At least, she has permanent custody for the time being."

"So Holly is visiting you?" Maren's thoughts were confused. Hadn't she read that Kyle's daughter was recuperating from a near-fatal auto accident?

Kyle tensed. Anger flashed in his gray eyes. He was careful with his words, but Maren could read the quiet wrath smoldering beneath the surface of his gaze. "Holly will be with me a few months—longer if I get my way." He set his cup on the table, and his shoulders slumped. "You must have read that Holly was nearly killed just before Christmas?"

Maren nodded silently, understanding for the first time the pain she had witnessed in Kyle's clear eyes. "It was a horrible accident," Kyle whispered. "For a while I wasn't certain whether Holly would pull through it." His voice had thickened, and he was forced to clear his throat. "Anyway, I just wanted you to know that she'll be at the house."

"And you still want me to come?"

"Of course."

"Don't you worry about setting the wrong kind of example by throwing our affair in her face?"

"Are you worried about what she thinks about you?"

"Yes. Aren't you?"

"No." He shook his head as if to relieve himself of a great sadness. "Holly and I don't communicate very well."

"This won't help..."

"I think it will. Holly needs to see that I can care for someone other than myself," he stated thoughtfully.

"And you're sure that I won't intrude?"

"Not a chance..."

Maren sighed in deliberation. Her love for Kyle overcame her fears. "Then I'll see you tonight."

A relieved grin broke across Kyle's rugged face. "I knew you'd see things my way," he said as he pulled a tie from the closet and knotted it around his neck before shrugging into his jacket.

"Your lack of confidence will lead to your undoing," Maren predicted, with just the trace of a smile.

"No, I don't think so," Kyle replied with a wink. He put his keys in his pocket. "I believe that my 'undoing,' as you so aptly phrased it, will come from a beautiful woman with a razor-sharp tongue."

Maren laughed, and the rich sound echoed against the rafters of Kyle's apartment. He took her arm, opened the door and held her tightly to his side as they walked to the elevator.

THE DAY WAS MORE HECTIC than Maren had predicted. Jan called in sick, forcing one of the production personnel to answer the telephones. Maren worked with Ted Bensen on the proposed sites for the location shots on "Yesterday's Heart." Of the three sites, only one was suitable for the Depression setting.

By the time Maren got back to the office, it was after three and her meeting with Elise Conrad and Kyle was scheduled for four. Fortunately Elise's office was nearby. Maren had just finished adjusting her lipstick and combing her hair, when the woman taking Jan's place stepped meekly into the office.

"Ms. McClure—I hate to bother you. I know that you're leaving, but this one guy keeps calling and insisting to talk to you." She handed Maren a stack of telephone messages. They were all from Brandon. "He's adamant about talking to you."

Maren disguised her dismay when she accepted the memos by smiling at the girl. "Thanks, Cary, I'll give him a call."

After the young girl had exited, Maren glanced regretfully at the clock before sliding into the desk chair and dialing the phone. It was several seconds before Brandon answered.

"Hello, Brandon. My secretary told me you wanted to get hold of me."

"Maren? What the devil took you so long?"

"I was out of the office," Maren replied, wondering why she bothered to explain herself to him. "What's up?"

"That's what I'd like to know," Brandon replied somewhat angrily. Maren could picture the indignant arch of his brow. "The physical therapist seems to think he's done all he can for me."

"That's great," Maren replied with genuine enthusiasm.

"Oh, yeah, you think so. Now you won't have to fork out for the therapy."

"The money has nothing to do with it, Brandon. I was just relieved that you were back on your feet again."

"If you can call it that," he spat out.

Maren closed her eyes. The recovery she had been praying for obviously hadn't occurred. "Are you still having trouble?" she asked quietly.

"They told me I could never play tennis again."

"They've told you all along that might be a possibility," she reminded him softly.

"Tennis is more than just a game for me."

"I know that, Brandon."

"I was good. I was damn good! If it hadn't been for the accident…I'd probably have been number one last year."

The guilt within her twisted in her heart like a dull blade. "And the physical therapist says you can't play?"

"Not professionally."

"I assume the orthopedist concurs."

"Who knows? I never can get a straight answer out of that guy! He seems to think that it's all in my head. Easy for him to say."

"Have you talked to a psychiatrist?" Maren asked patiently, knowing the answer before Brandon replied.

"A shrink? Are you kidding? I don't need someone to psychoanalyze me, Maren. I need my legs back!"

"Wait a minute. The therapist says you can't play professionally. But you still can teach, right?"

"I don't know," he pouted. "I don't want to teach. I want to play—I have to."

"Maybe you will," Maren encouraged. "Look how far you've come. A year ago you thought you might never walk again."

"Well, it doesn't help to have the therapist back out on me."

"Back out? What do you mean?"

"He seems to think that he can't do anything else for me. He wants to send me packing with a list of exercises."

Maren tried to remain patient. "It sounds to me as if you're making real progress. You knew that it would come to this."

"That's easy for you to say," he shot back hotly. "You've never had your career…your entire life, ripped away from you, have you?"

Maren's free hand clenched into a tight fist. "No, Brandon, I haven't. But I know that you have to work with the doctors and not against them in order to make the most out of the situation!"

"Yeah, well, tell that to them."

"What is it you want me to do?"

"Talk to the therapist, or get another. I'm on the verge of making it all work, I can feel it, but I've got to have help!"

"Why don't you talk to your doctors?"

"Because they won't listen to me! Damn it, Maren, is this too much to ask?"

Sighing, she replied. "No, it's not. I'm just not sure I'll have any influence."

"People with money always have influence!"

Maren bit back the hot retort forming on her tongue. She'd never let Brandon know how expensive his treatment was. Nor had she told him how tight her own pocketbook was. She had hoped that he might recover more quickly if he wasn't burdened by the knowledge that her financial condition was far from wealthy.

"I'll see what I can do," she agreed, glad that the trying conversation had come to an end.

"Good!" With this final remark, he hung up. Maren slammed the receiver into the cradle of the telephone.

Hot tears welled in her eyes as she thought about the hopelessness of her situation. "Damn it," she mumbled to herself as she pounded a small fist on the desktop. "Damn it, Brandon, why won't you help yourself?"

Looking up to the ceiling, as if in supplication, her shoulders slumped with the weight of her guilt. Whether or not Brandon fought for his independence wasn't the issue. It made no difference. It was her burden to help him, and she would shoulder it with all the strength she could find.

Plucking a tissue from a box on her desk, she dabbed at her eyes and vowed to herself to find some way to get Brandon back on his feet and able to earn his own way in the world. There had to be a way to slowly help him support himself.

Kyle's vicious accusations the first night she had been with him entered her mind. "You still love him," Kyle had accused, speaking of the unknown man who had wounded her.

"Not true," she whispered in the office alone. Her voice caught. "The only man I love is you," she said, wishing she were strong enough to confront Kyle with those same words.

BY THE TIME MAREN HAD finished with the business in the office, she was already late for her appointment with Kyle. Ted Bensen had been bending her ear with production problems on the Mirage videos for nearly forty-five minutes before Maren could break away from him.

In the parking lot, before she could slip behind the wheel of her car, Joey Righteous had caught up with her, demanding information on his video for "Restless Feelin'." He was angry, but Maren was able to calm him down by taking him into her office and reassuring him that the video would be finished by the time he left on his tour.

Snarls in traffic were another delay. By the time she made it to Elise's office, Kyle, Ryan Woods and the attorney for Sterling Recording Company had gone.

"We hit a snag," Elise explained with a thoughtful frown. She was a woman of fifty-odd years with perfectly styled dark hair and snappy brown eyes.

"What kind of a snag?" Maren asked before dropping into one of the soft chairs surrounding Elise's desk.

Elise adjusted her reading glasses. "The price was reasonable. As a matter of fact, the entire offer on Festival seemed aboveboard."

"I don't understand." Maren stared at her attorney as Elise studied the legal document lying on the desk.

"It has to do with the employment agreement. I wanted Sterling to guarantee you three years of employment. *And* I wanted you to be able to purchase a large block of Sterling Recording Company shares with the money you'll receive for Festival."

"Kyle wouldn't go for it?" Maren guessed.

"He was advised against it, by that Woods character and Bob Simmons." Elise paused, seemingly intrigued with a particular clause in the contract. "Before I could convince them that we wouldn't budge on this issue, Sterling excused himself. Said he had to go back down to La Jolla." Elise shrugged her round shoulders. "So this Ryan Woods told Sterling that under no circumstances was he to talk to you about the contract, not until he and I and Bob Simmons come to terms."

"Bob Simmons is the recording company's attorney?"

"Right. He drew up the agreement."

"So what should I do?"

"Nothing. Not until I sort this out with Simmons." She tapped her pencil on the desk. "And I'm going to give you the same advice. I know you might come in contact with Sterling because you do business with him. Whatever you do, don't discuss this contract. Just until I understand what Simmons and Woods want."

"You act as if you don't trust them," Maren observed.

Elise shook her head and rubbed her jaw. "No—it's the other way round. They acted as if I intended to pull a fast one on Sterling Records. Can you imagine that?" Elise's dark eyes took hold of Maren's.

"I don't know why," Maren stated honestly.

Elise waved off the serious mood. "Everyone's cautious these days, especially a person as famous as Kyle Sterling. He's a prime candidate for any number of lawsuits in his business. Someone complains about the copyright of a song—or bootlegged copy of an album..." Maren's heart seemed to stop beating, but Elise continued. "...or that Sterling Records stole another company's artist. Who knows? The point is, they have to be careful, and so do we. Until I get everything straightened out with Simmons, you should avoid talking about the offer—to anyone."

"Do you think that Sterling Records will do everything we want?" Maren asked cautiously.

Elise pursed her uncolored lips. "I don't know. From the way I read Kyle Sterling, he was more than willing to extend the employment agreement. It was the stock in Sterling Recording Company that seemed to be the real bone of contention." Elise saw the concern in Maren's blue eyes. "Don't worry about it. Simmons promised to get back to me by Tuesday. This time next week we should have everything wrapped up, and if I get my way, you'll be a very wealthy woman!"

CHAPTER TEN

ELISE'S WORDS RANG in Maren's head as she drove southward, and she vowed to take the attorney's advice and avoid the subject of the sale of Festival with Kyle. Negotiations were too strained as it was, and there were always the lingering doubts he had concerning the pirated tapes. Though he hadn't mentioned the subject lately, it was always there, distancing Maren from him.

Maren returned to Kyle's manor by the sea with more than a trace of trepidation. Not only was the impending sale looming over her head, but there was also the meeting with Holly to consider. As Maren drove through the wrought iron gates protecting the estate, she considered the delicate situation. The thought of confronting Kyle's daughter made Maren more nervous than she would like to admit, even to herself. What would the child think of Maren and her relationship with Kyle? Would Maren be able to handle the tense situation? Kyle had admitted that his relationship with his daughter was already strained. It was possible that Maren's unwelcome presence in the house would only add to the problem.

With a vow of determination, Maren got out of the car, reached for her briefcase and walked up the flagstones through the garden near the front door. Resolving to try her best to get along with Kyle's daughter, she reminded herself that Holly was still recuperating from the latest in a series of operations. She smiled as she pushed the doorbell. Chimes echoed throughout the house.

It was several minutes before the heavy front door was tugged open by a round Hispanic woman with a cautious smile and graying, black hair neatly coiled atop her head.

"You're Maren," Lydia guessed before the visitor had a chance to introduce herself.

"Yes." Maren smiled with the ease and friendly manner she had acquired as head of a small production company. She was accustomed to meeting wary strangers. The stiff-spined housekeeper used her round body as a barrier to the entrance of Kyle's home. Obviously she was protective of Kyle and his estate. Piercing dark eyes roved over Maren distrustfully. "You must be Lydia," Maren surmised. Her clear blue gaze was steady and without pretense. "It's nice to meet you." Maren offered her hand to Lydia with a sincere smile. The Mexican woman took Maren's palm cautiously, but a slow grin spread over her round face.

Satisfied that the strange woman with the deep blue eyes was entirely different from Rose, Lydia moved slowly out of the doorway and ushered Maren inside the house. "Come in, come in," she invited with a merry grin and a twinkle in her black eyes. "Can I get you something to eat…or drink, perhaps?"

"I'm fine," Maren replied, but the kindly woman refused to be put off.

"Nonsense," Lydia persevered with a shake of her head. "How about a glass of iced tea? I have fresh lemon."

"You're twisting my arm," Maren said with a low laugh. She knew in an instant that she and Lydia would get along famously. The other hurdle to overcome was Kyle's daughter. Maren realized that winning Holly over wouldn't be so easy.

"Good." Lydia seemed pleased. "I was getting Holly a glass anyway. She's out on the deck, if you'd like to join her."

"Where's Kyle?"

"He had to go into town, but he promised to be back soon. He's been expecting you." Lydia turned toward the kitchen. "I'll bring the tea out to the deck," she called over her shoulder, and Maren was left with the distinct impression that the housekeeper *wanted* Maren to visit with Holly.

It's now or never, Maren decided as she crossed the familiar living room and opened the door leading to the covered deck.

Holly, wearing a lemon-colored T-shirt and cutoff jeans, was reclining on a chaise lounge. One leg was propped against the soft cushions of the lounging chair, and the girl was attempting to paint her toenails. Maren was surprised to note the healthy color of Holly's complexion and the girl's sure movements. Maren had guessed that Holly would be frail from her recent surgery, but it appeared that whether Holly would admit it or not, she was recuperating very well under her father's careful supervision.

At the sound of the door opening, Holly lifted her intense green eyes toward the intrusion. There was a light of expectation in her eager gaze, but when she saw Maren the gleam faded and genuine disappointment surfaced.

"Hello," Maren greeted warmly. She closed the door behind her and leaned against the railing. "I'm Maren McClure."

"I know who you are," Holly said rudely. "Dad told me you were coming." Holly's full lips drew into a pout as her insolent eyes moved away from Maren's face and back to an unpainted toenail.

Maren held her tongue at the girl's intentional rudeness.

So this was how it was going to be. Unless Maren straightened a few things out with Kyle's daughter, the weekend would turn into a disaster. Holly's angry frown stated more clearly than words how deeply she resented Maren's company. It was going to be a long, hard uphill battle to win the child's confidence.

'Your father said that you only got out of the hospital recently. It's good to see you up and on your feet."

"Is it?" The teenager's tone indicated her total lack of enthusiasm. "I'll bet."

Maren's fingers tightened around the railing until the knuckles blanched and she could feel the warm wrought iron press painfully into her palms. "Are you able to go to school yet, or do you have a private tutor?" Maren asked, eyeing the ignored stack of textbooks piled on the small table that also held a variety of shades of nail polish, cotton balls and nail files.

Holly sighed loudly and ignored the question. Maren tried again. "Do you always paint each nail a different color?"

With her brush poised carefully over her large toe, Holly lifted her eyes and impaled Maren with her frosty stare. "Look, lady," Holly said with a petulant frown, "you don't have to come out here and make chitchat with me. I really don't give a rip what you do with my dad, but you don't have to pretend that you're interested in me. It's no skin off my back."

"Are you always so defensive?" Maren asked, wondering if Holly was in her own manner trying to clear the air.

"Just tellin' it like it is." Once again she lowered her eyes to contemplate her toes.

Maren was thoughtful for a moment, not sure exactly how to handle the resentful child. She considered leaving well enough alone and going back into the house but thought better of it. No matter what Holly said, the girl was trying to get a reaction from Maren to understand where she stood with her father's latest girlfriend. Maren took one searching look at the calm sea as she gathered her poise to confront Kyle's willful child.

"It's not written in stone that you have to like me, you know," Maren said softly.

"What d'ya mean?" Holly asked, abandoning her task to give Maren her full attention. Though partially hidden, a slight trace of confusion knitted her brow.

"I mean that just because your father and I are seeing each other doesn't necessarily mean that you and I have to get along. If you would prefer, we could avoid each other."

"Oh, sure. Like right now, for instance."

"You mean that I'm intruding."

Holly paused, careful with the pretty woman whom she instinctively considered an adversary. This Maren was different from what Holly had expected. For one thing, she had guts, and Holly admired that. "Yeah, well, I guess so."

"Do you want me to leave you alone?"

"Why not?" Holly lashed out, her well-practiced mask beginning to slip. "I'm old enough to take care of myself."

"And smart enough to realize that you wouldn't want to," Maren ventured.

"As if you know anything about me," Holly baited, tossing her dark curls away from her face.

"I know enough about you to realize that you're not very comfortable living here with your dad. You don't really know what to expect from him and that scares you just a little."

Holly broke in. "I'm not *scared*."

Smiling quietly to herself, Maren was forced to agree.

"Maybe that was a poor choice of words. What I meant to say was that I know you miss your mom. That's natural. A girl your age needs a mother whom she can talk to and confide in."

Holly's full lips pulled into a disgusted frown. "Next I suppose you're going to tell me that you can be that person."

"Of course not." Maren's clear eyes held the young girl's distrustful gaze. "No one can ever step into your mother's shoes, and I wouldn't want to try."

"Sure," Holly tossed out contemptuously, but Maren's words sounded sincere. No matter how corny she came off, the lady seemed to mean what she said.

"I was hoping we could be friends…"

Holly rolled her eyes skyward as if asking for divine intervention. "Fat chance," she whispered.

"…but it's up to you. We can get along or not. The only thing I ask is a little polite civility from you, and I'll return the favor."

"God, don't you ever know when to lay off?" Holly asked angrily.

"I just wanted you to know that I'm not a threat to you."

"I *know* that already, so don't waste your breath."

A spark of indignation flashed in Maren's eyes, and Holly tossed her dark curls away from her small face.

"As I said before, the decision is yours…" Maren was about to continue, but the door from the kitchen opened and Lydia hurried out onto the deck with a tray of glasses filled with iced tea and sliced lemons.

"That looks wonderful," Maren said gratefully as she smiled at Lydia.

Lydia beamed under the praise and gave first Maren and then Holly a tall glass of the amber liquid. There was a third glass on the tray, but when Lydia didn't pick it up, Maren assumed it was meant for Kyle.

"Why don't you join us," Maren invited with a welcoming smile. "Holly and I were just having a get-acquainted chat.' Holly's round eyes widened, as if she expected Maren to tell Lydia of the girl's rude behavior.

"I can't right now," Lydia apologized with sincere regret. "I've got a chicken in the oven that won't cook itself." She hesitated, casting a knowing look from Maren to Holly and back again. "Maybe later," she suggested hopefully.

"Whenever you can take a break," Maren said after taking a long swallow of the cool liquid. She held up her glass and smiled. "Thanks."

When Lydia disappeared into the kitchen, Holly turned her condemning eyes on Maren. "You've got Lydia eating out of the palm of your hand, too, don't you?' she charged.

"I wouldn't say that. We've just met. I was only being pleasant."

"Why? To get in good with Daddy?"

Maren pursed her lips, shook her head and closed her eyes. "No, of course not. Your dad seems to think a lot of Lydia. I can see why. She's a very generous person."

"You can tell all that from just meeting her?" Holly's smirk indicated her disbelief.

Maren raised a knowing brow. "Oh, yes, Holly. That and much more. When I meet a person, I generally can see right through her," she said pointedly. "You'd be surprised what some people try to hide—just because they don't feel comfortable about themselves."

"You're talkin' about me," Holly accused.

After taking a swallow of the tea, Maren sighed. "I'm talking about a lot of people, Holly." She took a long look at the sea before continuing. "I know that you resent me, and I understand that, really I do. You've been through quite a bit lately, and the last thing you needed right now was having to deal with your dad's latest girlfriend, right?'

Holly didn't answer, but a telltale blush crept slowly up her neck. In Maren's opinion, that was some small bit of progress.

"Look, I'll stay out of your way, if that's what you want. But I don't think that would be fair to me, your dad or yourself."

Gritting her teeth against the tears threatening her eyes, Holly lashed out. "I don't care what's fair to *you!*"

"Then think about your dad and yourself. Like it or not, you're stuck with each other for a while and the fewer waves you make, the smoother sailing it will be."

"Oh, yeah? Is that what you really think? Or is that just a way to keep me quiet? You'd do anything to get in good with Dad, wouldn't you?"

Maren shook her head. "No one's paying me to like you, or to even try and get along with you—it would just be easier that way. And for that matter, you may as well know that I do like you. I'm not really sure why," Maren admitted to the surprised child, "but I'd *like* to be your friend." A glimmer of triumph flickered in Holly's eyes but quickly faded when Maren added, "However, if it doesn't work out, it won't kill me." She picked up her empty glass and walked into the kitchen. "See ya later," Maren called in a cheery voice, leaving Holly to consider the unlikely woman to whom her father was attracted.

MAREN WOULD NEVER HAVE believed it, but the weekend that had started so badly with her confrontation with Holly did improve. When Kyle returned to the house, he was enthusiastic to see both Maren and his daughter. To her credit, Holly did seem to try to rise above the barriers she had erected between herself and Maren.

It was evident to Maren that the relationship between Kyle and his daughter was not as tense as Kyle had said. Maren noticed that a spark of expectation and love would light in Holly's eyes whenever Kyle would give the child his attention. There were arguments, of course, but the hostility that Holly had worn self-righteously on her slim shoulders seemed to have evaporated.

After dinner, Holly went upstairs to study, and Lydia refused Maren's offer of help with the dishes. "Come on," Kyle invited, "let's go for a walk on the beach." The look of longing in his clear gray eyes couldn't be denied.

Dusk was beginning to settle on the calm waters of the Pacific. Frothy waves broke against black rocks before running toward the beach. Purple shadows lengthened against the white sand and darkened the clear water.

The twilight was breathless. The usual breeze from the ocean had disappeared, but the smell of saltwater lingered in the quiet air.

"I'm glad you came," Kyle admitted, taking Maren's hand in his as they reached the bottom of the cliff. "I had a sneaking suspicion you might not show up."

"Why?"

He shrugged his shoulders and stared out to sea. "Maybe it's because you keep running away from me…" Serious doubts clouded his gaze. He watched the flight of a solitary gull as it circled above the waves, and then, as if dragging himself out of a distant pain, he looked down on her and smiled. "What do you think of Holly?"

Maren returned his grin, and a dimple enhanced the

smooth contours of her face. Her dark brows arched at the question. "I think she's a handful."

"That's evasive."

"And the truth."

Kyle frowned as he pushed his hands, palms facing outward, into the back pockets of his gray corduroy slacks. "I suppose you're right," he conceded reluctantly. "She hasn't had much of a chance."

They started walking near the edge of the tide. "You blame yourself," Maren said quietly, guessing at the burden of guilt he silently bore.

"I'm her father."

"But she has a mother..."

At the mention of Rose, Kyle's head snapped upward. Anger, like a bolt of lightning, flashed in his eyes. "Not much of one," he said through clenched teeth, and then, as if to quell his storming rage, he shook his head and pushed his fingers through his thick hair. "I'm sorry," he whispered. "Rose and I haven't seen eye to eye, not since day one."

He sighed in exasperation. "My marriage was doomed from the start," he admitted, letting his thoughts revolve backward to a time in which reality consisted of twangy guitars, managers and night after night in towns he'd never heard of. "When I met Rose, I was only mildly successful...still playing for peanuts. I'd had one song that had made a move up the charts, I think.

"Rose's career was just beginning to take off, and I was flattered that she would even notice me." He paused, as if looking for a reason for his actions. "I was young, and I didn't have my head screwed on right. Anyway, we got married, and the media loved it—not to mention the public relations people." He frowned in disgust. "If I'm fair about it, I'd have to say that marrying Rose was the single most important thing I did to advance my career."

"You got married for your career?" Maren asked, masking the disbelief in her voice. Knowing Kyle as she did, Maren would never have thought he could do anything so callous.

"I didn't think of it that way, not at the time. I convinced myself that I really cared for her. She *acted* like she felt the same. As I said, it was mutually beneficial." He squinted into the gathering sunset, and his mouth turned down in disgust with himself.

Maren swallowed with difficulty. "You weren't in love?"

Kyle shook his head. "Who knows?" His jaw tensed. "I'd say not, wouldn't you?"

"I didn't know you then."

"You wouldn't have liked me if you had." His voice was flat and emotionless. "I don't think I liked myself, and after a few months, I didn't have any use for Rose. The feeling was mutual." He sighed contemptuously and stopped walking. "I suppose that was my fault, too."

"I don't understand," Maren replied, not knowing what to say.

He stretched out on the sand and studied the tide. Maren sat quietly next to him. "Neither do I," he admitted. "That whole period of my life doesn't make much sense." His gray eyes drilled into hers, and she noticed the pain of fifteen lonely years. "The marriage brought us national attention, and we did everything in our combined power to use it to our advantage. It worked. Suddenly the public couldn't get enough of our music. Record sales skyrocketed, and our egos didn't suffer much, either."

Maren reached for a handful of sand and let the sparkling granules sift through her fingers. "If you were having trouble, why didn't you slow down?"

"I don't know. Maybe the marriage wasn't that important. We were arguing all the time, and then Rose turned up pregnant." Kyle's eyes narrowed in disgusted agony at the memory. "You should have seen her when she told me. She'd been to the doctor in the morning. When she got in to the studio where I was working, she threw some prescription at me and shouted out the news. 'Well, now you've done it. I'm knocked up. What're we going to do about it?' As if there were any question." He pounded his fist angrily into the sand.

Maren's eyes reflected her despair. Why would any woman react so negatively to having Kyle's child? To Maren, there could be nothing more precious than the thought of carrying Kyle Sterling's baby. Her stomach knotted at the picture Kyle was painting.

"I talked her out of the abortion, and I think Rose was relieved. When Holly was born, she even showed a little interest in the baby. I thought everything might work out, and I tried to convince her to give up singing to stay home with the child. That was my mistake. Rose threw a fit, and told me if it was so important, I could stay home and take care of the kid."

"And you didn't like the idea?"

"I thought it was ridiculous—and now I wonder. Maybe I was wrong. I'm sure Holly would have been better off with me. I should have known that Rose wasn't cut out to be a full-time mother. She needed the night life, she loved the fame and she was addicted to the glitter."

"And you weren't?" Maren asked cautiously.

"I don't know." He grimaced as if studying a puzzle he couldn't begin to understand. "I guess I was too hard on

Rose. I didn't want her to go back on tour because I couldn't stand the thought that Holly would be raised by a complete stranger. I thought that a child needed to be with her mother, no matter what. The trouble was that Rose was being pushed by her manager. He wanted her to work longer hours, take more tours, rush through another album."

Kyle stood and stretched his long frame as he squinted into the sunset, as if he were searching for the answers to his life. "Maybe things would have been different if Rose had allowed Lydia to look after Holly. Since Lydia had helped raise me, I knew that she would take good care of my child. Lydia had always loved Holly. But Rose would hear none of it. In Rose's estimation, Lydia wasn't good enough for Holly."

Maren stood next to him, and he let his fingers touch the soft strands of her hair. It shimmered in the dusk, framing her face in delicate coppery curls. Her brow was lined with anxiety as she listened to his story.

Kyle felt compelled to tell her about himself; he felt inexplicably drawn to her as he had never been drawn to a woman. The complexities of his life didn't interfere; nor did he care for the moment about Festival Productions, pirated videos or sales agreements. All he wanted was for Maren McClure to understand and trust him. And he needed to trust her, though he knew it would be a mistake. Her incredible blue eyes sought his, encouraging him to continue.

"I guess the fights increased after Lydia left. Rose and I had nothing left in the marriage except our child. We stuck it out because of Holly." His voice had taken on a new dimension, and his quiet rage was replaced by scorn. "A couple of years later—Holly was about three at the time—I caught Rose with a member of the band, a kid about eighteen. Their affair had already been going on for a few months, and I had suspected as much, but it still came as a shock to me.

"Rose indignantly demanded a divorce, and I agreed. The only thing I wanted was custody of Holly. Rose flipped. I don't really understand why. Maybe Rose's motherly concern was deeper than I suspected. Anyway, Rose refused to give up Holly. We argued, and she promised that if I fought her, she would give me a vicious custody battle that would throw us and our child onto the front page of every scandal sheet in the country."

"So you gave in," Maren guessed in a hushed voice. Tears burned at the back of her eyes and threatened to spill. The agony on Kyle's rugged features was deep and tortured. How long had he borne the scars of a past he couldn't change? The emotions he expressed reached out to Maren, and she wanted to soothe him, comfort him, hold him to her breast and whisper words of solace to him long into the night.

"I hate to think of it as giving in," he replied. "I did what I thought was best for Holly, and I've regretted it ever since." His voice quieted. "You might have noticed that Holly and I don't get along very well."

"I don't think it's as bad as you make it."

"Only because we've made tremendous strides in the last couple of weeks."

"Because she's been living with you?" Maren asked.

"Or because Rose rejected her!"

Maren's heart stopped. "What do you mean?"

"I mean that now, right after the kid's latest surgery, Rose decided to leave her high and dry!" The anger burning in his eyes sparked.

"If you don't want to talk about it..."

"But I do!" He clutched her shoulder in a death grip. "I've been trying to tell you about Holly for a long time." Seeing the startled look in her eyes, he released her arm. "Oh, hell! What do you care?"

"I do care, Kyle," she reassured him, touching the tips of her fingers to his chin. Her voice was low and husky. "I think I care too much..." Her blue eyes caressed his. "I want to know everything about you," she admitted.

Kyle rubbed his temple. The quiet of the night was disturbed by a rush of wind off the sea. Its breath, now cool with the night, ruffled Kyle's dark hair. "You know about the car accident?"

"I read about it."

"Then you know that Rose was at the wheel when the car skidded into oncoming traffic?" His voice was deadly.

"Yes," Maren whispered. According to the newspaper article, Rose had been speeding in the rain. The oil-slickened streets had become dangerous for ordinary traffic. When Rose applied her brakes at a tight corner, the Jaguar had slid and slammed into a car heading in the opposite direction. At the time of the article, no one expected Holly Sterling to survive.

"Rose's carelessness nearly killed my daughter!" Kyle's teeth clenched, and his hands balled with his barely controlled rage. His eyes had turned vengefully dark.

"But I thought that Holly recovered."

"She has—but not thanks to Rose." His voice was flat and self-condemning. "Or maybe that's my fault, as well. Even after her first stay in the hospital, she wasn't completely well. Her most recent surgery was to correct a problem with scar tissue in her uterus."

"But she's all right now?" Maren asked hopefully, thinking of Holly's future.

"We're not sure. Right now, everything looks fine, but if Holly starts having problems again, she might be forced to have a partial hysterectomy."

Maren swallowed back the lump forming in her throat. The thought of a fifteen-year-old girl suddenly facing a future without the ability to bear children was devastating. Shadows of pain darkened Kyle's eyes. "And you blame yourself," she thought aloud.

"Holly's my child, Maren. I should never have let Rose get custody."

"Oh, Kyle—"

"I should have protected her!"

"You couldn't have known…"

"But I did know, damn it! I knew Rose wasn't fit to care for her, but I let it happen. I didn't fight hard enough for my child. You said it yourself, I gave in, and I never intend to give in again. I'll never let Holly suffer at the hands of her mother anymore. I let Rose and her threats about causing a scandal intimidate me. I should have let the gossip columnists write whatever they damn well pleased and fought for my kid!"

"We've all made mistakes," she offered.

"Maybe so. But that was the last one I'll make concerning Rose."

Maren let the silence speak for itself. Kyle needed time to let go of his anger. No words from an outsider could still the storm of emotions raging within him. She watched him noiselessly and waited until she noticed the tight muscles in his jaw softening.

"Now that Holly is living with you," she said, touching him on the forearm, "maybe things will be better."

"This is only a temporary arrangement," Kyle replied. "Rose was offered the lead in a movie about a country-western singer. It's being shot on location in Texas, and that's why Holly's here. Even though Holly had barely recovered from her last surgery, Rose took off for Texas the moment she was offered the part." He let his forehead drop into his hand and rubbed his brow. "I've asked my attorneys to start proceedings for me to gain permanent custody of Holly."

"Does Rose know that?"

"Not really, but she must suspect…she knows how I feel about that kid."

Maren was hesitant. "And what about Holly. What does she want?"

"I don't know."

"Have you asked her?"

"Not yet. I thought I'd wait until my attorney tells me how good my chances are of getting custody." He placed a comforting arm over her shoulders and tried to relieve some of the genuine concern in her eyes. "Don't worry—somehow I'll make it work," he promised, kissing the top of her head. "I believe that if you want something badly enough, you can get it."

They walked back toward the steps. Above them, high on the cliff face stood the proud hacienda. Warm lights illuminated the windows and invited them back inside.

CHAPTER ELEVEN

ONLY A FEW INTERIOR lights welcomed Maren into the dim rooms of the hacienda. Once in the hallway, Kyle wrapped his arms possessively around her waist and pulled her tightly against his lean frame. "Stay with me tonight," he suggested huskily. "I want to make love to you until dawn and wake with you still in my arms." His lips brushed her eyelids, and her blood began to race in her veins.

"But what about Holly…and Lydia?"

"Holly's already asleep, and Lydia's gone for the night. It's only you and me."

"Kyle—"

"Stay with me."

It was impossible to deny what she, too, needed so desperately. "How could I possibly refuse?"

"Would you want to?"

Seductive indigo eyes held him transfixed. "Never," she whispered. His mouth captured hers hungrily, and his palms pressed urgently against her back, kneading the soft muscles until she moaned in expectation. The light fabric of her cotton blouse was a frail barrier to the warmth of his touch.

As if on cue, he lifted her from her feet. One arm supported her back, while the other captured the bend of her knees as he carried her upstairs. She twined her arms about his neck content to bury her head in his shoulder and hold him dearly. He smelled so tantalizingly masculine. The scent of him mingled with the tangy odor of the sea, awakening feminine urges deep within her.

He didn't hesitate, but carried her into the master suite. Softly kicking the door shut, he strode across the room and through another door to deposit Maren in a sunken tub made of gray marble and rimmed in blue tile. When she began to feebly protest, he shook his head and smiled, conveying to her how desperately he wanted to please her. After deftly unbuttoning her blouse, he slid it off her shoulders. Slowly he unfastened her bra and placed the flimsy garment atop the shed blouse.

Her nipples, ripe with desire, hardened under his watchful stare, and she had to suck in her breath when his fingers touched her abdomen and lightly brushed against the waistband of her jeans. Slowly, sensually, he slid the zipper down before lowering the pants over her hips and down the length of her legs. Her skin heated when his fingertips brushed against her, and she moaned in contentment when, at last, he removed all of her clothing. She lay naked in the tub, peering into his eyes as his gaze roved restlessly over the soft contours of her body.

He turned on the faucet, and the tub began to fill. The touch of his eyes was far hotter than the water in the tub. Without looking away from her elegant form, Kyle reached for the sponge and submerged it in the water. Maren shivered as the water crept slowly up her skin.

Gradually he squeezed the sponge over her breasts before lathering them with soap. His hands slid invitingly against her skin, teasing her nipples until the breasts became swollen with desire. Maren shifted in the water and closed her eyes with a soft sigh. She felt her breasts becoming engorged and the nipples becoming taut under the wet caress of his hands. A warm tide swirled in her bloodstream, starting in the deepest part of her and rushing upward through her body in ever-increasing fervor. She moaned his name.

Kyle slowly washed her hair and her back, letting his fingers graze the soft flesh of her buttocks. Her eyes were only half open, the indigo irises observing him through the veil of her thick black lashes. Her auburn hair clung to her face in wet ringlets, making her appear innocently seductive. Her rosy skin gleamed from the water. Long slender legs, high firm breasts and a face that was as vulnerable as it was strong enticed him.

She smiled lazily upward, and her blue eyes twinkled playfully.

"You're a witch," he muttered, as he leaned over the tub and his lips found hers.

"And you love it," she murmured, returning his heated embrace.

He stripped off his clothes and tossed them aside before wrapping his arms around her waist and dragging her from the bath. Water spilled over the sides of the tub as he pulled her upward and pressed her warm body against his.

His tongue probed her mouth, and he groaned with the savage need ripping through his loins. Gently he carried her to the bed and using the weight of his body, forced her against the cool coverlet. Her body moved against his fluidly. The dewy water acted as if it were oil, allowing his muscles to glide over hers. He couldn't wait. Capturing her eager lips with his, he ran his anxious fingers down the slippery hill of her breasts, past her abdomen, to gently part her legs.

He shifted until he was positioned over her, where he

could stare into the blue intensity of her eyes in the moonlight. Moving his aroused body suggestively over hers, he touched her as intimately as had the bathwater.

Maren groaned in frustration, and her fingers dug into the lean muscles of his back. The bittersweet torture was driving her mad with desire. Her heart thudded painfully in her chest, and her breathing had become erratic. She sighed into his open mouth and thrilled when his tongue touched the soft recesses behind her teeth, plundering the sweetness therein. His fingers were as warm as the water had been, teasing her, toying with her, until at last his body covered hers and she felt the whirlpool within her turn molten.

As he came to her he whispered her name in the darkness. She joined him recklessly, allowing herself the luxury of his physical love. She needed to be touched by him, wanted all of him—for as long as possible. The love within her grew as he murmured her name.

"Love me," she pleaded, praying that his desire for her was more than physical. But her cries were lost in the night as he blended into her, shuddering as his need was fulfilled. She tasted the salt on his skin as her teeth sank into the hard muscles of his shoulder.

When their heartbeats had quieted, and their breathing had slowed, Kyle propped himself on one elbow to gaze down on her. "What happened to you, Maren?" he asked softly. Noticing the confusion in her eyes, he repeated, "Your marriage—the man who hurt you. What happened?"

Her chest became constricted. She didn't like to think about Brandon. Especially not now, not after making love to Kyle.

"It was a long time ago," she said, turning away from him.

His hand cupped her chin and forced her head back in his direction. Concern shadowed his eyes. "Tell me about it."

"There's not much to tell." When he didn't press her, she closed her eyes for a moment and sighed. "It's a part of my life that I'd rather not dwell on," she admitted.

"Because you're still in love with him?"

"I don't think I ever did love him."

"I find that hard to believe," he said, a steely edge to his words.

"Why?"

"Look at you," he replied gruffly. "Every time we get near the subject of your marriage, you clam up." She shook her head as if to deny his accusations, but he wouldn't let it rest. He seemed obsessed with it. "I don't understand what's going on, Maren. For the most part, you seem like a pretty together lady—in your business, dealing with Holly, anything—but the minute the conversation gets too close to that marriage of yours, you put up these false walls to protect yourself."

Maren started to protest, but Kyle placed a silencing finger to her lips. "There's no use denying it, Maren. Something in that marriage of yours isn't quite what you'd like me to believe."

Angrily he sat up and then stalked across the room, grabbing a thick robe from his closet and throwing it over his shoulders. As if in explanation he said, "I think more clearly when I'm not touching you." He sat on the corner of the bed and eyed her. "Damn it woman, I don't understand you, not at all." Raking his fingers through his dark hair in impatience, he stared at her. His eyes were dark and condemning, his lips compressed into a determined line. "What are you doing here—playing me for a fool?"

Rage sparked in her blue eyes. "Of course not."

"Then explain yourself. Doesn't sleeping with me mean anything to you?"

"It means a lot to me," she whispered.

"But not enough to give me the truth?"

"I've never lied to you, Kyle," she whispered defiantly.

'Then why don't you tell me what it is you want from me."

She took in a deep breath before sitting up and holding the sheet over her breasts. If only she could tell him how much she loved him… "I don't want any more than you're willing to give," she said evenly, ignoring the pain twisting in her heart and pushing back the threat of burning tears. "But what about you? What do you want from me? My body? My undying affection? *Or my production company?*"

"I'm not going to be deterred by your accusations. I just want to know about that ex-husband of yours."

"Why?"

"Because I think there's something you're not telling me, and I don't have the time to waste on another man's woman."

She felt her hand snap backward, but before she could slap him, Kyle's hand took hold of her wrist. "Another man's woman?" she repeated incredulously. She let her eyelids fall shut and smiled grimly to herself. "Is that what you think?"

Releasing her arm, he shook his head. "Quite honestly, Maren, I don't know what to think." His hand dropped slowly to his side. "You turn my head around…"

"And you don't like it," she finished for him with a catch in her voice.

"I don't understand it. And what's more," he continued, his temper flaring in his steely gaze, "I won't be played for a fool."

She tilted her head defiantly upward. "You don't understand me at all."

"Because you won't let me."

Tossing back the covers, she reached for Kyle's shirt and slipped into it, then walked out of the room and onto the deck facing the sea. Kyle's deck lay above the deck off the living room, and the view of the dark Pacific was just as breathtaking. Maren hoped she would absorb some of the tranquility of the calm sea.

Taking deep breaths of the sea air, she attempted to clear her head and let her indignation dissipate. Why did it matter what Kyle thought of her? How had she let herself become so hopelessly in love with him when she was still irrevocably bound to Brandon? Dear God, how had she let her entire life be turned inside out by Kyle Sterling? She pounded her small fist on the railing and shook her head in desperation. A few weeks ago her most urgent problem had been a few unsigned contracts from Sterling Recording Company. Tonight the problems with the contracts seemed light-years distant. Even her concerns over the sale of Festival had vanished with the night.

Leaning against the railing, she stared down at the blackened sea. The night wind blew across the tranquil waters of the Pacific and touched her face with its cool breath before catching in the coppery strands of her hair and lifting them away from her face. Maren didn't notice. Her thoughts were too turbulent; her emotions too raw. Powerful floodlights secured to the cliffs cast their ghostly illumination on the water, exposing the waves as they crested over the craggy rocks near the shoreline and ran in frothy rivulets to the shadowed sand.

The bedroom door opened and closed. Bracing herself

against the railing, Maren continued to stare at the sea. She felt the rugged strength of Kyle's arms encircle her abdomen. His warm breath whispered familiarly against her ear. "You know that you mean much more to me than just the beautiful owner of a company I'm hoping to acquire." Maren's throat became dry, and her fingers tensed over the railing. Her heart fluttered as he kissed her softly on her neck and her cool skin quivered at his tender touch. Everything seemed so right with him. "From the first time I saw you, sipping champagne at Mitzi Danner's party, I knew that you were incredibly alluring. I was intrigued." The admission was whispered quietly, as if he were talking to himself.

"So intrigued that it took you nearly a year to find me?" she threw back callously. His words were burning a hole in her heart.

"I didn't want a woman complicating my life—because of Holly."

"So you ignored me?"

"You left the party early. I did look for you," Kyle replied. Maren remembered his aloof stance at the party that night. She envisioned his quiet, understated manner, his brooding gray eyes and his rakish smile. She had been as wary of him as he had been of her.

"That was nearly a year ago," she whispered, her long fingers clenching. "Don't expect me to believe that I captivated you then. Too much time has passed, and you've been in my office since…"

"As I said, I didn't need or want a woman complicating my life…" His voice was as persuasive as the clear California night. Maren had to fight the urge to turn around and let her arms twine around his neck. She wanted to cling to him and never let go, but she couldn't. Not yet.

There was still Brandon to consider. She closed her eyes to erase the memory of him.

"And you do now—want a woman to complicate your life?"

"Not just any woman," he replied into her hair. "Maren, I want you." Maren felt the lump in her throat begin to swell uncomfortably. He sounded sincere. She pressed her eyelids more tightly together but couldn't stem the tears from pooling in her eyes.

Her voice trembled. "So what do you want to know about Brandon?" she asked softly.

She felt his arms release her before forcing her to turn and face him in the shadowy night. His gray eyes drove into hers, as if searching her soul. "I need to know what he means to you."

"Nothing," she responded with a sigh. "I thought I loved him once…"

Kyle's jaw hardened and his eyes turned dangerously cold. "But now you're not sure?"

Maren was forced to smile despite the tears in her eyes. "I grew up believing that love was eternal," she explained. "Either I was incredibly naive or I wasn't in love."

"You can't make the distinction?"

"Not easily."

His eyes narrowed in the darkness. "Why do I still get the impression from you that you can't let go of him…not entirely at least?"

"Because I can't," she admitted, her unwavering blue gaze filled with honesty and pain. She saw the anger surfacing in his stormy gray eyes, and she touched the tips of her fingers gently against his shoulders. He flinched under her touch. "Let me explain," she insisted.

"Please do." His voice was flat. All emotion was hidden.

"Brandon and I were married when I was still in college. I was young, and I thought I was in love. I managed to finish my senior year, but Brandon was too restless. He dropped out of school to become a professional tennis player..."

Kyle inclined his head. Vaguely he remembered a flash in the pan by the name of Brandon McClure. The man had had an incredible serve, which was accompanied by an equally explosive temper. In Kyle's opinion, Brandon McClure never had a chance. He was his own worst enemy. Tennis was a game of complete concentration and skillful manipulation. With only a couple of obvious exceptions, few hotheads made it into the top ranks of the pros.

"What happened?" Kyle demanded.

"To make a long story short, it wasn't long before I realized that he was having an affair. The woman was someone I knew and worked with." She paused. "There were other women. He admitted as much."

"So you divorced him?" Kyle's voice was low. The question seemed dangerous.

Maren took in a deep, ragged breath and tore her gaze away from Kyle's angry gray eyes. The pain of the divorce still bothered her. She looked toward the dark sky, and moonlight brushed a silvery sheen into her dark hair. "No. We separated for about six months, I guess. It was my fault. I opposed the idea of divorce and let it drag out. Even when we finally agreed to actually go through with the proceedings, I didn't feel comfortable about it...as if in some way, *I* had failed."

"And you never got over that feeling?" Kyle guessed.

Maren shook her head from side to side and pinched her lips together to hold back the sobs of regret that were forming in her throat. "No," she whispered. "A while back…it had been several years since the divorce was final, Brandon called and I suggested that we spend the weekend together skiing in Heavenly Valley." Her hand slapped the railing as the memories that she tried vainly to forget came back to her.

"I realized it would probably be a mistake. He was talking about reconciliation, and I knew at the time that too many years had passed. But I decided to go because…"

"You still loved him," Kyle accused.

"No!" She pursed her lips together in determination. "It wasn't love that made me consider starting over with him. It was pride: stubborn, foolish pride, because I'd failed! Nothing as heroic as love was involved.

"I wasn't with him more than half an hour when the first argument started. I determined then and there that it would never work out, and I was relieved. But I decided to spend the rest of the afternoon skiing because Brandon had already bought the lift tickets."

As she gazed into the distant night Maren tried to construct her thoughts so Kyle could understand the helplessness of her situation with Brandon—why she couldn't let go of him. "Brandon started skiing down the most difficult run, racing down the slopes as fast as he could. I could tell that he was tired, but he wouldn't give up. I think he was trying to work off some of the anger…"

"What anger?"

"His anger at me."

"For refusing to go back to him?"

She shrugged her slim shoulders. "I don't know. But he was angry with me. Anyway, he wouldn't listen to reason when I tried to stop him. He pushed me aside and told me that he could do anything he damn well pleased. Rather than cause a scene, I gave up and let him go."

"And he fell," Kyle said, remembering the accident. Maren's story reminded him of an article he'd seen in the sports page of the *Times* a couple of years ago. At the time, he hadn't made the connection between Brandon McClure, the bad-tempered tennis pro and Maren McClure, owner of Festival Productions. But why would he? They were divorced at the time and the article had made no mention of Brandon's ex-wife.

"Right," Maren agreed, her small shoulders slumping beneath the soft fabric of Kyle's oversize shirt. The horrifying memory of the accident flashed vividly before her eyes.

Kyle's voice seemed far away. "From what I understand, he'll never play tennis again—not professionally." At least that was the speculation at the time. Since the first report, Kyle had read nothing about Brandon McClure.

"It's worse than that. He may not be able to play at all, or walk without the aid of a brace." She felt suddenly tired, drained of her strength.

"Maren?" The coldness in his voice forced Maren to rotate and look at him. "Do you feel responsible for what happened to him?" Undercurrents of tension charged the cool night air.

"Partially," she conceded.

"That's ludicrous!"

"I've told myself the same thing a hundred times over, but I just can't seem to convince myself."

Leaning against one of the posts supporting the roof, Kyle studied her. He folded his arms over his chest and his square jaw jutted into the darkness. Deep lines of concern webbed from the corners of his eyes. "So how does this affect you now? It was all in the past: unless there's something you haven't told me."

Kyle stared at her, noting every reaction on her elegantly sculpted face. He sensed that McClure still had a hold on her and it involved more than guilt. Gritting his teeth together to cut off the possessive feelings entrapping him, he waited.

"It isn't just in the past," she admitted, rotating to face him. She noticed the tense angle of his jaw, the flexed muscles straining in his chest and the glint of steel in his eyes. "Brandon always had a way of living beyond his means..."

"I can believe that," he cut in.

Ignoring the sarcasm in Kyle's voice, Maren continued: "Even the money he won on the tour couldn't begin to support his lifestyle. At the time of the accident, Brandon was in debt and had let his major medical insurance policy lapse. Only a small policy was left to pay a portion of the hospital bills."

"So you've been supporting him," Kyle concluded, his lips thinning in controlled rage. No wonder the profits from Festival Productions had been bled from the company. Maren had been using that money to support Brandon McClure. Kyle's thoughts turned dark. *"Do you still live with him?"*

"Of course not," she replied, surprised by his accusation. "I told you that part of it is over!" She saw his muscles relax slightly. "Brandon's in a rehabilitation center working with a physical therapist."

"I assume he doesn't have a job and you're footing the bill."

"He's only been walking with the brace for a few months," Maren snapped, wondering why she felt so suddenly defensive of a man who had done nothing but hurt her. She let out her emotions in an angry sigh. "I think he'll be able to work again soon. Until he does, I have to help him."

"Why?"

"Because he doesn't have any other family," she replied. "Haven't you been listening to me? It's my fault he went skiing that weekend. If it hadn't been for me, he'd probably still be playing tennis, for God's sake!"

She was shaking with the intensity of her emotions. She felt chilled to the bone. Kyle opened his robe and folded her against him, letting his arms and the soft folds of cloth protect her from the night air.

Softly he kissed the top of her head. She let her arms tighten around his naked torso and leaned her head on his chest. "I think your husband's career was over before it began," Kyle stated reassuringly. "I read about him; he couldn't control his hostility. It worked against him rather than to his advantage."

"Your opinion."

"The truth."

The protests forming in her throat died. For years she had been deluding herself that Brandon would have made it on his own. The gravity of Kyle's face and his firm words helped convince her that Brandon would take advantage of her as long as she gave him the opportunity. She had only to remember Brandon's last near-frantic call.

"For the time being," she said, "Brandon is my responsibility."

"Until when? Until he decides he can make it on his own? Or *you* get tired of carrying the burden? *When?*"

"It will work out," she said vaguely.

"When Brandon McClure decides that he's tired of sponging off his ex-wife."

She was tired and her voice was bitter. "I don't see that it's any concern of yours what happens to Brandon. It won't affect my decision to sell Festival Productions one way or the other, and that's why I'm here, remember?"

"Is it?" he asked in a throaty whisper. With one long finger he traced the length of her bare arm and a shiver of anticipation darted down her spine.

His embrace became more possessive, and his eyes drilled into the mystery of hers. "Tell me again," he persuaded, "why you're here."

With a surrendering sigh, she leaned heavily against him. "I'm here because I want to be," she admitted, listening to the steady cadence of his heart. This is where I belong, she thought, alone with Kyle in the night, letting him hold me.

"Come on," he whispered. "Let's go to bed."

His arms supported her as they walked through the door and back into the warmth of the rambling hacienda.

CHAPTER TWELVE

"I WANT YOU TO MARRY ME."

Kyle's voice was the first sound she heard as she awoke. Maren opened her eyes and stared into the dark gaze of the man she loved. She smiled and stretched.

"I thought we weren't going to discuss marriage."

"Only because you're so damned independent." Kyle sat up in the bed and ran his hand over the stubble of his beard.

"Should I consider that a compliment?" she teased.

"Damn it, Maren, I'm serious. I want you to marry me and live with Holly and me here in La Jolla." His tanned brow was creased and his coffee-colored hair, streaked from the sun, was rumpled. He clasped his hands behind his head and stared up at the ceiling. "I've been thinking about this all night. It's the only answer."

"And what about my work?"

"We could handle it here."

"I don't think—"

"Sure, we'll have to be in L.A. once or twice a week to supervise what's going on, but there's no reason you can't work out your ideas and those sketches here."

"There's a lot more to it than that," she stated, trying to quiet her racing heart. Kyle had asked her to marry him! It was what she wanted most, and yet it couldn't be. Not now. "I'm involved with the actual shooting of the sequences and some of the editing, not to mention hiring the actors, renting the soundstages..."

"But don't you have people who can supervise that sort of thing?"

"To some extent..."

"And once you've sold the company, things will be that much easier," he suggested.

His words had the effect of salt on an open wound. She stiffened in the bed. "Elise advised me against talking with you or anyone from Sterling Records about the offer, until we can come to some sort of an agreement."

He looked at her as if she were out of her mind. "And just how are we supposed to do that if we don't discuss the offer?"

"Elise thought she could straighten things out with Bob Simmons."

"And then he'll want to discuss it with me, in private. It doesn't make a hell of a lot of sense, Maren. We can wrap this thing up this morning." He turned to face her. "I thought you were the kind of woman who made her own decisions."

"I am."

"Then why the hell do you have to rely on Ms. Conrad?"

"Because she's my attorney!"

"Do you really think I would try to pull a fast one on you?" His silvery eyes impaled her. "Don't you trust me?"

"Kyle, this has nothing to do with trust...it's business!"

She rolled over and started to get up, but he caught her wrist, forcing her back on the bed. "This is not business... not anymore...this is *us*."

"You're clouding the issue."

"And you're avoiding it!"

She jerked her hand free of his grasp and got out of bed. "Maybe you're right," she allowed, struggling into his bathrobe and seating herself in a chair across the room. She stared at him with intense indigo eyes as she brushed her hair away from her face with her fingers and crossed her shapely legs. "You want to talk business? What about right now?"

"Fine with me." He rolled off the bed and pulled on a pair of khaki-colored jeans.

"Why don't you start by telling me exactly what you have in mind for Festival, if I decide to sell?"

"It's in the offer..."

"Refresh my memory."

"Only the ownership will change. You can still run the operation any way you wish, with the exception that Festival will be in the same building as the record company and you'll spend most of your time working from the library here."

She arched her eyebrows elegantly. If only she could believe that his proposal of marriage had nothing to do with his desire for the company. He'd married once to promote his career. Would he marry again to bolster the income of Sterling Records? Dear Lord, she hoped not!

"I'll pay you a fair price for your company," Kyle said, breaking into her thoughts "Even Elise has agreed about that."

Maren nodded, tapping the tips of her fingernails on the arm of the chair.

"I've been honest with you, Maren. I need your talent as well as your company. Elise mentioned that you wanted a three-year employment agreement. It's yours. As far as I'm concerned, you're the talent behind Festival Productions. Without you, Festival is just another production company, and they're a dime a dozen." He sat on the edge of the bed, his eyes holding her unwavering blue gaze. Resting his forearms on his thighs, he stared at her. "We can work together," he said softly, "after we're married."

She tried to speak but couldn't find her voice. She had to shift her gaze away from his penetrating stare. "You tried that once before," she reminded him. "It didn't work with Rose."

"Rose has nothing to do with this!" Every muscle in his body became rigid. "Haven't you been listening to what I just said?"

"I'm trying, Kyle," she replied, her voice wavering and tears filling her eyes "Dear God, I'm trying."

"Then hear what I'm saying. I want you to be my wife, and it has nothing to do with also wanting the production company." His dark gaze grew deadly, and the lean muscles in his forearms flexed. "I made a mistake with Rose, and I'll be damned if I ever make that same mistake again. I want you to live with me because I don't want to live without you. I *love* you, Maren."

The tears pooling in her eyes began to run down her cheeks. How long she had waited to hear those words, and how desperately she wanted to believe them. He stood and unhurriedly walked across the room. "Can't you see how much you mean to me?" Lowering himself to one knee he touched her shoulders. As she stared into his brooding eyes she thought she would like to drown in his gaze. Her love for him was overpowering, and she could never find it in her heart to tie him down with a marriage he didn't want.

"Maren, please marry me," he said. His fingers slid under the folds of the robe and his thumbs moved seductively over her soft skin. How easily he could coax her.

"I don't want to rush into anything" she replied quietly,

hoping to stop the tears streaming down her face. "This is the eighties. We don't have to get married."

"Unless we want to."

"It's not that I don't want to marry you," she reassured him, softly touching his chin. "I just need a little time to think it over."

His smile was wistful. "All right," he agreed reluctantly. "Now let's go downstairs, and you can tell me how far you've come on the Mirage videos."

"We're going to work at this hour of the morning? It's Saturday."

"I've got to convince you that you can live here and still do your work," Kyle reminded her. "And I've only got a couple of days to prove it."

Wiping away her tears, she laughed. "Give me a couple of minutes to shower and change, fix me a huge breakfast and *then* I'll get to work."

"Lady," he responded with a widening grin. "You've got yourself a deal!"

SATURDAY AND SUNDAY PASSED too quickly, and Maren realized that she was beginning to feel a part of Kyle and his intimate family. Holly's hostilities slowly evaporated, and Lydia seemed elated that Maren was in the house. During the day Kyle took Holly and Maren sailing, and in the evenings they walked along the beach.

The meals were a time of laughter and warmth, especially when Lydia was able to stay and sample her own talents. Everything the elderly woman prepared was superb, and Lydia positively beamed when Maren insisted on helping her in the kitchen in order to discover the secrets of Lydia's culinary skills.

If Holly disapproved of her father's relationship with

Maren, she managed to hide it. Several times the young girl caught Kyle holding Maren in a loving embrace, but Holly only smiled at the intimate couple.

The only black spot on the remainder of the weekend occurred just before Maren left. She was packing her clothes into her suitcase when Kyle came into the bedroom. "I hate to see you leave," he stated, watching Maren's movements as she leaned over the bed and folded a blouse into her bag.

"Oh, but I must," she quipped, looking behind her and sliding a suggestive glance in his direction. "That president of Sterling Records becomes positively unglued if I'm late with anything."

He caught the look of provocation in her eyes and noticed the way her jeans hugged her hips. "You're going to have to marry me sooner or later," he responded mentally calculating how long it would take to strip off her jeans.

"Why's that?" She locked the suitcase and turned to face him, balancing herself on the edge of the bed. "And don't give me that lame excuse of making an honest woman of me."

He lifted his palms in mock surrender. "I wouldn't dream of it."

"Well then?"

"I think it would be best for all of us."

The laughter in her eyes faded. "I don't think Holly would appreciate me stepping into her mother's shoes."

Kyle strode across the room, pushed the suitcase off the bed and sat next to Maren. His gray eyes held hers in a smoky embrace. "Holly adores you…"

"She *tolerates* me." Maren let out an uncomfortable sigh. "I'll admit, that's progress and a lot more than I expected, but a far cry from adoration."

Attempting to rise, Maren felt strong hands grab her arm and pull her forcefully onto the bed. She fell onto the comforter and felt the persuasive strength of Kyle's body stretched near hers. Her auburn hair fell away from her face in tangled disarray, and her clear indigo eyes searched his. Her skin was flushed, and Kyle knew she was the most intrinsically beautiful woman he had ever met. This one woman had changed his entire outlook on life.

"Why won't you consider my proposal?" he demanded, his hands tightening behind her back. She felt each of his lean muscles pressed supplely against hers. His warm breath fanned her face, and though she tried to ignore it, her heart began to thud irregularly.

With all the determination she could gather, she replied. "I think it's time for total honesty, Kyle."

"I'd agree."

One of her delicate dark brows cocked. "Would you?"

He smiled and gave her a short shake. "Out with it, woman. What's on your mind?"

"There's more to it than worrying about becoming a stepmother to Holly," she admitted.

"I figured as much."

"How much of this...proposal has to do with the buyout of Festival?" She felt his arms tighten rigidly around her.

"None."

"Then why do I get the feeling that you're holding something back from me...that something about Festival Productions is bothering you? If it's not the sale, then what?" Confusion clouded her gaze, and Kyle was forced to unburden himself.

"Of course I want you to sell Festival to me, and I expect that you will, once we change the terms of the offer to satisfy Elise." He released her slowly and propped his head on one elbow so he could study the slightest reaction on her face. "Ryan Woods thinks that he's found a pirated copy of Mitzi Danner's latest release."

Maren's eyes widened. "The video of 'Going for Broke'?"

"Right."

"That's impossible," she stated, her mind whirling. That tape was barely back from editing.

"Not according to Woods." Was it his imagination, or did a tremor of fear darken her eyes?

"We haven't even sent the finished product over to Sterling Records yet."

"I know."

Anger replaced disbelief. "So you assume that someone at Festival is ripping you off?"

"I don't know. I haven't seen the tape myself, but Ryan Woods seems pretty sure of himself, and he knows his business."

"There must be some mistake..."

"I don't think so." Kyle's voice was as calm as the steely look in his eye. "But I'm waiting to see the evidence myself..."

"Evidence?" Maren cried. "Good Lord, Kyle, you make it sound as if I'm some kind of criminal!" She pulled herself off the bed and stood up before glaring down at him. "Why didn't you tell me?"

"I wanted to be sure." Dragging himself to his feet, he towered over her, accepting the anger in her gaze.

"Are you?"

"No, not yet."

She ran trembling fingers through her hair. "But you expect to discover something," Maren guessed.

"I don't know. I'm not certain that someone from

Festival's involved. The only thing we can do is wait until Ryan somehow finds a way to get a copy of that tape."

"Dear God…"

"Okay, so I told you my secret," he stated, drawing her attention back to his hard face. "What about yours?"

"I don't have any…"

"I'm talking about Brandon."

Every muscle in Maren's body froze. She hadn't expected her ex-husband to be included in the conversation. Lifting her eyes to meet his condemning gaze squarely, she managed to hide the fact that her stomach was doing somersaults. "What about Brandon?" he charged. "How long do you intend to support him?"

"Until he can get a job on his own."

Sparks of anger lit his cold gaze. "If he wanted to be employed, I'm sure he could be." Kyle's lips drew into a frown of disgust. "What I'm *not* sure of is how badly you want to be free of him."

Maren's rage matched that of her attacker. "That's a low blow, Kyle. You know that I'm only helping Brandon until he can get back on his feet again."

"No matter how long it takes?' Kyle charged.

"Until *I* know for certain that he could hold a job if he wanted to."

Maren grabbed her suitcase and strode angrily out of the room and down the stairs. She could hear Kyle's footsteps behind her, but she refused to turn and face his angry stare. Attempting to appear as calm as she could under the circumstances, she pushed open the kitchen door, hoping to track down Lydia and Holly so she could say goodbye.

Both Lydia and Holly were seated at the kitchen counter. A textbook was lying open-faced in front of them as they sipped lemonade and chuckled merrily to themselves. Holly began to murmur a simple phrase of butchered Spanish, and Lydia laughed so hard she had to wipe the corner of her eye with her apron.

"*Dios,* girl." Lydia smiled. "Have you ever thought about studying French instead?"

Holly giggled and closed the book. "How do you say 'I've had enough'?"

"What's going on in here?" Maren asked with an interested smile.

"Lydia's teaching me Spanish," Holly replied, sliding her instructor a mischievous glance.

"Not me," Lydia denounced fondly. "You're a lost cause."

Pretending to be miffed, Holly mumbled. "Oh, yeah, just wait. When I ace the test, guess who'll want all the credit?"

"And I'll deserve it," Lydia added with a warm smile for the girl. Maren laughed, but felt a growing sadness when she realized how attached she'd become to Kyle and his small family. She heard him enter the room on her heels, and she knew that if she didn't make her farewells hastily, she might not find the heart to leave.

"I just came to say goodbye," she announced regretfully.

Holly's smile faded. "Will you be coming back soon?" the girl asked, hoping to appear uninterested. Lydia's worried gaze studied Maren, communicating the elderly woman's concern for Kyle's daughter.

"I don't know," Maren admitted honestly. The argument with Kyle was still burning in her heart. She glanced at him and penetrated his brooding stare. He cared for her. She could see it as clearly as if it were written on his face. Maren smiled and touched Holly lightly on the arm. "Of course I'll be back, I'm just not exactly sure when.... I've got a job, you know."

"Yeah, just like Mom," Holly replied thoughtlessly.

The comment settled like lead in the room. An awkward silence followed, and Kyle's eyes, dark as night, watched Maren intently.

Lydia nervously twirled the pencil she had been using while helping Holly study. She cleared her throat before speaking. "Are you sure you can't stay for dinner?... There's plenty of food." Lydia's dark eyes were hopeful.

"I'm sure there is," Maren agreed. "And really I'd love to, but I just can't. Not tonight."

Kyle's silence charged Maren with the lie, but she ignored him and didn't bother to protest when he took her suitcase from her hand and held the door open for her. "This is your decision, you know. You could stay if you wanted."

"I think we both need a little time to sort things out," she objected. Her cool gaze held his firmly. "If you're right about the problem at Festival, I'm going to find it."

A look of concern crossed his face. He looked at her profile, pondering the gentle contours and the intelligent depths of her eyes. A soft sea breeze ruffled her hair, and he wished to God he could find a way to make her stay with him. In frustration he rubbed the back of his neck. "Don't go jumping off the deep end on me," he warned. "Not until we're sure about this thing. It might get sticky." Together they walked outside toward Maren's car.

"Are you trying to say 'dangerous'?" she accused flatly.

"I just want to know that you'll be careful. I wouldn't have brought any of this up to you, but you insisted."

"Now you sound like a private eye on one of those ridiculous detective shows. You're the one who started this," she reminded him.

"Not me, one of your employees."

"You *think.*"

He opened the car door for her and placed the suitcase on the backseat. She slid into position behind the steering wheel, pausing as she poised her keys at the ignition. The car door shut, and she had to squint against the blinding glare of the sun through the open car window. "I wish you'd reconsider," he suggested in a rough voice filled with intimate memories.

"You know that's impossible." She started the car, but before she could put it into gear, his fingers had captured the sun-gilded strands of her reddish hair, forcing her to look up again. In silent promise, he kissed her upturned lips.

"I'll miss you," he vowed, wondering at the dull ache pounding between his temples as he watched Maren wheel the sports car down the long driveway. Pushing his palms into the back pockets of his jeans, he wondered if there would ever be a day when she would trust him enough to stay with him.

KYLE HAD BEEN AS GOOD as his word. Elise had called the following week and been happy to report that the offer was completely satisfactory. As a show of good faith, Kyle had offered Maren a bonus program that would allow her to use the money to purchase shares of Sterling Recording Company stock. The attorneys for Sterling were rewriting the offer, and it would be ready to be signed by the end of the month.

Maren was so swamped with work that she didn't have a chance to breathe. Everything that could go wrong with the Mirage video did. There had been lighting problems in the soundstage, some of the costumes had been lost for nearly two days before being found hidden in a trunk near the location site and a small accident with fireworks exploding at the wrong time had shorted out the amplifiers. Fortunately no one had been hurt.

"I tell ya," Ted Bensen had stated at a meeting earlier in the week. "It's almost as if this Mirage sequence is jinxed. If I didn't know better, I'd swear we were being sabotaged!"

Maren had dismissed his complaints as a way for Ted to vent his frustrations. She couldn't blame him for being concerned: the problems were unlikely, but not inexplicable. Maren remembered the first video she had done for Mirage. Compared with it, the problems with "Yesterday's Heart" seemed insignificant.

What bothered her more than the puzzling events happening to the Mirage video was Jan. The secretary's attitude had become frigid, and try as she might, Maren wasn't able to communicate with her. Jan's work hadn't suffered, but her remarks to Maren about the impending sale of Festival were severe.

"Why do you think we've had all these problems with the latest Mirage video?" Jan had asked with a knowing glint in her brown eyes. "Why now, I'll bet Kyle Sterling is behind all this. He's trying to find a way to force you to sell!"

"That's ludicrous," Maren had replied indignantly. "He knows I intend to go through with the deal."

"Sure," Jan had responded with a frown. "But you haven't done it yet, have you? I think Sterling is just hedging his bets!"

Maren had pushed aside Jan's pointed comments and attributed them to overwork and a lousy situation with Jake. No doubt the secretary was feeling very insecure, and the fact that Festival was going to be sold didn't help the situation.

The first break in Maren's seven-day work weeks came nearly three weeks from the time she had left La Jolla. Fortunately, despite the unlikely delays, Maren had been able to accomplish more than she had hoped in the twenty-odd days and had even started work on Joey Righteous's video, once Kyle had signed the contract. She had seen Kyle fleetingly during the long three weeks. He had called several times and had been able to come to L.A. to watch the location taping of "Yesterday's Heart." But their time together had been short, and all too quickly he had returned to La Jolla, leaving her alone and taking with him the signed agreement of sale for Festival Productions. It had been a difficult decision for Maren, and more than once she had experienced the uncanny feeling that she had made an irreversible mistake in agreeing to sell the one thing she had worked so hard to create. In handing Kyle the signed document, Maren had given Kyle the opportunity to free himself of any commitment to her.

With her work load slightly less burdensome, Maren decided to take Kyle up on his open invitation. She deserved a small vacation.

It was evening by the time she had packed. She decided to take the scenic route along the coast back to La Jolla. That way she wouldn't have to concentrate on the snarls of traffic that backed up the freeways, and she would be able to consider all that had happened to her in the last few weeks.

The drive was pleasant and carefree. Wind from the Pacific Ocean blew through the Torrey pines that clung tenaciously to the parched bluffs overlooking the sea north of La Jolla. Maren let out a contented sigh as she drove southward and noticed that the final rays of a dying sun turned the blue waters of the Pacific various shades of brilliant gold.

In the short time she had been with Kyle, Maren hadn't felt that the problems between them had been resolved. Perhaps her agreement to sell Festival Productions would change all that. She certainly hoped so. Elise Conrad, Maren's attorney, had assured Maren that Kyle's offer to buy out Festival was not only legal, but also more than equitable. In Elise's estimation, Maren would never get a better offer. She advised her client to sell and escape from the rigorous daily routine of running the business. Reluctantly Maren had agreed. The one shining spot in the entire transaction was that Maren would finally be able to pay off Jacob Green and get out from under his slippery thumb.

Before leaving for La Jolla, Maren had called Brandon. It was a stilted conversation, and though he did admit that he felt better physically, he wasn't able to accept the idea of working at a desk job for the rest of his life. He'd consulted several career analysts, but none of the employment they had suggested appealed to him. After the action and glamour of the tennis circuit, a dull job of pushing papers just didn't cut it.

Brandon had indicated that his physical therapy sessions were nearly finished and that he hoped Maren would consider letting him reside in the condominium they had shared when they were married. Though it was her part of the divorce settlement and she now rented it to an elderly couple, Brandon reasoned that she could drum up some excuse to evict them. After all, what was he to do? He couldn't very well support himself, at least not yet.

Maren had hung up the phone with trembling hands. A wave of nausea rushed up her throat as she realized that Kyle had been right. Brandon had been using her, playing upon her sympathies and guilt all along. Her ex-husband was avoiding taking any responsibility for his own life.

When she considered all the guilt she had borne over Brandon's unfortunate accident, a new feeling of self-awareness took hold of her: His accident wasn't her fault. Maren didn't *owe* Brandon anything.

And so, soon she would be working for Kyle, she mused to herself as she passed through the familiar gates guarding his estate. She found the thought pleasant, if a little unnerving. The largest step of all had already been taken. Filming was complete on the first Mirage video, and editing would be finished within a couple of weeks. A celebration was planned for the first showing of the tape.

Maren turned off the car motor, and a pleased smile spread over her face. The only thing she hadn't been able to accomplish in the last few weeks concerned Mitzi Danner's videotape of "Going for Broke." Maren had come across no evidence to indicate that Mitzi's tape had been duplicated. She was still bothered by Kyle's accusations, but had come to the conclusion that Ryan Woods, whoever in the world he was, had made a mistake—an incredibly big mistake.

Maren walked briskly to the front door with newly felt confidence. Perhaps things were going to get better. Before she could knock on the door it was pulled open and Lydia greeted her with worried eyes.

"Thank God you're here," she murmured, hastily making the sign of the cross over her breasts.

"What's wrong?" Maren's heart leapt to her throat. The anxiety in Lydia's dark eyes and the pained expression on her face made Maren's pulse race.

"Come in, come in," Lydia insisted, moving out of the doorway. She rambled for a minute in rapid Spanish before realizing that Maren couldn't understand a word she was saying. "*Dios,*" she whispered. "It's Holly."

Maren's eyes widened in horror. She grabbed Lydia's arm as she imagined a gamut of horrible accidents occurring. Her heart felt as if it had stopped beating. "What's wrong? Has something happened?"

Lydia nodded gravely. "That woman called!" she spat out.

"What woman—who called? Is Holly hurt?"

Lydia attempted to allay Maren's worst fears. "She bleeds, but it's from the heart," the elderly woman whispered. "That mother of hers…" Once again communication was broken by Lydia's rapid stream of Spanish.

"Hold on, Lydia. Calm down and explain to me what happened—*in English.* Where's Holly now?"

"She's down at the beach…I think…. She wouldn't talk to me…."

"What about Kyle?"

"He's with her."

Maren's worries subsided slightly. Slowly she let out a gust of air. "Maybe I shouldn't intrude."

"It wouldn't be intruding. Holly needs you…"

"She's got her father."

"She needs a woman who cares for her," Lydia stated emphatically.

"Like you."

"*Dios,* no!" Lydia replied, shaking her graying head. "I am like the grandmother…with you it's different." She took Maren's arm and hustled her toward the back door. "You go. Maybe you can talk some sense into her."

More to placate Lydia than anything else, Maren decided to track down Holly and Kyle. If there had been some family disturbance with Rose, Maren doubted that she could help and secretly thought it better for father and daughter to work it out alone. However, she slowly descended the weathered steps and squinted into the dusky twilight. Several hundred yards northward she spotted Kyle and Holly sitting on the beach. Maren took her time approaching them.

"Lydia insisted that I come looking for you," she stated when she was still several feet away from the two huddled figures. Kyle looked up, and the lines on his face indicated the strain he had been enduring. Holly refused to raise her eyes, but Maren noticed the wet tracks from recent tears on her cheeks. Maren's heart ached for the sad girl with the trembling lower lip. "If I'm intruding…"

"I'm glad you're here," Kyle interrupted, but Holly refused to comment. "Maybe you can explain a few things to Holly," he suggested, his gray eyes pleading.

Maren took a tentative seat near the girl. "Maybe I can. I was a fifteen-year-old girl myself once," she allowed, rubbing the toe of her tennis shoe into the sand.

"Did your mom work?" Holly charged, her frail voice catching on a sob.

"Yes, she did," Maren admitted. "She was a schoolteacher. Taught English at the high school I attended. It was a terrible burden. I *never* got away with anything."

Holly lifted a suspicious eye, as if to see if Maren were bluffing. The sincere look on Maren's studious face convinced her that Maren was for real. "Did she ever miss your birthday?" Holly asked in a voice so low it was lost in the surf.

Maren frowned as she thought. She studied the disappearing horizon before turning to Holly. "I don't remember. I doubt it. She was pretty big on birthdays, Christmas and all the other holidays. I think I'd remember if any of them were skipped."

"Yeah, I though so," Holly sniffed, stiffening her spine.

Kyle placed a comforting arm over his daughter and pulled her against his side. The look he cast Maren was filled with the pain he was bearing for his child.

"Is that what happened?" Maren asked softly. "Did your mom forget your birthday?"

Holly had trouble trusting her voice. When she replied, it quavered. "Oh, she remembered all right. It's just that she thinks she has to stay in Texas longer than she planned and…well…she won't be able to see me on my birthday. I'm going to be sixteen…and…she promised me a big party." The tears Holly had been fighting slid silently down her cheeks. "She doesn't love me," the girl said flatly.

"Oh, I doubt that," Maren responded, with a gentle smile. Slowly she reached out and touched Holly's curly hair. Kyle's eyes reflected his surprise. "I'm sure your mother loves you very much," Maren maintained as Holly broke into sobs. "Some people have difficulty expressing their love…"

"She's sending me a birthday present," Holly interrupted angrily. "But she can't seem to find the time to come home!"

Maren hesitated, finding it hard to defend Rose. "Look, Holly, I know that sometimes it's hard to understand your mother. But you have to think about it from her perspective. Her career is very important to her…"

"More important than I am!"

"I don't think so." Kyle eyed Maren suspiciously, but Maren continued. "She probably knows that you're safe and well cared for here with your father, and right now she can't afford to let her career slide. Soon you'll be grown and out of the house, and what will Rose have other than her career?"

Holly let out a ragged sigh, and her teeth sank into

her lower lip. "You act as if you understand her—why would you?"

"I'm only trying to give her the benefit of the doubt…and, if it's a party you want, I know one where you'll be an honored guest…" Maren's eyes held Kyle's confused gaze. The angle of his chin warned her that she had better know what she was doing.

"What party?" Holly asked, distracted at least partially from her own misery.

"Well, it might not be as grand as a sixteenth-birthday party, but I'm planning a celebration next week because I've just finished a very important piece of business." Kyle's eyebrows lifted in interest. "And the best part is that I think all of the members of Mirage will be there."

"Really?" Holly sniffed back her tears.

"Really. What do you say?"

Kyle looked as if he were about to interfere, but the determination in Maren's gaze deterred him.

"Oh, Maren," Holly sighed, temporarily forgetting her woes. "Is it all right if I bring a friend?"

"Of course."

In a gesture overflowing with gratitude, Holly wrapped her small arms around Maren's shoulders and smiled. "Thank you," she whispered. "I…I'm sorry I gave you such a bad time the last time you were here."

"It's all right…"

Abruptly Holly stood. "I'm going to call Sara right now. She'll be out of her mind!" With that she cast one last smile at her father, turned and raced back toward the house.

A cryptic smile spread over Kyle's thin lips. "It seems that you've just won another victory," he decided as he watched his daughter disappear up the stairs along the cliff face. "Holly thinks you're wonderful."

"Of course she does," Maren said with a slow-spreading grin. "I just offered her the chance of a lifetime: to meet J. D. Price, teenage heartthrob and hunk *extraordinaire*." Her laughter warmed the night.

"So you think you bribed her?"

Maren shook her head. "*Bribe* has such a distasteful connotation. I prefer to think that I charmed her."

"Just like her old man?"

Maren smiled wickedly. "Well, maybe not in the same manner." She sobered as a thought struck her. "Holly went to the doctor last week, didn't she?" Kyle nodded. "Well, what's the prognosis?"

Kyle closed his eyes. "Dr. Seivers seems to think that she's fine. Her uterus seems to have healed properly and though there's a slight chance that more problems could arise, he's not worried."

'Thank God," Maren whispered in relief.

"You really care for her, don't you?"

"Yes," Maren admitted with a shy smile. "I was only kidding before. She's the one who's charmed me."

Kyle's arm reached out in the darkness. Moon glow caught in her eyes and he pushed on her wrist, causing her to lose her balance. She fell back on the white sand, her hair framing her face in tangled waves of auburn silk. Leaning over her, Kyle studied the finely sculpted shape of her oval face and the mystery in her blue eyes.

"I've missed you," he admitted in a voice as rough as the sea. Leaning forward, his lips brushed softly against her throat. At the tenderness in the gesture, she gasped. Her love for this man seemed to overflow into the night.

Watching him through a dark fringe of lashes, she was forced to concede the truth. "And I've missed you…hopelessly." She lifted her head and captured his lips with hers, feverishly showing how desperate her longing had become.

"How long can you stay with me?" he asked, dark gray eyes holding hers fast.

"As long as you want me to..." she sighed.

"Forever?"

One word hung in the air between them, drowning out the sound of the relentless tide.

"Oh, Kyle," she answered, yearning with all her heart to accept his proposal and share her life with him. There was nothing she wanted more in this life than to share his darkest secrets, love his only child and sleep with his arms wrapped securely around her breasts each night.

"I'm serious, Maren. You know that. Please marry me."

How could she refuse that which she most wanted? On this lovely star-studded night, lying on the silver sand, his body pressed urgently against hers, she could find no objections to his request. "Of course I'll marry you, Kyle," she sighed, giving in to her most intimate desires. "I'd love to." She closed her eyes and felt the warmth of his lips molding impatiently to hers.

"Dear God, Maren," he said, lifting his head to contemplate the enigma in her eyes. "You don't know how long I've waited to hear those words."

She wrapped her arms around his neck, and he kissed her once again. A warmth, starting in the deepest region of her soul, began to spread slowly through her body. How many nights had she lain awake aching for this man? Now at last, he was hers.

CHAPTER THIRTEEN

THE WEEK PASSED BY in a flourish and rush of activity. Maren spent every waking moment at the office, and she was so absorbed in the final editing of the Mirage video and planning for the celebration that was to take place that she had little time to notice anything else. It was Friday afternoon before she could catch her breath, and the party was scheduled for the next day.

At four o'clock Jan came into the office carrying cold drinks from a nearby fast-food stand. "You're an angel," Maren said gratefully as she accepted the opaque paper cup and took a long drink.

"You've called me a lot of things," Jan remarked with a sad smile. "But that's the first time you referred to me as an angel."

"An oversight on my part," Maren thought aloud. "But it doesn't matter. When all the dust has settled on the buyout, you should be getting a raise."

Jan's smile quivered. "How did you arrange that?"

"I'm in tight with the boss." Maren laughed, giving Jan a broad wink and playful smile. She felt lighthearted and incredibly happy. There was a disturbed light in Jan's large brown eyes, and Maren imagined that things weren't going well for Jan. The secretary seemed nervous—as if she wanted to get something off her chest.

"So tell me," Maren prodded gently. "How're things with you and the baby?"

Jan perked up at the mention of her pregnancy. "As well as can be expected, I guess. I did have a little trouble last week, but it wasn't anything serious."

Maren's smile faded. "What kind of trouble?"

Jan waved off the concern in her employer's gaze. "Nothing really. Last Wednesday morning I bled—just a little."

"Why didn't you stay home?" Maren asked, astounded. "You could have had the day off—or the rest of the week, for that matter."

Jan shook her head and bit her lower lip. "I had too much work to do..."

"Cary could have handled your work. Look, I don't want you jeopardizing your health or the baby's..."

"It's no big deal...I saw the doctor, and he seems to think everything will be fine if I just take it easy..."

"Are you?" Maren demanded, trying not to sound overly concerned. Jan's worries about her pregnancy explained the secretary's nervousness and anxiety. Jan was worried sick about losing the baby. It didn't seem fair. First Jan had trouble with Jake...now this.

Tears clouded Jan's gaze, and she tried vainly to hide them by wiping her eyes with the back of her hand. "I wish you wouldn't worry so much about me, Maren." She bit at her lower lip. "There's something you should know."

"What's that?" Maren asked quietly.

"Oh, God, Maren, I wish—" The telephone rang before Jan could finish her thought. Jan started to get up to answer it, but Maren waved the secretary back into her chair.

"I'll get it," Maren said with a heartfelt smile. Jan looked tired and distraught. At least Maren understood her worries. Setting her soft drink aside, Maren picked up the receiver. "Festival Productions, Maren McClure speaking."

"What happened—did you get a demotion?" Brandon's voice charged with a nervous laugh.

"Not exactly." Maren's tone was frigid, and Jan knew immediately that her boss was involved in a private conversation. Ignoring Maren's gestures for her to remain in the room, Jan hoisted herself out of the chair and waved at Maren, before silently mouthing her goodbye.

"I'll see you tomorrow," Jan whispered as she left the room, smiled at Maren and shut the door thoughtfully behind her.

"I hadn't heard from you in a while and I thought I'd call to check up on you," Brandon stated with a nervous laugh. "What's new?"

Maren's spine stiffened. "I was going to call you, as a matter of fact," she replied.

"Oh?" Brandon's voice was interested but wary. He could sense a difference in his ex-wife.

"I wanted you to know that I'm planning to get married this summer."

There was a surprised gasp on the other end of the phone. "Anyone I know?" he asked, with just a hint of sarcasm.

"Kyle Sterling." Why was she so reluctant to give Brandon that bit of information?

"*The* Kyle Sterling? Jesus Christ, Maren!"

Maren broke the uneasy silence that had settled over the stilted conversation. "So, I've been giving some thought to you."

"Nice of ya," he retorted angrily.

"I've decided to give you ownership of the condominium, Brandon. Since I don't use it, I don't really need it, and the couple who rent it are planning to move at the end of their lease, which is in about six weeks. I've already had the papers drawn up. You can pick them up from Elise Conrad, at her office." Once again there was weighty silence as Brandon considered Maren's offer. She silently prayed that he would accept the condominium they had shared when they were married. It held too many memories of the wasted marriage, and Maren never had the heart to live in it. As it was, she had rented it and used the income to pay for Brandon's medical needs. She would only be too glad for him to accept that piece of real estate, which still reminded her of the painful divorce.

"Is this the kiss-off?" Brandon asked.

"I think it's time we went our separate ways."

"Easy for you to say. You're marrying into big bucks, so you don't want to bother with a cripple!"

"Brandon, you're not a cripple. I've talked with your doctors and your physical therapists. They all seem to think that you're fine. And your career counselor says he can put you into a job as soon as you're willing. I think…"she paused, wondering just how to handle him, and then decided that honesty was what he needed. "…I think it's time you decided what you want to do with your life."

"And what would you say if I told you I wanted you?" he asked softly.

"I'd say that you're wrong. We tried, Brandon. It didn't work. *You're* the one who decided that." When he didn't immediately respond, she concluded: "It's up to you whether you want the condo or not. Just give Elise a call. Goodbye." With finality, she replaced the receiver. "Thank God it's over," she murmured as she pulled herself upright and hurried out of her office to look for Jan. Maren had been left with the uncanny feeling that Jan had had something she wanted to discuss with her before the conversation was cut off by Brandon's untimely telephone call.

When Maren entered the reception area, she realized that Jan must have left for the weekend. The clutter on Jan's desk had been cleared and there was no sign of the blond secretary. Whatever it was that Jan had wanted to say would just have to keep.

Within a few minutes Ted, from production, stopped in with the finished product of the Mirage video.

"Better late than never," Maren quipped as she accepted the cassette. "How does it look?"

"See for yourself," Ted suggested with a smile and a weary raking of his fingers through thinning blond hair. There was a satisfied look in his eyes.

"That good, is it?" Maren asked as she placed the cassette into the recorder and watched as J. D. Price and the rest of Mirage sang and acted out the lyrics of "Yesterday's Heart." A pleased grin stole over Maren's lips. "It's a winner," she thought aloud.

"You bet it is," Ted agreed.

"Now we'll really have something to celebrate tomorrow," she replied, rewinding the tape and watching the video a second time.

"It should be a big day," Ted surmised, lighting a cigarette.

"It will be interesting to see Mirage's reaction to this tape," she said, mentally noting that Kyle's reaction would be just as worthwhile.

"I think J.D. will be pleased."

"Let's hope so," Maren murmured as she took the cassette from the recorder and locked the black cartridge in the file cabinet. "We'll find out tomorrow night, won't we?"

"We'll knock 'em dead," Ted predicted as he turned to go. "And let me tell you, it's been a long time coming. After that unscheduled blowup with the fireworks, I was ready to throw in the towel."

"Good thing you didn't."

"I guess so. See ya tomorrow." He ambled out of the office leaving Maren to turn out the lights and lock the door.

SATURDAY DAWNED PERFECT for sailing. The party, which was primarily to celebrate the buyout of Festival Productions by Sterling Records, was to be held on Kyle's yacht, at his insistence. After an afternoon of sailing around Santa Catalina Island, the yacht would return to her private berth near Long Beach. At that time, Maren planned to unveil the Mirage tape, hoping that everyone involved with the making of the video would get to see it.

Invited guests streamed onto the yacht under the brilliant Southern California sun. Some of the guests were dressed casually in beachwear, while others stepped onto the deck in glamorous gowns and dripping in jewels. When the eclectic group seemed complete, the gleaming white vessel set sail for the short trip.

Maren was in a festive mood. She was dressed casually and felt as carefree as the wind. Mingling with the guests, she accepted congratulations on the sale of the production company. And for the first time in several years, she felt unburdened with thoughts of her ex-husband. She was free to love again, and she was hopelessly in love with Kyle.

Sunbathers crowded the polished wood deck, while other guests clustered in the main salon, drinking champagne and sampling a lavish display of hors d'oeuvres. Liveried waiters were prompt to refill a glass or offer the trays of appetizers. Champagne flowed from a fountain near an extraordinary seafood buffet.

"You really know how to throw a party," Maren teased when Kyle made his way over to her. A flash of white teeth warmed his tanned face.

"Thank you." He placed a possessive arm around her waist and leaned over the railing to watch the prow of the yacht knife through the clear blue-green water.

"Who're you trying to impress?" Maren asked, her eyes twinkling mischievously.

"Just one lady," he admitted with a devilish grin.

"You didn't have to host a party to impress me," she sighed. The wind caught in her hair and pulled it free of her chignon. Salt sea spray caressed her face. "I was already interested."

He leaned with his back to the railing, and his gray eyes roved over the crowd milling on the deck. His smile broadened as his eyes rested on his daughter. She and her friend were sunning themselves while sitting in lounge chairs. "I've got some good news," Kyle announced, letting his eyes linger on Holly.

"Oh?"

"Well, actually, it's good news for me, but it might be a difficult adjustment for Holly." His lips drew into a contemplative frown. "Rose called this morning."

At the mention of Kyle's ex-wife, Maren's stomach knotted. "She wanted to talk to Holly?"

"That's the surprising part. She didn't want to speak to Holly at all. As a matter of fact, she didn't want Holly to know about the conversation until she'd worked out a deal with me."

Maren was instantly on guard. "What kind of a deal?" she asked anxiously.

The waiter interrupted Kyle's response by offering slightly unsteady glasses of champagne from a silver tray. Kyle accepted one for himself and handed another to Maren. When the slim steward disappeared into the crowd, Kyle continued. "It seems that Rose has finally seen the light."

Maren took a drink of her champagne. "What do you mean?"

"Rose has taken up with some singer in the movie. He's not playing the lead, but that's beside the point."

"What is the point?" Maren asked, raising her brows in anticipation.

"Rose assured me that the new man in her life is not just a casual fling. But there is a problem. She wants to cut a record with him, and she's going to move in with him. He lives somewhere near Dallas and the last thing he wants is Holly."

Maren raised her eyes to meet Kyle's angry gaze. "So Rose is going to give you custody of Holly after all—just because this guy doesn't like kids." Maren couldn't hide her surprise. Her heart bled for Holly.

"That's about the size of it," Kyle admitted grimly.

Maren disguised her disgust. "Good. Holly deserves to be with you."

"With *us,*" Kyle amended. "She'll be with us."

"And I'm thrilled about it," Maren said honestly, with tears shining in her eyes. "I can't think of anything that would make me happier than living with you and your daughter."

Relief flooded Kyle's ruggedly handsome features. "You're a very special woman, Maren McClure," he stated, taking her into his arms and kissing her softly on the lips. "Do you think that I could persuade you to drive to Las Vegas with me tonight so that we can quit talking about getting married and just do it?"

"What about Holly?"

"She's staying the weekend with Sara. We'd be alone until Monday."

"It sounds like heaven," Maren murmured, closing her eyes. She didn't realize how tired she was. The last six weeks had been frantic and she couldn't think of anything more perfect than spending a quiet weekend alone with Kyle.

"Consider it," Kyle suggested, just as Grace, his secretary, approached them and offered her congratulations. The plump woman seemed genuinely pleased. "This one," she pointed accusingly at Kyle, "needs a woman looking after him."

Maren laughed aloud. "I'd say you've done a pretty good job of that."

"At the office, yes. But he needs more than that. Good luck to the both of you," Grace said with a satisfied smile as she turned back toward the refreshment table.

"You've been spreading rumors about us," Maren accused with a merry laugh. "And I love you for it."

"Guilty as charged," Kyle replied, finishing his glass of champagne. "But the only people I told our little secret to were Grace, Lydia and Holly."

'So she did know about it! That little stinker. When Holly boarded the yacht, I thought she looked like the cat who ate the canary, feathers and all!" Maren looked deeply into Kyle's amused gray eyes. "So tell me, how did your daughter take the news?"

"Very well. As a matter of fact, I think that she and Lydia had a little wager about it."

Maren's dark brows arched elegantly. "Is that so. Did Lydia give up on Spanish and start teaching Holly the techniques of gambling?"

"Why don't you ask Holly," Kyle said with a laugh. The

sound of his laughter was rich and managed to touch the darkest corners of Maren's heart. When he tightened his arms around her waist, Maren imagined she could die in the warmth of his gentle embrace. How was it possible to love one man so desperately?

Holly strode up to Maren and her father. "So when are you going to make the official announcement?" she asked.

"Any day now," Kyle replied.

"I'm so happy for you," Holly said, looking at Maren. "This old guy needs someone to keep him in line."

"Old?" Kyle repeated with a vexed look crossing his face.

Holly ignored his mock anger. She threw her small arms around Maren's neck and hugged her. "It's wonderful," the girl whispered to Maren, and Maren had difficulty holding back her tears. She felt as if her heart would burst with happiness.

The white vessel rounded Santa Catalina Island just as the sun sank into the horizon. By the time the yacht was docked back at Long Beach, it was dark and all of the guests had wandered into the main salon. The room was thick with cigarette smoke as everyone waited to witness the first showing of "Yesterday's Heart." A crowd huddled around the screen in a tight semicircle. All five members of Mirage had their eyes riveted on the screen.

Maren slipped the tape into the recorder. In a flood of sound and visual effects, the throbbing music of Mirage dominated the room and the screen offered an image of a spurned lover singing angry lyrics while walking down an empty street during the Depression. The editing was perfect, and J.D.'s charisma blended with the pouty disdain in Janie Krypton's intriguing eyes.

When the tape had ended, there were roars of approval

from the crowd: "Let's see it again!" "That was great!" "What an inspired idea!" All of the comments were enthusiastic, and Maren felt as if a great weight had been lifted from her shoulders. The room was filled with smiles and the popping of champagne bottles being uncorked until Holly Sterling turned her confused eyes on her father.

"What's the big deal?" she asked, aware that members of Mirage were eyeing her warily.

"What do you mean?"

"I've already seen that video," Holly stated weakly.

Kyle's smile fell from his face. The clatter of voices hushed. "I don't understand."

"I saw that video yesterday at Jill's house," she said, her round eyes searching for Maren.

"Are you sure?" Kyle asked as the cold hand of suspicion climbed up his spine.

"Daddy, I told you. I saw 'Yesterday's Heart'!" Holly repeated.

"What's going on here?" J. D. Price thundered. "You told me you wouldn't release the video until I approved!"

"And I meant it," Kyle said evenly.

Price stopped dead in his tracks, his thick brown brows pulled into an angry frown. "What are you trying to tell me, Sterling. If you haven't released it, how did she see the video?" Price's brilliant blue eyes sparked with vengeful fire. "What the hell are you saying—that the tape's been *pirated?*"

"I don't know," Kyle replied, his gray eyes searching the crowd for Maren.

"I'll sue!" Price roared. "Goddamn you, Sterling, I'll sue you for every cent you've got!"

Maren's knees sagged and she had to lean against the

wall for support. What was happening? Dear God, had Kyle been right all along? Was someone really stealing her tapes and duplicating them for the black market?

Angry members of Mirage separated Kyle from Maren, but when his wrathful gray eyes found hers, she felt as if a dull knife had been thrust into her heart and slowly turned, to let her bleed slowly in an agonizing death. Without completely understanding her motives, Maren ran from the room and out onto the deck. She took deep gulps of sea air before she managed to get hold of herself. A nauseous feeling rose in her throat and her hands were shaking, but she was able to make it down the walkway to the dock. She raced to her car and roared out of the parking lot.

She couldn't remember the drive to the office. She had driven mechanically, her head pounding with questions she couldn't answer. *Who* would steal the tapes? *Why? How?* Her hands were still shaking when she unlocked the door of Festival Productions, raced up the stairs and switched on the lights. All she could think about was the unspoken accusation in Kyle's dark eyes as he had stared at her across the crowded salon. *It was as if he thought she were the culprit.*

Tears began to stream down her face as she realized that everything was lost to her. Her business was sold and the love she had basked in was gone. A raw ache took hold of her, tearing her apart from the inside out. Opening the file drawer, she counted the copies of "Yesterday's Heart." None of the cassettes was missing. Slowly she placed each cassette in the recorder, watching to see that it hadn't been mismarked. Everything seemed in order. "Get hold of yourself," she whispered.

She huddled on a corner of the couch, wrapping hr arms

around her legs and resting her forehead on her knees. "There has to be an answer," she told herself. Something didn't add up. Ted had just finished editing the Mirage tape yesterday and yet, Holly insisted that she had seen that very tape the same day. How could it happen? Carefully examining the past two weeks, Maren slowly found a possible answer. It occurred to her that on Wednesday, Ted had mentioned that he had an edited version of the Mirage tape but wasn't happy with it. The tape was too rough and needed the final editing for polish. He had left the tape in the offices overnight and reworked it later in the week. The editing changes had been minor and only a professional would have noticed the slight variations in the scene sequences. That rough version *had* to be the copy Holly had viewed.

But who? Who would do this to her?

Lost in her confused thoughts, Maren didn't hear the intruder until the sound of heavy steps racing up the stairs caught her attention. Maren lifted her head, and her heart leapt to her throat as she rose to face whoever was entering her domain. The tears she attempted to keep at bay fell from her eyes as she recognized Kyle. She wanted to run to him, to let her head fall against his chest, but the wariness in his eyes forced her to remain still.

"I figured you'd come here," he stated. A pain, as raw and naked as the night itself, lingered in the silvery depths of his gaze.

"I had no idea..." she whispered, but the hard jut of his jaw cut off the rest of her plea.

"Let's go," he ordered, the strain around his eyes overshadowing his rough command. "One of your employees...I think her name is Jan, is in the hospital."

"But she was on the yacht," Maren objected, concern for her friend evidenced in her words.

"I know." Kyle's voice was gentler. "She collapsed on the floor just after you left the salon."

"Dear God," Maren cried. "The baby."

Most of the drive was spent in silence. Maren was numb from the agonizing events of the evening. When Kyle finally parked his car in the hospital parking lot, Maren spoke.

"Do you know…did she lose the baby?" she asked.

"I didn't know there was a baby involved," Kyle replied. He placed a comforting arm on her shoulder. "But she was hemorrhaging pretty badly."

Maren closed her eyes and took in a long breath. "Let's go."

Kyle's grip on her arm tightened. "The reporters have already gotten wind of all this," he warned.

"Great," Maren replied. "Wouldn't you know?"

There was pandemonium at the hospital, and when Kyle and Maren entered the lobby, several reporters shoved microphones in Kyle's face. The questions all had to do with the rumored pirating of several Sterling releases, to which Kyle replied a stern, "No comment." Flashbulbs popped until a security guard for the hospital hustled the reporters out of the building and Maren and Kyle were led to a waiting room.

"Where's Holly?" Maren asked, concerned for Kyle's child. How was the young girl reacting to all the commotion over the tape?

"She's at Sara's house. Lydia is going to pick her up in the morning."

Maren's pained blue eyes searched his. "God, Kyle, I'm so sorry about all of this…"

"It's all right," he whispered, clutching her hand. "You didn't know." His gaze was filled with the conviction of the trust he felt for her.

"You're incredible," she whispered. "How did you know that I wasn't involved?"

"Oh, Maren," he sighed. "Don't you realize how much I love you, how much I trust you? I've known all along that you couldn't be a part of this." Relief took hold of Maren.

"Are you Maren McClure?" a young intern asked Maren as he strode purposefully into the waiting room.

"Yes."

He looked at the chart he was carrying. "Jan Sommers wants to see you." The young man observed Maren through thick glasses. "I advised her against seeing anyone, but she's absolutely insistent about talking to you." His myopic gaze was severe. "Please make it brief."

Maren asked the question uppermost in her mind. "What about the baby?"

The doctor shook his head and frowned. "We couldn't save it," he said wearily. "As for Ms. Sommers, I've given her a sedative that will begin to put her to sleep very shortly."

"I won't stay long," Maren whispered, understanding the intern's concern.

Kyle took Maren's arm and led her to Jan's room. The lump forming in Maren's throat refused to dissolve as she saw Jan's thin form lying on the hospital bed. "Hello, Jan," she whispered, reaching for her friend's hand.

Jan turned her head to face Maren. Black smudges darkened the skin around her eyes. "Maren," she whispered, her eyes filling with lonely tears, "I lost the baby."

"I know," Maren replied in a throaty whisper.

"I wanted that baby," Jan said, taking her eyes away from Maren's comforting gaze. "I really wanted him."

The words of reassurance stuck in Maren's throat. "You should rest," Maren stated. "I'll stay with you."

"You shouldn't," Jan sobbed.

"Of course I should; you're my friend…" Jan held up her palm to cut off the rest of Maren's explanation.

"No…no, I'm not. Just listen to me a minute. There's something I want to tell you, something I've tried, but couldn't." Maren's eyes widened with the realization of what was to come. She had to fight to keep the nausea at bay. "I was the one who took the tapes," Jan admitted with a ragged sigh.

"I don't think you should be talking about this right now," Maren interjected, looking down at the wan form on the bed. "You're tired."

Jan impaled Maren with her tortured gaze. "No, Maren, this is something I've got to say. Right now, while I have the courage. I took those tapes. Last month it was 'Going for Broke' and last Wednesday I stole 'Yesterday's Heart.'"

"But, Jan, *why?*" Maren asked, shocked and unaccepting of Jan's tearful admission.

"For Jake."

"Oh, Jan, no."

"Look, Maren, you know that I would never have done anything of the sort. It was Jake's idea and I refused. Even though I was pregnant with his child, I wouldn't stoop to theft. Then…well, then he threatened me. He said that if I didn't help him he would beat me."

"Why didn't you go to the police?" Maren gasped.

"I started to…after one of our fights, but he caught up with me and I ended up with bruised ribs. I…I almost lost the baby." Jan wept bitterly at the memory. "I didn't want to lose my child and I was stupid. It was wrong and I should never have done it and I don't expect you to forgive me. I just want to make a full confession and implicate

Jake. It doesn't matter if he tries to hurt me now...there's no baby to protect."

Maren fought the sobs threatening to erupt from her throat. Her fingers wrapped over Jan's thin hand. "There's nothing to forgive, Jan." The secretary's eyes blurred and she turned her head aside. "I'll call Elise Conrad in the morning, Jan. Maybe she can help you out of this."

"I really don't care, Maren. I just want to see Jake get his," Jan sighed as her lids became heavy.

"Do you know where we can get hold of him?" Kyle asked, against Maren's better judgment.

"I think you can find him at our old apartment. I moved out yesterday and he's already got another girlfriend. I guess he's been seeing her for the past couple of months. Maybe it was because I was pregnant...who knows? I'm...I'm very tired."

"Are you all right?" Kyle asked Maren, who was visibly pale.

"Fine," Maren lied. "I just had no idea...poor Jan."

Kyle called the police while Maren had a cup of coffee in the lounge. When she was certain that Jan would be all right, Maren let Kyle take her home.

Within a few hours the police called Kyle's apartment and informed him that they had arrested Jacob Green, who, upon hearing the evidence against him, confessed to stealing the tapes. He also admitted that he had coerced Jan into helping him by threatening her with physical and mental abuse.

After resting fitfully in Kyle's embrace, Maren finally fell asleep in his arms just before dawn. She didn't wake when he left the apartment, and it was not until several hours later that his loud reentry finally roused her.

"What time is it?" she asked groggily, noticing the sun streaming in the windows of Kyle's apartment.

"Late." He watched her as she stretched on the bed. There was still a trace of sleep in her eyes, and it made her seem incredibly soft and vulnerable.

"Where have you been?" she asked, pulling herself to a sitting position against the pillows. The sheet draped away from her body, showing off the lacy slip she had used as a nightgown. The sculpted ivory lace only partially hid the seductive curve of her breasts.

"I've been busy, dear lady, and I've accomplished a lot," he said with a smile as he eased himself onto the bed next to her.

"Tell me all about it."

"Gladly," he said, gently nuzzling her neck.

"First of all, I think your friend Jan is off the hook. Green's confession to coercion, coupled with the fact that Jan implicated him, should be enough to save her—or at the very least put her on probation. I'll see to it that she gets a good lawyer," Kyle said thoughtfully.

"That's wonderful."

"Also, Green admitted to trying to sabotage the Mirage video. He was the one who engineered the explosion. He stole the costumes."

"And the lighting problem?" Maren asked.

"He didn't admit to that. It was probably just coincidence."

"It doesn't matter," Maren said. "The important thing is Jan." Maren looked up at him with eyes filled with love. "You're incredible," she whispered. "What about Mirage?"

"Ryan Woods managed to calm down J. D. Price. We offered Mirage a more lucrative contract and it seems that J.D. has reconsidered. He's not going to sue after all."

"You *have* been busy, haven't you?"

"Well, we're going to have to see how it all turns out. There's going to be a lot of adverse publicity."

"Until Jacob Green is exposed to the press."

"That might take a few days," Kyle observed. "Oh, there is something else I wanted to discuss."

"What more?" Maren inquired.

"It's good news," he said silkily as his lips brushed against the top of her shoulder and pushed the strap of her slip down her arm.

"Sounds interesting," she responded, imitating his seductive tone.

"Lydia has promised to watch Holly for the entire week—while you and I spend our time honeymooning on the yacht…"

A provocative grin spread over Maren's lips, and a wicked twinkle lit her indigo eyes. "Honeymoon?"

"That's right. You and I are going to be married as soon as possible—you've been putting me off too long."

"You won't hear any arguments from me."

His lips gently touched hers. "Then we'll be married this afternoon."

"I can't wait."

The pressure on her mouth increased, and she tasted the sweet promise of his words. Surrendering to the happiness welling within her, Maren wrapped her arms possessively around Kyle's neck. "I love you, Maren," he groaned, holding her close. "And I'm going to make sure that I never lose you."

"Promise?" she asked, looking into his clear gray eyes.

"Forever."

* * * * *

[illegible]

[illegible] only [illegible]

[illegible]

[illegible] week [illegible]

[illegible]

[illegible] the afternoon.

[illegible]

DARK SIDE OF THE MOON

CHAPTER ONE

THE HEAVY DOOR swung violently outward, letting the late afternoon sunshine pour in to the stark marble building, filling a small space of the gloomy interior with the warmth of late Indian summer. A moist Pacific breeze full of the promise of the ocean met Jefferson Harmon as he strode out of the turn-of-the-century courthouse, and his near-black hair ruffled in the wind. His jaw was set squarely, and his hazel eyes glinted with fierce determination. He paused only slightly as he noticed the swarm of newspaper reporters and television cameramen that were milling along the steep cement steps of the building. A dark look of savage anger crossed his aristocratic face, but was quickly, professionally disguised. Damn that Lara, he thought to himself; summoning the reporters must have been her idea. She knew how he hated facing the press when it came to issues involving his personal life. The oath that had been forming in his mind never made it to his lips.

From habit, Jefferson shifted the deep-set scowl his features formed into a pleasant, though restrained, smile. Although he squinted against the bright glare of the rapidly lowering sun, he presented a poised and self-assured image. All of the anger that had been threatening to overcome him in the last few hours was well hidden behind his hazel eyes. Only those who knew him well would notice the dangerous gleam of determination in his gaze and the square angle of his jaw that remained rigidly set in proud resolve.

To appear more at ease than he actually felt, Jefferson casually pushed one hand into the pocket of his navy-blue suit pants. Repressing the urge to loosen the knot of his expensive silk tie, he grinned at one of the reporters that he knew from his days in politics. Jefferson appeared every bit the successful man that he was—or had been—as he descended the steps under the hazy California sun.

"Hello, John," Jefferson called to the reporter, and flashed his famous smile. He mentally braced himself for the barrage of questions that his affable greeting invited.

The press took their cue and converged upon their subject. Reporters shoved and elbowed their way closer to Jefferson, and traffic along the palm-lined street slowed to watch the spectacle. Questions, some louder than others, were tossed in his direction, and he fielded them with the ease of someone accustomed to being in the public eye. Microphones, wielded almost like weapons, were shoved into Jefferson's outwardly calm face as he smiled into the cameras.

"Mr. Harmon?" The portly, middle-aged reporter who had been greeted by Jefferson earlier began to speak. "Is it true that your divorce from your wife, Lara, is final as of today?"

Jefferson's smile faded slightly as he answered the bespectacled man with the busy, graying moustache and homey grin. "That's right, John," Jefferson admitted, deciding it was time to end the hastily convened press conference before the questions became too personal. With a wave, he pressed through the throng of reporters and headed toward his parked car. Jefferson hoped that his gesture would dismiss the crowd. He was wrong.

"What about the custody of your daughter, Megan, Mr. Harmon?" This time it was a shrill woman's voice that called out to him. "What about her? Has Mrs. Harmon retained custody?"

There was a hitch in Jefferson's long, easy stride, and he felt every muscle in his body tense at the mention of Megan. Relax, he told himself, trying to retain his escaping composure. He whirled to face the smartly dressed young woman with the cold, calculating eyes.

"We're still working on that," he offered politely, flashing her his most disarming smile. The smile still intact, he muttered a mental oath at his scheming ex-wife, Lara. She was probably still in the courthouse, watching him from the window, enjoying the scene that she had created—at his expense. A muscle in Jefferson's jaw twitched at the thought, and once again he turned toward his silver Mercedes. If he could just get to the car before his temper took complete control of him, he would be all right. The sporty car was parked near a palm tree, not more than a hundred yards away. He walked briskly toward the auto.

"But, Governor!" The insistent young woman with the brassy blond hair relentlessly pursued her story. "Won't you please tell us a little more about the divorce?"

In his pocket Jefferson's fist clenched, but he willed it to uncoil just as he reached the waiting Mercedes. He leaned against the silver car casually, and his gaze traveled over the faces of the reporters that had followed him en masse from the courthouse steps. "I'd prefer not to comment about the divorce at this time," he responded crisply. There was just the slightest edge to his voice, and he hoped that the commanding tone of his voice would dissuade the asking of any more impertinent, personal questions. Why, he wondered, after two years, would anyone still make the unpleasant mistake of referring to him as governor?

"Then—" a new voice beckoned him, and he turned to face a young, and obviously green newspaper reporter "—could you comment on the rumor that your wife has a drinking problem?" The young man was anxious, and hungry for a story. Jefferson could read it in the eager brown eyes and nervous twitch of his cheek.

Jefferson's deep, hazel eyes turned the color of tempered steel and impaled the young man that had made the mistake of asking too private a question. "No." He jerked the car door open and began to slide into the soft leather interior. As the next barrage of questions assaulted him every muscle in his body froze.

"What about the rumor that both your divorce *and* Mrs. Harmon's drinking problem were caused by your affair with that girl before you were married. Is it true that you really never got over her? If so, why did you marry Lara Whitney? Do you still see that woman?" Jefferson's eyes darkened and narrowed as he glared at the impertinent young man. The reporter sensed a change in his subject's attitude and, smelling a story, pressed his advantage. "Mrs. Harmon publicly claims that you never really forgot that *other* woman, and that you married Mrs. Harmon on the rebound. Is there any truth to your ex-wife's accusations?" Jefferson looked away from the interested eyes that were watching his every move and quickly settled behind the wheel of his car. The young man continued to badger him. "You know the woman that I'm talking about, Governor Harmon. She…was a conscientious objector to the war… or something…." The hard, condemning voice trailed off, as the reporter hurriedly scanned his notes. The young newspaperman knew that he'd made some trivial mistake...a vague error about the girl and the scandal of ten years past. What was it? Didn't he have that woman's name?

Jefferson's response to the inquiry was to slam the car door shut, flick on the ignition and roar out of the parking lot. His anger got the best of him, and he ripped the gears of the Mercedes mercilessly. His calm exterior dissolved into a contemptuous frown as he left the anxious reporters behind him. Perhaps his ex-wife, Lara, would be so good as to offer her opinions to the press about the farce that she had called marriage.

As he turned the wheel of the car he thought involuntarily of his young daughter. If it hadn't been for Megan, he wouldn't have continued the charade that his marriage to Lara had become. Jefferson's face softened as he recalled his five-year-old daughter and all of the suffering that the child must have borne in her life. As his fingers tightened around the steering wheel, Jefferson promised himself that he would fight Lara tooth-and-nail for custody of the only bright spot in their otherwise grim sham of a marriage.

THE AFTERNOON IN THE office had stretched longer than Andrea had expected. As the hours in the confining cubicle slowly ticked by, she felt her stomach tighten into a knot of anxiety and uncertainty. That morning, after the Nielson ratings had come out for the previous week's shows, the president of Coral Productions had immediately informed the office staff of an emergency personnel meeting, slated for four-thirty.

Andrea shifted uncomfortably in her desk chair and eyed the clock. Four-fifteen. The waiting would soon end.

Now, as she sat staring vacantly out of the window toward the hazy hills in the distance, she could see the writing on the wall, she could almost envision the headlines: Coral Productions Loses Three Shows; Bankrupt Company Closes Its Doors. The tension that had been building in the small suite of offices had been charging the air. Everyone involved with Coral Productions was on edge, because each person understood that his job, along with the operation of the company as a whole, was on the line.

An early edition of the local paper sat folded on Andrea's desk. While passing the final minutes until the meeting convened, she opened the tabloid in an effort to occupy her worried mind. Her misty green eyes scanned the columns on the front page: the economic recession was still waging war with the American people, and unemployment had jumped another percentage point for the month of September. She pushed an errant lock of blue-black hair behind her ear and lifted her eyes from the disturbing news. Never in all of her thirty years had she considered that the state of the economy could affect her. Not personally. She pursed her full lips tightly and rubbed the back of her neck with her fingers. That was the problem with being born rich, she decided, one never expected the money to run out.

To avoid thinking about the pressing problem of her potentially uncertain employment, she quickly flipped past the national news. She took a sip of her cold coffee and nearly choked as her eyes met the headlines in the social section: Harmon Divorce Final: Custody of Child Still Undecided. Beneath the bold, black letters, Jefferson Harmon, his jaw square and determined in the dull image of a black and white newsprint photo, stared back at her.

"No," she whispered to herself. "Not again." She

regarded the image of the tall, broad-shouldered man and fought the urge to toss the newspaper into the trash basket. Ten-year-old emotions ravaged her body—the same emotions that tore at her each time Jefferson's famous face reappeared in the public limelight. She willed the tears that were burning the back of her eyes to dry as the memories of pain and suffering, guilt and betrayal, love and deceit, came flooding back to her. "I can't go through this again—not again," she said to herself as her small palm slapped the disquieting article. Memories, wild and fanciful, brimming with love and the taste of salt air, began swimming in her mind.

How distant those warm, enticing summers seemed now. While she was lost in thought, her fingers reached out to touch the flat, cold image of Jefferson's face and traced the familiar line of his jaw. The picture didn't do him justice, she mused distractedly as she remembered a younger man, dashingly good-looking, with a smile that was slightly off center and eyes that were intelligent, kind, disturbing—eyes that could darken to stormy gray when he became challenged or angry. How many times in the past had she witnessed the darkening of his deep-set, hazel eyes?

Ignoring the time that was passing, Andrea skimmed the article. Her throat became dry, and she bit her lower lip as her eyes touched on the printed words. Familiar phrases, some that haunted her nights, leapt up at her to scorch her mind: brilliant young lawyer...marriage to prestigious wealth...short term of governor...controversial resignation...scandalous past...

"Hey, Andrea!" Katie's soft voice called through the door of Andrea's small office and broke into her reverie. "Better get a move on. The meeting's in five minutes!"

Andrea's startled green eyes broke from the article to her wristwatch to confirm her friend's announcement. "I'll be there…. Save me a seat," she managed to say at last.

"Sure," Katie answered, a confused look in her clear, blue eyes. She shrugged her slim shoulders and hurried off down the hallway toward the conference room.

Hurriedly Andrea folded the newspaper and set it on the corner of her desk. Although the evening tabloid was not normally a scandal sheet, the article on Harmon read like a vicious gossip column. His famous life, dissected anew, was splashed before the public eye with short, explicit references to his personal and political career. The newspaper story left Andrea feeling naked and vulnerable. Would the pain never end? Would the past never stop chasing her?

"Dear God," she whispered almost inaudibly. "Will I ever get over him?" For several long moments, she stood gazing vacantly at the newspaper, remembering endless lost hours of making love in the warm Pacific rain. She felt the grit of sand scrape against her bare feet and heard the lonesome cries of marauding seagulls over the relentless pounding of an angry, northern surf.

With difficulty Andrea swallowed the tears that threatened to spill and forced her thoughts to turn to the present, and the immediate problems with her job. She couldn't—*wouldn't*—let herself fall victim to the past. Never again. Her fists balled at her sides as she regained her composure, and defiantly she willed her feelings to retreat to the past. She quickly picked up her pen and notepad and hurried down the hall to the conference room.

The small central room where the meetings of Coral Productions were held was thick with the haze of blue cigarette smoke and the scent of stale coffee. Nervous chatter buzzed around the table as Andrea entered the room and slid into a vacant chair. The other employees of Coral Productions, a secretary, the bookkeeper and three other scriptwriters—the "office personnel"—were already seated or sprawled around a small table strewn with Styrofoam cups of tasteless black coffee and half-full ashtrays. In the middle of the table was another copy of the newspaper that Andrea had just read. Again Jefferson Harmon's face stared blankly up at her, and Andrea had to force her eyes away from the unsettling photograph.

Andrea was relieved that Bryce Cawthorne, one-time character actor and now president and owner of Coral Productions, hadn't yet arrived. So far the ax hadn't fallen, and all of the talk about closing down the company was pure conjecture. She managed a thin, encouraging smile at Katie Argus, the other woman on the scriptwriting team, but the furrow of Andrea's dark brows, and the shadow of anxiety in her large, sea-green eyes belied her outward equanimity.

"Are you okay?" Katie asked, her bright blue eyes searching Andrea's delicate face. "I didn't think that you'd make it before Bryce got here. Is anything wrong? You look a little pale."

"I'm fine," Andrea replied with a faint smile. "Just a little concerned."

"Aren't we all?" Katie observed, almost to herself, while her long, brightly polished fingernails tapped against the glass tabletop. Her full lips pulled into a pouty frown of concentration, and even her deep tan seemed to have paled against her sun-streaked golden hair.

"Not me," a well-modulated male voice announced from a distant corner of the room. "I'm not worried." Jack Masters shrugged his shoulders with indifference and slumped into a chair opposite Katie. An anxious line of concern etched his forehead and belied his casual exterior. "It isn't my fault that Nicole Jamison can't act her way out of a paper bag."

"I don't see that Nicole has anything to do with shutting down production," Katie snapped back irritably.

"It's simple," Jack explained, lifting his palms skyward. "She should never have been cast as the virginal do-gooder bride in *Pride's Power.* The character of Justin Pride would never have fallen for and married a woman like Nicole. She's just not right for the part of Angela. Justin would want a strong woman, proud and yet vulnerable, virtuous to the point of self-sacrifice—not some scheming bitch like Nicole Jamison. She's about as innocent as Mata Hari!" Jack pronounced sarcastically.

"And just about as old," Katie murmured, half to herself.

"It doesn't matter," Andrea pointed out, trying to be heard over the snicker of laughter at Katie's dry attempt at humor. Andrea examined each of the faces surrounding the small table. As senior writer she had a small edge of influence over her coworkers, and the fact that she had worked the most closely with Bryce Cawthorne gave her better insight into some of the problems that the small production company faced. "At this point we're only second-guessing ourselves. Whether it was a case of poor casting, a lousy time slot or anything else, the fact is that *Pride's Power* has continued to slip in the ratings. Last week it was polled in the bottom twenty. Who knows why? Maybe the public has become saturated with nighttime soaps."

At that moment the door to the room flew open and banged against the wall. Bryce Cawthorne, his perennial frown in place, strode into the room. Under his arm was the latest dismal set of Nielson ratings. Ignoring the captain's chair that had been reserved for him, he hoisted his small, wiry body onto the lowest filing cabinet. From his perch he looked over the tops of his bifocals at all of the anxious eyes that had followed his dramatic entrance. He pulled the ratings sheet from under his arm and began listing the current shows produced by Coral. It didn't take long.

"*Night Sirens,* our latest police production…and our newest hopeful, climbed to number 42. *Dangerous Games* fell off another three ratings points to 46. And, our feeble attempt at nighttime drama, *Pride's Power,* tumbled down to 57." After an audible groan from Bryce's captive audience, there was an unsettling silence as the weight of Bryce's somber announcement settled like lead on the shoulders of everyone in the room. Bryce continued. "From what I understand all three shows will be canceled at the end of the season." Bryce tossed the disturbing ratings sheets up in the air. The assembled staff watched them land with a smack in the middle of the table, next to the newspaper article on Jefferson Harmon.

Andrea's eyes stopped for a moment on the picture of Jefferson before returning to Bryce's furrowed face. He shook his head in confusion. "I don't know what to tell you…." His eyes moved around the table. "I don't understand it. I thought we had a winner in *Pride's Power.*' He rubbed the back of his neck with his hand and attempted to uncoil the tension in his shoulders. "We just can't afford any more flops…not even one!"

Andrea bit at the corner of her lower lip. She was probably the person in the room closest to Bryce, and yet even she had trouble asking the question that was uppermost in everyone's mind. "What exactly are you saying, Bryce?"

Andrea could feel the sting of tension in the air as all eyes focused on the owner of the company. Bryce rubbed his palms on the knees of is worn designer jeans. 'I don't know," he admitted, shaking his balding head. "I came up with a couple of ideas for new shows, but most of them were scrapped immediately by the Powers That Be in the broadcasting company. It seems that they're not interested in airing any more situation comedies, detective shows and, least of all, night soaps."

Bryce was depressed. Andrea could tell by the droop of his usually straight shoulders. "They didn't like any of your ideas?" Andrea was amazed. Since his retirement from acting, Bryce Cawthorne had become something of a Hollywood legend when it came to creating new and interesting ideas for television. Until two years ago, when the ratings had begun to sour, it seemed as if Coral Productions could do no wrong.

"The only real possibility is with an independent cable network. I've been talking to some of the sales people at ITV, and they are very interested in presenting a weekly special about an interesting, controversial public figure.... It might work...it definitely has possibilities...."

"Like who?" Katie asked, eyeing her boss with interest.

Bryce leaned backward and stared at the ceiling, lost in speculation. "Oh, I don't know...I've just been kicking the idea around a little, but it should be someone who is a household word, who creates a bundle of public interest...someone that people like...or hate, I suppose. For example, there's Sondra Wickfield..."

"The wealthy philanthropist who allegedly shot her lover?" Andrea asked.

"Right, or, I don't know, maybe that country singer who had an affair with the Spanish nobleman," Bryce continued, warming to his subject.

"You're talking about the people that grace the front pages of the scandal sheets," Andrea observed, and her eyes flickered from Bryce to the picture of Jefferson Harmon and back again.

"No, not necessarily," Bryce countered. "Think of it as human interest stories." His tone was placating, and Andrea began to feel a coiling uneasiness grip her.

"I don't know," she began, but Bryce's stern look of challenge halted her argument.

"We're talking about saving the company, Andrea! Face it, we're fighting for our lives...*your* job! I'm only attempting to give the public what it wants, and right now there's a barely tapped gold mine in revealing the intimate lives of the famous."

Andrea knew that the argument was going in Bryce's direction, and she wisely withheld further comment. She realized that to push Bryce when he was this desperate, would only make him all the more adamant.

"That's right," Jack chimed in, siding with the boss and eager to get in on the conversation. "There are a lot of personalities that the public is dying to hear about. Take, for example, Jefferson Harmon," Jack continued, pointing his finger at the newspaper. "Now, there's a guy that we all want to know more about!" Andrea's heart leapt to her throat as her green eyes, wide with concern, moved from Jack's finger on the newspaper back to Bryce.

"Exactly!" her boss stated, and Andrea felt her heart sink. "Harmon is a perfect example of the kind of interview and examination that the cable company wants. Andrea, what do you think?"

Vaguely Andrea heard her name. "What?" she asked, and she could feel the color rush to her cheeks.

"About the new show, what do you think?" Bryce prodded, his gaze pinioning her.

"Ah, well, I guess it's a good idea," she managed to say, hoping to get a grip on herself and avoid angering Bryce any further.

"But you have some reservations?"

"No, I was only questioning the choice of guests. It...it would be important that anyone we cover be an interesting, powerful personality. Someone who is newsworthy today...." Was she rambling? She wondered, forcing herself to smile stiffly at Bryce.

"That's why I think Jefferson Harmon would be a perfect choice. Perhaps his should be the first story in the series," Jack continued. "Have you seen the headlines this afternoon?" Jack asked the group around the table. He flagged the newspaper in the air theatrically. "How about all of this interest in his divorce and the custody of his kid?"

Andrea knew that she had to stop the speculation about Jefferson, before the pain and embarrassment of ten years past caught up with her again—just as it always did whenever Jefferson Harmon's name was splashed across the headlines.

Andrea cocked her head to one side and calmly looked Bryce in the eye. "Don't you think that Harmon is yesterday's news?" she inquired, and though her voice was even, she could feel her stomach fluttering. The color drained from her face, but even so, she hoped that she was masking the disturbing sense of dread that was climbing up her spine.

"Not this guy!" Jack asserted. "He's been in and out of

the papers ever since he began his political career. Remember all of the ruckus about him and that college girl, back, when was it, about ten years ago?"

"That's ancient history!" Andrea snapped, and an unguarded defiance lighted her light green eyes. Andrea's angry tone wasn't lost on Bryce.

"Not necessarily," Bryce interposed, ending the simmering argument. It was obvious to her boss that Andrea was upset, though she attempted to mask it. Her usual sparkling complexion was drawn and wan, and there was a disturbing look in her eyes. Was it fear? Bryce wondered. It seemed impossible. In the eight years that Andrea had worked for him, she had proved herself to be unafraid of any challenge he offered. And yet, something was definitely wrong with her. She was nervous, stiff. And from time to time her gaze would wander to the newspaper that Jack held in his hands. Bryce puzzled for a moment, but decided that her anxiety stemmed from the fact that, like most of the employees, Andrea realized how desperate the situation had become for Coral Productions. Everyone was on edge. "Okay, people," Bryce sighed, "the bottom line is this: I've got to find a way out of this mess, and if it means taking a chance on a new program, then we'll do it!" Bryce surveyed the group of people around the table. All of the eyes that met his severe gaze seemed in agreement with his statement. "All right, that's it, then. Let's go home."

The group began to head out of the door. Andrea slid out of her chair, but before she could leave the room, Bryce's hand on her sleeve held her back. As she turned to face him he released her arm. When they were alone, he asked, "Is there something wrong—something that I don't know about?" His gaze had softened, but his dark eyes still probed hers.

"Nothing," Andrea replied, but even to her ears the words didn't ring true. Yet how could she tell Bryce, or anyone for that matter, about the lie that she had been running from for ten long years.

"You're sure?" He seemed unconvinced.

"Well, I am a little worried about the company," she hedged, hating herself for her deceit.

"Don't be. It will work itself out."

"You didn't sound so sure of that in the meeting."

"It was all just part of the show to keep you writers on your toes," he retorted with a fatherly smile.

"Convincing show, I'd say."

They walked out of the room together and, for the first time, Andrea noticed the deep lines of age that had crept up on Bryce Cawthorne over the past eight years. The corners of his eyes were ridged with a webbing of crow's-feet, and lines of worry were etched irregularly across his forehead and neck. His voice was sober as he stopped at the door of her small office.

"You were planning a vacation for the next three weeks?"

"That's right, but if it's inconvenient and you'd prefer me to stay, I can take the time off later, after everything is ironed out."

His hand, raised like a flag of surrender, stilled her. "No, no, by all means, go. I think it would be better for all of us if you got away between the seasons. If we do go ahead with the new program, I'll need you back here to help with the nuts and bolts." He shook his balding head as he leaned, cross armed in the hallway. "Go, and don't give the rest of us a second thought. You look like you could use some time off!"

"I look that bad, do I?" she asked with a grim smile.

"Of course not! But I think that it would do you some good to get away. You worry too much."

"I've had a good teacher," she pointed out.

Bryce raised his finger and scored an imaginary "one" in the air as his dark brown eyes twinkled. "Take care of yourself, Andrea, and get some rest. Just be sure to leave your number with Carol in case I have to reach you."

"I will," Andrea promised to Bryce's retreating figure as she snapped out the lights to her office, reached for her purse and tucked the newspaper under her arm. The article on Jefferson Harmon was hidden deep in the society pages, and Andrea almost tossed it into the trash. But then she thought better of it. Something inside her forced her to take the article home to reread in the privacy of her apartment, to think about the times she and Jefferson had shared, long before their lives had become complicated, long before they had bitterly parted ways.

CHAPTER TWO

THE RINGING OF THE telephone startled Andrea and interrupted her pensive thoughts. She had been sipping a rare blend of tea and gazing through the leaded glass windows of the redbrick town house at the gray, threatening sky that seemed dark against the hills of the park. It felt good to be home again; even the somber, overcast skies of bleak November didn't dampen Andrea's spirits, and she felt more at ease than she had in the past few weeks. Her vacation to her parents' Canadian home was exactly what she had needed.

At the second ring of the insistent phone Andrea turned to face the intrusive instrument. She had only been on Vancouver Island for six days, and expected no calls. Her parents had telephoned just last night from Hawaii, and the only other person who might call was her sister, Gayla, who lived near Seattle. Buoyed by the thought that the caller was probably Gayla, Andrea hurried to the telephone.

"Hello!" she called cheerfully into the receiver.

"Hi! It sounds like your vacation has brightened your mood," Bryce's voice boomed to her over the wire.

Andrea felt a little deflated, but tried not to let her disappointment show. "I suppose it has," she agreed distractedly as she leaned against the wall and twisted the telephone cord nervously. Bryce Cawthorne wasn't the kind of man to waste time or money on long-distance phone calls merely to pass the time of day. There had to be a reason for his call. Perhaps, after all, he had decided to close the doors of Coral Productions. Andrea was sickened by the thought, but rather than wait for the bomb to drop, she took the offensive in the conversation. "What's up?" she asked.

"Good news, I hope," he replied.

"That I could use," she said with a rueful smile.

"Remember the new show that I brought up in the meeting?"

"The interviews with celebrities?"

"The very same!" At his words Andrea experienced a sinking sensation. There was something in Bryce's voice that triggered her unease. He continued, "Well, I think I've sold it to ITV. It's somewhat tentative. They've agreed to air five shows, and if the public likes those, ITV will broadcast an additional ten shows."

"Sounds good…" Andrea murmured, still twisting the cord of the phone and waiting for the forthcoming hitch. She had a gut feeling that Bryce was holding something back…some piece of information that she might not like.

"It's the break we need," he continued fervently in a lowered voice.

"So…do you want me to come back to California to work out the details?"

"No." He paused. Here it comes, Andrea thought. "But I was hoping that you could help me out a bit."

"You know that I'd be glad to." What did he want? Already she knew that she would regret her agreement to help him.

"Okay," Bryce said with a sigh. "Here it is, we have to

make sure that every one of the shows is a hit—we don't dare miss with one."

"I understand that. What do you want me to do?"

"We've come up with a few possibilities for the interview, and for the most part, the people concerned have agreed—with only a few reservations."

"But..." Andrea prodded, biting her lower lip.

"But the one man that we really need for a leadoff story hasn't been available to us."

Andrea couldn't sustain the suspense any longer. "You're talking about Jefferson Harmon, aren't you?"

There was a surprised snort on the other end of the line. "How did you know?"

"Why else would you call?" Andrea retorted. "I'm up here in Victoria, and you've learned that Harmon has a retreat on a private island nearby. Right?" Andrea's stomach was twisted more tightly than the phone cord.

"Yeah.... You know, it's just kind of a coincidence, your being so close to him."

Andrea drew in a long, steadying breath. "So what exactly do you want?"

"The problem is we can't reach the man. I've talked to his ex-wife's secretary, his one-time press agent, even the incumbent governor. But it seems that they can't, or won't, give me a number where he can be reached. I was hoping that you could talk to the phone company up there, see if they could contact him—or maybe go see him personally."

"If the man has taken so many precautions to ensure his privacy, don't you think he might be a little upset to have me knocking on his door?" Andrea replied in what she hoped would seem a reasonable tone of voice. "Why don't you just get someone else? Harmon obviously doesn't want to be bothered!"

"Precisely my point! He grants no interviews, avoids the press at all costs, wraps his privacy around him like some God-given cloak and the public eats it up! They can't get enough of him. It's his penchant for secrecy that works against him. It makes the public want to explore him.... Get to know him, just get an inkling into the psyche of the man. What made him renounce his governorship? How does he feel about his ex-wife, his kid, American politics today?"

"And you expect me to persuade him to agree to the interview?" Andrea asked, shocked.

"No. Leave that to me. All I want is a chance to talk with him. If you can somehow find a way to get in touch with him and have him call me—that's all I need."

"You make it sound so easy."

"Are you with me?"

Andrea swallowed. Her mouth was dry. "Of course I'll try," she agreed hesitantly, "but I doubt if I can do anything."

"You might be surprised," Bryce commented enigmatically. "We're just lucky that you're up in Victoria, so near to him. Boy, that's one helluva break!"

As Andrea hung up the phone Bryce's parting words began to echo in her mind: A *coincidence*...a lucky break that she was so close to Jefferson Harmon and his private isle. If Bryce only knew, she thought wryly to herself as she picked up her cold cup of tea and sipped it slowly. Was it coincidence that she was here, alone, less than ten miles from Jefferson's summer home? Or did she come of her own will, hoping to meet him again? Although it was early November, she had suspected Jefferson might retreat to the island after the news of his divorce hit the papers. Was it fate that lured her to him, or was it her own free will that tempted her to find a means of communicating with him?

Though she loathed the idea, she knew in her heart that she had never really stopped loving him. And, although she had maintained her distance from him since his marriage, she had never stopped thinking about him. Did she secretly hope that she would get just such an opportunity to see him again? Was the reason that had prompted her to arrange this hasty visit to her parents' Canadian home because she suspected that Jefferson might be nearby? God, she hoped not. She wanted to believe that the reason she had come to Victoria was expressly to get some sorely needed rest from the hectic pace of Southern California and her job. But try as she might, she couldn't shake the feeling that she had secretly wished for an excuse to see Jefferson again.

It seemed so wrong. While Jefferson was married, Andrea had wished only for his happiness, and when the rumors that the marriage was foundering had surfaced, Andrea grieved for him and his wife. No matter how much pain she might have suffered in loving Jefferson, Andrea had sincerely hoped that he had found happiness with Lara Whitney. Andrea had no illusion that Jefferson would ever be able to love her, and she prayed that Lara Whitney would prove to be the woman that Jefferson could cherish.

Or was Andrea kidding herself? How many times had she seen pictures of the strikingly beautiful Lara on the arm of Jefferson and inwardly wished that she could trade places with his wife? How many empty nights had she lain in the loneliness of her bed and longed for him, while hating herself for the thought. Though outwardly she had told herself that she had only wished for Jefferson's happiness, hadn't she cried for hours in teary anguish the night his child was born? Hadn't she lain awake trying to understand why she felt ripped to the bone in her desperation? It wasn't that she was not happy for him; it was good to know that he had a child, a little girl of his own to love. But she couldn't banish the feelings that somehow she had been betrayed, and she felt painfully envious of the woman who had borne his child. Hers was an intimacy Andrea could never share with Jefferson.

Over the years Andrea's pain had lessened, and when confronted with pictures of Jefferson's famous child, Andrea was forced to smile. Megan was thin and fine boned like her beautiful mother, but had the same haunting and piercing eyes of her father. She was a beautiful girl and seemed to carry herself with a maturity that extended far past her five years.

So now the opportunity to see Jefferson presented itself again, if only Andrea was strong enough to accept the challenge. It was a difficult and emotional decision. Although it had been over ten years since she had talked with him, she was still nervous at the thought, as evidenced by her suddenly perspiring palms. Could she face him again?

With sudden decisiveness she set down her teacup and dialed the number that had lingered, stagnant, in her mind. She slammed the receiver down as the recorded message told her that the number she had dialed was nonworking. Quickly she dialed the operator. But she couldn't get through with the operator's assistance either. After nearly half an hour of frustration, Andrea hung up the phone. She realized that there was no way for her to hide behind the impersonality of a telephone conversation with Jefferson. He had apparently pulled all of the right political strings to ensure his privacy, and if the telephone company did have a number where he could be reached, Andrea had been unable to coerce it from any one of the four operators that she had spoken with.

The question loomed before her, as threatening as the purple clouds that hung over the city: could she face Jefferson Harmon again, after all of the bitterness and suspicions of the past? Would he agree to see her? Or would she again feel the rejection and pain that she had suffered at his hand? Was she strong enough to accept his rejection? Could she contend with a door slammed in her face?

Andrea didn't bother to change her clothes; instead she reached for her raincoat. Armed with the frail excuse supplied by Bryce Cawthorne and Coral Productions and the naked truth that she had to see Jefferson again, Andrea ignored the winter gales of the sea squall that whistled through the city streets. She set out for the marina, hoping to find some money-hungry sailor who was crazy enough to take her to Jefferson's private retreat. Though the wind had picked up considerably in the late afternoon, Andrea was fortunate enough to find one young sailor foolhardy enough to fight anything the stormy sea had to offer—for the right price, of course. She was reluctant to take the brash young man up on his offer, but could find no one else willing to ignore the storm warnings and take her to the island.

Andrea's conscience argued with her judgment, telling her that it was dangerous to sail in such rough water, and that it was ludicrous to knock on Jefferson's door after ten long silent years. Her mind reasoned that he might not even be on the island, and that the terrifying journey would all be in vain. Despite the logical arguments that her mind put forth, Andrea knew that she had to see Jefferson while she still had the courage to look into his dark, arrogant eyes.

What seemed more ridiculous than any of her arguments against the short sea voyage was the fact that she was anxious, almost eager, to see him. Once more she wondered if she had subconsciously willed an excuse to seek him out.

The rain was pelting down furiously, and she nearly slipped as she stepped onto the tiny, pitching motorboat. As she tied her hair back from her face with a leather thong, the sailor of the small craft eyed her speculatively.

"Not dressed for sailing, leastwise not in a storm the likes of this," the bearded young man observed while unleashing the moorings that held the rocking boat to the dock. His watery blue eyes traveled up the length of her calfskin boots, across the heather-colored tweed of her skirt, over the ribbing of her cashmere sweater, to meet her steady gaze.

"This trip was a sudden impulse," she responded with an innocent shrug of her shoulders.

"An impulse? To weather this storm? You've got to be kidding!" He rolled his eyes toward the dark heavens.

Andrea smiled patiently, reticent to give the prying sailor any other information about herself. He adjusted his stocking cap and started the engine of the boat. With a lurch they were off, and after maneuvering past the other docked vessels of the marina, they were out of the harbor. Andrea hiked the collar of her coat up farther on her neck to block the chilly rain from her face and shoulders.

The dull gray clouds continued to pour rain, and the boat pitched recklessly in the leaden water. Rain and salt spray moistened Andrea's face and curled the wispy tendrils of hair as they slipped from the thong that was intended to hold her long, ebony tresses away from her neck. Anxiously her tongue rimmed her lips and tasted the salt of the sea.

"This Harmon fella. He expecting you?" the seaman asked.

"Why do you want to know?"

The sailor shrugged his shoulders and sipped from a thermos that Andrea suspected held brew stronger than coffee. "Oh, I don't know, but from what I hear, he's the kind of guy who likes his privacy."

"Doesn't everyone?"

"I suppose so, but with him, it's different. Takes it all real personal, if you know what I mean. I don't know how he'll react when he finds a stranger dumped on his doorstep."

Andrea chose to ignore the remark and instead squinted her eyes against the rain to search the darkening horizon for the island. She knew that it would look different from her faded memory of it, as she had only visited the isle in late summer, long ago. Daisies had been in bloom, the sand had been warm, and a lazy, caressing sun had warmed her bare skin. But now, in bleak November, as her destination loomed before her, a rocky mountain rising from the sea, she felt a chill of apprehension skitter down her spine. Andrea experienced a dry, tight knotting in her stomach that couldn't be explained solely by the rocking of the small craft on the stormy sea.

Vivid memories flooded her mind, trapping her. Memories flavored with the romanticism of the passing of time. Memories that had drawn reality out to the abstract and distorted the events of a much younger, happier time in her life. Where were the fields of clover that had scented the air? Where were the lush, verdant oak trees that stood imperially on the island? In the gray of winter, with the wind howling and the rain beating mercilessly down on her, Harmon Island looked far more foreboding than welcoming. *What am I doing here?* she wondered crazily, and for a moment was sorely tempted to tell the young man guiding the vessel to take her back to the safety and warmth of the town house in Victoria.

It was nearly dusk by the time the sailor had managed to settle the boat against the mooring of the wooden dock near a shallow, rain-drenched strip of beach. It took some convincing, but Andrea made the man promise to wait for her, at least for an hour. He was reluctant to stay because of the increasing tempo of the storm, but at the prospect of a little extra money he agreed to wait. He hoisted his thermos in the air as a salute to her before heading into the shelter of the boat's cabin.

Andrea drew in a long, deep breath of cold air and started to climb the wooden staircase that led from the tiny beach up the face of the cliff toward the interior of the island. The gray sky and dark waters of the sea added to the early onset of evening, and Andrea was careful as she ascended the slippery steps. It was difficult to remember clearly, but she hoped that upon reaching the top of the slick steps, she would be able to see the house. It occurred to her that the last thing that Jefferson might want on this stormy night was to confront her. She remembered their last bitter quarrel. Andrea grimaced at the thought, and hoped that she hadn't made the precarious voyage across the rough waters of the sound for nothing.

Once she had mounted the stairs, and the face of the cliff no longer guarded her from the force of the gale, the wind angrily whipped her wool skirt against her thighs. The wet, rough fiber added to her discomfort, and she vaguely chided herself for not wearing her more practical jeans. But, then, she hadn't expected that the storm would rage so severely, nor did she remember that she would have to hike so far to get to the immense house.

She looked back for a moment to survey the wild,

crashing sea below her. The frothy white waves thudded against the small stretch of beach near the dock, and the tiny boat rocked crazily against its moorings. Why had she come here? Her rational voice reprimanded her. Ignoring the doubts that crowded her mind, she continued to pick her way carefully down the sandy path. How would Jefferson react to her intrusion of his private refuge? A shudder of apprehension darted up her spine and lingered, but she tried to repress the feelings of trepidation that began to capture her with the oncoming stormy night.

The rain continued to beat down on her in gusty sheets of water as she hurried onward. Once around a bend in the path, Andrea stopped, her pale green eyes caught in fascination at the sight of the regal house that guarded the island. It was more impressive and stately than she had recalled. A mansion by Andrea's standards, it seemed to rise out of the very ground that supported it. From its spectacular appearance, Andrea guessed that it had been built over a hundred years ago. The foundation was hewn from the stone of the cliff, carved from the smooth, solid rock of the island, and the imposing two floors that stood over the foundation were masoned of stone, the color of a dove's underbelly. Only the arches and the roof were composed of darkened, weathered timbers.

The roofline was immense, fitted with wooden gables and turrets that stretched upward to the dreary, nightlike sky. Large paned windows of leaded glass winked from almost every angle of the house, glass eyes that watched the turbulent sea. The warmth of fire glow illuminated the otherwise somber manor, and after a moment's hesitation, Andrea hurried to the broad double door of the house and knocked deliberately against the ancient wood. She felt cold apprehension grip her and wondered vaguely if she could be heard over the whistling gales of the wind.

JEFFERSON HARMON LOOKED up from the newspaper article that he had been studying intently. He gazed into the red, dying embers of the fire and listened to the sounds of the night. His dark, near-black eyebrows drew together in concentration. Was it his imagination, or had he heard a faint rap on the front door? Impossible. He paused for a moment, and then decided the noise must have been a tree limb knocking against the walls of the house in the storm. He chided himself at his own case of nerves. He was upset, and he knew it, ever since the phone call from Lara only hours ago. Damn that woman for making such a mess of the divorce and dragging Megan into the middle of it all.

After straightening the newspaper, he once again became absorbed by the article about his ex-wife that recounted her late-night dancing date with a wealthy young European and the subsequent automobile accident that had put both of them, as well as a few innocent motorists, into the hospital overnight. Luckily it appeared that no one was injured seriously…a fact confirmed by Lara only a few hours before on the phone. The newspaper reporter was sympathetic to Lara Harmon, driver of the ill-fated vehicle. Jefferson was not. His scowl deepened as he continued to read.

The knocking began again, and this time, instantly alerted, Jefferson pulled his long body from the comfort of his favorite leather chair and quickly made his way to the front door. Who could possibly be here, in the middle of a Pacific tempest? He discounted it being anyone he knew—all of his friends respected his privacy and would have called in advance. Who then? The only logical explanation was that some poor fool had stupidly been caught in the storm and landed on the island rather than attempt the rugged journey inland. It had happened before, but Harmon was in no mood to try and make small talk with anyone, much less some idiot who didn't even have sense to stay on dry land when a storm was brewing. Jefferson was in a foul mood, and he knew it, but found it impossible to dispel. Reading the article on his ex-wife had made him irritable, and talking with her only served to make him feel tired and frustrated. The last thing he needed at this moment was a stranger on his front porch. It would be difficult to keep his anger in check, especially with some inexperienced blowhard sailor.

Jerking the door open roughly, Jefferson was stunned by the sight that met his eyes. A woman—young, near thirty he guessed—was standing, straight as an arrow, on his front porch. The fact that rain cascaded over her, and that cold, northern winds had obviously tousled her hair and chilled her body as well, didn't seem to concern her. The collar of her raincoat, which was fashionable and totally impractical, was hiked around her neck, and she was clearly soaked to the skin. Still, she held her head regally high, as if she anticipated his hostility. An image of another woman, another time, began to form in his mind.

As the light from the house spilled into the evening and touched upon her face, Jefferson drew in a long, steadying breath, for not only was she the most intrinsically beautiful woman that he had ever laid eyes upon, but she was a vision of the very woman who had haunted his nights and fired his blood: Andrea Monroe. Jefferson had all but forgotten the depth of her femininity.

It wasn't that she was gorgeous in the classical sense—

quite the opposite. Her features were perhaps a bit too large for her small, clear face. But the combination of round, deep-set sea-green eyes, surrounded by thick, black lashes, her short, straight nose, and the wide, voluptuous curve of her mouth, gave her a look of sensuality coupled with an innocent vulnerability that instantly captivated him. Perhaps it was the sparkle of raindrops in her tangled hair, or maybe the startled look of hesitation in her intelligent green eyes, but whatever the reason, Jefferson Harmon suddenly realized that she was the most strikingly provocative woman that he had ever had the misfortune to meet. Her guarded gaze locked with his, and he saw in her eyes an unmistakable, proud defiance.

Oh, God, Andrea, Jefferson thought inwardly. Why now? Why, just as he was trying to pull his life back together, had she come to complicate things?

The shock of the door opening had startled Andrea, and for a moment she hesitated, awestruck. The man in the doorway was certainly the object of her quest, and yet, confronted with the powerful physical presence of Jefferson while touched by his memory, Andrea faced those nagging doubts that had been working on her ever since she had first read the article about his divorce, over a week ago. The man standing before her was just as foreboding as she remembered. Even dressed casually in faded western jeans and a wool work shirt, he exuded the strength of his personality. He was taller than she recalled, and he carried himself with a proud authority that hinted of arrogance. His face was stern and commanding, but roguishly handsome. Severe hazel eyes, shielded by thick, ebony brows and dark, straight lashes, bore down upon her with inquisitive but uncompromising dominion. And in the depths of those glaring eyes a flash of recognition gleamed.

The mutual silence between them was broken only by the sound of the wild surf pounding relentlessly on the shore, hundreds of feet below them. He looks older and somehow more vulnerable, Andrea thought as she stared past his indifference and delved into the private depths of his soul. He's been scarred.

"Jefferson?" Andrea asked, her voice rough from the cold wind. She attempted to look him squarely in the eye, and hoped she appeared outwardly calm. The mixture of the tempestuous storm, the blackness of oncoming night and the strong virility of the famous man before her had shattered her poise. It's been so long…too long, she thought. Deliberately, she refused to be intimidated by the force of Jefferson's physical presence.

"Andrea? What in God's name are you doing here…in this storm?" he inquired, his dark gaze dropping from her face to study the rest of her rain-drenched frame. Although fully clothed, Andrea felt suddenly naked, as if the man she was addressing could see to the very core of her being, into her mind and through her soul—just as he had always done.

His dark eyes lifted. "Did you come here looking for me?"

"Yes… I…"

"Why?" he demanded tersely. "Are you a reporter now, searching for the latest scoop on my life? If so, the interview is over!"

Andrea felt herself inwardly cringe. "I'm not with the press," she stated evenly, and knew in her heart that if she mentioned Bryce and Coral Productions, she would get no further with him. Besides which, now that she had seen him, she wanted to see more. She hadn't exactly lied—she wasn't a reporter.

"But you did come looking for me?" Serious questions shadowed his eyes.

"Yes." She stared deeply into his probing gaze and wondered how she would ever be able to broach the subject of the interview. It seemed almost petty, when she considered all of the love and hate that had bound Jefferson and her together and thrust them fatefully apart.

Jefferson's face softened slightly. "I'm sorry," he murmured quietly. "Please come in. You look like you could use a good, strong drink and a warm fire." A smile lit up his harsh face, and for an instant Andrea remembered the charismatic young governor who had used the flash of his slightly crooked smile or the edge of his razor-sharp wit to lure hesitant voters to his party.

"There's a fire in the den," he remarked, leading the way through the large, exquisite marble vestibule toward the rear of the house. Andrea nodded in mute agreement, remembering the intimate evenings alone with him in just that den, and knowing the way to its cheery interior without his direction. She followed him as he led the way, and smiled uncomfortably to herself at the alluring enigma he presented. If only she could touch him again, talk to him the way that she once had....

She snapped her mind back to the present and tried to focus her thoughts on the house rather than the man. The old manor was filled with classical, formal antiques, beautiful and yet cold. Jefferson Harmon himself held that same formal, cold wariness in his eyes, but also exuded a warm, comfortable country charm that seemed to reach out and grasp her. She noticed that he was clad in stocking feet, and yet he carried himself almost loftily as he walked. The man still intrigued her, and frightened her just a little. Perhaps she had made a very serious error in judgment in coming here to meet with him face-to-face. She had suffered his rejection once already in her short life—could she face it again?

"Take off your coat," he commanded, "and lay it over there." He pointed to a worn leather chair near the fire. "I'll get us a drink, and you can explain just what it is that made you brave that god-awful weather to come and visit me after nine, make that ten, years. Somehow I don't expect that you're here asking for contributions to your latest crusade for mankind and against the violence of war."

Andrea smiled in spite of herself, ignoring the bite in his words. She took the proffered drink and set it on a corner table. After removing her coat, she warmed her palms against the coals of the fire and then took a long swallow of her brandy. "You're right, Jefferson. I'm not here soliciting anything…not really."

"Oh?" Once again he flashed her the charming, off-center smile.

"No. I—I came here because I wanted to see you," Andrea admitted with a sigh, her voice uneven.

He stared for a moment into the amber depths of his drink, and his smile faded into a scowl. "Why now, Andrea? After ten years, why now? Is it because of the divorce?" he asked, his hazel eyes touching hers. "Here, let me help you with that," he continued, and set his brandy on the table near hers.

Andrea had been struggling with the leather thong that had restrained her hair. But her fingers, stiff from the cold, wet weather, fumbled at the rain-swollen knot. Jefferson came up and stood behind her, his strong, sure fingers working against the leather.

"Damn," he swore under his breath, and the warmth of the air that had passed from his lungs brushed Andrea's chilled neck. "When you decide to tie a knot, you really do a job of it, don't you?"

"I didn't realize that it would get so wet, or swell so much. The storm was more severe than I had imagined," Andrea attempted to explain.

"Obviously," was the dry retort. "You still don't look like a lunatic, and if I remember correctly, you're far from it. But only a madwoman would attempt to brave that storm!"

Andrea couldn't disagree with his logic, and she found it difficult to think of anything other than the strong fingers that brushed against her neck as Jefferson worked at the thong. Although he didn't outwardly acknowledge the intimacy of his touch, Andrea could feel her skin warming when his hands seemed to linger against her neck.

"Ah, well, we really don't have much of a choice here," he began, admitting defeat. "This calls for drastic action."

"What do you mean?"

From deep in his pocket he pulled out a silver jackknife, and in one swift stroke, cut the confining cord. Involuntarily Andrea's hands flew to her throat, and she whirled to face the man she had once loved so much.

Her quick reaction and the startled look in her eyes arrested Jefferson. There was something about Andrea that was alluring, captivating and yet distant and wary. Who had she become during the last ten years, and why was she here?

"I didn't mean to frighten you," he asserted as he snapped the knife closed and put it back in his jeans pocket. He returned the brandy snifter to her slightly trembling hands.

"You didn't."

Doubtful, he cocked a black eyebrow. He took a long

swallow of his drink, and Andrea watched the fluid movement of his throat as he swallowed the smooth liquor.

Jefferson stared at Andrea in the deepening silence. Even the wind from the storm seemed to have become a distant, vague memory as his eyes took in all of her. "Well," he finally said, breaking the heady, thick silence, "I could start out the conversation with something like, 'Long time, no see,' or 'Gee, Andrea, what have you been up to for the last ten years?' or even something as inane as 'I certainly didn't expect to run into you tonight,' but I've never been one for small talk, and I realize that you didn't come here to apologize...or just to check on my health...." His smile was affable, but there was an underlying determination to his words. "What is it that brings you here?"

"I told you that I wanted to see you again."

"All right, I'll buy that, but why tonight, in this storm?"

"There is a reason," Andrea admitted, unable to look into his eyes. "I told you that I wasn't a reporter, and I'm not. But I do work for an independent production company, Coral Productions, and, to make a long story short, we've run into a little financial difficulty—"

"And you're looking for additional capital?" he guessed.

"No."

Again silence. All of his attention was directed at her. He regarded her pensively over the rim of his glass, and the warmth of his gaze steadied her.

"Coral Productions is promoting a new show for cable television. It's about faces in the news...in-depth interviews with people of celebrity status, like you. Coral Productions would like you to be the lead interview.'

Andrea's declaration stung the air, and the warmth in

Jefferson's eyes cooled as his face hardened. "Pardon me?" he whispered.

Andrea took in a deep, sharp breath. "I said that the company wants you to be the first feature story in our series."

He stepped farther away from her, as if to regard her entire body with his condemning gaze. Jefferson's jaw clenched, and Andrea could tell that every muscle in his body had tightened. His legs, dark silhouettes against the scarlet embers of the fire, tensed, and his fingers clutched the empty brandy snifter in a death grip. "That's why you're here?" he accused.

"That, and the fact that I wanted to see you again."

He snorted derisively. "You expect me to believe that you purposely stayed away from me for ten years, and just coincidentally you want me to go public with my life.... You can't be serious, Andrea. I thought you knew me better than that! What do you take me for, a fool?"

"Oh, no...you don't understand."

"I think I do. Let me get this straight. Isn't Coral Productions responsible for that piece of trash on Saturday nights—*Pride's Passion?*"

"Power," Andrea corrected. *"Pride's Power."*

"No wonder you're in trouble."

Andrea attempted to protest, but his sharp gaze cut her off. "It doesn't matter. Whatever the reason, Coral is in trouble, and wants to do an interview show. And I assume that your boss, Bryce Cawthorne, right?—" Andrea nodded in confirmation "—knows about our past relationship and hoped that you could persuade me to talk to him."

"He doesn't know anything about us!" Andrea shot back at Jefferson.

"Sure he doesn't. He just happened to send you up here to find me, and he doesn't know that we knew each other…intimately? You expect me to believe that? Come on, Andrea, give me a little credit."

"Bryce thinks it's a coincidence that I came to Victoria."

"Was it?" Jefferson asked, his hazel eyes pinioning hers.

"I don't know," she admitted honestly. "I knew about the show before I came up here, but I tried to dissuade Bryce from considering you."

"I'll just bet you did," he mocked.

Andrea stiffened, and her green eyes darkened in rage. "It's not important whether you believe me or not. That's the way it was. You have to know that I don't want this interview any more than you do! I don't want all of the scandal and you and me and Mart dug up again! It's over now! Dead and gone!"

Andrea could sense Jefferson appraising her, mentally calculating everything about her. "Okay, Andrea, you've got my undivided attention, so why don't you explain what, exactly, brought you here, and why you expect me to believe that you're not in cahoots with Cawthorne." His voice was brittle, and Andrea could feel the anger simmering beneath his words.

"I came to Victoria, to my parents' town house, for a vacation, to get away from the pressures at work and just to think. I didn't expect for Bryce to call me with orders to contact you, but he couldn't get hold of you. You're not listed in the book, you know. Anyway, he called me, and I told him I'd talk to you."

"That's it?" he demanded.

"All of it."

"All right, let's just say that I believe you," he agreed affably, and Andrea was reminded of his infamous courtroom charm. "Let's assume that you don't think that Bryce knows of our past friendship," he suggested, caution underlying his smile.

"You don't have to assume anything. It's the truth!"

"You're sure?"

"He couldn't." Why didn't she sound convincing?

"Why not? The man can read, can't he? Your name and mine were linked very closely in the press, weren't they?"

"But that was ten years ago," she protested feebly, suddenly realizing that he knew something that she didn't.

"And Bryce Cawthorne has the memory of an elephant." Jefferson saw the first traces of doubt cross Andrea's face.

"What are you saying?" she demanded.

"I'm stating that your boss lied to you, pure and simple. He called me yesterday with his ridiculous idea, and I hung up on him."

"But he told me that he couldn't get hold of you."

"Did he?" Jefferson laughed mirthlessly. "He's more conniving than I suspected."

"But how..."

"I don't know. Lara probably gave him the number. That sounds like something she would do." A grim smile twisted his lips into a thin, uncompromising line.

Embarrassment and confusion flooded over Andrea, and she could feel the stain of color on her face. Tears of frustration burned at the back of her eyes, but she refused to cry. If Bryce had lied to her, he hadn't much cared for her feelings, and if Jefferson was lying to her now, well, it didn't much matter. "Look, I'm sorry if I've inconvenienced you at all, Jefferson. Here's my card...Bryce can be reached at the number on the left, if you reconsider." Her voice began to waver, but she continued bravely on. "I'm sorry about everything," she whispered, and her throaty voice trembled with emotion.

"Don't be."

"I...look, it was probably a mistake for me to come here in the first place," she admitted.

"I don't think so," Jefferson argued, condemning himself mentally. What was he doing, what was he hoping for? Why did he feel so attracted to Andrea, just as he had in the past? Had he forgotten all of her lies, the disillusionment he had suffered at her hand? Then why, in God's name, did he feel an urge to comfort her, to touch her, to make love to her until dawn?

From her position sitting on the couch, Andrea pulled her eyes upward to meet the unwavering gaze of the man standing determinedly before her. She wanted to apologize and hurry out of the room to hide in the night. But something in his eyes made her linger. Was it tenderness or wariness, passion or loathing? Andrea was too tired to guess. She stood up and reached for her coat.

The warm, gentle touch of his hands on her shoulders surprised her. "Don't go," he suggested huskily.

"I have to go."

"You can't think that you can find a boat to take you back in this storm."

"No, there's someone waiting for me." She started to turn, suddenly feeling the warm, delicious pressure of his fingers near her throat.

"Who?" he challenged, his voice growing rough.

"A sailor, I don't know his name. He said he would wait an hour," she glanced at the bold, Roman numerals on the clock face over the fireplace mantel. "I've really got to go," she whispered breathlessly, but remained standing in the inviting den, allowing Jefferson's warm fingers to caress the light fabric of her sweater and promise higher, more intense sensual delights.

"Stay," he persuaded, his dark eyes deepening with passion.

"I can't," she persisted. "Please, don't touch me. I can't think when you touch me. I've never been able to."

"Don't think," he advised, while his thumbs touched the silken skin of her throat. "Just listen to the wind."

Andrea closed her eyes and concentrated on the whistle of the northern gale. She felt as if her entire body were beginning to melt in the heat of his hot, persuasive touch, and when his lips descended to find hers, she let herself fall into his arms and returned the passion of his kiss with an intensity that had lain dormant for ten years. Her heart fluttered wildly in her chest, and a warm, moist heat coiled within her body. She found herself willingly trapped in the velvet touch of his embrace.

His hands, large, strong and sensitive, kneaded warm circles of moist desire against the small of her back, and she felt her skin quake when his fingers tugged at the bottom of her sweater and touched her lightly, tentatively, flesh to flesh. The passion that was seducing her took her swirling backward in time, and she knew that if she didn't stop him soon, she would be lost to him forever.

"This is crazy," she sighed into his open mouth.

"I know."

She felt her knees collapsing, and his weight, gentle but sure, forced her onto the soft mat of carpet before the fire.

"Oh, Andrea," he moaned, "it's been so long…so long." His lips, warm and inviting, brushed over her neck, and his hands, eager with long-denied passion, wound themselves in the thick, wet strands of her blue-black hair.

She let her arms move upward to encircle his neck. It all felt so right: the hungry possession of his body over hers, the radiant heat from the dying fire, an inner glow inspired by the brandy and the stormy wind whistling far in the distance.

His lips whispered promises as they swept over her face and touched her cheeks, her eyes, her throat. And his tongue, with a claiming passion long hidden, traced the outline of her lips, the length of her jaw, the lobe of her ear. Without thought she felt her body arch up to meet his, to invite him boldly closer.

With a moan of surrender Jefferson let his hands slide upward over the soft, silken texture of her abdomen to slowly, erotically, caress a breast. Instantly Andrea felt her nipple stiffen and her breasts strain against the lacy bra that held them confined. "Let me love you," he whispered into her hair.

"Please…please…" she begged, gasping for breath. "Oh, Jefferson—I need you."

Her plea was as desperate as the feeling of renewed, torchlike passion that was blinding him. He knew he should stop and control himself. He knew all too well his vulnerability where Andrea was concerned, and yet he couldn't resist what he had dreamed of, longed for and yet denied himself because of her lies…all of her lies. Blood thundered in his temples as he pulled the sweater off her body. For a moment he hesitated, studying her perfect body in the shadowed fire glow. If it was possible, she was more beautiful than he had remembered. And as he gazed into her eyes, heavy with awakened passion, he felt a damnable urge to make love to her endlessly. But he stopped himself.

Rational thought took command of his body. Why had she come here tonight? What did she want of him? Was she really as willing as she seemed…or was she using her body as a means of getting him to do what she wanted—

be it the interview or anything else. Jefferson knew only too well what he could be talked into doing just for the sake of Andrea Monroe.

His desire ripped savagely through his body, but the fact that Andrea had lied to him in the past, and had waited ten long years to resurface, gave him pause. Don't do it again, his reason told him. Don't let her use you.

Andrea's eyes watched Jefferson's face. As surely as the tide went out to sea, he willed his passion to subside. She could read it in the straight, hard angle of his jaw, the glint of determination in his eyes. Slowly he rolled away from her to lie on his back and stare at the ceiling.

"You and I have a lot to talk about," he said with a sigh. "And I think it's time that we ironed out some of the problems of the past."

"Do you think it's possible?" she asked, suddenly feeling empty.

"I don't know," he admitted, pinching his lip between his teeth and drawing his brows together. "I just don't know."

CHAPTER THREE

"I'VE GOT TO GO," ANDREA stated after a few heavy moments of silence. She had pulled her sweater back over her head and disappointedly noted that Jefferson hadn't attempted to stop her from getting dressed. Furtively she looked at him, seeing his long, lean torso and the taut muscles that strained rigidly in the shadowed fire glow. He stared vacantly up at the cross timbers of the ceiling, lost in thoughts of the past.

"You're not going anywhere," he advised.

"I have to."

"No, you don't. You may have been foolish enough to brave that storm once, but I'm not letting you attempt it again. If something should happen to you, I don't want it on my conscience."

"You don't have to worry about that."

"Look, Andrea." Jefferson's voice was cold and emphatic. "I wasn't the one who came knocking on doors in the middle of a raging tempest." He propped himself up on one elbow and stared down at her, his eyes narrowing as he surveyed her. "Now that you're here, I think we should talk. It's long overdue!"

"But I told that sailor I would be back within the hour."

Jefferson's eyes slid to the clock face. "You've already missed that appointment by about twenty minutes."

Andrea curled her legs beneath her as if to rise. "Really, I have to go. I gave you Bryce's card, and I would appreciate it if you would call him—as a favor to me."

Jefferson's hand reached out and manacled her wrist. "I don't see that I owe you any favors to begin with, and I think you're being foolish. Let the seaman go. Stay with me."

"I...I don't know," Andrea murmured, and bit at her lower lip. All of her senses begged her to stay, to listen to him, but something in her conscience told her that staying with Jefferson would only make it more difficult to leave later.

"We could use some time together," he coaxed, and his hand over her wrist loosened enough to let his thumb slide seductively up and down her forearm. "Admit it, Andrea. You really would like to stay with me."

"Of course I would, Jefferson. I'm not foolish enough to try and hide that fact. But I don't know if it would accomplish anything. I was hoping that, at the very least, we could become good friends again."

"And at the very most?" he asked, his hazel eyes twinkling.

She pulled her eyes away from his gaze and stared into the fire. "I don't know," she admitted in a rough voice.

"Let's find out," he coaxed. "Stay."

"I can't!" she admitted with a finality that even he understood. His thumb abruptly stopped its intimate caress of her arm and pulled away.

"Have it your way," Jefferson agreed, icily. Still, his dark eyes challenged her decision. She felt at once angry and helpless. He knew she didn't want to go, but he was willing to let her make her own choice.

He watched her as she silently slid into her wet raincoat,

and he mentally chastised himself for the burning longing that still lingered in his mind. It was impossible not to mistrust her. Although she had seemed vulnerable, perceptive and incredibly drawn to him, he had to remember that she had left him without so much as a look over her shoulder after all the publicity of their affair had become front-page news. And that brother of hers, Martin, with his left-wing ideals and underhanded scruples, had used both Jefferson and Andrea to his own best advantage: to champion a cause that had nothing to do with them. Jefferson's jaw squared at the thought, and his eyes darkened in quiet rage.

Was it possible that Andrea would attempt to use him again? Would she be so bold? It seemed incredible that after ten years of silence she would come to him again, unless she wanted something in return. Even after ten lost years, she didn't seem to be the kind of woman who would give herself so easily to a man, and yet she had yielded to him with no protest. Did she actually think that he would believe that she might still care for him? When he had halted the passion of their lovemaking only moments before, he had seen the unmasked look of disappointment surface in her intent green gaze. And her face, caught in relief against the onyx color of her hair, was as quietly reproachful as he had remembered. Damn her for her beauty, and those haunting eyes that seemed to pierce right to his soul.

Andrea gave an embarrassed pull on her raincoat and cinched the belt tightly over her slim waist. She felt the dark, inquisitive probe of Jefferson's eyes on her body, but she avoided his gaze. She wondered fleetingly how she could have let things get so one-sided and out of hand. It was true that she felt the same attraction for and fascination with Jefferson that she had as a college girl, but she had matured since then and, hopefully, learned from her mistakes. Then why had she felt a welling sense of disappointment when he had forcefully pulled away from her?

Without a word Jefferson led her out of the stone manor and escorted her down the path toward the steps. In the time that had passed, evening had set in, and it was difficult for Andrea to find her way. Twice she stumbled on an exposed tree root, and only Jefferson's strong, aloof touch kept her on her feet. The wind raced over the ridge of the island, blowing cold, salty spray and minute particles of sand against Andrea's face. Her hair, dark as the stormy night, streamed out behind her in windswept tangles.

The stairs had become treacherous in the darkness, and Andrea picked her way carefully down the steep steps, grateful for the wooden railing that gave her a modicum of balance as she descended. At last she fumbled on the lowest step and felt the soft, wet sand of the beach crunch beneath her boots. In the darkness Andrea could barely make out the small boat that was tied securely to the dock. Shuddering from the cold, she hurried to the craft.

Jefferson was at her side, and although he hadn't uttered a word since they had left the den, Andrea could feel his simmering anger and imagine the square outline of his determined jaw.

Although Andrea was walking within inches of him, Jefferson had to shout to be heard over the crashing of the sea. "You really expect to make it back to Victoria in this?" he shouted incredulously. "You'll never make it!"

"I've got no other choice," she shouted back.

"Sure you do. Wait until the storm dies down!" She began to shake her head, and Jefferson caught hold of her forearms, gripping them tightly and shaking her. "For

God's sake, Andrea, just this once use your head. Stay with me—at least until it passes."

Andrea hesitated, and at that moment a large wave crashed against the dock, sending white spray up into the air and down on Andrea. The icy, frigid water drenched her in its wet, cold plume.

"That does it! You're not going!" Jefferson swore emphatically. "I was going to let you have your bullheaded way again, but not now. It's just not safe!" Andrea began to protest, but Jefferson continued. "I'll tell the skipper, you wait here. I'll only be a minute."

Before Andrea could argue, Jefferson stepped onto the boat and slipped into the cabin. He was back in a matter of seconds, and Andrea could see the look of disgust that crossed his features. "Come on, let's get out of here," he advised, taking her arm and nearly pulling her down the weathered wooden planks of the dock. "Your friend was in no condition to go anywhere."

It took nearly twice as long to climb up the staircase as it had to climb down. Andrea felt chilled to the bone from the arctic winds that pressed cold fingers through her clothing and propelled her upward. By the time that she got back to the house, she was exhausted and nearly frozen.

"You know, Andrea," Jefferson said, after slamming the broad wooden door of the house, "I gave you credit for more brains than this."

"What do you mean?" she shot back at him.

"I mean, not only do you tempt fate by challenging the worst storm of the year, but you do it in one of the poorest excuses I've ever seen for a boat. To top matters off, you hire a drunk!"

"The choice was restricted."

"To a drunken madman?"

"Yes!"

"And you couldn't wait for the weather to clear?" he accused, tossing his wet poncho on a hook near the door.

"I..." She sighed, her voice catching. The long day and the strain of seeing him again were taking hold of her. "I was afraid."

"Of what? Certainly not the storm—or that questionable excuse for a skipper!"

She drew a long breath into her lungs to steady herself. "That wasn't what I was concerned about."

"What then?" he thundered, grabbing her elbow and leading her back toward the den. She ignored his question, aware only of the strong persuasion of his touch at her elbow. Through the light fabric of her raincoat and the thin sweater, she imagined his fingers against her skin.

Once back in the warm den, with its cherrywood walls, deep, plush burgundy carpet and comfortable leather furniture, Jefferson strode over to a closet near the bar and pulled out a large, rust-colored terry-cloth robe.

"Change into this," he commanded, tossing the robe at her. "You can put your clothes over the fireplace screen for now. We'll wash and dry them later." His eyes skimmed over her body in a quick head-to-heels appraisal. "I'll try to find you some slippers that fit while I'm changing into dry clothes." He strode to the door of the den and stopped short, as if a sudden thought had occurred to him. "There's a telephone on the desk, in case you need to inform someone of your whereabouts." His hazel eyes regarded her intently. "I mean, in case someone is waiting for you." There were questions in his gaze, but he didn't bother with them. "And if you need another drink, you know where the bar is." His face softened slightly. "Fix me one, too: bourbon."

"I remember," she murmured with a hesitant smile as Jefferson's footsteps retreated in the long, dark hallway of the ancient, Tudor home.

Andrea tugged off her wet clothes and hung them carefully over the screen. She pulled on the long, warm, comfortable robe and cinched the belt around it tightly. The sleeves were much too long, and she rolled them upward in order to free her hands.

Taking Jefferson's advice, she padded barefoot to the bar and poured them each a strong, neat bourbon. Her eyes traveled over the leather-bound editions on a nearby bookshelf, and her fingers encountered a light covering of dust on the books—proof of their disuse. A pity, she thought to herself. So grand a home used as a hermit's refuge. So large a library idly gathering dust. So alluring a man wrapped within himself. If only things had turned out differently for them, perhaps Jefferson would be as she remembered: softer and warmer somehow, free of the mistrust that she could sense in his quiet gaze. What had happened to him, to her? How had something so wonderful gotten so tangled in bitterness?

Andrea felt the winter's chill climb up her legs, and she hurried back to the chair near the glowing fire. She tossed another moss-laden log into the flames and heard the hiss and pop of the fire as it reignited against the new wood. She settled into the worn oxblood leather of the antique chair. Carefully she tucked her feet beneath her and buried them in the soft folds of Jefferson's robe. A faint scent of his aftershave tingled in her nostrils, and bold, vivid memories began to overtake her. Absently she swirled the amber-colored liquid in her glass and gazed into its clear depths, trying to piece together the memories that assaulted her…

IT HAD BEEN A LONG, HOT spring; a spring rare even for Southern California, and Andrea had found herself hoping to go home to her parents' summer town house in cool, well-groomed Victoria as soon as the term was over. She was restless, as were many of the local students, not only from the incredible heat, but also with the bitterness and unease of a war that no one seemed to want, and somehow was impossible to end. Her older brother, Martin, was graduating soon, and he would be eligible for the draft when his student deferment had run out.

It was nearly June when Andrea and a few friends, Martin included, had gone to the political rally. Several politicians who had succeeded in the primary had come to speak with the students in the open arena of the outdoor amphitheater. It wasn't intended that the rally become a heated debate, but the two candidates had immediately squared off and verbally attacked each other.

That was the first time that Andrea had seen Jefferson—from a distance, as one of the spectators in a crowd of nearly two thousand. He was a young lawyer at the time and was considered a dark horse candidate for the California State Senate—the youngest man ever to have won his party's nomination in the primary. The moment Andrea had seen him, she had sensed in him a difference from the other, blander politicians. She knew of him only what she had read—his reputation as a brilliant corporate lawyer preceded him. It seemed that he had just the right combination of charm, looks, savvy and ruthlessness to propel him quickly up the ladder of success. Although only twenty-six years old at the time, Jefferson Harmon had become a household word in California. The young lawyer with the tanned, masculine face, graced with a comfortable flash of a smile and thick, neat hair, had wooed the public, especially the young, female voters, over to his camp. Even from a distance Andrea had felt his magnetism. When he smiled at the crowd, she felt that it was a message sent to her alone.

When the topic of the debate began to encompass the Vietnam war, a few hecklers in the crowd began to shout obscenities at the raised podium. The shouts calling for an end to the war interfered with the debate. Martin, himself a conscientious objector, yelled pointedly at the politicians, urging them to stop the war.

Jefferson's principal opponent, a rotund, white-haired gentleman, ignored the remarks thrust in his direction. He was the incumbent, and as such, he was accustomed to the antics and catcalls of a young crowd of restless college students. His feathers remained unruffled as he attempted to swing the argument away from the topic of the war and on to safer, more stable ground.

Jefferson, however, was distracted by the audience, and more than once his keen, hazel eyes surveyed the crowd to sort out the leaders. Often, while searching for Martin, who was shouting at the top of his lungs, Jefferson's gaze found Andrea's—or so she imagined.

The rally continued in the relentless sun, and the audience quieted. Jefferson's concentration fell neatly back in place, and he managed to come out a victor in the debate, at least in Andrea's estimation. Sometime during the heated discussion he loosened his tie, tossed off his jacket and rolled up his sleeves, never once missing a point in the debate. Andrea was mesmerized as she watched him talking, arguing, blasting shrewdly at his opponent, seemingly unaware of the sweat that trickled down the length of his throat, past his open collar. Andrea wondered just how far the beads of sweat traveled, and found herself blushing at the thought.

When the debate ended, Andrea felt disappointment spread through her as she watched Jefferson Harmon take a long drink from a cup near the podium, sling his coat over his shoulder and hurry down the steps to the back of the amphitheater.

"Come on, Andie," Martin was saying to her. "Let's go see if we can talk to those guys personally."

"What guys…the politicians?" she gasped as her heart fluttered.

"Sure, why not? They're the ones pulling all of the strings in the country. Let's just see if they'll talk to us."

"Right on!" a friend of Martin's agreed. "They owe it to us. Those are the guys that are sending all of us to the front lines."

"But I don't think that state senators have much influence about the war," Andrea objected. "You should be talking to someone in Washington."

"You've got to start somewhere," Martin replied. "Let's just go see what these guys have to say for themselves."

Martin and a few of his friends headed out in search of the politicians, and Andrea followed. It wasn't so much that she approved of what Martin's friends were doing, but she was intrigued, and hoped to catch a closer glimpse of Jefferson Harmon.

Although the crowd hurried toward the politicians, a long, black limousine carrying the incumbent was already heading out of the winding road of the campus.

"Too bad," Martin said roughly under his breath. "I really wanted to corner that guy."

"We're still in luck," Martin's friend Dave had rejoined. "That Harmon guy is still here…over there!" Dave pointed a long finger at Jefferson. "Wouldn't you know it, he's talking to the ROTCs."

Somehow Andrea felt a compelling need to defend the young political newcomer with the intense hazel eyes. "There's nothing wrong with that, Dave," she shot out unexpectedly. "Some people want to become officers in the military and the Reserve Officer Training Corps, and others, unlike you, need the money to help them get through college. Not everyone is born with a silver spoon in his mouth!"

"How would you know about that?" Dave goaded, pulling on the strands of his thin beard. "You've never had to work a day in your life!" His dark, condemning gaze moved from Andrea back to Martin. "You'd better watch out, my friend," he cautioned Martin, "it looks like little sister is becoming a warmonger!"

"Cut it out," Martin shouted, ignoring the simmering argument between his sister and his friend. "Let's go see what Harmon has to say."

Jefferson was just moving away from the crowd of would-be young officers and heading toward his car. He was still holding his jacket over his shoulder, and in the other hand he held a bottle of cola.

"Hey, Harmon," Martin said, accosting Jefferson, and Andrea visibly cringed. "Why don't you cut out all the double-talk and let us know how you really feel about the war."

Jefferson smiled affably and tossed his empty bottle into a nearby trash can. "Personally, I don't like war, *any* war," he stated while casually throwing his jacket into the backseat of his old BMW. His broad shoulders strained against the cotton of his light blue oxford shirt, and a smear of sweat pasted the fabric against his back.

"And so what do you propose to do about it?" Martin asked. "That is...if you're elected."

"Whatever I can," Jefferson admitted. "But I don't think I'll have a helluva lot of influence. The California State Senate is a far cry from congress."

"Cop-out!" Dave muttered, and Jefferson's hazel eyes snapped. He began to open the door to his car, and his eyes rested on Andrea's embarrassed face for just a moment. He seemed to hesitate, but then, as if thinking better of a betraying thought, he settled comfortably behind the wheel.

"What about your old man, Harmon?" Martin persisted. "Wasn't he an officer in the army?"

"A major," was the clipped reply. Jefferson's eyes darkened.

"So you grew up living off the backs of enlisted men—draftees. From what I understand, your old man made quite a fortune in his time! How does it feel to know that he made the bucks, while other men died?" Martin taunted, leaning against the door of the clean black automobile and sticking his face nearly inside the open window.

"Cut it out, Martin," Andrea whispered loudly as she tugged on her brother's arm and attempted to pull him away from the window. Once again Jefferson's penetrating gaze encompassed her.

"Listen to your girlfriend," Jefferson advised Martin as he started the car and his charming grin faded. "You don't know what you're talking about."

With those final words Jefferson jerked on the steering wheel and maneuvered the car out of the parking lot, past the lace-leafed trees, in the direction of the intricate mass of freeways of Southern California.

"Bastard!" Martin shouted at the car, and kicked at the dusty ground in his frustration. "Damn bastard politician! He's supposed to be different, but they're all the same!"

Not so, Andrea puzzled to herself, as she shielded her eyes against the glare of the sun and watched the sporty black car drive past the campus gates.

It was later that summer when Andrea chanced to meet Jefferson again. The incident on campus had lingered in her memory, and she couldn't quite seem to forget Jefferson Harmon and his winning, intimate smile. And although Martin seemed to hold a personal grudge against the man, Andrea attributed it to the fact that Martin had a chip on his shoulder when it came to politics. Martin blamed all the politicians for the Vietnam war. He had applied for another student deferment, hoping to enter graduate school and avoid the draft. But he had been refused, and unless he reported to the draft board within the next two weeks, he would be considered guilty of draft evasion. Even his hastily acknowledged status of conscientious objector to the war fell on deaf ears, as far as the military was concerned. And although his parents had the town house in Victoria, on Canadian soil, Andrea's father was adamant that his son do his national duty and join the armed forces. Martin was, after all, an American citizen, as were his younger sisters, Andrea and Gayla.

Andrea was torn. She didn't much care for Martin's political leanings, and yet she understood his concern and resentment. She didn't think of him as a coward, as did her father, but thought of him as what he was: a young man anxious about his future and his country's commitment to a foreign war that seemed fruitless and painful. Besides which, at the time, Andrea was barely twenty and somewhat naive.

Martin had been gone for several days on the pretense of meeting with the draft board. It was early September, and Andrea's mother and father had already moved back to California to enroll Gayla in her last year of high school. Andrea had stayed in Victoria, feeling restless. University studies didn't start for another three weeks, and she preferred swimming in the calm waters of Deer Lake during the Indian summer days on Vancouver Island to the heat and mayhem of the outskirts of L.A.

It was while browsing in the market, looking over the vast array of fresh fish, vegetables, shellfish, fruits and meats, that Andrea noticed she was being watched. At first she didn't see anyone staring at her and tried to shake off the feeling, but it persisted.

The open-air market was bustling with activity: shopkeepers in white aprons displaying their wares, curiosity seekers and tourists browsing over the interesting produce and exotic samples from the ocean. And everywhere was the smell of the salt sea from English Bay.

Andrea carried a small basket over her arm and was gathering a few groceries to sustain her until she had to leave Vancouver Island later in the month. Already she had picked up a loaf of fresh-baked sourdough bread and a brick of cheese. She was studying a display of razor clams when the distinct feeling that she was being watched again climbed up her spine. Instinctively she raised her eyes. They clashed with hazel eyes she had seen only once before, but immediately she recognized the face of Jefferson Harmon.

He was studying her as if attempting to place her face in some distant cog of his memory. She found the power of his gaze mesmerizing, spellbinding. He was dressed casually in faded, low-hanging jeans that showed signs of age and a simple cotton pullover that hid none of the tense muscles of his chest. Yet dressed in comfortable, worn clothes, a pleasant smile on his face, he still retained the same commanding presence that he had so forcefully demonstrated while speaking to the college spectators in California. Andrea guessed he stood no taller than six feet, but somehow he seemed to tower over and stand out from the crowd of shoppers in the busy fish market.

Andrea could hear the quiet noises of the city, but they seemed to be droning in the distance. The occasional honk of an automobile horn, the busy clatter of merchants displaying their wares, the familiar sound of a large ferryboat plowing slowly through the salty sea—all the sounds that normally commanded her attention were subdued when Jefferson spoke to her. She felt as if she were alone with this commanding man who stared so intimately into her widened eyes.

"You're Andrea Monroe," he surmised, to Andrea's amazement as he gave her a quick head-to-heels appraisal. She was surprised, but tried to stifle the urge to shrink under his studying gaze. Instead, she angled her face upward to meet his arrogant gaze.

"That's right." Though she tried vainly to hide the fact, she felt awkward and incredibly young in the presence of such a famous man. Although he could only be a few years older than she, he seemed light-years ahead of her in maturity. She managed a feeble imitation of his warm, knowing smile.

His hazel eyes darkened. "You were with your brother last May in the amphitheater at U.C.L.A."

Once again Andrea was surprised, and it must have registered in her large, green eyes, because when Jefferson noticed her reaction, the severity of his gaze appeared to soften. How did he know of her and Martin? *Why* would he know them?

"How do you know who I am?" she asked, lines of concentration etched across her smooth forehead.

"Your brother isn't one to just lie back and take things sitting down. He makes a lot of noise. Especially about his feelings on Vietnam. It doesn't go unnoticed," Jefferson observed with a dismissive shrug of his shoulders.

"What do you mean?" Andrea asked, a trickle of fear running in her blood. Was Martin in some sort of trouble because of his left-wing ideals? "Is someone spying on Martin?" she asked indignantly.

Jefferson's smile broadened. "You've been seeing too many movies about secret agents. Nothing as sinister as spying against your brother is going on...at least not that I know of." He picked up two tart, red apples from a stand, paid for them, handed one to Andrea and polished the other against his jeans.

"Then how do you know who he is?" Andrea persisted.

"Aside from the fact that he's written nearly a dozen letters to me—not exactly fan mail, mind you—and the fact that he's made the local news on campus, I made it my business to find out about him."

"You were spying!"

"You've got an overactive imagination." A twinkle of amusement lit his eyes.

"Then what would you call it?"

"Curiosity," he said with a lift of his broad shoulders.

"Why?" she demanded, not sure what to believe. He seemed to be toying with her.

"Come on," he directed, with an affable, off-center grin, "and I'll tell you all about it. Then you can fill me in, tell me what a beautiful girl like you is doing up here."

"Don't you know why I'm here? If you've been checking up on Martin, certainly you must know about me also," she tossed out with a touch of sarcasm. What was it about Harmon that tempted her so? she mentally asked herself. No matter how hard she tried to deny it, she was attracted to him. Was it his looks? His infamous courtroom charm? His teasing hazel eyes? His fame? *What?* No matter the cause, Andrea realized that she was more strongly bewitched by the roguish man standing before her than she had been by any man before. She sensed that he was compassionate and warm, but yet she felt that getting to know him might somehow become dangerous. It galled her to think that Jefferson Harmon, just because he was a political contender, had the *nerve*...the *influence*...the *power* to check up on Martin. Perhaps Martin was right all along. Perhaps Jefferson Harmon was just another scheming politician.

"Your folks live up here in the summer, don't they?" he prodded, touching her bent elbow, and guiding her through the tight, noisy throng of shoppers.

"You've been doing your homework," she replied frostily.

A smile, oozing with country-boy charm, illuminated his face, just as he intended it to. Once out of the confining marketplace, and back in the bright, near-blinding sunshine, Jefferson bit into his apple and watched her as he swallowed. A warm breeze, flavored with the tang of the ocean, blew across the bay. It pushed Andrea's long, wavy black hair away from her face and pressed the lightweight cotton of her pastel halter dress against her bare legs.

"So, it seems that you know why I'm here," Andrea pointed out, shielding her eyes with her hands to ward off the glare from the sunlight reflecting on the water. "What about you? What is it that brings California's favorite son up to the northern beaches of Victoria?"

"Vacation," was the simple reply. His eyes moved from her innocent face to skim the clear, blue water.

"From politics?" she asked, pressing to find out more about him.

"And everything else."

"But I thought that you, along with the rest of the contenders, would be campaigning hard and heavy. The election is in early November. That doesn't give you much time."

Jefferson nodded vacantly, as if his mind was on something other than the conversation. "Everyone, including a politician, needs some time to himself—to relax."

"So you decided to find the quiet life in Canada?" she inquired dubiously. One black, sculptured eyebrow raised to show her disbelief.

Jefferson pulled pensively on his lower lip, and his thick, near-black hair ruffled in the breeze from the sea. "Not exactly. My family owns an island up here, complete with a large house. I came up to spend a quiet weekend."

"Alone?" she asked, feeling her breath become tightly constricted in her throat.

"Does that surprise you?"

"No… I suppose not, but I do think it's strange that a person who came to the northern Pacific seeking solitude would come down here to this madhouse at the market."

"One has to eat," he pointed out. His smile was as gentle as the mild summer's day, and when he looked down upon Andrea with his commanding dark hazel eyes, she felt for a moment as if she might melt into the liquid warmth of his gaze.

Her voice faltered, but boldly, she continued. "What I do find surprising, almost incredibly so, is that up here, in all of these people," she waved theatrically to include the milling crowd of the market, "you bump into me. It seems highly unlikely."

"And suspicious?"

"I didn't say that."

"But you thought it," he perceived, noticing that her lips seemed to be trembling slightly. He tossed his apple core into a nearby trash can, and seemed to weigh his next words. "There's really nothing strange about it at all. I found you today because I wanted to. I don't leave a helluva lot to chance, and I wanted to meet you. I followed you here."

"What? From the town house? Why?" Andrea was incredulous.

"I wanted to see you alone, and I wasn't in the mood to make small talk with your family, especially that brother of yours. Just as I got to the town house, you were leaving. So I followed you to the market."

"But *why* did you want to see me? I don't even know you!"

"That's the mystery, isn't it? I can't even tell you for certain. Maybe it's because I find it hard to believe that your brother, Martin, could have such a beautiful and bewitching sister. And because, when I first saw you on the campus, I did you a disservice by thinking that you were just one more face in a crowd of angry young students bent on heckling me. I made a mistake, and I'd like to apologize by offering to take you to dinner."

"You don't have to apologize. It was an easy mistake," Andrea managed to say feebly. "But, thanks anyway." Andrea heard the polite words passing her lips, and crazy thoughts that she would like to take them back crossed her mind. In her heart she wanted nothing more than to spend some time alone with Jefferson Harmon. It was an insane idea, and she was intelligent enough to realize it.

"You're going to pass up a dinner and a sunset horseback ride on Harmon Island?" he asked, his dark eyebrows rising. Andrea sensed that Jefferson Harmon was not often discouraged.

"I…I think it would be best." Still, she hesitated, and he sensed it.

"Do you?" His voice was soft, seductive.

"Look, Mr. Harmon—"

"Jefferson," he persuaded, touching her naked arm with his sensitive fingertips. Andrea felt a ripple of heated blood climb up her arm to beat erratically at the base of her throat. Jefferson's eyes lowered as he watched her pulse, and a deep, scarlet flush spread up her neck and cheeks.

"Jefferson," she managed, his name catching in her throat.

"Do you have other plans?"

"No."

"Then you must be afraid of me," he challenged.

"No, but…"

"But what?"

"I don't even know you!" she blurted out.

"And you never will, unless you make the effort. What do you say?"

"All right," she agreed breathlessly, wondering if she was thinking at all. It wasn't like her to be so bold. After all, what did she know of the man?

The quick drive to the redbrick town house, with its elegant two stories and imposing, formal facade, was a blur in Andrea's mind. And the fast motor launch to the private island seemed to take no time at all. She had the uneasy feeling that she was making the worst mistake of her life, and yet she also thought that perhaps she was taking the most wonderful chance that opportunity had ever presented to her. There was something magical and spellbinding, tantalizing perhaps, in the feeling of adventure and romance that surrounded her. The ride over the clear blue water in the speeding motorboat was exhilarating, and in those moments while they crossed the shimmering stretch of water toward the island, Andrea felt as if she had known Jefferson all of her life.

CHAPTER FOUR

IT HAD TAKEN ANDREA SOME time to feel comfortable in the large stone house that commanded the island. Although her family had never been poor, she was unprepared and unaccustomed to the gracious display of wealth and power that dominated the mansion Jefferson called a summer retreat. She found it impossible not to linger over the elegant, formal antiques or the magnificent view of the sea that almost every window of the manor revealed.

The meal, prepared by a middle-aged live-in housekeeper, was excellent. Andrea had ravenously eaten the broiled Pacific salmon and steamed rice, all the while being charmed by Jefferson. His low voice, soft and seductive, vibrated in her ears, and his eyes seemed to follow her every move, as if touching her. The delicate meal, along with two glasses of clear, dry Riesling wine, and the low, enchanting conversation, seemed to wrap Andrea in warm, seductive folds of intimacy.

After the meal, without words, Jefferson took Andrea by the hand and led her to the rear of the house, and then to the stables. A large bay gelding, with a blaze of white that tapered to velvet pink at his nose, perked up his ears at the sound of Jefferson's entrance.

"Do you ride?" Jefferson asked, cocking his head in the direction of the large bay.

"A little."

"Bareback?"

"Never!" she gasped, eyeing the large horse dubiously.

"Then it's high time that you learned," Jefferson decided as he placed a bridle over the bay's broad head. "It's really very easy, and I can guarantee you that there's no better horse to practice on than old Monarch here." Jefferson gave the horse a good-natured slap on its rump before gently leading him from the musty stables and out into the clear air of the paddock that bordered the back of the manicured estate.

"I don't know," Andrea hedged, staring at the gelding with mounting uncertainty. She had ridden several times in her life, but always with a saddle, and on a considerably smaller horse. Monarch's imposing frame and heavily boned stature made Andrea's confidence waver.

"Don't worry about it. Just hang on to me," Jefferson instructed with a gleam of amusement in his hazel eyes. Andrea noticed something else in his gaze. Although it was hidden, she was aware of his smoldering desire. Unexpectedly she felt an answering passion igniting her blood.

She tried to keep her wandering mind on the conversation. "You aren't really serious. You don't think that he can hold both of us?" she asked, motioning to Monarch.

In answer, Jefferson smiled devilishly and, hoisting himself onto the bay's wide back, he swung his leg over the horse. In one lithe movement, he was astride the horse. Monarch's only response was to stamp one foot impatiently and give an inappreciative flick of his pointed, dark ears. Jefferson patted Monarch's shoulder, leaned down and offered his outstretched hand to Andrea in an invitation to mount the horse. Andrea couldn't help but suck in her breath as she extended her hands to Jefferson's and their fingers entwined. A tingle of apprehension darted across her shoulder blades. Was it fear of the horse—or the man?

With a strength that Andrea found astonishing, Jefferson lifted her onto the horse. The only movement that the bay made was to swish his tail against Andrea's slim, bare leg; naked because her dress was hiked daringly up to the swell of her hips as she sat astride the horse.

"Aren't we too heavy for him?" Andrea asked, tugging at her hem with her free hand, and trying to ignore the tension and excitement that she felt building in the air. Her bare legs were pressed against the horse's flanks, and she could feel his warm, soft coat move against her thighs and calves.

"Not for Monarch. He's a draft horse, part Belgian. That accounts for his size and strength," Jefferson explained as he loosened his grip on the reins and urged the animal forward. In his other hand, he pressed Andrea's fingers against his hard stomach. He let the bay walk slowly, letting Andrea get a feel for Monarch's steady, lumbering gait. They went past the paddock and into the wooded, unkempt portion of the island. The path through the stands of Douglas firs angled sharply downward, but the horse proved surefooted. Andrea's body was forced to hug Jefferson's as the pull of gravity pressed her, muscle for muscle, against him. Her arms were wrapped securely around his lean, hard torso, and her legs outlined his. Andrea couldn't ignore the warmth and rigid power of Jefferson's abdominal muscles as they tightened against her touch, nor could she deny that her own breathing, pulsating against the back of Jefferson's neck, had become as erratic as her thudding heartbeat.

The woods seemed to wrap both horse and riders in its

intimate folds of darkness. Filtered light, the last, ghostly rays from a rapidly lowering sun, permeated the branches of giant firs and shaded the forest in a dusky, ethereal glow. Shadows lengthened against the cracked bark of the trees and hid the wildflowers that scented the air.

As the bay picked his way carefully down the stony path, the crashing of waves against ancient rock echoed against the wooded hillside. All too quickly the dark intimacy of the woods gave way to the open air and roar of the surf against the beach. Monarch pranced sideways nervously and raised his head proudly in the air. He paused for a moment, twitching his ears, his muscles tensed in anticipation, and his pink nostrils flared into the wind. The signal from Jefferson came swiftly; he compressed his legs against the bay's broad shoulders and urged Monarch into a gallop. The long, powerful strides of the horse made short work of the narrow strip of dry land. Soon Andrea felt the sting of cold seawater against her legs as the horse found more stable, wet sand near the frothy edge of the tide.

Jefferson guided Monarch in the direction of the setting sun, letting the horse race on the surf's undulating edge. The animal thundered down the beach, his strong legs plowing through the cold water of the sea. Andrea lowered her head against Jefferson's shoulders for protection, and her long, ebony hair streamed out behind her, unfurling in the wind. She felt an exhilaration entering her lungs with each breath of salty air that she inhaled.

Monarch continued on his murderous race until the strip of sandy beach disappeared into the hillside. Only as he began to climb the steep path at the opposite end of the beach from where he had entered did the horse begin to slow down. Monarch seemed to know the path by instinct, climbing steadily upward, his labored breathing disturbing the solitude of the oncoming night.

And then Jefferson finally pulled upon the reins and let the horse pause.

"Come here," he commanded her as he slipped from Monarch's dark back and helped Andrea do the same. His arms slipped around her waist, and for an unsteady moment brushed against her breasts. She felt the air whisper in her lungs at his light touch, and quickly he released her to touch only the tips of her fingers with his.

They left the horse to nibble at a few blades of grass that had surfaced in the sandy soil. Jefferson led Andrea to the edge of the cliff. He stood next to her and let his arm drape loosely over her shoulders as he pointed out the winking lights of a passing ship on the horizon.

"I used to stand here…in the summer, on this very spot, and watch the ships against the sky," he admitted roughly.

"Why?"

He snorted in self-derision, as if he hated to answer. "I was always hoping that my father would be on the next ship. He never was." Seemingly embarrassed, he shrugged his shoulders as if to dismiss his thoughts.

Andrea felt her heart turn over, and involuntarily she leaned closer to Jefferson. Never would she have imagined that he had ever felt the pain of loneliness. The sun had settled into the clear waters of the calm Pacific, and vibrant colors ranging from deepest amethyst to brilliant orange illuminated the night sky and reflected against the sea.

Andrea felt a strange tremor pass through her body as Jefferson's hands, gentle but persuasive, rotated her shoulders, forcing her to face him. In the depths of his gaze she found smoky passion. "Andrea," he murmured against the night before letting his head dip lower to hers. His voice was rough with an emotion that was foreign to him, and his fingers nearly trembled as he reached up to cup her chin.

Her eyes, full of innocence and longing, looked deeply into his, pleading to understand him. Her lower lip quivered in anticipation and fear, and she wetted it unconsciously with her tongue. Her provocative gesture made him close his eyes for a moment and hesitate slightly. And then, tenderly, expertly, with a flaming passion that he thought had been lost with his youth, he pulled her tightly against him. His lips, tasting of salt, brushed tentatively against hers, teasing her with a promise of higher, more savory delights. She answered by letting her head fall backward in surrender. Her long thick hair tumbled over his arm as his lips pressed desire and possession upon hers. As if by instinct she let her mouth open to him in a shuddering sigh.

"Oh, God," he whispered, pulling his mouth from hers and holding her breathlessly against him as if nothing could make him take his arms away. "I must be out of my mind."

Gently he released her and took a step backward, as if to put distance between their aching bodies.

"Is something wrong?" she asked, wide-eyed and innocent.

He seemed almost angry as he kicked at the sand and ran his hand roughly against the back of his neck. A breeze ruffled his hair, but couldn't erase the grim, determined set of his jaw or the blazing passion in his gaze. "No… nothing's wrong," he snapped back sarcastically. "Here we are, all alone on the island, and you couldn't be more than twenty, and all I can think about is seducing you. Now what could be wrong with that?" he asked rhetorically and added a contemptuous curse, aimed violently at himself.

"Nothing," she answered honestly. "There's nothing wrong with it."

"I don't think you understand, Andrea," he replied, coming more closely to her. He touched her arms with his warm fingers, at first lightly, but suddenly possessively. "From the first time that I laid eyes upon you, back in that amphitheater at U.C.L.A., I've *wanted* you, needed to make love to you. All my interest in your brother was only an excuse to find you, to *have* you. God, Andrea, I thought I would go crazy with wanting you." He closed his eyes with his confession, and his fingers dug into the soft flesh of her upper arms. "It's as if I can't rest until I make love to you—forever."

Her smile was wistful, knowing, and it seemed to antagonize him further.

"Don't you hear what I'm saying?" he demanded, giving her a short shake. "I'm trying to tell you that I followed you up here with the express purpose of seducing you. I…I want to sleep with you!"

"I know."

His eyes rolled upward to the heavens, and he shook his head in frustration. "Then why did you come with me?" he asked. "Do you enjoy torturing me?" His breath, laced with the sweet flavor of wine, fanned her face, and she let her eyelids droop as she leaned against him.

"I'm not torturing you."

"Oh, God, Andrea," he moaned, slipping his arms gently around her small waist and holding her breathlessly against him. "If you only knew." His words, spoken in a prayerlike manner, ruffled against her hair. The purple shadows of twilight began to settle restlessly against the hillside, and only the shimmering half-moon kept darkness at bay.

"I understand," Andrea murmured.

"You couldn't possibly. You don't know what you're saying."

Oh, yes I do, she thought to herself, but you're not listening, Jefferson. *I'm saying that I love you.* Andrea felt her heart hammering wildly within the confines of her rib cage, and she knew that her blood was coursing through her veins more heatedly than ever before. She experienced a warm melting sensation curling within her, struggling to be set free.

"I do know...." The air rang with her honesty.

The space between them became thick and heavy with unspoken words. Andrea could hear Jefferson's heart thudding, pounding deeply in his chest, and she felt the rigidity of his self-control begin to melt as it slipped from him.

His lips, burning with need, found hers. His tongue, tasting of sweet maleness, rimmed her lips and tenderly probed the warm invitation of her mouth. Andrea's thoughts began to swim, and she felt her knees weaken as Jefferson pulled away from her. He watched her face in the silver moon glow, his questioning gaze driving into hers, searching for any shadowing of doubt that might flicker in her trusting eyes. He found none.

"Andrea, I want you so desperately," he groaned, closing his eyes and gritting his teeth against the rising fire in his blood. "But—" his eyes opened with renewed resolve "—I need to know that you want me, and that you understand what this means to me, to us."

She hesitated only slightly, and then, while her misty green gaze was still woven with his, she disengaged herself and stood. Then she drew her hands upward to rest at her neck. With quivering fingers she slowly loosened the small satin ribbon that held the loose bodice of her halter in place. Her gaze never left his eyes as the thin fabric dropped and she felt the cold embrace of the sea air against her bare skin.

Jefferson stiffened and took a step backward to gaze at her. Her skin seemed pale and innocently soft in the silver moon glow. The dress had fallen to her waist, and her breasts, softly rounded and unrestrained, tightened in the cool air. The wind swept her long, raven hair away from her face as she stood on the ledge over the blackened Pacific.

"You don't know what you're doing," he muttered through tightly clenched teeth.

The blush that started at her neck colored her cheeks, but her eyes met his calmly. "I do."

Jefferson swallowed with difficulty. "Andrea," he whispered, casting her name over the waves, "I don't think…"

"What?"

The innocence of her question reached to the deepest core of him. A tortured expression clouded his face. "Look, Andrea, I'm sorry, I should never have brought you here. I don't know what's gotten into me…."

The color drained from Andrea's face when she finally understood what he was saying. He was rejecting her. He had brought her up to the ledge to tease her, nothing more. He probably had lots of women, much more sophisticated and mature than herself. All his tender words had been empty and meaningless. As the realization hit her, a look of horror widened her eyes and tears began to burn behind her eyelids. She lowered her gaze in order to avoid the direct intensity of his eyes, and her fingers fumbled with the bodice of her dress. Her movements were unsure as she tried to retie the satin ribbon around her neck.

Jefferson's voice was husky but calm. "Let me help you with that…."

"No!" He had started toward her, and she wrenched away from the touch of his fingers against her neck. She tried to muffle a sob and failed.

"Andrea?"

She turned her back to him and closed her eyes, vainly willing her tears to stop. She didn't want to cry, but the pain of his rejection was as sharp as a knife twisting in her heart. Her small shoulders shook in her attempts to control the sobs that were threatening to explode.

"Oh, God, Andrea," Jefferson sighed. She stiffened. The last thing she wanted was his pity. "I'm sorry."

"For what?" she tossed out shakily. "For bringing me here to your lonely retreat? For trying to seduce me? Or…for failing?"

"What?" He seemed sincerely confused.

"You know what I mean," she accused, astounded at the bitter sound of her words. Her ragged emotions and anger finally got the better of her. "This was all some sort of game to you, wasn't it?"

"Andrea, no…."

"And I was stupid enough to fall for it. You brought me up here just to embarrass me, didn't you?"

"What are you talking about?" he asked, clearly stunned.

She spun to face him, swallowing back her tears. "I'm talking about the fact that I'm Martin Monroe's younger sister, and you're using me to get back at him!"

"I would *never* use you, don't you know that?"

"Then I guess I don't understand what's happening

between us. I thought—I thought that you wanted to make love to me," she whispered, her voice catching.

"I did. I *do!*"

"But then why?"

Jefferson's voice was thinly patient. "Andrea, I was trying to control myself."

"That much was obvious. It wasn't very hard, was it?" she countered angrily, and hating the spiteful sound of her voice. Her emotions began to overtake her, and she wanted to lash out at him for rejecting her. She knew that she was being unfair, but she didn't care.

"It might have been the hardest thing I've ever done in my life," he admitted in a hoarse, self-condemning whisper.

"Don't," she cried, trying to stem the flow of tears down her cheeks. Why was he torturing her so? "I…I don't want to hear it!" As if to escape from anything else he might say, Andrea turned and began to run down the path that was parallel to the ledge. She knew that she was being irrational, but she had to get away from him. She needed to put some space between them, to think and sort things out for herself. She heard the thudding sound of her own footsteps in the sand, the pounding of her heart, the crashing of the waves along the shore, and from somewhere nearby Monarch's soft nicker. There was another sound as well. Jefferson was following her. Her feet skimmed over the sandy trail until they caught on an exposed root. She started to fall, but Jefferson's arms, strong and powerful, caught her as she stumbled. Together they fell to the ground.

"Dear God, Andrea," he whispered, "what do you think of me?"

Her voice was raspy and breathless both from her sprint

and the intoxicating nearness of the man holding her. "I don't know what to think."

One of his fingers reached upward and brushed a silvery tear from her cheek. His face twisted into a frown of repentant pain, and with a moan of surrender he buried his head in the tangled strands of her hair. His hot breath against her bare shoulders warmed her flesh and forced a sigh from her lips. "Dear Andrea," he murmured, "what am I going to do with you?"

Love me, she pleaded silently as his lips moved down her forehead to her eyes. He tasted the salt of her tears, and once again an unknown anguish contorted his features.

"Don't cry, sweetheart," he pleaded, and the hot persuasion of his lips found hers. "Don't ever cry for me." He kissed her again on the lips, and his tongue gently eased into her mouth. Sparks of liquid fire leapt through her as his tongue found hers and molded against it. She felt the weight of his torso against her breast, the crushing ecstasy of his arms around her and the soft, cool sand against her back.

She wound her arms around his neck, enjoying the warm sensations flowing through her. She didn't resist when his hands found the ribbon supporting her dress and untied it. He pulled his lips from hers as he slowly, seductively lowered the bodice to once again expose the full ripeness of her straining breasts. As his eyes seared a path over her skin and down her throat to gaze at the beauty of her nakedness, she felt her nipples respond. A blush of excitement and shyness tinged her skin, giving it a rosy glow in the twilight.

With a groan of pleasure Jefferson surveyed her. His lower body lay across hers, and his stiff arms held him away from her, enabling him to embrace her with his eyes. If he had any doubts about the sanity of the situation, he cast them aside, secure in the excitement and surrender he found in her mystifying gaze. Still supporting himself with one hand, he lazily reached forward. One strong, male finger drew an imaginary line from the hollow of her throat down to linger on her breastbone. The movement was slight, but Andrea felt as if he were controlling her entire being in the tiny, slow circles he drew against her skin. Just when she thought she would cry out with her aching need, his fingers traveled up the swell of her breast to tease and fleetingly touch her nipple.

A soft moan came from somewhere in the deepest reaches of her, and she knew that her hands were working on the bottom of his shirt, tugging it out of the waistband of his jeans. He pulled the shirt over his head and cast it somewhere in the night. Her fingers moved up his silky arms, revelling in the taut, corded muscles of his shoulders. She touched him boldly, as she had never touched a man before. Her palms were flat as she rubbed the firm muscles of his chest and traced the outline of hair around his male nipples.

In response he lowered his head and captured one of her nipples in the warm, soft cavern of his mouth. Involuntarily Andrea sucked in her breath, and dizzying sensations of pleasure swept through her entire being. She held on to his head, pressing him ever more close to her. Her thoughts were distant and vague, and she was aware only of the warm, glowing sensations he was creating within her. She wanted the magical moments never to end. *I love you,* she thought desperately to herself. Dear Jefferson, if only I was brave enough to tell you that I love you.

She felt his hands move over the fabric of her dress, kneading pleasurable circles of passion against her bare legs. The light cotton fabric that separated her flesh from his added to her bittersweet torment as it was pushed and molded against her hips.

"Love me, Jefferson," she pleaded into the night. He paused only slightly, and that was to look into the pale green depths of her eyes. He saw no fear, only honesty and simmering, undeniable passion.

"Oh, yes, little one. Let me love you as no one has before."

His hands, which had crept up the hem of her dress to lovingly touch her thigh, stopped their seductive motion at her response.

"No one has ever…"

"What do you mean?" he asked quietly, pressing a gentle kiss to her temple.

"I mean that this is the first time," she sighed. "Does it matter?"

He regarded her silently, but the passion remained in his eyes. "Are you sure?" he asked. "Are you sure this is what you want?"

"Oh, yes, Jefferson, oh, yes." She pulled his head back to hers and opened her mouth in sweet invitation.

"I must be out of my mind," he said aloud, but the passion of the girl lying seductively on the sand and the warm, late-summer night overshadowed his reason. His hands resumed their enticing exploration, and Andrea felt a white-hot lava begin to burn in her.

She reached for the button of his jeans, and soon they were both naked in the night, their bodies touching, caressing, embracing in the moon glow. A light dusting of perspiration created a smooth film over them, and when Jefferson moved over her, Andrea was breathless in anticipation. She felt the gentle nudge of his knee parting her legs, and sighed in relief as he settled himself against her.

Slowly, gently, forcing himself to be in control, Jefferson entered her. She gasped at the twinge of pain, but his steady rhythm eased her through the first uncomfortable spasm and pushed her into warm, liquid union. His mouth never left hers, and his hands continued their uncompromising kneading of her body. She found herself blending with him, encouraging him with her hands. His hot body over hers and the cool sand beneath her touched her skin. She felt hot licks of flame bursting within her while her breath came in short, quick gasps, and as his motion quickened, so did her response. The ache grew and consumed her until at last Jefferson pushed her over the brink of yearning to satisfaction and she moaned quietly beneath him.

The sounds of the night seemed to be amplified to her as afterglow settled upon her. The waves below them, her hammering heart, Jefferson's erratic breathing, all seemed to weigh against her.

"Do you have any idea how beautiful you are?" Jefferson asked, stroking a strand of black hair out of her eyes.

"Tell me."

"It would be very easy to fall in love with you," he admitted. "Too damned easy."

Andrea sighed contentedly and pressed her body more closely to his. Everything seemed right with the world.

THAT WAS HOW IT HAD ALL started, Andrea mused idly as she regarded her empty glass. It had been nearly ten years ago, and she could still visualize those warm, seductive summer nights filled with lovemaking and the brilliantly hot, cloudless days of walking on the beach. She remembered laughing into each other's eyes, running from an occasional rain shower, sleeping soundly in the cradle of

Jefferson's strong arms. Was it as romantic as it seemed? Or had her memory been colored with the passage of ten long, lonely years? Had it been a special, magical time, or was she the victim of her passion?

The sound of Jefferson's footsteps broke through her pensive thoughts, and she pulled her eyes from the empty glass toward the door. His anger seemed to have disappeared for the moment, and his eyes, though wary, held hers in a commanding but friendly embrace.

His dark hair was still wet, evidence of a quick shower, and, for a moment, Andrea was mesmerized by his bold features. In one hand he carried a tray of food—cheese, bread, pieces of ham—and in his other hand he held a pair of slippers that had to be at least four sizes too large for Andrea's small feet.

"This is the best I could do. I'm not really prepared for visitors here," Jefferson stated half-apologetically as he set the tray of food on a nearby table and handed Andrea the worn, scruffy slippers.

"Everything looks fine to me."

"Are you hungry?"

"Not really," she admitted with a weary sigh.

"Tired? Or just too nervous to eat?" he guessed, as he cut a thick slice of ham, and offered her a makeshift sandwich.

Her eyes raised to his. "You have to admit, this isn't exactly a normal situation."

He smiled in spite of himself. "I guess you're right. I knew that Bryce Cawthorne, cuss that he is, would find some way to get at me. He doesn't exactly lie down and die when you give him no for an answer. But I never, not in a thousand years, would have guessed that it would be you he'd send to track me down. Especially on a night like this."

"Then you did expect someone?"

His smile pulled into a frown. "I knew that Cawthorne would find a way to try again."

Andrea took a bite of her sandwich. "So you think that he's persistent?"

"At the very least! What I didn't realize was that he would be able to get *you* to go along with him. For one thing, I thought you knew me better than that. Why would I consent to an interview...especially now?" He grimaced at the thought, and his eyes narrowed suspiciously. "I should have expected something like this from Cawthorne...but then, I didn't know that you worked for him." His eyes impaled her. "I didn't have a chance to keep up on your whereabouts." He set the remainder of his sandwich aside. "Did I?"

"That was the way you wanted it," she reminded him.

"I don't think so." He sat on the floor and leaned against the chair where she sat, curled in his warm robe. He stared into the fire.

"Don't you remember?" she asked hesitantly. The light mood in the room had changed. She could sense that Jefferson was baiting her, deliberately leading her into the past, and she knew that it was dangerous emotional territory he intended to dissect.

"Why don't you give me your version of the story," he suggested in a rough, deep voice.

"The story?" she repeated innocently.

"Don't play games with me, Andrea. You're a big girl, now...sophisticated. Don't pretend to be the naive innocent you once were. I wouldn't believe it! You know what I'm talking about." His narrowed eyes seemed to study the flames that shadowed his face. "I want to know exactly how you interpret our final days together, and just what happened between you and me."

"You know very well," she replied, her throat constricting and her words raspy. He reached for his drink and as he swirled the amber colored liquor he looked listlessly into the small whirlpool he had created.

"Do I?" he prodded. "Why don't you explain it to me?"

At that precise moment Andrea knew the feeling of fear that must have come over each witness who had been called to the stand for cross-examination and interrogation by Jefferson Harmon, the lawyer. Although he seemed dispassionate and lost in thought, Andrea knew instinctively that he was coiled, patiently waiting to trap her. He would encourage her to say just the wrong thing, and then he would pounce mercilessly upon her.

Her silence encouraged him to speak quietly to her, and the seductive ring of his voice against the low howling of the wind made her stomach knot in dread and her breathing become labored.

"Come on, Andrea, you remember, don't you? It was late in the fall, you had already gone back to school, and the election was just over, isn't that right?" He didn't wait for her to respond. He could feel her strained composure electrifying the air. "Wasn't that about the time that Martin found out about us?"

She closed her eyes, vainly trying not to recall the angry, embarrassing scene with Martin and her parents. It seemed so far away. "I guess so," she stammered breathlessly.

"You know so!" Jefferson blasted, and then, in a softer voice, "Would you like another drink?" The question was sudden, jarring Andrea from her uncomfortable reverie, and the pain of those half-forgotten memories came crashing around her.

"Yes...thank you," she murmured politely, wondering

how she could change the course of the intimate conversation. She didn't want to remember the humiliation, the rage, the agony again. Only the bitterness that had forced her away from Jefferson would resurface.

Jefferson strode over to the bar, and just as he was pulling out a bottle with an expensive label, he paused dramatically. "That's right!" he said, almost to himself, as if a sudden thought had struck him.

Andrea rose to the bait. "What?"

"I remember now, it *was* in November, about this time of year. The election was over, I was a senator, or would be in January, and your brother, Martin, was visiting you at U.C.L.A. He'd just completed basic training at the time!"

Andrea swallowed with difficulty. "Jefferson…don't," she pleaded, watching his disciplined theatrics with increasing horror. Dear God, he's enjoying this, she thought desperately to herself, he's actually enjoying dredging all of this up again!

"Don't what?" he shot back at her, pouring a stiff drink and walking back to hand it to her. "Don't talk about the past?" he asked levelly, watching her blanched face. "Don't bring up the subject of that pitiful excuse you call a brother?" he demanded. Her eyes darkened in rage and began to fill with tears. "Or don't remind you of the fact that you left me high and dry, all alone, to face your family, the other members of the senate…and the press?" His mouth had hardened into a tight, drawn line as he remembered the loneliness and shock he had felt when his affair "with a left-wing radical war objector" had splashed across the headlines coast to coast.

Jefferson ignored Andrea's outstretched hand and set the drink on the nearby table with such a force that some of the liquid sloshed onto the table, blurring the print of an open newspaper and smearing an image of Lara's face. Jefferson's grimace hardened.

"I didn't mean to hurt you—or anyone," Andrea attempted to explain, closing her eyes as if to shut out the pain.

"Then, why, Andrea? Why did you lie, and for God's sake, why did you run away from me? If only I could have talked to you!"

The torment in his voice pushed her deeper into her despair. "I, I couldn't face you. I couldn't face anyone. Can't you understand that? I was only twenty years old!" Andrea cried. "Dear God, Jefferson, how could I face you?" she asked, the tears beginning to stain her cheeks. She let them run, unashamed of the emotions they so poignantly displayed.

"Then why did you lie to Martin?" he persisted, forcing himself to look away from her anguished, tear-stained face. He couldn't let her get to him—not again. It would be too damned easy to hold her, to caress her, to kiss back those tears.

"I didn't lie! Not to anyone!"

Jefferson bit at his lower lip and studied her ruefully. "Then why don't you tell me what happened when Martin got out of basic?" Feeling himself getting caught up in the emotions he had purposefully buried, Jefferson silently cursed himself. Unfortunately Andrea's emotional performance was getting to him, no matter how much he attempted to dissuade himself. He damned himself mentally, knowing that he had always been weak where she was concerned. Why had he even let her into the house tonight? She was destroying all of the walls of bitterness that he had built to surround himself for the past ten years of his life, and he knew instinctively that with the collapse of those walls would go all his self-control and restraint. He reminded himself that no matter what, he couldn't trust her…not again…not ever!

"It…it was a difficult period," she began, her dry throat burning with raw feelings that threatened to strangle the words of explanation that she had begun to whisper. Jefferson's cool hazel eyes never left her face. "Martin came to see me…of course he hated the army. He had orders to Vietnam." She sighed wearily. "He was frightened, and appalled that my father wouldn't condone his desertion. Martin wanted to come up here to Canada and apply for citizenship, but my parents had both suffered through World War II, and they thought that he was being disrespectful to his country—a traitor."

"So what did that have to do with us?"

"You have to remember that Martin blamed the country, or, more specifically, the politicians for the war." Andrea's shoulders sagged at the memory, and a painful shadow crossed her pale green eyes. To Jefferson she was incredibly alluring, and he felt his heart twist for her. Was she really suffering or was it a well-practiced act? he wondered silently.

Andrea's voice was barely a whisper as she continued. "He found out that I had been seeing you, and, although I never admitted it, he surmised that we had been sleeping together." Andrea's memory flashed, and she saw once again the look of shock and disgust on Martin's face when he realized that his accusations were true. And something else had registered in his eyes—was it satisfaction?

"He thought that we'd slept together? Did you try to deny it?"

"No."

"So what happened?"

"First he told my parents." She sighed, remembering the tears of her mother and the stern, ashen face of her disapproving father.

"Martin told your parents?" Jefferson repeated. "Nice guy, wasn't he?"

Andrea's eyes plunged into Jefferson's derisive gaze. Her chin tilted defiantly, and she seemed to collect herself and become cold.

"Is that why your parents called me?" he asked, aware of the stiffening of her spine and the proud toss of her hair as she shook it out of her face.

"I…I guess so."

"But that's not all of it."

"No. He had a friend, an editor for a left-wing campus paper, and Martin told him about our affair."

A rage, deep and primeval, started to flame within Jefferson. His lips compressed into a thin white line as he continued to question Andrea. "What else did Martin tell his *friend?*" he asked slowly, his hoarse voice threatening to explode.

"You know the answer to that!"

"I want to hear it from you!"

Andrea drew in a shaky breath and closed her eyes, as if she wanted to hide from the truth. "He told his friend at the paper that—that I had been pregnant."

"Go on."

"And—and that I had been forced to have an abortion…" she admitted as a sob ripped through her words.

"And that I forced you?"

"Yes…yes, because of your career and my…no, my brother's political leanings!"

Jefferson came over to the chair in which she was

nestled. He put each of his hands on an armrest, imprisoning her within the aged leather as if he expected her to attempt to escape. His angry eyes roved restlessly over her face, calculating her emotions, before resting in the depths of her green gaze.

"But you weren't pregnant, were you?" he asked slowly, trying not to shout out the question that had stolen so many nights of his sleep.

She shook her head negatively, allowing the sweep of her ebony curls to brush against the pale whiteness of her skin. "How did you know?" she whispered.

"I thought I knew you well enough, and I hoped that if you had been carrying my child, you would have had the decency to tell me about it. What I didn't expect was that you would leave me hanging, avoiding me, letting the press conjure up anything they so pleased about us!" He rose from the chair, trying to assuage the intimacy he felt every time he was near to her. He attempted not to see the soft invitation of her eyes or the dusky hollow between her breasts, partially exposed by the overlapping lapels of the robe.

Andrea was expecting the next question, but when it came with such unmasked vengeance she felt her confidence ebb from her. "Why did Martin lie, Andrea?"

"I don't know."

"But surely you have an opinion. You can guess."

Again she shook her head, trying to dispel the agonizing image of her brother as he had been then: young, loud and full of hate. And she tried not to dwell on his image today or the jagged, white scar that cleaved his once-handsome face. "Who can tell?" she asked rhetorically. "It's been ten years, Jefferson. I don't know what he thought or what he was feeling. Maybe he thought that somehow you could help his cause, keep him out of the war. Perhaps he thought that you could use your influence to help him."

"He knew how I felt. I had answered his letters. There was nothing I could do!"

"Well, then, I don't know. Perhaps he thought that if he drew attention to your situation, something would prevent him from going to Vietnam."

"That's crazy!"

"He was scared, damn it!"

Jefferson halted his scathing reply and took a swallow of his drink. He looked once to the floor and then at Andrea's downcast head. His voice, full of suspicion, was flat and emotionless. "Did you put him up to it?"

Andrea's lowered eyes flew to Jefferson's face. "Of course not! I didn't want anything to do with it—with any of it. I couldn't believe what he'd done!"

"And yet you stand up for him now?" Jefferson's lips curled in disgust. "After he used you—used us!"

"He's my brother!"

"He's a jerk!"

"Oh, Jefferson, don't—"

"Why not? It's the truth! That bastard of a brother of yours told lies, vicious lies about you, went AWOL to disgrace your family and nearly ruined my reputation as a member of the senate. What else could you call him? I don't doubt that he was scared, Andrea, but a lot of us get scared, and we don't lash out at everyone or everything. He had no right to try and destroy any of us!" Jefferson threw out, vehemently. His gaze knifed through her. "And what about you. Why did you run away?"

Andrea's oval face drained of color. "I couldn't face you. I couldn't face another argument, another confrontation about Martin," she whispered.

"So you hid!"

Andrea remembered the reverberation of her father's voice, the look of utter humiliation in her mother's blue eyes, the shaming knowledge that she had wounded them both irreparably. "My parents enrolled me in a private school in Oregon," she sighed. "They wanted to shelter me from the press, to avoid any further scandal."

"I don't doubt that. The article in that left-wing, radical college paper somehow made it to the national press, and I can bet who was responsible for that. Oh, yes, your brother did quite a job on us, didn't he?" he suggested as his eyes darkened with a boiling wrath. Andrea found it hard to meet his demanding stare as he continued to speak.

"And why didn't you call me?" Jefferson asked suddenly.

"My parents...didn't want me to see you again."

"And you agreed?" he asked, incredulous.

"I had no choice!"

"You hid, Andrea! You hid behind the lies that your brother contrived!"

"No, no, you don't understand!"

"You bet I don't!" His large fist crashed against the gray stone of the fireplace. "How can you possibly sit there and try to defend your brother after all of the cruel lies that he told about you and me? Don't you remember the public embarrassment that you suffered...that I suffered?" Jefferson asked, accusingly, his voice harsh and his dark eyes knowing.

Andrea's defiance tightened her face. "That's what this interrogation is all about, isn't it?" she charged. "Your main concern at the time, as well as now, was your reputation, your public standing. Martin was scared, worried for his life, and all you could see was that he was tarnishing your image as a public figure! This entire argument is about your career, isn't it?"

His voice was low, deathly quiet, as he tried to hold on to the remnants of his patience. "It has nothing to do with my career," he growled, the intensity of his words slicing through the air. "If I had cared so much about my career, would I have ever resigned as governor?"

"That was different!"

"How?" The question thundered from his voice and echoed in the rafters.

"Because of your *wife.*" Andrea stammered, feeling her pulse jumping and her nerves beginning to stretch to the breaking point.

"My *wife?*" he whispered callously, and his gaze moved involuntarily to the sodden picture on the end table. He shook his dark head sadly, for a moment lost in thought. "My wife wasn't the cause of my decision to withdraw from public office!" Contempt distorted his arrogant features as the firelight shadowed his intense gaze. His deep voice lowered an octave. "I thought you knew me better than that," he whispered, leaning against the broad mantel of the fireplace. "But then, I've been wrong about you before."

"What's that supposed to mean?" she breathed.

"It means that I thought you were stronger than you actually proved to be. It means that I expected you to stand by me, to publicly refute the lies that your brother propagated. But, no. You couldn't handle anything that tough, could you? You left me to stand alone. The fact that you ran away only added fuel to the fires of gossip!"

"I was only twenty years old!"

"You weren't a kid, Andrea. You were a mature *woman!*"

Andrea felt the truth of his words pierce her, and all of the excuses that she had made for herself seemed feeble and weak. "My parents…they wouldn't let me see you," she repeated. "They wanted to protect me from you. They were afraid of the press."

"This has nothing to do with your parents!" Jefferson interrupted, his hot words knifing through the air. "This only involves you and me!"

"Then why do you insist on bringing up Martin?" she shouted back at him, her raw emotions reflected in the raspy, desperate tone of her voice. "Why do you continue to badger me about him?"

"Because I have to know!"

"*What? What* is it that you want from me?"

His voice was dangerous when he responded. "I want to know how on earth you can still call him your brother after what he did to us?" Jefferson's fingers curled tightly over the drink, and he refused to take his gaze off her face as he finished the warm liquid in one swallow.

Andrea closed her eyes, avoiding his scrutiny. She realized that her shoulders were shaking, but she tried to keep a fragment of her poise. The headache that had been building ever since Jefferson's intense questioning began was throbbing mercilessly at her temples, and Jefferson's dark, unguarded stare pierced her to the heart. Her voice quaked when she spoke. "It's been hard," she admitted, biting the tip of her thumbnail and feeling her breath pass raggedly out of her lungs. "But I've had to forgive Martin."

"Why?"

"So that he could forgive *me!*" she breathed, letting out the incriminating truth.

"I don't understand."

Andrea's eyes studied her glass, looking into the clear

liquid as if seeking the answers to his questions. "Too much time has passed. We—he and I—we had to bury the past." She pressed the cool glass to her lips before finally taking a steadying swallow. She didn't want to think about Martin or his buddies or the anguish and physical pain that he had found during the war. She didn't want to remember how much he had suffered, nor did she want to confess her own sins.

"Because you're older…he's older? That makes what he did right?" Jefferson challenged, sensing deep, heart-wrenching emotions savagely tearing at her.

"It will never be right," Andrea whispered, as if no one was with her in the room. "But then, Martin will never be the same again…not ever."

Jefferson hesitated, seeing the blanched and pained expression that crossed the beauty of Andrea's face. Though she tried to hide her agony, Jefferson's probing gaze sought it out. His dark brows drew together pensively, and he waited for her to explain her enigmatic statement.

"Because of Dad's insistence, Martin eventually went back to the army. Within several months he was sent to Vietnam, to the front lines of the war."

"And?" Why did Jefferson have the feeling that he really didn't want to know the outcome? All the muscles in his body tensed, became wary, as if waiting for some unknown attack on his senses.

"This time Martin followed orders," Andrea stated grimly. "At first he seemed to adjust, at least that's what my folks said. His letters home appeared to be normal." Another sip of bourbon interrupted her story. "But then we got a…military cable. Martin had been injured." Andrea felt tears well within her at the memory. "My parents were frantic. It took nearly a week to get any further information about him. No one seemed to know if he was dead or alive." Andrea paused, and Jefferson felt a weakening sense of dread skitter up his rigid spine. "It was a land mine. According to the army, Martin was lucky—he survived. Several of his buddies weren't so fortunate," Andrea choked out through the streaming tears that fell over her cheeks. She didn't endeavor to hide the wet stains that reflected the glow of the fire. Nor did she try to disguise the guilt that had weighed so heavily on her fragile shoulders.

"His injury was serious?" Jefferson surmised.

Andrea's eyes, shining with pooled tears, probed deeply into his. Slowly she nodded, the words strangling in her throat. When she did speak, her voice was barely audible over the storm. "It's been a nightmare," she confided. "The shrapnel caught him and embedded itself in his right side. Fortunately, the pieces that hit his abdomen and chest didn't penetrate any of his internal organs. He has scars, of course, and his right hand has lost most of its mobility—it's nearly useless, despite several operations. But, but…"

"What?"

Andrea bit at her lower lip. "Oh, God, Jefferson. Martin's *blind!*"

Jefferson stiffened, and Andrea's voice cracked with ravaged emotion.

The strain of the night caught hold of Andrea, and she leaned heavily in the chair. She rested her forehead in her palm, closing her eyes to the black, tormented thoughts that gripped her. Finally, with a self-deprecating smile twisting her pale lips, she continued. "And do you know what the worst part of it all is?"

He waited, not wanting to hear. Something angry in her voice made his dread mount.

"All the while that Martin was over there, in Vietnam, fighting for his country, *my* country, I refused to write to him. Not one lousy letter. Because," she sobbed, tears stinging her throat, "because of the lies and the gossip that he had spread about you and me! I couldn't find the compassion in my heart to even write him one damned postcard!"

"It's not your fault," Jefferson asserted. "You can't blame yourself." He tried to find adequate words to console her, hoping to find a way to lessen the guilt that she had borne on her slim shoulders.

"If only I could believe that," she sighed. "But, I never will. Martin was in a foreign country, fighting a war that no one cared for, and all *I* could think about was my damned reputation!"

Jefferson couldn't take any more. He was beside the chair, and his large, strong hands took both of hers in their tender grasp. "Don't torture yourself," he pleaded, forcing her eyes to meet the kindness and understanding in his.

"I'll never forgive myself."

"You were young. You said so yourself."

"And you pointed out that I was a woman, capable of making my own decisions, my own mistakes."

"We all make mistakes."

Coaxingly he pulled her out of the chair to sit next to him on the floor before the fire. He cradled her gently in the strength of his arms and rocked her softly. "It's all right," he murmured into the thickness of her shining black hair. "It's all right now. You're with me…."

CHAPTER FIVE

IT WAS WELL AFTER MIDNIGHT by the time Jefferson found himself in his bedroom, alone. It had taken him over an hour to calm Andrea and convince her to try and relax. He hoped that she would forget about her brother—at least for a while.

Thoughts, like demons, continued to play in his tired mind. He made a contemptuous sound, directed at himself, as he pulled on his pajama pants and played back all of the words of comfort he had whispered to Andrea in the cozy solitude of the den. The warm, seductive mood cast by the dying embers and the vulnerability of the woman in his arms had brought out tender, caring words of love that he couldn't possibly have meant. Somehow he had been able to calm Andrea, but now he could feel in his body all of the tension and guilt that had been lying dormant in hers. *God help me,* Jefferson thought as he flopped down on the large, oak bed and gazed, unseeing, out the window and into the windy, dark night. The rain had stopped beating against the roof, but still the gusty wind whistled against the interior of the island.

She was still in the shower. Jefferson could hear the hot water gushing through the ancient pipes of the house, and he could imagine the warm, clear rivulets of steamy water as they cascaded over her thick, raven hair to slide caressingly down the naked length of her creamy skin. The wayward thought issued restless stirrings in his body, and the same aching need that had bothered him since he had first seen her standing drenched on his doorstep, assailed him.

Angrily he rolled off the worn patchwork quilt, not caring that the bedclothes were rumpled or that his bare feet encountered the icy chill of the hardwood floor. He paced restlessly, rubbing the back of his neck, before finally resting at the foot of his bed to gaze thoughtfully out of the window at the ghostly clouds crossing the pearl-like moon. The dark clouds, tangled as thickly as Jefferson's conflicting emotions, partially hid the moon and shadowed the island in the murky night. The sandy strip of beach, usually visible even in evening, was imperceptible to the naked eye.

All of the promises that Jefferson had uttered passionately to Andrea while she was lying vulnerably in front of the scarlet embers of the fire came back to haunt him. All of the whispered words of care and affection rang incessantly in his ears. Did he mean them? Could he possibly? After all of the years of doubts and mistrust? How could he fall victim to her so easily all over again? Why couldn't he just forget that she was sleeping in the next room?

A low moan from the pipes made Jefferson acutely aware of the moment when Andrea turned off the water in the bathroom. In his mind, brilliant, vivid flashes of imagination convinced him that she was stepping out of the tiled shower and buffing her body with the thick pile of the cherry-colored towel.

"Stop it!" he muttered aloud to himself, slamming a palm onto the oaken frame of the bed. He was being a damned fool! She had betrayed him once, and she would do it again. Why else would she wait ten years to show up?

In frustration, he threw himself back on the bed, forcefully attempting to drive all haunting thoughts of Andrea from his mind. It had been a long night, full of false promises and soul-searching. First the phone call from Lara, reinforcing Jefferson's concerns over the welfare of his child, and then Andrea, out of the past, out of the night, into his home...like a sea witch.

Andrea pulled on the T-shirt that Jefferson had given her as a substitute for a nightgown. She tried to ignore the smell of it. It seemed to exude that special, clean, virile scent that was uniquely Jefferson's. Andrea closed her eyes for a moment, breathing in the lingering scent, and found herself thinking about Jefferson's warm embrace and the soft commanding pressure of his fingertips against her body.

With a jerk she opened her eyes, discovering that she was blushing at her own image in the steamy mirror. Don't do this to yourself, she cautioned, knowing full well that all of the loving words that Jefferson had whispered to her in the den had only been to calm her. When she had quit sobbing against his shoulder, the gentle words had silenced, and the consoling motion of his hands against her shoulders had slowed. She had sensed that if she would have given him the slightest invitation, the gestures of solace could have heated into passion, and that Jefferson would have made love to her before the fire.

As it was, she hadn't encouraged him, afraid of the outcome, knowing that he would be able to see with his probing eyes what must be so utterly transparent: that she loved him with the same ardor of ten years before. She loved him.

After quickly drying her hair with the towel, she left the creamy-white tiled bathroom and padded, barefoot, into the bedroom that Jefferson had assigned to her. It was large, and the ceiling was comprised of open beams and aged, wooden planks. The walls were rough plaster, colored only with splashy seascapes. The bed, sitting regally in the center of the room, was a massive four-poster, complete with down-filled ticks that seemed to caress Andrea's skin in their lightweight fluffy thickness. This was the first night that Andrea had slept alone in the immense Tudor home, and involuntarily her thoughts rambled to Jefferson's room and the nights of unleashed passion that they had shared together beneath the soft folds of a handcrafted patchwork quilt. Andrea couldn't help but wonder how often he had shared his bed, *that* bed, with his wife.

Don't think about it, she warned herself as she closed her eyes against the soft comfort of the downy pillow. After a few restless moments she drifted off to a fitful, dream-filled sleep in which erotic images of Jefferson sifted through her subconscious.

Jefferson found sleep elusive. His mind, reeling with conflicting thoughts of Andrea and her brother, seemed to throb with contempt for his ex-wife and worry he felt for his daughter, Megan. The crowded images, along with the disturbing knowledge that Andrea was only an unlocked door away, made sleep impossible.

After three hours of frustration, he could stand the charade no longer. The wind had died in the darkness, and the silence in the large house seemed deafening. With anger and hostility aimed primarily at himself, Jefferson threw back the rumpled sheets and quilt and determinedly strode across the room to the doorway. He hesitated only slightly, and then, with his jaw set squarely in determination, he walked down the corridor, his footsteps echoing against the wood. He didn't attempt to quiet his tread; it would have been a foolhardy, useless gesture in his own home. Andrea would soon find out that he was coming anyway.

He opened the door to her room with a jerk, but the old hinges creaked only slightly, and Andrea seemed undisturbed. Jefferson's heart began to thud recklessly against his chest as his eyes became accustomed to the half-light and he could see her face serenely resting upon the pillow. The storm had quieted, and the moon cast a thin stream of silver light through the window. In the dim ethereal glow Andrea rested peacefully, her oval-shaped face surrounded by tousled black hair, a stark contrast to the milky-white pillowcase.

Jefferson reached out and grabbed the doorjamb to steady himself against the wave of emotions that washed over him as he looked down upon her. Resolutely he fought the growing urge to walk over to the bed, throw back the covers and crush her pliant body to his. Why, in heaven's name, after all of the torment that he had suffered at her hand, did he still feel the urgent, pressing need to make love to her? Why did he ache to feel her warm, supple body pressed rapturously beneath his until they were both spent in silkily perspiring afterglow? Earlier in the evening she had been so willing, so yielding against him. He felt the traitorous heat in his loins begin to swell at the vivid memory.

Andrea's dream gave way to wakefulness, and her eyes fluttered open against the darkness. For a moment she was disoriented. The large, unfamiliar bed with its cozy down coverlet was strange. The moon, silver and pale through the lead glass window, and the dull, constant thudding of distant waves crashing relentlessly against the shore were foreign to her. Where was she? Cold air in the room touched the light T-shirt that she was wearing, and she felt her nipples respond and tighten. Involuntarily she hiked the warm, feathery comforter more tightly around her neck, and she moved her head into a more comfortable position against the pillowcase. Still groggy, she blinked and realized that she wasn't alone. Her eyes locked with that of a man standing near the door.

The scream in her throat died before it reached her lips, as conscious, rational thought overcame her and she recognized Jefferson, the elusive lover of her dreams. Her cloudy mind, still drugged with sleep, instantly cleared. Jefferson's hazel eyes, shadowed in the dark room, reached out to her, begged for her understanding. Without breaking his gaze, she read his mind, and she rolled over slightly before pulling the coverlet open and boldly inviting him into her bed. The honesty and promise in her misty eyes assaulted him, but after a moment's hesitation and a great deal of self-deprivation and grit, he slowly inched backward out of the room. His eyes did not leave hers until he shut the door and she was alone again.

Andrea watched his retreating figure silently, and bore his rejection painfully. He was clad only in pajama bottoms, and the stark nakedness of his bare chest, strident with lean, supple muscles, stood out in the semidarkness of the room. When he slammed the door of her room, effectively closing her away from him, Andrea cringed. She was sure that she could hear the clap of the door along with his anger echoing down the long corridors of the ancient house and reverberating in the night.

Jefferson spent the remaining few hours until the light of dawn in restless frustration, torturing himself with thoughts of Andrea. Conflicting emotions ripped him, and one moment he would decide that he could trust the raven-haired beauty, only in the next moment to discard the idea. Although his simmering passion for her refused to subside, he denied himself the pleasure of her bed, and waited impatiently for the long, dark hours of the night to slide toward morning. When the first dim rays of dawn pierced the darkness of his bedroom, he was still without a solution to his aching need for her.

His mind kept reminding him that Andrea was once again obviously setting Jefferson Harmon up for a fall. Why else would she appear on his doorstep so soon after the finality of his divorce, begging to see him? Angrily he remembered that Andrea had left him torn and naked to the world once before…ten years past. At the time she didn't seem to give a damn that he alone had to battle the scandal, including the pressures from both the public and the press. She had never once had the compassion within her to let him know that she was alive…that she was safe.

All of Jefferson's attempts to pursue her had been thwarted, largely by her protective family. Her parents, shocked and shaken at the scandal, had effectively cut off all means of communication between their daughter and her lover-politician. Clay and Sylvia Monroe had been adamant, refusing him entrance into their home, denying his requests to see Andrea again. Although at the time Jefferson wanted desperately to bridge the abyss of misunderstanding that Martin's lies had hewn, it had been impossible. Andrea's parents made it clear that they never wanted their eldest daughter to see Jefferson Harmon again. In their opinion Jefferson was merely a scheming, egocentric politician bent on using and abusing their daughter.

Eventually Jefferson had given up his quest of Andrea, vowing to himself that he would never let another woman touch him or control his emotions with the same intensity as he had allowed Andrea to do. Until last evening Jefferson had been able to keep his promise to himself, but the sight of Andrea again had shaken all of ten years of bitter resolve.

After Andrea had left him, and he had no means by which to find her, Jefferson had decided that he would banish her from his memory forever, or at least until she decided to seek him out. And it had worked, until last night.

So here she was, planted as firmly back in his life as if she had never left him—despite all of his efforts to the contrary. The thought that bothered him more than anything else was the knowledge that he *wanted* her back in his life. But how could he trust her?

The flimsy excuse that her boss had supplied Andrea with didn't wash with Jefferson. There was no doubt that Andrea was sent with a message from Bryce Cawthorne, but there had to be more, much more, to the story. Jefferson had dealt with Cawthorne in the past, and Jefferson knew that the ex-actor, despite his flamboyant Hollywood lifestyle, was not necessarily a gambler. Bryce Cawthorne expected more from Andrea's visit to Harmon Island than one lousy phone call from Jefferson. It was obvious that Cawthorne wanted this interview, and badly. Cawthorne, with or without Andrea's knowledge, was banking on the intimacies of the past affair to aid his cause. Jefferson knew that Andrea's employer assumed that she would be able to persuade Jefferson, by any means possible, to do the interview.

Jefferson's reasoning explained only too well Andrea's willingness to surrender before the dying fire and in the morning darkness of her bedroom. She gave in much too easily. It wasn't that Jefferson doubted the flames of desire that blazed in Andrea's intelligent green eyes. Nor did he discount the fluttering beat of her naked pulse. It was her motives that bothered him and interrupted his sleep.

Although the thought tasted bitter to his mind, Jefferson realized that he no longer knew Andrea Monroe. In the last ten years she had matured and grown up. What kind of woman had she become? Was it possible that she would stoop to anything, including sleeping with a man she didn't care for, just to further her career?

Jefferson closed his eyes and gritted his teeth together in disgust at the incriminating thought. He didn't want to imagine Andrea as a callous businesswoman to whom hopping into bed with a man was all part of a "business deal." And yet, he no longer knew her....

Pushing the bedclothes aside, Jefferson rolled over to sit on the edge of the bed, lost in thought. How desperate was Andrea? How far in debt were Bryce Cawthorne and Coral Productions? Were they really on the verge of bankruptcy, as Andrea had hinted, or did Bryce Cawthorne just smell the opportunity to sell expensive advertising minutes by splashing Jefferson Harmon's life before the American public? Jefferson's eyes narrowed suspiciously as he pulled on his jeans. Moving with swift decisiveness, Jefferson pulled on a work shirt and rolled up the sleeves. He had a lot to accomplish this morning. He had to find a way to probe more deeply into Andrea's mind in order to read her soul. If she really did care for him, that was one thing, but if she was indeed the fraud that he suspected, Jefferson intended to find out about it and expose her for the liar she was. Two could play this game of deception.

Andrea slowly opened a sleepy eye to the invasion of sunshine that was saturating the room with its golden rays.

Groggy, she lifted her head and then remembered where she was…and with whom. The morning air was frigid, and the sheets, when Andrea moved against them, felt like ice. Quickly she slid out of the bed, tugged on the oversized robe and slippers and hurried over to the window to survey the damage of the storm.

From her vantage point on the wooden window seat, Andrea watched the cold gray Pacific, calm after the zeal of the night's tempest. Pieces of debris from the sea had been deposited by the wild tide and were scattered along the sandy strip of beach below the cliff. Closer to the manor, above the rage of the water, fir branches that had broken loose from the trees near the stables littered the grounds, along with small dark shingles that had been torn from the roof of the house by the storm in its fury.

The turbulence of the Pacific Ocean had always fascinated Andrea, and now, as she watched the calm waves belie its wrath, she was once again in awe of its power. The changing face of the sea served to remind Andrea of the varying moods of the volatile yet kind man who resided in the house, the only man that she had ever truly loved.

A disturbance on the beach caught her eye, but only proved to be a slight altercation between two vying seagulls. Shifting her gaze to the left, Andrea found that she was unable, from her window, to see the dock, as it was hidden by a protruding edge of the cliff. She opened the window and craned her neck, but still she was unable to spy the aged wooden pilings or assure herself that the motor launch and the sailor were still docked and waiting for her. Cold sea air, freshened by the scent of recent rainwater, filtered into the room and felt invigorating against her skin.

She squinted against the morning sun as she remembered, hazily, that Jefferson had entered her room sometime late in the night. Her brow furrowed as she wondered if she had misread his intentions. It had seemed evident at the time that he had come into the room intent on making love to her, but something had stopped him. Perhaps in her slumbered state she had been too willing to comply. Perhaps it was too soon after his divorce, but for some unknown reason, Jefferson had rejected her once again. The sting of that refusal still burned hotly in her memory and against her cheeks. A feeling of deep humiliation and embarrassment welled within her as she realized that she and Jefferson had drifted too far apart on the seas of mistrust to ever be able to accept each other again.

Andrea pinched her lower lip against her teeth. It was obvious that she should have listened to the more sensible side of her nature and never have come to the island in the first place. Neither Bryce's requests, nor her own girlish fascination with Jefferson, should have colored her judgment. But they had. And she had succeeded in accomplishing nothing other than baring the disturbing emotions that she had kept safely locked within her for nearly ten long years.

Suddenly Andrea understood that it would have been better for her to have left the island last night, while she had the chance. The stormy sea would have been preferable and much less heart wrenching than the storm of emotions that had battled within her ever since she had looked once again into Jefferson's enigmatic gaze.

Impatiently she closed the window and smoothed the wrinkled bed. Fortunately, she decided, she was leaving the island today, within the hour, and she would be able to put some much-needed distance between Jefferson's compelling magnetism and the traitorous desires of her body. Why was it that her body seemed always to overshadow her mind when she was close to him?

She plumped up a pillow, pulled the tick over it and mentally forced the feeling of disappointment welling within her because she was leaving the island back to a far corner of her mind. Rather than dwell on the unsettling predicament and intense emotions that existed between Jefferson and herself, Andrea cinched the belt of the oversize robe more tightly around her waist and hurried downstairs. For a brief moment she thought of awakening Jefferson, but decided against it. What more was there to say?

Her clothes were still in the den, draped over the fireplace screen, and although they were probably wrinkled, they certainly would be dry and warm. She imagined herself running into the den, tugging on the skirt and sweater and sneaking out of the house before Jefferson's eyes met the morning light. She felt a twinge of guilt at the thought—the least she could do was say goodbye—but she dismissed it. Better to be gone when he awoke rather than face him when the wound of his rejection was still so open and fresh.

Andrea hurried quietly down the hall, past the closed door of Jefferson's room, to the head of the stairs. Hiking the long robe over her ankles, she began to descend the polished rosewood steps. The arguments of the night before pounded relentlessly against her head, and the comforting words of passion and love that Jefferson had murmured into her hair while they lay in an embrace before the fire seemed to haunt her. Andrea knew that she had to avoid Jefferson. All of the caring words, the whispered promises, the loving endearments, were said only to placate her in the darkness, and wouldn't stand the bright light of the new day. She didn't want to bring up everything that he had promised—not now. She couldn't bear to have him feel obligated to her because of some thoughtless promise in the night, and she knew that she couldn't stand the punishment of his denials. She knew that he had uttered words he couldn't possibly have meant, and he knew the same, but she just couldn't stand the thought of *hearing* it spoken aloud—from the same lips that had been so compassionate and forgiving in the night.

She was almost at the bottom of the staircase, her hand poised against the carved banister, when his voice called out to her. At the sound of her name, uttered by the man who meant so much to her, she froze, but after that first arresting, heart-stopping second, she collected her poise and rotated to face him.

Jefferson was standing on the landing above her, casually leaning over the railing, and regarding her with tired but intense eyes. He seemed weary, though he attempted to smile, and she surmised that he had slept no better than she. The flash of his familiar half smile, shadowed in the darkness of an overnight's growth of beard, seemed to welcome her, touch her.

"What are you doing up so early?" he drawled. His hastily donned plaid shirt was rolled up at the sleeves and gaped open, exposing an expanse of muscular, tanned chest and a mat of thick, curling black hair. Andrea moved her gaze from his bare skin upward to meet his direct and inquiring gaze as he continued to speak. "I know," he said with a wink. "You got up early because you wanted to surprise me with breakfast in bed!"

"Dreamer," she laughed back at him. His lighthearted tone was somehow infectious and chased away all of her restless doubts. "You can't be serious."

"Oh, but I am. I always awaken ravenous…or don't you remember?"

Her voice seemed to catch. "It's been a long time," she murmured.

"Too long," he agreed, never letting his eyes move from the feminine contours of her face. Andrea felt the house beginning to close in on her with his shadowed gaze.

"I think that I had better get ready to go."

"Why?" Slowly he began to descend the stairs. She waited, feeling her breath begin to constrict in her throat. "The least that you could do is have breakfast with me." He was standing one step above her, leaning against the banister, whisperingly close to her.

"Oh, Jefferson," she sighed, trying to get hold of her composure. "What's the point?"

"I think we have a lot to talk about."

"We tried that last night!"

"And you don't think we accomplished much?"

"Do you?" Her dark brows lifted as she turned to face him.

"You can't expect to solve ten years' worth of problems in one evening,' he countered, rubbing his chin.

"I don't *expect* anything."

"Then why did you come here?" His voice was low and commanding, and his fingers found the soft flesh of her upper arm. She felt a warmth ooze from her at his touch.

"We went through this last night. I came here as a favor to my boss."

"Cawthorne?" Jefferson asked, his fingers tightening on her arm and a dark, guarded look deepening his gaze. "Do you grant him many?"

His abruptly savage tone startled her. "What?" she asked, hoping that she was misreading him.

"*Favors,* I asked you if you grant many to Bryce Cawthorne."

Her eyes narrowed as she caught the meaning of his words. "What are you suggesting…that I sleep with my boss? Dear God, Jefferson, is that what you think of me?" Angrily she pulled her arm out of his imprisoning hold.

"I don't know you…not anymore."

"So you just automatically think that I sleep with Bryce?" She was incredulous, indignant and incensed.

"Let's just say that it seems more than a little peculiar that you would wait for ten years in absolute silence, not once trying to contact me, and then, the minute your boss asks you to call on me, you jump at the chance." Jefferson leaned back against the railing, crossed his arms over his chest and cocked his head to one side, waiting for her response.

Her lips had thinned with her anger. "That's not exactly how it went."

"No?" His eyebrows raised as if to say, "enlighten me."

"You were married, remember?"

A dark cloud passed over Jefferson's face and wiped away his self-assured smile. "How could I ever forget?"

"I don't think that your wife would have appreciated my calling to chat with you about old times. Do you?"

"Lara has nothing to do with us," he maintained, his face muscles tight with strain. "And besides, what about the two years before I married Lara. Where were you then?"

Andrea shifted uncomfortably on the stairs, and some of her rage seemed to quiet. "I told you. Those two years were difficult for me, for my whole family, because of Martin."

"So you did," was the brief, succinct reply.

"Look, Jefferson," she began, her palms rotating expressively skyward. "I'm not trying to say that I handled the situation very well, but I'm not apologizing for my actions, either. I was too young, and it was a long time ago. Too many things have happened to you and me since then. I'm sorry I came here last night. It was a mistake."

"Do you honestly believe that?" he asked more gently.

The honesty in her light eyes challenged him. "I don't know what to believe."

Jefferson's lips pressed together thoughtfully, and his hand against the railing tapped nervously while he stared at her in ponderous silence.

"Perhaps we should start over."

Her heart stopped. "What?"

"Let's just start getting to know each other again. Today. What do you say?"

The change in his mood surprised her, but there was a wariness in his gaze that stopped the ecstatic surges that had begun to run through her blood. "I'm—I'm leaving soon."

He shrugged dismissively. "Not without eating. How about breakfast?"

The lightheartedness of his banter infected her and reminded her of a happier, more carefree time in her life. "All right," she agreed after only a moment's hesitation. "If you're doing the cooking."

"So much for my romantic fantasy of having breakfast in bed, served by a dark-haired sea witch," he said mysteriously as he took her hand and led her into the kitchen.

"You're living in the wrong century," she chided. "Don't you realize this is the nineteen eighties? You should be the one serving me breakfast in bed."

"Gladly," he replied fervently, and his face sobered.

"I don't think so," she quipped with a laugh that

sounded as false as she felt. The burning sting of his rejection in the moonlight was too painful to be so easily forgotten. She wouldn't give in to temptation again.

The atmosphere in the cheery kitchen seemed to thicken with his probing, watchful stare. She knew that he was reading her thoughts. "I'm sorry about last night," he admitted, noticing the flaming blush on her cheeks.

"It's all right."

"No, I should never have come to your room."

Andrea lifted her chin slightly. "Why did you?" she asked as a trace of indignation lit her pale eyes.

"I wanted to see that you were all right."

"No, Jefferson, that's not the reason that you were there, and we both know it. I don't expect much from you, but I do think that you owe me honesty. It was something we shared together in the past, and no matter what has come between us, I hope that now, today, we can be open with each other.

"The reason that you came into my room last night was because you wanted to make love to me. Don't try to deny it. A woman can read the passion in a man's eyes. But for some reason the minute that I awoke and offered to love you, you changed your mind." Andrea's short speech had rolled off her tongue before she could really consider it. Jefferson had listened, not interrupting her. For a moment the silence was intense and oppressive as Andrea waited for his response.

"It's not a step to be taken lightly."

"I agree."

Again tense silence filled the room while they stood staring at each other. It was Andrea who managed to find her voice and drag her eyes away from the magnetic, enigmatic gaze of the man who still intrigued her beyond the limits of rationality.

"I thought you wanted breakfast."

"I do."

"Then just point me in the right direction, and I'll get started," Andrea suggested.

"I thought you expected me to cook."

Andrea's lips quirked into a smile. "Some other time. For now, why don't you go and get cleaned up, and I'll see if I can fix us some kind of a meal."

"You won't try to run out on me?" he asked pointedly as his fingers scraped against the thick hairs of his chin.

"Promise."

"Good."

In a moment, he was gone and she heard his feet treading overhead. Rather than allow herself to think or puzzle over him and his erratic behavior the night before, she busied herself in the kitchen. It was an immense room, equipped to handle even the most sophisticated of banquets. The countertops were made of cool dove-gray marble, and copper pots swung overhead from exposed beams in the ceiling. A cooking island graced the middle of the room and had the luxury of a small sink inlaid against rust-colored tile. The floor was of polished oak, with only one spot of wear beginning to mar the shiny patina near the sink. Andrea thought that the kitchen, though old, was every cook's dream, and she considered it a pity that it was no longer used to prepare lavish feasts.

While Jefferson was upstairs she put together a decent, if somewhat meager, meal from the leftovers she found in the pantry and refrigerator.

"Efficient, aren't you?" Jefferson noted as he walked into the kitchen and took in the domestic sight of Andrea frying slices of ham.

"Years of practice," she called over her shoulder as she pulled a hot tin of biscuits from the oven.

"You cook like this for yourself?"

"Hardly," was the dry reply. "I barely have time for toast and coffee before I head for the office. It's a forty-minute drive."

They sat opposite each other at the small café table near a bay window. After Jefferson ate heartily, he sipped the strong black coffee and regarded Andrea over the rim of his cup. Even after what must have been a mostly sleepless night, she carried herself with a serene pride that enhanced her natural beauty.

"Do you live alone?" he asked, setting his cup on the table.

"Yes. I had a roommate once, but it didn't work out."

A muscle twitched in Jefferson's jaw. "Why not?"

Andrea shrugged. "Different lifestyles."

"Were you good friends?"

"Not particularly. Why?"

Jefferson frowned into his cup. "Just curious."

"Sally liked to hang out at the singles bars. I didn't. It became a problem, and I moved out." Andrea smiled in spite of herself, noticing the relief evident on Jefferson's face. Once again his eyes were searching her face, studying her intently.

After the dishes were done, Andrea became adamant about leaving the island.

"I've got to go," she stated, heading for the den to pick up her raincoat.

"No, you don't."

"I can't expect the sailor to wait for me all day long, can I?" she asked, pulling the thick curtain of her hair from beneath the collar of the pewter colored coat.

"You don't have to worry about him," Jefferson replied with an indifferent shrug.

"Why not? Do you think he's too hungover to get me back to Victoria in one piece?"

"No."

"Then?" Her question was tossed over her shoulder as she shrugged more comfortably into her coat and hiked the collar closely to her neck. Though the day was filled with shafts of November sunlight, it was still chilly, and Andrea had no doubt that the ride over the water toward Vancouver Island would be a cold one.

Jefferson's arm reached out and found hers before she opened the door. "I sent the seaman home, Andrea."

She whirled on him. "You did *what? Why?*"

"I wanted more time alone with you," he admitted hating himself for his deception and duplicity. Why was he suspicious, and why did he want her so?

"Don't you think you should have asked me first?"

"I didn't want to disturb you."

"Right. Just like you didn't want to disturb me last night?" she accused sarcastically.

His jaw hardened. "I'm sorry about that."

She glared at him for only a minute before jerking free from him, opening the door and running down the sandy path that led from the front of the estate toward the edge of the cliff. Once in sight of the sandy strip of beach she stopped and surveyed the gray tide frothing against the aged wooden moorings. The boat was gone.

She knew that Jefferson was beside her—she could feel his eyes boring into her—but she was angry and afraid. Angry that he had manipulated her, and afraid that being manipulated was exactly what she had wanted and expected of him.

"You should have asked me before you let my transportation leave."

"You're right, but you were sleeping, and the man was in a hurry to be on his way." The lie slid over his tongue easily. Too easily, he thought. But how could he explain to Andrea that he had sent the seaman packing just so that he could gain more time alone with her, to try and understand her, to try and trip her up in her own set of lies?

"But I owed him money."

"I took care of it."

Bewildered, she stared at the dark sea. "And how am I going to get back to Victoria?"

"I'll take you there."

"When?" She found herself wishing that he would say never, but she knew that the sooner she left Jefferson, the better it would be for her.

"I'm leaving myself this evening. I'll take you back then. Is that all right with you?"

"You haven't left me much choice, have you?" she countered.

"Did you really want one?"

"I like making my own decisions."

"Come on," he suggested, ignoring the rebellion in her eyes, "let's take a walk on the beach."

"Now?"

"It's a beautiful morning for it. Why not?"

He touched her lightly on the neck and she felt the anger and indignation of a few moments before begin to flow from her body. He was standing behind her, and his arms closed around her waist. "Come on," he prodded gently, lightly kissing her cheek. "Let's get to know each other again."

CHAPTER SIX

AN UNSEASONABLY WARM breeze pushed Andrea's hair away from her face and pressed her rough skirt against her legs as she walked with Jefferson down the desolate ribbon of sand that served as a weak barrier between the jagged, rocky cliff and the blue ocean. Although she and Jefferson were alone, they walked slightly apart from each other in solitary concentration.

They were nearly to the far end of the beach before Jefferson reached down and picked up a rotten slat of wood on the sand and hurled it back to the sea from which it had drifted. Andrea couldn't help but notice the athletic slant of his body as he tossed the driftwood, nor could she ignore the passionate play of feelings that was evident in the tense, angular planes of his face. Jefferson stopped walking in the wet sand and watched the driftwood float in the foam of the tide before scratching the back of his head. He began to speak softly over the noise of the waves.

"Why haven't you asked me about Lara?" was his surprising question.

Andrea felt her own footsteps falter at the name of Jefferson's beautiful ex-wife. She bit her lip and shrugged her shoulders in feigned indifference. "I don't know. I guess I didn't want to pry."

"Even after the interrogation I gave you last night?"

A rueful smile that didn't light his eyes flickered over his grim lips.

"Some things are better left unsaid, I suppose."

"Meaning that you're not interested?" Jefferson asked, thinking once again of the importance of the interview and Bryce Cawthorne.

"Meaning that I don't want to invade your privacy."

"You, the woman who wants me to do a national interview on television?" he scoffed.

"That's not me. It was Bryce's idea," Andrea maintained, not realizing that she had squared her shoulders automatically at Jefferson's accusations.

"It doesn't matter," he sighed. "I want you to know."

Andrea wondered if there was a way she could escape the intimacy of the conversation. The thought of Jefferson being married to another woman had always caused her pain, and she wasn't sure that she wanted to see more deeply into the secluded and intimate corners of his marriage.

"I'm not sure that you should be telling me any of this," she thought aloud, avoiding his intense gaze.

"Why? Do you intend to run back to Bryce Cawthorne with all the juicy tidbits of information that I give you?"

"Of course not!"

"Good." There was still a flicker of doubt in his eyes, but he pushed his hands into his back pockets and once again began walking, head bent against the wind. To Andrea he looked older and more strained as he began talking about his wife.

"It was two years since I had seen you," Jefferson began, thoughtfully. "I had given up hope of ever seeing you again. The way I figured it, you didn't want to see me, or you would have made some attempt to contact me."

"I told you my parents put me in a private school."

"Save it, Andrea! You were over a thousand miles away from your father and mother. If you really would have wanted to get in touch with me, you could have called or written, for God's sake."

"I wanted to, really." Andrea sighed.

"Then why didn't you?" he demanded.

"I was afraid. My parents told me that you—"

"That I was just a cheap politician interested in taking advantage of you until another girl caught my interest, right?" His voice hardened, and his face muscles became rigid. "They told you that you would never be able to avoid scandal with the likes of me, isn't that so?"

Andrea's silence incriminated her. Jefferson gave his head a stern shake and muttered under his breath, "I thought so. They probably also told you that all I was interested in was a career."

Andrea closed her eyes against the truth Jefferson spoke, remembering her father's rough, uncompromising words about the evils of men and politics. Jefferson's next question startled her.

"Did they ever tell you that I had come looking for you?"

Andrea's footsteps on the sand suddenly stopped, and she turned her eyes upward to Jefferson's. The shocked expression on her face wasn't lost on him.

"I didn't think so," he snorted, and kicked violently at a rock on the beach. Then he looked beseechingly toward the cerulean sky. "Oh, hell, what does it matter anyway?"

Tentatively her hand reached out to touch his bare forearm. "You came to see me?" she asked quietly.

He jerked his arm roughly away from her sensitive touch. "Of course I did, Andrea. Damn it, I'm not exactly the bastard your parents made me out to be!"

"I always knew that."

Disgust was evident in his condemning look. "You couldn't prove it by me!"

Andrea felt her anger beginning to surface. One moment Jefferson was tender, the next unyielding. She felt as if she were caught in the middle of his conflicting storm of emotions. Her patience, worn thin by the depth of her feelings for such an uncompromising man, snapped. She turned on her heel as if to head back to the house. "Look, Jefferson, all of this bickering isn't getting us anywhere. I understand that you feel I ran out on you ten years ago, and I guess you have that right. But what I don't understand is why you continue to bring me up just to push me down. One minute I think that you want to get along with me, the next minute we're arguing again. I'm tired of it, and I'm going back to the house to wait for you. Or better yet, I'll call for a launch to come and get me. That way I won't be of further inconvenience to you!"

"Don't go."

"I'm not about to stay here to suffer any more of your sarcastic remarks about the past. It's over… Let it go!"

"And what about the future?"

"I haven't really given it much thought," she admitted, "other than to worry about my job."

"Is it that serious at Coral Productions?"

"Would I be here if it weren't?" she murmured.

"Now, that's an interesting question," he mused. "What do you think?"

"I don't honestly know." Her clear green eyes clouded with the question.

Jefferson took Andrea's hand in his and urged her to continue walking with him. At first, she made a feeble attempt at resistance, but finally found herself walking near him, letting her shoulder touch his, letting his fingers control hers.

"I was going to tell you about Lara."

She didn't comment, and an uneasy feeling began to grow in the pit of her stomach. She didn't like the easy way his ex-wife's name rolled off his tongue.

Jefferson's mouth pulled into a tight frown as his eyes narrowed in memory. "I met Lara a little over a year after the scandal about us had occurred. At first I thought it was going to be the same type of situation, because the minute that the papers got wind of the fact that I was dating one of San Francisco's socialites, they dredged up all of the business concerning you and me, including the alleged pregnancy and abortion." A muscle that had been twitching near the corner of Jefferson's jaw became rigid.

"Lara must have known about you, because while I was dating her, the gossip sheets were covered with speculations as to what had become of you." Andrea nodded at the memory. Even in the small town of Forest Grove, Oregon, she had seen articles in the papers, and several of her close friends had realized who she was and what her relationship had been to California's youngest and most attractive male senator. Andrea pushed the faded memory aside as Jefferson continued to speak.

"It wasn't that Lara was so fascinating, although at the time we got along. It was the timing that was important, I guess," he said with evident disbelief in his own words. "Anyway, at that time in my career, especially after the national coverage of my romance with you, my campaign manager advised me to change my image, to become more of a conformist, avoid rocking the boat politically. One of his ideas, which I discounted at the time, was that I marry and start a family—establish a more stable personal life that would reflect well on my public image."

"No!" The disbelief in Andrea's voice couldn't be disguised. "You married because it was a politically sound move? I—I don't believe it!"

"People get married for many reasons, Andrea."

"What about love, Jefferson? Isn't that the best reason?"

"I couldn't say—not personally."

"But to further your career—"

"It's no worse than knocking on someone's door in the middle of the night, dredging up old, near-forgotten memories…for the sake of a career, is it?" Jefferson demanded, his fingers tightening around Andrea's hand.

"But *marriage,* Jefferson. You can't possibly compare what I've done in the last few hours to what you did—marrying for the sake of your career!"

"I gave up on believing in love when you left me," he asserted.

Andrea was silent and her stomach was churning as she realized how deeply and irretrievably she had scarred the man that she loved. No words could assuage his bitterness. No explanation would suffice. No embrace could ever erase his disdain for love.

"There's more to it than that, anyway," Jefferson began again, interrupting Andrea's dark thoughts.

"What?"

"Lara. She wanted to get married, was anxious, in fact. I guess it was balm to her frail ego that she could snare an up-and-coming politician. From the moment we were married, she was more interested than I in my political aspirations." He shook his head in disgust. "I even think that she fantasized about being the first lady. Ridiculous!"

His eyes grew darker and looked almost deadly. "It was

a mistake from the beginning. She didn't care for me any more than I cared for her. I suppose that I was as much to blame as she, because when I realized what a mistake I had made, rather than admit it and seek a divorce, I just engulfed myself deeper in my work, my career. For a while it worked. I kept myself busy with political meetings, and she kept up a lively social schedule. It wasn't much of a marriage, but we both kept out of each other's way, for the most part."

"Then what went wrong?" Andrea asked, clearly puzzled.

"She got pregnant."

Andrea swallowed with difficulty. "You didn't want the baby?" she stammered, remembering the lies that Martin had spread about a false pregnancy.

Jefferson smiled sternly. "No, that wasn't the problem. Although the baby wasn't planned, I was really very happy about it, and I thought that Lara was, too. She seemed happy, at first, until she lost her figure to the pregnancy...." Jefferson's dark brows drew together in concentration, as if he were still trying to piece together a puzzle. "I didn't really understand it...not at the time.

"When Megan was born, I was ecstatic. It was the first time that I had ever found any real happiness or satisfaction in the marriage. Lara probably understood that, too. But the more hours I spent with Megan, the more I wanted to have with her. She became the single most important thing in my life—even more valuable than my career."

An inner tension, boiling and threatening to explode, was evident on Jefferson's sharp features. He rubbed his chin thoughtfully, as if trying to calm himself, as he squinted into the horizon. Andrea could feel Jefferson's strain flowing into her, through the warmth of his coiled fingers, and she felt as if she were an unwanted intruder into the dark, private corners of his life. A cold feeling of dread settled against her shoulder blades.

"It doesn't take a doctorate in psychology to understand why Lara began drinking," Jefferson whispered, and Andrea felt a wave of shock ripple through her at the mention of Lara's alcoholism—a condition, never proved but often speculated on by the press. "Although it was never my intention, I neglected her," he admitted. "After the baby was born, everything changed. Lara was still very much in the social spotlight, a privilege that she had always held dear, but she wanted more from me than she ever had in the past, and I suppose she really did deserve more attention. I just didn't realize it, not at the time. All of my love and my attention revolved around Megan, and of course, my political aspirations." He closed his eyes as if he wanted to shut out the truth. "You see, other than Megan, the only other importance I saw in my life was becoming California's governor."

Jefferson and Andrea had come to the end of the narrow strip of beach, and he gently led her up a gradual, sloping path. She didn't speak, not wanting to ask him about his life with his ex-wife and daughter. She was afraid to know, and yet she was very intrigued.

"It was a stupid goal."

"No," Andrea shouted without thought, once again remembering Jefferson as she had first seen him, the incredibly perfect aspiring political contender. Jefferson was *meant* to be a leader.

"I had my priorities twisted," Jefferson continued, ignoring her vehement protest. "I should have looked into my life and found what was valuable. I should have realized what I was doing to Lara."

"It wasn't your fault!"

"No? She wasn't an alcoholic when I met her. I have to assume some of the responsibility of her illness. At that time I did nothing to try and discourage her feelings of inadequacy. Without knowing it I was partially to blame."

Jefferson shook his head in disgust, and Andrea knew that his contempt was aimed at himself. "Suddenly my little world began to fall apart, or so I thought. I should have seen it coming, noticed the warning signals, but I didn't. Instead, what had started out as an acceptable, if stagnant and loveless marriage, had smoldered into a living hell. Lara and I began to fight bitterly. We were constantly at each other's throats.

"Somehow we managed to hide most of the battles from Megan and the press. And it was my opinion at the time that, for Megan's sake, it was better for Lara and I to stay married. And Lara knew it. She thought that I would never want to divorce her because it would reflect badly on my career, but the only reason that I stayed married to her was because of Megan.

"It wasn't long before Lara began taking lovers, but I was so angry about the poor mother she had become that I didn't give a damn who she slept with, as long as she was discreet. My only concern was that Megan would find out, or that the press would get wind of it." Jefferson's eyes smoldered in suppressed rage. "I never wanted either of us—me or Lara—to hurt our child!" He looked prayerfully up at the sky. "I was a fool in that respect. How I thought I could hide anything from the press was a mistake." He shook his head and pushed a wayward lock of dark hair out of his eyes.

"It was during the gubernatorial race that I began to suspect that she had a drinking problem. I was too blind to have seen it before, but suddenly it was very apparent. I found hidden bottles…she was often unclear in her thinking…her speech was thick. Damn!" His palm slapped the worn jeans over his thigh. "If only I hadn't been so wrapped up in my work…in *myself!*

"I suggested psychiatry. She ignored me, and told me that I was being ridiculous. Somehow she managed to pull herself together during the election, and despite a flurry of rumors instigated by the opposition, I was narrowly elected as governor. That's when I made another mistake. I had tried to convince myself that after we had moved into the governor's mansion, and she began practicing the role of governor's wife, she would snap out of her depression and put her bottles and her lovers aside. I was wrong."

"So you decided to resign?" Andrea asked, her voice catching.

"Not quite. I suggested counseling again, but of course, it fell on deaf ears. But then, within a year of taking over the responsibilities of governor, I decided that I had to find a way to overcome her alcoholism, no matter what the cost. It didn't matter that I didn't really love her. I had always cared something for her, and she was Megan's mother—my wife."

Andrea felt herself cringe at the intensity of his words. He was speaking as if he were alone, talking to himself. For a moment he was silent, but finally spoke again, this time posing a question.

"Have you read the clippings about my ex-wife lately?" he asked, a tinge of acrimony touching his words as his eyes sought and found Andrea's gaze.

"Some."

"Then you know that I failed. I tried everything money could buy, from expensive drying-out sessions at secluded hospitals in Marin County, to a private nurse in the governor's mansion. But I was stupid!"

"Why?"

"Because I didn't realize that money couldn't buy Lara's willingness to combat the alcohol. And the worst part of the entire mess was that Megan was becoming increasingly aware that, at times, there was something wrong with her mother! Do you know, can you possibly imagine, what it feels like to try and explain to a four-year-old child that her mother is sick because she drinks too much? It wasn't possible to hide the truth, even if I had wanted to. Megan is a bright child and she could see the effect of the booze on her mother. She could *sense* how deep and traumatic Lara's problem was!" Anger and suppressed rage surfaced on his face, darkening his eyes. "How long could I protect my daughter with feeble excuses and vague answers to her questions?" Jefferson's stony gaze impaled Andrea.

"I don't know..."

"Neither did I! There seemed no way to battle the problem effectively and it was beginning to have adverse effects on Megan. What little family life we had shared together was being destroyed, day to day. The harder I tried to persuade Lara to get help, the more determined she was to fight me, and the more bitter she became." He paused, thoughtfully. "I suppose, in retrospect, that I was a catalyst for Lara's rebellion. For the first time since we were married, Lara was commanding most of my attention. I was paying more attention to her than I was to my career...or even Megan.

"When I realized that everything else I had attempted to do for Lara had failed, in a final effort to save the marriage, I decided to resign the governorship. It seemed to be the right thing, the only thing I could do to protect my family…my child. My turbulent personal life was making a mockery of my responsibilities as governor, and I felt that it was in the best interests of both the state of California and my family to resign and end the speculation and gossip about my family. I had hoped that a more quiet, peaceful life would bring Lara out of her moody depressions and, perhaps, give a more normal, stable existence to Megan. I was foolish enough to believe that it just might work. We certainly had enough money, and I knew that I could always go back to practicing law."

"But the resignation didn't go as planned," Andrea guessed, feeling icy wisps of dread tease her spine.

Jefferson shook his head as if trying to dislodge an unpleasant memory. "It backfired! When I told Lara about my intent to resign, she lost what tenuous control on herself she had maintained. She was livid, appalled that I would even consider such drastic, socially unacceptable action, and she tried her best to talk me out of it. I don't really think that she took me seriously. Not at the time. She wasn't convinced until she saw the actual resignation on television. To Lara, it was the ultimate humiliation, a public admission of my *failure*—a social embarrassment!"

"Oh, dear God," Andrea murmured fervently, seeing all too well in her mind's eye the pain and humiliation that Jefferson had suffered. For a while she and Jefferson walked in silence, picking their way up the overgrown path. Jefferson seemed lost in his own dark thoughts of the past, and Andrea sensed the simmering tension that had taken hold of him with his reminiscence. So intent had she been on his story that she hadn't realized their eventual destination. Now, as she stepped over the final small crest in the hill, she stopped dead in her tracks. Jefferson was leading her to the same fateful ledge where they had first sealed their love, ten years ago. She felt as if all of the air had been driven out of her lungs as her eyes looked over the calm expanse of ocean, just as she had when she was barely twenty. She wetted her lips, hoping somehow to alleviate the parched feeling in her throat.

"You remember?" she asked, in a raw, emotion-filled voice. She lifted her eyes to witness his reaction. Why was he bringing her here, back to the place where all of the love and pain had begun?

The severe smile that curved over his lips didn't reach the hazel depths of his eyes. "Yes," he whispered, pulling her nearer to him, "I remember." For a moment he drew his eyes away from her captivating gaze and looked skyward in supplication as he shook his head. "I've tried to forget," he admitted. "But I couldn't. You don't know how many times I wished I could forget you—hoped that I could erase you from my mind." His whisper was filled with self-deprecation. "You couldn't begin to guess how much I wanted to forget you." At the thought his entire body tensed, and Andrea was pressed forcefully against his long, hard frame. His strong arms wrapped more urgently around her, crushing her against him. "I wanted to forget you," he moaned. "Dear God, how I tried."

Andrea felt as if he were about to say more, to explain his feelings for her, but if so, he quickly changed his mind. His palms spread across the small of her back, pushing every inch of her body against his. They stood on the ledge together, her legs braced by his, her breasts crushed against his chest, his chin resting against her forehead. Andrea could feel his tense muscles against her, warming her in spite of the cool November breeze that ruffled his hair and lifted her skirt.

Andrea floated backward in time on distant memories. The salty air, cool and fragrant, touched her face, just as it had in the past. Jefferson held her impatiently, rigidly against him, the way he had in her dreams. The surf roared in the distance, just as it had when this man had first taken her.

Slowly, as if his thoughts had taken the same path as hers, his grip on her slackened, and his hands came upward to cup her chin. His head lowered, and his lips, cool when they touched hers, quickly heated with smoky desire.

"I want you, Andrea, just as much as I did the night that we first made love." Andrea felt her knees weaken as his lips brushed slowly, seductively over hers in unhurried, lazy strokes. Involuntarily she let her head fall backward, grateful for the feel of his kisses against her face and throat. She sighed into the wind and slowly clasped her hands behind his neck.

His kisses, soft and insistent, moistened a trail down the soft column of her throat to rest where the neck of her sweater barred further exploration. He pinched the sweater between his teeth and pulled it away from her neck, allowing a cool whisp of air to float downward against her shoulders. She shuddered and he released the sweater, only to bury his head between her breasts. His words, torn from his throat to burn against her skin, were muted. "Let me love you again," he pleaded. "Let me make love to you, here, as we did in the past, until we can forget everything else."

It was a plea, and Andrea wanted desperately to give in to him, to recapture all of the beauty and love of the past, if only it were possible. She felt her resistance weaken and her muscles begin to relax in his embrace. He must have sensed her invitation because she felt his breath, hot and damp, against her sweater.

Andrea sighed as Jefferson lifted his head to capture her

mouth with his. Their lips met and molded together in a wet, sweet embrace. Andrea hardly noticed the sensation of falling backward. She was only vaguely aware of the feel of cool sand through her clothing; so intent was she on the feel of the man bending over her, the man pressing her against the ground, the man she had never stopped loving.

A passion she had once suspected of having died began to live in her again. Familiar yearnings, buried for ten years, spread throughout her body, warming her against the early November morning. His lips, erotically familiar, kissed a path of forgotten promises across her cheeks and neck. She felt a new, pulsing warmth in her veins curl upward through her body until a soft, rosy blush colored her skin. Willingly her mouth parted in silent invitation to his insistent tongue, and she felt a shudder of anticipation quake through her as he explored the most intimate regions of her mouth. Her tongue met the passion in his and rose to intimately entangle with it. He groaned as he felt her submission.

"Let me love you," he whispered against her ear, repeating his pleading demand, as he slid the coat, which had been unbuttoned, off her shoulders.

"Jefferson… I…"

"Shh, don't think, just love me," he persisted as he continued to kiss her.

I do, she thought to herself. I always have. Oh, God, Jefferson, if only you could guess how fervently I love you! Her response never got past her lips, because she knew that it didn't matter. It hadn't mattered in the past, it couldn't possibly now. They had no future together. And yet they had today, this morning, right now, beneath the warm Pacific sun.

His lips were persistent as they seemed to melt against her throat. They moved slowly, insistently against her chin. Despite the cowl neck of the sweater, he plunged onward, pulling the warm fabric away from her neck to allow his enticing lips to seek and find the pulse that fluttered deep in the hollow of her throat. His tongue rimmed the delicate circle of bones at the base of Andrea's throat and moved restlessly against the confinement of her sweater.

An aching need began to bloom within Andrea's body. Warm bursts of liquid fire raced through her veins and flooded her senses. The gentle persuasion of Jefferson's hands moving in circular patterns against the small of her back and his hot lips rubbing insistently against the barrier of her sweater began to arouse a yearning that Andrea couldn't deny. Involuntarily she arched against him.

Jefferson pulled his head away from her neck to gaze into the passion-clouded green depths of her eyes. A smile of satisfaction softened the planes of his face. "It hasn't changed for you, either," he murmured. "You want me as much as I want you."

"I've always wanted you," she admitted, saying what she had attempted to deny for ten years.

"You are a witch, aren't you?" His eyes never left her face as he tugged the cashmere sweater from the waistband of her skirt. Slowly his fingers wedged between the soft fabric and her warm flesh. She closed her eyes against the sweet, passionate desire that was growing within her at his persuasive, gentle touch. She sighed contentedly as Jefferson lifted her torso from the ground and pulled the sweater over her head. For a moment their gazes locked, and then he let his eyes move over her partially nude body. He gasped at the sight of her breasts, two softly rounded mounds, pushed together by the filmy white fabric of her bra. He groaned and let his face fall between them, softly kissing the top of one and then the other. His hands pushed the soft flesh more closely to his cheeks as he sighed against her.

Andrea let out her breath, and she cradled Jefferson's head against her as if she never wanted to let go. Her fingers entwined in the thick curls of his hair as she kissed the top of his head and murmured his name over and over.

With agonizing languor his thumbs moved against the lacy fabric of her bra, enticing her nipples to strain against the silky garment. The intimate circles his thumbs created started a whirlpool deep within Andrea, and she felt as if the center of her being was being slowly drawn from her.

Jefferson lowered his head and took the clasp of her bra in one hand. His lips grazed and teased her skin as, slowly and surely, he unhinged the wispy material and the bra parted, letting Andrea's breasts free to feel the cool Pacific air and the heat of Jefferson's torrid breath. He took one soft globe in his hand and kissed it as he kneaded the soft flesh. Torrents of lava singed her blood as he softly took a nipple in his mouth. His tongue caressed it, sliding wetly against the taut, ripe skin.

With his free hand he reached behind her and pushed against her back, pressing the firm muscles forward, thereby thrusting more of her breast into his expectant mouth. It was as if he couldn't get enough of her—as if he wanted to devour every inch of her. His tongue stroked and teased at her breast, nudging her higher and higher in the euphoric satisfaction that he wanted her, needed her—perhaps loved her.

He found the other breast, and as if to apologize for ignoring it, he took it hungrily in his mouth to suckle and nip at with renewed fervor.

The ache that was growing in Andrea spread upward and a sleek film of sweat converged in dewy droplets over her skin. Her fingers reached up and began to unfasten the buttons of Jefferson's shirt expertly, as if it had been only yesterday when she had last undressed him. The shirt parted and slid unnoticed to the ground.

Andrea opened her eyes to gaze at him. His physique was as muscular and athletic as she remembered: tanned to a deep bronze that was darkened by the thick, near-black hairs on his chest. Her fingers caressed his flesh, and electric currents seemed to pass from him as she touched his darkened male nipples. He lifted his head and boldly she pulled him down on her, letting her lips taste the salty maleness of his chest as she kissed the flattened muscles. He groaned when she took a male nipple in her mouth and gave him the same pleasure he had sparked in her.

"Dear God, Andrea," he sighed, "what are you doing to me?" He closed his eyes and fell victim to the pleasure that she was creating. His voice was rough with denied passion. "What have you always done to me?"

He rolled backward on the sand and pulled her over him. His hands dipped below the waistband of her skirt to brush against the hill of her buttocks, only to retreat for an instant. and then, in a moment of total abandon, Jefferson jerked the skirt off her and pushed her legs free of her boots. Savagely he ripped off her panties and held her against him, naked in the sun.

"Undress me, Andrea," he whispered into her ear. "Take off my clothes and let me lie with you naked to the world."

A thousand tingling sensations coursed through Andrea's body as she slowly undid his belt and lowered his jeans from his body. Thrills of excitement awakened within her as she touched his skin and slid the pants off him. Her eyes roved boldly over his body, noting the way his muscles tensed at her light touch and the glowing film of perspiration that glistened against his tanned skin. She saw all of him and realized just how anxious he was for her. But he waited, slowing the pace of their lovemaking, expanding the sensual experience.

"Come here," he whispered as she finished undressing him. He was still lying on the ground, propped by only one elbow. She lifted her gaze, and as her eyes locked with the stormy intensity of his, Andrea reached up and touched one lean, firmly muscled shoulder. His muscles tensed expectantly, displaying the flat contours of his chest and stomach.

As Andrea watched him Jefferson swallowed with difficulty but held her gaze steadily. He held his lower lip in his teeth as if attempting to restrain himself. With one finger he touched her cheek and brushed away an errant strand of wayward black hair that had been caught in the brisk morning wind.

"This is the time to stop," he told her, giving her one last avenue of escape.

"Do you want to?" she asked, suddenly chilled.

Again the muscles in his arms flexed, and he expelled a gust of wind from his lungs. For a moment he seemed suspended in time, but just as quickly he came to life. His smile was almost boyish in its charm. "Do I want to stop making love to you?" he echoed as he grabbed a fistful of sand and let the minute crystals slide through his fingers. "I don't think I could."

"Then don't—not ever," Andrea whispered, letting her palm caress his cheek.

He took her hand in his and pressed a wet, passionate kiss to her hand before gently pulling her to him. "I won't," he promised as he rolled her onto her back and she felt the cool, damp sand press against her. Her hair splayed out in shiny black ringlets on the ground, and Jefferson paused for a moment to gaze upon her. He looked down past her wide, smoky-green eyes, past the alluring tilt of her chin, past her rosy-tipped breasts, taut in the autumn air, to rest on her soft, warm flesh. Then slowly his eyes took in the rest of her, including the seductive curve of her hips and the tight, firm muscles of her calves. Lying naked in the morning sun, embracing him as she had in the past, Andrea appeared more alluring and inviting than Jefferson could ever have imagined. He silently damned himself for his impetuous need of her. She was beginning to capture him, body and soul, just as she had in the past. Was it possible to ever get enough of her? he wondered to himself as his passionate gaze swept over her supine form. Could he use her, make love to her, until he was satiated, and somehow drive her out of his mind forever? She seemed so willing. Wouldn't it be wiser to keep her on the island and make love to her until he was exhausted and she was expunged from his blood?

Another look into her deep, unguarded stare, and Jefferson cast all of his conflicting emotions and lingering doubts to the cool Pacific wind. There was something about Andrea Monroe that set her apart from any woman he had ever met, and Jefferson knew instinctively that it would be impossible for him to ever get enough of her despite whatever seemingly insurmountable barriers had grown between them. As man and woman they were physically attracted to each other—mutually entwined. He hadn't been able to get her out of his mind for the last ten years, and he knew that the next ten would be no different. She was part of his blood.

Slowly Jefferson lowered his body over Andrea's form. His fingers started well down the length of her leg, lightly stroking the curve of her calf and the outside of her thighs. Her reaction was to suck in her breath and close her eyes, thinking only of his fingers and the hot path that was being traced over her rib cage to linger at her throat. He kissed her neck, the hollow between her breasts and the soft skin of her abdomen.

When she moaned with pleasure, his hands traveled up the inner sides of her thighs, gently touching the muscles in warm, sure strokes. Andrea shifted her hips upward, feeling the coiling heat in her body begging for release. Jefferson's hands took hold of her hips and he kissed the skin near her navel before gently pushing her legs apart with his knee. Still he didn't take her. This time, after waiting for ten long, agonizing years, he was going to make her want him with the same urgency that controlled him.

"Please..." Andrea murmured, knowing that he could soothe the ache that was burning within her. "Jefferson, please..."

His eyes fell from the passion of her gaze to embrace the white soft fullness of her breasts. The cool autumn nip of the sea air and the persuasive touch of his hands made her sigh in yearning. Expertly he toyed with her, letting his inflamed eyes and gentle fingers tease her until she thought she would go insane with her desire for him. His lips dipped and brushed her sensitive skin until at last, just as she thought she would cry out with desire, his mouth descended over hers and he settled comfortably between her parted thighs.

She moaned against him, holding his head firmly in her hands and entwining her fingers in his thick, rich, near-black hair. She pressed him more tightly to her, as if she would never let go. Her body arched against him as the burning passion in her veins melted to the deepest core of her. Her breath became shallow, and her heart thundered in her chest.

When Jefferson realized her need, the teasing and game playing were finished. It was as if the moment that she felt herself lost to him, he sensed her completc surrender and could deny himself no further. She felt him press close to her, sealing her to him. There was only one weighty pause in the lovemaking, and Andrea opened her eyes to see a flicker of hesitation cross his hazel gaze, but in a minute it was gone, and once again Jefferson's impassioned lips found hers in a bruising, insistent kiss. The kisses that plundered her lips were urgent demands that fired her pulse and fueled her need.

His hands and fingers stroked and caressed her as she felt the weight of his body settle upon her. In one breathless instant he broke the fragile barrier that he alone had crossed in the past. He came to her, pushing himself against her, filling her need in deep, swift strokes that drove her further and further into a dizzying, sensual pleasure that took her breath away. She felt the air constrict in her throat as hc gently lifted her into a reeling, pleasure-filled world that warmed her from the inside out.

His breathing became labored as the tempo of his sweet rhythm increased into a throbbing, burning, unyielding demand that enticed a warm, moist response from her most feminine core.

"Oh, Andrea," Jefferson groaned, his voice raw in his despair, "I've wanted you for so long…so long." His voice trailed off and was lost against the sound of the crashing waves and Andrea's own labored breathing. The intensity of his desire increased until she felt herself begin to melt and Jefferson's answering explosion of surrender.

"Oh, God," she sighed nearly inaudibly as she lay spent in his arms. Was it happiness or fear that forced a lump into her throat? Tears filled her eyes.

It was in the long, silent moments afterward, when her rapid breathing had slowed, and the serenity of afterglow had begun to fade that Andrea came floating back to the present and the realization that she, once again, had willingly been captured in the same alluring trap that had ensnared her so completely in the past.

CHAPTER SEVEN

"IT'S TIME FOR US TO leave." Jefferson voiced the dread that had been welling in Andrea the entire afternoon. After their lovemaking above the calm Pacific Ocean, Andrea had found it difficult to think of anything other than spending time with Jefferson, and all too quickly the peaceful day was gone.

Dusk was brewing as Jefferson loaded his suitcases into the motor launch that was moored in a sheltered cove not far from the dock. He helped her into the small craft and then manuevered the boat away from Harmon Island and toward the distant lights of Victoria. Even through the purple-colored dusk, the lanterns of the city were visible, and soon the small vessel had crossed the gray stretch of saltwater that separated Jefferson's Canadian retreat from the larger land mass of Vancouver Island.

As Jefferson docked the boat in the marina he took Andrea's hand and helped her out of the craft. "I'll take you to dinner," he suggested. His face was cold, as if he dismissed the afternoon as something in the past.

"It's not necessary," Andrea murmured, beginning to feel a twinge of the loneliness that was bound to assail her when Jefferson was gone. Hurriedly he hailed a passing cab.

"Of course it is," he refuted. His smile, though distant, was sincere, and Andrea was forced to answer with one of her own.

"If you insist."

The drive to the town house was quick and silent. While Jefferson waited downstairs, Andrea hurried up the polished staircase to shower and change. It felt wonderful to wash the salt and sand from her long black hair and skin.

The emerald green jersey dress was perfect for the evening—sophisticated yet sexy. Its soft folds molded to Andrea's curves, displaying just the right hint of femininity. The wide boatneck showed off her collarbone and a little shoulder, and the slit of the skirt flirted at Andrea's knees, exposing a touch of her leg.

Jefferson's appreciative glance as she hurried down the stairs gave Andrea some of the confidence that had been ebbing from her since twilight had descended upon the city. Somehow it had seemed that once in the charming city of Victoria, Jefferson had become withdrawn and brooding again. Andrea could feel the barriers that they had broken during the day begin to build between them.

"What are you trying to do to me?" he asked as she reached for her coat.

"What do you mean?"

"Oh, Andrea," he sighed, taking the coat from her hands and tossing it over the arm of a velvet side chair. Passionately he pulled her against him, holding her so tight that she found it difficult to breathe. His kiss, burning with renewed desire, took the wind from her with its fire. She felt drawn into the circle of his intense need.

When the kiss ended, it was Andrea who backed away from his embrace, forcing herself to get a grip on her emotions. With only a touch of Jefferson's hand, or a lingering kiss from his lips, she fell victim to him.

He felt her restraint, and as he helped her with her coat, his voice whispered into her ear. "Regrets?"

"About today?"

A curt nod was his only response as he opened the door and they stepped into the ghostly glow of the lanterns.

"No. I have no regrets," she replied.

He cocked a dark, questioning black brow over his stormy hazel eyes.

"Really," she explained, hurriedly.

"But...?" he prodded, sensing her hesitation.

"But it reminds me of the past, and I'm not sure that either one of us should think about it."

"We can't escape it."

"But we don't have to *relive* it."

"Then you do have regrets," he stated with finality.

Only that things hadn't turned out differently for us, she thought to herself. Andrea hiked the collar of her coat more closely to her neck to ward off the chill of the night. Without a thick bank of fog the temperature of the town had dropped considerably since nightfall.

Jefferson noticed Andrea's gesture to ward off the cold, and though his lips were set in a thin, grim line of determination, he placed a comforting arm over her slim shoulders and rubbed his hand up and down her upper arm, as if to give her warmth. Rather than take a cab, he insisted that they tour the waterfront on a double-decker bus, and before long Andrea felt the tension and strain begin to leave her body. Both she and Jefferson became swept up in the charm of the London-like city with its illuminated, ivy-covered brick buildings, horse-drawn carriages and incredible view of the ocean. They stopped to eat at a local fish-and-chips house on the waterfront and spent a relaxing evening drinking imported beer and eating the specialty of the house. The small restaurant, with its weathered pine interior, checkered tablecloths and candles lighting the tables, seemed homey and charming. A cheery fire near the bar added warmth and character to the old establishment.

Andrea secretly wished that the evening would never end. She was swept up in the romance of the tidy little pub, the smiling man seated opposite from her and the dark promise of the night. From their table she was able to look across the black water into the night, or see the reflection of the fire in the paned windows.

Jefferson glanced at his watch and tossed his napkin onto the table. "I've got to go soon," he whispered.

"Can't you stay?" she asked impetuously.

His smile was harsh as he took her hand in his. "No. I have an important matter to clear up."

"Megan," Andrea guessed, her eyes meeting his.

"Yes. Megan." He drew his hand away from hers and rubbed his chin savagely as he looked out over the black water. "I have to get her away from Lara before something happens."

"You're afraid for her."

"Yes. Wouldn't you be?"

Andrea didn't know what to say. "I don't think that Lara would hurt her."

Jefferson's eyes sparked. "Of course she wouldn't! Not intentionally! But haven't you been reading the papers? Lara was in another car accident just two nights ago. It was her fault, because she was drunk again. How long do you think it will be before Megan is injured?" he threw out vehemently.

Andrea blanched. "I...I don't know."

"Damn right, you don't. No one does. But I can't take any chances. Not anymore. I was telling you about my marriage earlier today, but I didn't finish, did I?"

"You don't have to explain."

"But I think you should know! You were the one who needed an interview, remember?"

"But I don't want to intrude."

"Don't you?"

"Look, I think that it's time we left."

Andrea began to rise, but Jefferson's hand reached out and pulled her back into her seat. "Stay. I want you to know how it all ended."

Noticing that other patrons in the tiny restaurant were beginning to cast interested glances in their direction, Andrea decided to sit back in her chair to avoid causing a scene. The last thing that she needed was the press to get wind of the fact that she was seeing Jefferson again.

"I think I was beginning to explain about my resignation."

Andrea nodded, avoiding Jefferson's piercing stare.

"That night," Jefferson began, in a voice devoid of emotion, "after I had officially resigned, I got home quite late because I had decided to clear my personal things out of the governor's office right away. Megan was in bed, and Lara was waiting for me. She had been waiting for some time and had been drinking for hours." He paused, and all of the muscles in his face became rigid with the memory.

"We quarreled bitterly. Lara was as drunk as I had ever seen her, and she was loud. She shouted accusations at me, and insults and taunts. I tried to talk her into going to bed, but she was too interested in venting her wounded pride and belittling me. The argument became heated, and I didn't realize it, but Megan had awakened. She had come down the stairs and was standing on the landing, just staring at us, watching us verbally tear each other's throats out." Jefferson's face clouded with self-disgust and pity for his child. "The look on Megan's face made me realize that I had to get her away from Lara and her drinking problem.

"For some time, Lara was remorseful about the fact that Megan had witnessed her in such an intoxicated state. Lara even allowed herself to be committed to a private hospital to combat her alcoholism. But in the end, when she came home, she couldn't control herself."

Andrea felt as if someone were twisting a knife in her stomach as she watched the play of emotions contort Jefferson's angled face.

"Her behavior became so intolerable that I demanded a divorce—and custody of Megan. I was afraid for Megan's safety when she was alone with Lara. I had finally realized that I would never be able to help Lara, and that the marriage couldn't be saved. Divorce was the only way to save myself and my child from being destroyed by Lara and her alcoholism."

Andrea listened to Jefferson's story with difficulty. She tried to hide the tears in her eyes, but failed. All of the years that she had silently wished that she could exchange places with Lara Whitney Harmon came hauntingly back to her, and she felt enormous guilt for those emotions. Suddenly she felt pity for the woman who had become Jefferson's wife.

Jefferson's arm stretched across the table and he touched her wet cheek. "Tears? For whom?"

"You...your child...your wife...I don't know," she breathed, and dabbed at the corner of her eyes with her napkin.

"There's no reason to cry."

"I know."

"Remember, you're a reporter after a story," he reminded her sharply.

"I'm not!"

"No?"

"I would never use you," she hissed, her eyes narrowing at his insinuations.

"You have in the past."

"Not I."

"Okay, your brother did."

"And you'll never trust me again," she whispered, suddenly realizing how deep the rift between them had become. Her eyes, wide with understanding and horror, stared at him accusingly.

At that moment the waiter came with the check. Jefferson paid the bill, helped Andrea with her coat and guided her toward the door of the small restaurant. The chill of the night couldn't match the cold feeling deep in Andrea's heart. All of the time that she had spent with Jefferson alone on the island had meant nothing to him. He was suspicious of her. He didn't trust her, and yet he had made love to her as if he meant every loving motion. And she had been stupid enough to fall for him all over again. In fact, he obviously thought that she had seduced him for her own interests: the interview.

Somehow they made it back to the town house. The cab ride was silent, with only a half smile or a quick response to the cabby's questions breaking the thick, suffocating stillness in the backseat of the cab.

At the doorstep she paused, only because of the pressure Jefferson placed on her upper arm.

"I didn't mean for everything to turn out this way," he offered.

"I know."

"Then you understand that—"

"No, Jefferson, I don't understand you at all. I thought

I did once, and I foolishly hoped that I could again, but I was wrong."

"I'm sorry."

"Not half as sorry as I am," she whispered, feeling tears again burning the back of her eyes.

"You understand that I can't do the interview."

"I never expected that you would."

She turned to place the key in the lock and found that her fingers were trembling with the feelings that were twisting her insides.

"Andrea."

She couldn't look at him, but held her palm out in protest. "Don't talk to me about anything. I don't want to think about it anymore."

"I wish that I could explain."

"So do I, but you can't, can you? You have a plane to catch."

She felt his hands on her shoulders and knew that he intended to kiss her. "No, Jefferson," she pleaded. "Don't." His lips found hers in a bruising kiss that stopped all of her protests. She tried not to react, attempted to show no emotion, but it was useless, and slowly her arms came up to entwine around his neck. They clung together for an endless moment before he slowly and determinedly pulled away from her.

"I'm glad you found me," he admitted earnestly. "I'll call you."

"You don't have to," she replied, fearing his response.

"I *want* to."

And then he was gone. He checked his watch and ran back to the waiting cab. Andrea stood on the porch and listened while the noisy yellow car ground its gears down the street and vanished into the darkness. Andrea had never felt more lonely in her life.

THREE DAYS AFTER JEFFERSON had returned to California, Andrea could stand the emptiness no longer. He hadn't called. No one had, not even Bryce, and the calm that Andrea had hoped to find on her vacation eluded her. She attempted to renew her acquaintance with the city, but the quaint tea shops, the glistening antique stores, the open-air markets, held no interest for her. Instead of unwinding in the city, she found herself growing tired of her inactivity. She needed to *do* something—anything—to keep her mind off Jefferson and the few hours they had blissfully shared together.

Her worries wouldn't leave her alone, and by the end of the week she was tired of brooding over the problems of her job and daydreaming about Jefferson. She scanned the newspaper every day in hope that she might read something about him, and then felt guilty at being just like the rest of the public, hoping to catch a glimpse of him.

Her last suitcase was packed, and there was still a week remaining of her vacation. On sudden impulse, before buying her airplane ticket to Los Angeles, she tried one final time to reach her sister in Seattle. She let the telephone ring several times before hanging up. Her dark, arched brows drew together pensively. Although she had attempted to call her younger sister several times during the two weeks that she had stayed in Victoria, she had been unable to contact her. Once she had gotten hold of her brother-in-law, Doug, but never Gayla. Doug had promised to have Gayla return Andrea's call, but either Andrea had missed the call or her sister hadn't attempted to reach her.

Andrea couldn't help but feel uneasy about the entire situation, and she thought fleetingly of taking the ferry to Seattle and dropping in unannounced on her younger sister.

There was something disturbingly out of character in her brother-in-law's voice—an uneasy restraint that was unlike Doug—which made Andrea discard the idea before it was completely hatched. Instead, she decided to try to reach her sister by phone once she was back on warm California soil.

Hurriedly, as if to ward off the chill of uneasiness that had begun to settle heavily on her shoulders, Andrea picked up her suitcase, marched out of the town house and locked the front door behind her. She huddled against the brisk northern wind as she waited watchfully on the porch for the taxicab that she had summoned. Pleasant memories of Jefferson kept filtering into her mind, but she resolutely tried to ignore them. Anxiously her eyes scanned the cross street for a sign of the taxi. Suddenly she couldn't get out of Victoria quickly enough to suit her. She was fidgety by the time the yellow cab screeched around the corner, and she breathed a muted sigh of relief as the door swung open and she slid into the black interior of the cab.

"Where to, lady?" the portly cabby asked, turning to eye her appreciatively as he stubbed out his smoldering cigarette.

Anywhere, she thought to herself, but instead smiled and replied, "The airport."

Tires spun against the wet pavement as the driver shoved the car into gear and pushed against the throttle. Puddles of water splashed nearly to the windows, and Andrea stared listlessly out into the approaching evening. She tried to convince herself that she was relieved to be leaving the stormy gray skies of Victoria behind her, but images of a warm November morning in Jefferson's arms wouldn't leave her restless mind.

IT WAS OVER A WEEK LATER that Andrea was back in the car driving on the concrete freeway network of Southern California. Her tired muscles rebelled at their cramped position in her tiny sports car. A week of cleaning, wallpapering and redecorating her small apartment in an effort to keep her mind from dwelling on Jefferson and the fact that he hadn't called left Andrea's muscles aching.

She had kept herself busy to the point of exhaustion during the final week of her vacation. Still, the nights of restless slumber were visible on her face. Her cheeks were more hollow than usual and dark circles under her eyes were evident despite her use of the most expensive cosmetics on the market.

The drive to Coral Productions was over too quickly. Although she was relieved to see the company was still functioning, and everything seemed "business as usual," she couldn't help but feel lingering wisps of dread tickle her spine. She thought it odd that Bryce hadn't telephoned her, and she wondered if Jefferson had explained his position about the interview to her boss. Chiding herself for her worries, she pushed open the plate glass door. The entire interview with Jefferson was probably forgotten, she reasoned. No doubt Bryce had found a suitable replacement for Jefferson, a different subject for the lead-in interview of the series.

Most of the office personnel hadn't, as yet, arrived at the production company. Andrea sneaked a peek into Katie Argus's office and was disappointed to find that Katie was late, as usual. After grabbing a cup of black coffee at the kitchenette, Andrea made her way toward her own office and smiled ruefully to herself as she noticed the desk, which had been clean when she'd left, covered with memos, letters, reports and brochures. Her office, usually tidy, was cluttered with accumulated work. Thank God, she thought to herself as she began to sift through the paper. At least she would be too busy to think about Jefferson.

"Well, look who's back!" Jack Masters's voice caught Andrea unawares. She looked up to see him lounging against the door frame, his tanned arms crossed over his chest.

"From the looks of it," Andrea retorted, her green eyes scanning the cluttered desk, "you missed me."

Jack's perfect smile extended to his eyes. "Of course we missed you—especially me!"

"Couldn't find anyone else gullible enough to get your coffee?" Andrea asked, lifting a dark brow.

"Are you insinuating that I take you for granted?"

"Me and the rest of the female population."

"Not fair, Andrea," Jack returned with an exaggerated wounded look. "I appreciate women—all of them."

"Sure you do," she agreed sarcastically. "What's been happening while I've been gone?" she asked.

Jack came into the office and sprawled into a chair near Andrea's desk. He reached for a paperweight on Andrea's desk and began rotating it nervously in his hands. He studied the hand-painted miniature carousel horse before lifting his eyes to search Andrea's perplexed face. His casual, lighthearted manner of a moment before had vanished, and his boyishly handsome face was set in stern, hard lines.

"I guess there's no reason to hide it from you. Things aren't going well here at all."

Jack's tension infected Andrea, and she felt her throat become dry. "Why not?"

"Did you happen to catch the last episode of *Pride's Power?*"

Andrea nodded thoughtfully as she mentally reviewed the episode that had aired the previous Saturday night.

"What did you think?" Jack's question was as penetrating as his guarded gaze.

"Well, it wasn't our best effort."

"It was rotten, a piece of garbage! And do you know why?" His brown eyes blazed furiously. "All because of Nicole Jamison! It galls me to the bone that she ever landed the part of Angela Pride."

Andrea sighed. They had been over this before.

"I don't think that solely Nicole can be blamed."

"Of course not. It's not her fault that she has no talent."

"Jack, don't you think you're placing too much of the blame on Nicole?"

"You saw Saturday night's program," he began slyly, sliding Andrea a sidelong look.

Andrea couldn't remember ever seeing Jack react so angrily. In Andrea's opinion he was usually too easygoing for his own good. But today, right now, he was barely in control of his simmering temper, and all of his hostility was aimed at Nicole Jamison. Andrea remembered that the story line for *Pride's Power* had originally been Jack's idea. Could it be that he was blaming the sultry actress as a scapegoat? Did he secretly feel that he was to blame for the poor ratings, and thus indirectly responsible for part of Coral Productions' financial problems?

Jack must have noticed the surprised, thoughtful look in Andrea's eyes, and some of his restrained anger seemed to ebb from him. "I'm sorry," he apologized, his affable smile neatly back in place. "I guess I'm overreacting."

Andrea's silence seemed to confirm this, and he felt a need to explain.

"It's just that it makes me so damn mad to see a good program scrapped, all because of a poor casting decision.

"Do you think that another actress could have saved the show?" she asked, eyeing Jack carefully.

"Maybe not. Who knows? But at least another actress—one with just a modicum of talent—wouldn't have butchered the part of Angela." He tapped his fingers nervously on the edge of the desk. "What did you think of the long speech—you remember, the first act, second scene—where Angela discovers that her nephew is actually her husband Justin's illegitimate son?"

"It was poor," Andrea was forced to admit honestly as she remembered watching Nicole struggle with Angela's lines of shock and dismay when confronted with the truth that her sister's ten-year-old child had been fathered by Justin.

The slim, fortyish actress with her hourglass figure, long, raven hair and frosty blue eyes, just didn't come across as the paragon of virtue that she was portraying. The speech, designed to depict despair, disbelief and yet compassion, was brittle and seemed insincere. Even with flattering lighting, a decent script and hours with the best makeup artist that money could buy, Nicole still seemed harsh and waspish, not anything like the sensitive and forgiving Angela Pride. Begrudgingly Andrea had reached the same conclusion as Jack: Nicole Jamison was wrong for the part of Angela.

"It wasn't poor, Andrea. It was a disaster!"

Andrea attempted to be equitable. "I don't think that we can blame Nicole entirely."

"She certainly doesn't help matters!"

"Okay, granted that Nicole doesn't embellish the role, what's the upshot of it all? You said that things weren't going well. Just what did you mean?"

"All three shows, *Pride's Power, Night Sirens* and *Dangerous Games* bit the dust. It's official."

Andrea sighed and leaned heavily back in her chair. She bit her thumbnail and asked the next question with difficulty. "So where does that leave us with the interviews for ITV?" The fears she had been propelling to the back of her mind began to resurface.

Jack shook his blond head negatively, and with a frown, placed the paperweight back on Andrea's desk. "Even that doesn't look good," he conceded.

"Oh?" Andrea hoped she seemed only interested and detached, but she could feel her pulse beginning to jump.

"No. Bryce is absolutely adamant that we get Jefferson Harmon for an interview, but apparently the man in question has politely but effectively refused."

"Certainly there are other personalities—"

"You would think so, but Bryce is intent on getting Harmon." Jack's eyes narrowed thoughtfully. "I don't suppose that you've kept up on him?" Jack took Andrea's silence as confirmation of his opinion. "I didn't think so. Well, it appears that his wife has gotten herself into quite a mess."

"You mean his ex-wife," Andrea said, correcting him.

Jack nodded his head and apparently didn't notice the lack of color in Andrea's blanched face. "Yeah. It seems, according to the local gossip tabloids, that not only is she out drinking and partying with a new man every week, but now she's got herself tied up in some sort of lawsuit."

"You mean for custody of the child?" Andrea surmised cautiously.

Jack nodded his head and waved his hand in the air dismissively. "That, too, of course. But there's something else. She was involved in a car accident a couple of weeks back." Andrea's mind whirled backward to the stormy night on Harmon Island and the soggy newspaper article on Lara.

"I read something about it," she responded calmly when Jack paused for a moment.

"Well, since then the occupants of the car that she hit are suing her."

"But I thought no one was injured," Andrea protested.

"It seems, or at least the other parties charge, that the car accident put a strain on an older passenger's heart. His subsequent heart attack, later that weekend, nearly killed him, and he is claiming the attack was the direct result of the car accident and Lara Harmon's negligence."

"But that's absurd!"

Jack shrugged. "People sue for almost any reason these days, you know." He surveyed Andrea with a sly gleam in his dark eyes. "Especially if they can blame a celebrity."

"Such as Jefferson Harmon's ex-wife?"

"Exactly."

"They can't possibly expect to win, can they?"

"Who knows? Harmon's got a lot of money, and he doesn't like publicity. Maybe the plaintiff's attorneys are banking on Harmon's privacy—hoping for a sizable, quiet, out-of-court settlement."

"I can't believe it," Andrea murmured. She hadn't been aware that she was holding her breath until it escaped in a trembling gust.

Jack noticed that Andrea was visibly shaken and pale. He hesitated only slightly before continuing the conversation, shrugging his broad shoulders as if to signify that what he was saying was inconsequential to him. "I'm only repeating what I've read recently," he said half-apologetically. "It looks like Harmon's newsworthy ex-wife is in more than a little hot water this time. The police report supposedly indicated that she was driving under the influence of alcohol at the time of the accident. Any way you look at it, the entire incident is a holy mess."

"I see," Andrea said, sighing wearily, only half listening to Jack.

"Wait. You haven't heard the best part!"

Andrea's lowered head jerked upward, and she felt her heart miss a beat.

"It seems that his ex-wife wants Harmon to defend her. Can you beat that?"

Andrea swallowed with difficulty and twirled her pen nervously in the air. "This is all very interesting, I suppose," she whispered in what she hoped was a calm voice. "But I really don't see what it has to do with Coral Productions."

"Don't you?" Jack stood up and stared quizzically down at Andrea. "That's the reason that Bryce is so hot after Harmon. Between our infamous ex-governor and his beautiful lush of an ex-wife, we have one helluva story. A story no one really knows, but everyone is curious about. It seems that no matter how hard Jefferson Harmon tries, he just can't keep his name off the scandal sheets. And the public is begging for more!" Jack was swept up in his rhetoric, and Andrea felt as if a sinister shadow had crossed his intense brown eyes.

"Old questions and new ones center around the man. He's just mysterious enough to whet the public's appetite. Why did he resign the governorship? What is the *real* cause of his ex-wife's drinking problem? How does he feel about his kid—or his ex-wife's latest lover? Will he defend her if she goes to court? Why did their marriage break up? Does he still love her? What truth is there to the charges that he never really got over that college coed?"

The pen that Andrea had been twirling dropped noisily to the desk top as she watched Jack's animated face. "And you honestly expect Harmon to give you an in-depth interview?"

"That's what Bryce wants."

"But what Bryce wants and what Bryce gets are two different things sometimes," Bryce himself announced as he strode into Andrea's office and leaned his wiry body against the windowsill. His solemn brown eyes softened slightly as he peered over his bifocals, and a warm grin spread evenly over his face. "Glad to have you back, Andrea. We missed you."

"So I gathered," Andrea said with a wan smile. She was grateful for Bryce's intrusion and the change in the course of the conversation. "From the looks of this office, I would hazard a guess that anything not demanding immediate attention was shuffled in here to welcome me back."

"Would we do that to you?" Bryce teased. For a moment there was an awkward silence and Bryce rubbed his palm against his jeans. His jovial face sobered. "I assume that Jack told you about all of the fall shows."

The mood in the room was subtly changing, and Andrea felt the tension that was quietly gripping Bryce diffusing the camaraderie of a moment before. "He mentioned that all of the shows were canceled."

Bryce shook his head and pursed his thin lips together. "That's right...every last one of them. Even *Night Sirens* was axed, although it had climbed steadily in the ratings."

"Why?"

"Pardon me?" Bryce's eyes fixed on Andrea's hollow face, and she felt suddenly transparent. His brow furrowed, and she wondered if he considered her question impertinent.

"I just wanted to know why the broadcasting company

cut *Night Sirens,* if it was moving up in the ratings. It's only been on for one season. I would think that the Powers That Be would give it at least one more chance to prove itself. Some of the longest-running programs on television got off to slow starts."

"My arguments exactly. But because of the shake-up in the management of the broadcasting company, the new president has decided to present a completely new lineup of shows to replace any that didn't break forty in the Nielsons."

"That's a tall order," Jack murmured. "They're going to need a bundle of replacement shows. And yet they didn't like any of our new ideas."

"Politics." Bryce squared his shoulders, and his lips thinned in determination. "For the past eight or nine months Coral has had a lousy track record, and the broadcasting company is edgy." He sighed wearily before continuing. "Well, there's no use beating a dead horse, is there? We've got to move ahead with our new ideas."

"That's what I was explaining to Andrea," Jack interjected. "I told her that we're all set with the interview series for ITV."

"Except for the fact that we haven't got our lead-in interview," Bryce reminded him.

Andrea could feel the muscles at the back of her neck begin to tighten and grow cold. "Harmon wouldn't do it?" she asked.

The lift of her eyebrows as she looked questioningly at Bryce and the question itself confused Jack Masters. He had just gotten through telling her about Harmon—why did she ask the same question of Bryce? He wondered. Suddenly, inexplicably, Jack felt himself an intruder in a very private conversation.

Bryce hesitated before answering, and Jack realized that

this was his opportunity to exit from the suddenly tense room. He started to back toward the open door. "Yeah, I was telling Andrea how interesting a character this Harmon guy is, but I guess she isn't convinced. Maybe you can change her mind," he stated skeptically. As he reached the door he tossed out a final statement to Bryce. "I'll be down the hall in Katie's office if you need me. We're going to start working on a series of questions for Sondra Wickfield." With these final words Jack left the office.

Bryce quietly closed the door to ensure that his conversation with Andrea remain private. Andrea felt her breath constrict in her lungs—she guessed what was coming. Trying to seem professional and unrattled, she started the conversation where Jack had left off.

"So, you were able to get Sondra Wickfield to agree to an interview?" she asked, straightening the piles of paper on her desk.

"Her attorneys think that the interview will help her by swaying public opinion in her favor. Even though she's still serving time, her lawyers feel that if they expose her lover as some sort of sadist—a real psycho with his women—that it will be to her benefit."

"What will the interview do for her?"

"Spring her, the attorneys hope. With enough public sentiment in her favor, there's hope that she might be paroled early. From what I understand she's a model prisoner."

Andrea sucked in her breath. "And the other personalities? Have you talked to any of them?"

"Yeah, no problem. Everyone's willing to talk for the right price—with one exception." Bryce wiped his receding forehead and hoisted himself up on the corner of Andrea's desk.

"Jefferson Harmon," she said, hoping her assumption was wrong.

"That's right. It seems that no amount of money will sway him." His dark, probing eyes bore down on Andrea, and she knew that her stomach was fluttering, but she held Bryce's intimidating stare.

"A man of principle?"

"Why don't you answer that one?" Bryce suggested as he folded his arms across his chest.

"What do you mean?" Andrea felt her heart thudding, and her palms beginning to sweat.

Bryce's smile wasn't convincing. "Let's stop playing games Andrea. I know that you knew Harmon in the past. That's why I called you in Victoria. You're the girl who was involved with him ten years ago. Good God, Andrea, were you actually an anti-war activist?"

"My brother was."

Bryce snapped his fingers together as if a thought had suddenly struck him. "That's the brother that was wounded in the war, right?" he asked, hopping off the desk and pacing restlessly between it and the window.

"Martin," Andrea answered, supplying Bryce with her brother's name. "How do you know so much about it?" She leaned back in her desk chair and surveyed her boss speculatively. It was as if she were seeing Bryce Cawthorne for the first time. Had Jefferson been right about Bryce all along?

"Before you left on vacation three weeks ago, I noticed your reaction to the article in the paper about Harmon's divorce. I thought it odd at the time, but I never dreamed that you were the college girl from his past until I did some further digging."

Andrea's shoulders drooped, but still she held Bryce's

gaze unwaveringly. Her voice was empty when she finally found her words. "You asked me to call Jefferson knowing what would happen, knowing about our past?" she accused.

"A little underhanded, wasn't it?" Bryce admitted with his most disarming grin.

Andrea's eyes sparked. "More than a little, I'd say."

Bryce held his palms outward. "All right, I should have leveled with you in the first place," he agreed. "But would you have done it? Would you have talked to Harmon… tried to persuade him?"

"I don't know…."

Bryce cocked his head to one side and lifted his shoulders. "This way I knew that you would get to him. After all, what did it hurt?"

"What did it help? He hasn't agreed to the interview."

"Not yet."

"But you think he might?" Andrea asked, incredulously.

"Don't you?"

"No!"

"Why not?"

"Because he's not the kind of man who likes to have his personal life splashed across the headlines or paraded on national television. You know that."

"Don't you think you could change his mind?" Bryce asked, pulling thoughtfully on his lower lip.

"No!"

"No?"

"Bryce, I wouldn't, *couldn't,* ask him to do something he doesn't want to do!" Andrea's dismay was evident on her face and in the tone of her voice. What was Bryce asking her to do? Was it her imagination, or was he different than she had remembered? How desperate for the interview with Jefferson Harmon was Bryce?

"And I wouldn't expect you to," Bryce reaffirmed, but the rigidity of his spine didn't slacken.

"Then you don't expect him to come through," Andrea surmised, and a giant wave of relief began to cascade over her.

"I didn't say that. There's got to be a way to get to him."

"But he doesn't want to do it!"

"Not yet, but people have been known to change their minds—especially politicians." Bryce cocked his wrist and looked at his watch. "I've got to get to a meeting at ITV. We'll talk about this later in the week."

When the door to the office closed, Andrea felt a shudder of fear jolt her. You're imagining things, she told herself, but she couldn't help but feel a welling sense of dread spread through her. Why was Bryce so adamant about Jefferson?

CHAPTER EIGHT

TWO DAYS AFTER THE confrontation with Bryce, Andrea finally found time to have lunch with Katie Argus. The pile of work on Andrea's desk had prevented her from socializing, and the mood in the office was so tense that Andrea had difficulty talking with the other employees at Coral Productions inside the building.

It was a warm day, warm enough to eat in the courtyard of the omelet house Katie had chosen. For the first time since returning to her job, Andrea felt the tension that had been building begin to dissolve with Katie's incessant chatter and sarcastic humor.

"I'm dying to hear all about your vacation," Katie said with a bright smile as they were seated at the parasoled tables in the brick courtyard. Although the walls of the adjacent buildings surrounded the courtyard, it was large enough to allow the winter sun to warm the backs of the patrons. Hanging baskets of flowers added just the right touch of fragrance and color, giving the enclosed patio a sense of privacy and casual charm.

"There's really not that much to tell," Andrea said.

"Don't hold out on me," Katie argued with a brilliant smile. "You've changed since you got back. My guess is it's a man!"

"You always have had an active imagination," Andrea

quipped back, and was relieved that the waiter came to take their orders.

Fortunately Katie was easily distracted, and Andrea took up the conversation, heading it in a different direction.

"So, how did things go at the office while I was gone?"

"Horrible," Katie admitted, pulling an exaggerated frown.

"Why?"

"Oh, who knows? Bryce was in one of his foul moods again and everybody suffered because of it."

"He's very worried about the company," Andrea suggested.

"I think there's more to it than that," Katie replied, accepting the plate that the waiter brought to her. She speared a piece of her mushroom omelet, dipped it in the sour cream sauce and swallowed it. "If you ask me, he's bugged about Jefferson Harmon refusing to do the interview."

"Why is it so important to have Harmon?" Andrea asked casually.

"Not only does Bryce want Harmon, but apparently so do a couple of the guys at ITV. It's only gossip, but Sheryl, Bryce's secretary, told me that Bryce promised the cable company that he would be able to get Harmon for an interview. That's really something considering the fact that Jefferson Harmon hasn't given an official interview since he resigned as governor. At least, not a personal interview."

Katie continued to attack her omelet feverishly, but Andrea's appetite had slowly diminished. She pushed the remains of her shrimp salad around in her plate.

"Why did Bryce promise something he couldn't deliver? Harmon hasn't agreed to the interview."

Katie tossed her blond hair and shrugged. "Beats me. Maybe ITV wouldn't buy the package of programs without being assured of a celebrity of their choice." Katie looked up from her meal to study Andrea thoughtfully. "According to Sheryl, Bryce could persuade Harmon to go along with him. Bryce seems to think that he's got some special pull with our mysterious ex-governor. I can't for the life of me figure out what it might be." Katie set her fork down beside her plate and lifted her glass of wine, but her eyes never left Andrea's blanched face. "Hey, are you okay? You look a little pale."

"Do I? Oh...well. You have to remember that I've been away from the California sun for a couple of weeks," Andrea stammered, trying to regain some of her lost composure.

"You haven't touched your salad," Katie accused.

"I guess I'm not very hungry," Andrea suggested with what she hoped appeared to be a genuine smile for her friend. But Katie saw through the ruse.

"Something's wrong, isn't it?" the blonde charged emphatically. "Are you going to explain it to me, or brood over your problems all by yourself?"

"It's really nothing...a problem with my family while I was in Victoria," Andrea lied, wincing inwardly. Katie was a good friend, and Andrea would have liked to pour her heart out to her, but how could she even attempt to explain the depth of her feelings for Jefferson? The secret that she had hidden for ten years was not easy to confess, not even to her best friend. After concealing the truth for so long, it was impossible to let it out now, especially since nothing had changed between herself and Jefferson.

"I didn't mean to pry," Katie apologized as she witnessed a dark, incomprehensible cloud cross Andrea's delicate features.

"You haven't. I'm just a little concerned about my sister in Seattle, that's all." At least the lie wasn't entirely fabricated, Andrea thought grimly.

"Gayla?" Katie asked, her honey-blond eyebrows arching in dismay. "What's wrong with her?"

"I'm not really sure," Andrea sighed, and then shrugged, as if to shake off her disconsolate mood. "It's just a feeling I have. I tried to reach her several times while I was in Victoria, and couldn't. I got through to Doug once, and even he seemed strange—uneasy. It's probably nothing," she admitted, but she didn't sound convincing.

"I wouldn't worry too much about Gayla if I were you. She's twenty-eight and can take care of herself. It sounds as if she and Doug just had some sort of marital tiff, if you ask me."

"I don't know," Andrea murmured.

"Don't worry about it. Now, let's get down to brass tacks. I don't buy the story that you're worried about your younger sister." Andrea began to protest and Katie amended her position. "I know, I know, you're concerned about Gayla, and you should be, but what's *really* bothering you?"

"I don't know what you mean."

"Sure you do," Katie pointed out. "We've worked together for a long time, been friends for years, and I know that there's a bigger problem eating at you. You've lost weight, color and apparently your appetite," Katie maintained, glancing at Andrea's plate. "If you don't want to talk about it, that's one thing, but don't try to lie to me with some overblown story about your sister."

Andrea had to smile in spite of herself. "You always could see right through me."

"It's easy, Andrea. You're transparent. You wear your

heart on your sleeve. My guess is that you've got a new man in your life."

"I wish it were that easy," Andrea sighed, wondering if she was making a mistake as she began her story. "There is a man, but it's not a new one. You see, the man I was seeing was Jefferson Harmon."

"What?" The stricken look on Katie's face showed her obvious dismay. "You must be kidding."

Andrea's wistful smile convinced Katie that she was telling the truth. "No, I was the college girl that was involved with him ten years ago."

"Oh, Andrea...."

"Bryce asked me to call Jefferson when I was in Victoria, but I couldn't find his number. Instead, I went to see him on his private island, the same island I visited years ago." Andrea sketched in the rest of the story, much of which Katie had read in the papers. Katie's expression darkened from shock to dismay and finally, to disbelief.

"You don't think that Bryce intends to use you to get at Harmon, do you? You aren't the special influence that he secretly holds?"

"I hope not," Andrea replied, still feeling vaguely uneasy. "Because even if I went along with any of Bryce's schemes, it wouldn't work. Jefferson's made up his mind."

Katie toyed with her napkin before lifting her eyes and giving Andrea a compassionate smile. "So, where does that leave you?"

"What do you mean?"

"I'm talking about you and Jefferson, for Pete's sake. Have you heard from him since you got back to L.A.?"

"I haven't seen him," Andrea hedged, but Katie was too quick to be put off.

"Has he called?"

Andrea bit at her lower lip before gently pushing aside her plate of uneaten salad. "Yes, he's called," she admitted sternly.

"And?"

"And *nothing!* He called twice, and it was very tense. He didn't ask to see me." Andrea pursed her lips together for a moment before tossing her napkin onto the table and rising from her chair. "Oh, he was polite, but it was very uncomfortable, and I felt worse after he called than before. It was almost as if he called me because he felt it was his *obligation!*" Andrea could feel the sting of tears biting at the back of her eyes, but she willed them back, refusing to break down in public over a man who thought so little of her.

"That doesn't sound like Jefferson Harmon to me," Katie observed as she rose from the table. "At least not the Harmon that I've read so much about. From what I understand of our ex-governor, he doesn't feel pressured into anything. That was why he was so popular as a politician. He was one man that stood up for what he believed, and couldn't be swayed by popular opinion or money."

Andrea couldn't trust herself to speak. Talking about Jefferson had only opened the wounds over her heart once again. With all of the feelings that she held for him, all of the love that welled within her, she wanted to believe everything that Katie was saying. Yet Andrea knew better than to be swayed by her emotions once again. Twice she had succumbed to her love for the man, and twice that love had been recklessly discarded by him.

Katie sensed Andrea's preoccupation and tried to turn the topic of conversation back to neutral territory, but Andrea only half-listened to her friend as the blonde rattled on about her latest romantic relationship with an up-and-coming producer. During the short drive back to the office Andrea's mind kept slipping back to Katie's earlier comments: *"Bryce seems to think that he's got some special pull over our mysterious ex-governor.... You don't think that Bryce intends to use you to get at Harmon, do you? You aren't the special influence that he secretly holds?"*

Andrea didn't want to believe that Bryce would stoop so low as to think that he could use her as a weapon against Jefferson. Would he? Andrea found the thought impossible, and yet the uneasy feeling burning in the pit of her stomach remained with her for the rest of the day.

The tension in the office continued to build, and when it was finally late Friday afternoon, Andrea couldn't wait to get home. Everyone in the office was on edge, including Jack Masters, whose usual affable grin had been replaced by a sour frown while he finished rewriting the final episode of *Pride's Power.*

Everything has changed, Andrea thought to herself as she locked her car and hurried up the short flight of steps to her second-story apartment. She kicked off her shoes and opened the sliding glass door to the redwood deck. It had been a warm, muggy day, and the promise of rain was thick in the air. The apartment seemed stagnant, and even the breathless air from outside helped cool Andrea's body against the stickiness of her clothing. After undressing she tossed her clothes into the hamper and started drawing a bath, hoping that the warm water would help wash away all of the tension from the office. The bathwater lapped lazily around her and she closed her eyes before sinking up to her neck in the warm water. Her black hair was twisted onto the top of her head, allowing her to submerge herself to her neck. For the first time in over a week she felt at ease. The sleepless nights she had spent finally caught up with her, and she began to doze.

A short while later her eyelids fluttered open in response to some distant intrusion that had interrupted her catnap. Something had disturbed her, and she was surprised to find that she had actually fallen asleep in the soothingly warm water. She listened for a moment before the doorbell chimed a second time. The hot water had cooled and was barely tepid. She shivered as she rose and stepped out of the tub onto the bare, blue tile.

"Just a minute," she called as she hastily pulled on her velour bathrobe and hurried to the living room, leaving a wet trail where her feet touched the creamy white carpet. The doorbell rang again insistently, and Andrea, piqued by the intrusion, hastened her stride. "I'm coming," she called out again more impatiently. When she reached the door, she unlocked it and jerked it open.

Her heart turned over as she recognized Jefferson standing on the porch, his shoulder propped against one of the black wrought iron pillars that supported the roof. His burgundy-colored tie was askew, his sport jacket rumpled and the shadow of a beard darkened his jawline. He looked tired and disheveled as he leaned near the railing.

"Jefferson? What are you doing here?" she asked, astonished to see him. She hadn't heard from him in over three days. Their last telephone conversation had been so stilted and tense that she never would have expected to see him standing, alone and tired and looking as if he needed a friend, on her front doorstep.

His dark, hazel eyes traveled up her body, and his off-center smile, tired but amused, broke across his face. "You look great," he said simply, letting his eyes caress her. In the thickly piled, indigo-colored bathrobe, her black hair curling and studded with diamondlike droplets of moisture and her skin flushed from the warm water of the bath, Andrea appeared more desirable and provocative than Jefferson had remembered. Though she had haunted his nights, his dreams of her had never lived up to the innocently alluring woman she was as she stood before him. He didn't really understand why he had come to see her after his long airplane flight from Colorado, but instinctively he had sought her out for comfort and companionship.

Andrea, recovering from the shock of seeing him on her doorstep, opened the door a little farther as she found her voice. One hand clutched at her robe. "Please, come in," she whispered, stepping aside to allow him to enter her home. "I...I wasn't expecting anyone," she apologized.

"Obviously," was his dry retort as his eyes dropped to the gaping lapels of the deep blue robe.

She regarded him silently for a moment, her puzzled eyes seeking answers in the contours of his face. Why was he here? She could feel his intimate appraisal of her, and she knew that he guessed she was wearing nothing under the velour robe. Dewy droplets of moisture still ran down her legs. She shivered from the water beading on her skin...or did she shiver from Jefferson's searching, silent appraisal of her. Seeing him again made her feel more alive, more sensual, more womanly, than she had since leaving Victoria. His presence seemed to dominate everything in the small, intimate living room.

"Nice," he murmured as his eyes ran over the eclectic pieces of furniture and wall hangings in the room. His smile was sincere as he looked at the assortment of belongings that Andrea had collected over the past ten years. The rose-colored couch was faded, an antique found at an estate sale. The side chairs were modern, in bold burgundy-colored stripes. Woven baskets from India were filled with leafy green plants, and copper kettles overflowing with books and needlework, crowded the corners of the apartment. Open-weave linen draperies, the color of faded jute, covered the windows, which also were graced with deep maroon blinds.

As he looked at the room Andrea could sense him puzzling over the pieces of her life that he had missed. He was looking at the most private reaches of her, studying every little detail, and suddenly Andrea felt the intimacy between them grow. He was seeing too much of her life in his omniscient gaze. She had to break the spell.

"Jefferson, why are you here?" she asked impulsively. His eyes left the contents of the room to meet her gaze.

"I didn't think that our phone conversations were very satisfying—or conclusive."

Andrea smiled wryly. "Whose fault is that?"

Jefferson shrugged, and his shoulders sagged wearily. "I'm not blaming you. I should never have called you when I was so upset."

"Then why did you?"

"I told you I would call you in Victoria, didn't I?"

"So you phoned because you promised that you would, because you felt obligated?"

His expression changed, and his lips thinned into a tight, uncompromising frown. "I called you because I wanted to, and for no other reason." Her black eyebrows lifted in an expression of doubt. "Oh, hell," he muttered, "I don't know why I'm trying to explain myself to you. My timing was poor. I shouldn't have called when I was so upset with the way things were working out with Megan. But damn it, Andrea, I just wanted to talk to you!" He bit out the last phrase as if it were an unwanted admission, and he dropped, without invitation, onto the faded, overstuffed couch.

Something in the uncomfortable way he slouched on the sofa made Andrea smile in spite of herself. It was true that she had wanted to see him and had hoped to hear from him. But after the last tense telephone conversation, when he seemed more distant and remote from her than ever—as far away as the dark side of the moon—she had all but given up on ever seeing him again.

"I've been unfair to you," he stated as he looked up at her.

"What do you mean?"

"I've been selfish and self-centered."

"No—"

"Just listen, will you?" he cut in. "Can't you even accept an apology gracefully?"

Andrea pressed her lips together and sat in one of the contemporary chairs that faced the couch. She folded her hands together on her lap, leaned against the back of the chair and inclined her head toward him, encouraging him to continue.

"I'm not very good at apologies—I never have been—but I'm sorry about not coming to see you sooner. I've been up to my ears in business meetings. As a matter of fact, I just got in from Denver a little over an hour ago, and, well..." He closed his eyes and thought for a moment. When he opened them again, Andrea could sense a look of bewilderment and confusion in his gaze. "How did everything get so fouled up?" he asked in a rough whisper. "Ten years ago everything seemed so simple."

"We were younger then," she said, thinking aloud.

"But not any smarter," he sighed. "We should never have allowed ourselves to get so far away from each other."

He rubbed the back of his neck and again lowered his eyelids.

In the past Andrea had witnessed a dozen different sides to the complex personality of Jefferson Harmon. She had known him to be loving, gentle and kind; she had been aware of his soft persuasion or ruthless determination; she had seen him filled with rage or passion; but never had she witnessed the defeat that was now evident in his deep voice He looked older than he had on the island, though it had only been a few, short weeks ago.

"Jefferson, are you all right?" she asked quietly. Why did she feel compelled to soothe his worried brow?

His smile was grim. "I'm fine," he murmured sarcastically and looked at the ceiling. "I'm just fine."

"Is something wrong?"

His eyes narrowed. For a moment she saw a flash of anger as his jawline hardened. But just as rapidly it was gone, as if he had willed his anger away. "Nothing's wrong," he answered flatly.

"Are you sure? Maybe I could help," she offered.

"This is one battle that I have to handle myself!" He snapped the words out bitterly, and for a second Andrea sat frozen in the chair, holding on to her knees, which were tucked under her. What did he want from her? Did he expect something? Why was he here, and why in heaven's name was he so angry?

"Is there anything I can get you? A drink perhaps?" she asked as she rose from the chair and hurried into the kitchen. She had to move, to get away from him. She couldn't bear to watch him stare blankly up at the ceiling, lost in thoughts that excluded her. "Is brandy all right?" she called through the doorway to the kitchen. She didn't expect a response, and none came.

Andrea poured the drink just to keep herself busy. She wanted to help him, talk to him, ease his pain. But although he had come to her home looking for her, it was as if he had retreated from her into the dark thoughts that were clouding his mind.

When she returned to the small living room, she noticed that he had discarded his jacket and tossed it over the back of the couch. Gone too, was his tie. His shirtsleeves were rolled up to expose his forearms.

"Thanks," he said as she offered him the drink. His eyes touched her face and slid down the slender white column of her neck to rest on the overlapping lapels of the robe and the soft tops of her breasts as she leaned forward to hand him the brandy. He took a long, satisfying swallow, but his eyes never left her as they watched her over the rim of his glass.

Andrea felt the mood in the small room begin to shift and thicken as she stood near him. She noticed the smell of his cologne and the way his hair curled near the back of his ears.

Her voice became dry. "Excuse me," she whispered hoarsely, trying to break the seductive spell that was building in the living room.

"Where are you going?" he queried. His fingers reached up to slide against her forearm and touch the sensitive skin of her inner elbow.

Andrea swallowed the lump that was swelling in her throat. Her eyes lifted as she searched for the excuse to pull away from him. "It's beginning to rain. I thought I'd close the sliding door to the deck and change into my clothes."

"Not on my account."

She ignored the implication. "I don't want the draperies or the carpet to get wet," she explained, knowing her excuse was feeble.

"Don't worry about that," he said, setting his drink on an antique end table. His voice was low and rough.

She ignored him and went over to the deck. The wind had picked up and was lifting the draperies to billow into the apartment. Small droplets of rain were running down the glass, staining the redwood slats of the deck. Andrea shuddered from the cool breath of the wind as it entered the room.

Just as she was pulling the door shut, she felt Jefferson's strong arms slide protectively around her waist. Her body responded to his touch, and her head fell backward as he began to kiss the wet tendrils of hair that surrounded her face and throat. Gently he pulled the pins from her hair, and it cascaded over her shoulders in soft waves of ebony silk. Andrea leaned against him as her skin came alive with his touch. The feel of his hands pulling her against him, the smell of the brandy on his breath as it whispered across her ear and the warmth of his long, hard body next to hers, seemed to wrap Andrea in a magical cloak of seduction.

"Do you know how long I've waited to touch you?" Jefferson asked as his hands slid under her robe. Andrea sighed in contentment as his palm pressed warmly against the tight skin of her rib cage. Her heart skipped a beat when his fingers moved upward to caress her firm breast.

Warm, liquid sensations began to swirl within her, and her weak knees began to give way. She leaned against him, content to feel the gentle, insistent pressure of his hand under the folds of her robe. Slowly he untied the belt that held her garment together, and when it parted, he moved both of his hands to cup her breasts and hold her near to him. In gentle, kneading strokes, his fingers embraced her breasts and his thumbs slid seductively over her nipples, sending waves of pleasure and desire through her body.

His hands dipped lower to run across her bare stomach. They pressed heatedly against her inner thighs, then pulled her roughly, insistently against him, allowing her to feel the desire that heated his loins and penetrated his heart. His hands were trembling as he turned her around to face him.. Slowly he pushed the downy, indigo garment from her shoulders.

"How can any one woman be so beautiful?" he questioned as his finger traced an imaginary line from the tilt of her chin, down her throat, to linger at the swell of her breast. He closed his eyes against the passion rising within him. His fist clenched in frustration at his side. "Why can't I seem to get enough of you?"

Ignoring the questions that neither one of them could answer, he wrapped his arms around her naked form and pulled her close to him. His lips found hers in a protective, plundering kiss that sparked fires within her only he could ignite. She pressed her lips just as urgently against his, demanding as much as he could promise. When their anxious tongues met to dance in silent union, a shiver of anticipation raced up Andrea's spine as the heat within her ignited.

As he kissed her, Jefferson's fingers inched down her spine, gently touching each vertebra before they stopped to linger at the swell of her buttocks. While her lips were still locked in fevered embrace with his, she found the buttons of his shirt and nearly ripped them off in her pressing need to touch him. When at last the shirt lay crumpled on the floor, she stood on her toes and pressed herself more tightly against him, inviting his further exploration of her aroused body. She reveled in the pressure of his hardened chest against the soft contours of her breasts.

"I'm going to make love to you, Andrea," Jefferson

whispered roughly against her ear. "And I'm never going to let you forget that you're mine—body and soul."

She thrilled at the protective, intense quality of his words. "I don't want to forget," she sighed before his hungry mouth captured hers and he pushed her gently onto the floor with the weight of his body. To ensure her comfort, he reached for a pillow from a chair and tucked it under her head. Once he had propped her against the pillow, he stood up, and lazily undid the belt to his trousers. His gaze never left hers as she watched his every move. She was content to witness the unveiling of his lean, hard legs as he stepped out of his pants. They were tanned and well-muscled and covered with the same dark hair that she saw on his chest.

Just as slowly, he slipped out of his underwear, and Andrea examined him boldly, unafraid to study all of him. He lay down beside her, and his fingers traced intricate patterns lightly against her shoulder. Shivers of delight sizzled through her body. "Make love to me," he commanded as he pressed his warm lips to her eyelids. "Make love to me as if this were our last night together."

Her hands, which had reached up to touch his chin, stopped, chilled by his words. "Is it?" she breathed, trying to ignore the welling sense of dread that his words had created.

His hands stopped their seductive movement. "Is it what?"

"Our last night together?" She couldn't hide the catch in her voice as fear settled upon her.

"Of course not," he sighed, nuzzling the soft skin of her neck. "I just thought it would be nice to let out all the stops." He paused for a second before repeating his throaty request. "Make love to me, Andrea."

Andrew slowly let out her breath and pushed any nagging doubts to the dark corners of her mind. She pulled herself onto him and rained kisses on his face and neck. A satisfied groan rumbled deep in his chest, and his fingers sank into the firm muscles of her back. Andrea's hands moved wildly through his hair as she boldly parted his lips with the sweet pressure of her tongue. Jefferson groaned again, and Andrea felt a shudder rip through the length of him. His hands slid caressingly down her body, rubbing her rib cage and hips in a gentle, persuasive motion that took hold of Andrea and warmed the deep core of her femininity.

Slowly she moved against him, allowing the feel of his soft chest hairs and light beard rub against her skin. She felt him sliding downward beneath her until his mouth found the supple mounds of her breasts. Lazily, he began to suckle, seeming to draw out all of her tension and fears. Instinctively she leaned over him, offering him the pleasure and comfort of her swollen breast. His mouth opened wider as she lay over him, and his tongue licked and caressed the smooth skin until she thought she would go mad with the longing that was spreading through her body. He murmured her name against the soft mounds, and his hands roved restlessly over the muscles of her back and hips, gently stroking her with sure, fluid movements.

A volcano was swelling within her, threatening to erupt at any moment. Warm, liquid lava was coursing through her veins, thundering in her ears. He slid beneath her once again, and his lips trailed hotly over her rib cage and smooth abdomen. She hugged the pillow more tightly to her as she felt his hot breath teasing her skin. His fingertips found the soft flesh of her inner thighs and he began touching her, petting her, exciting her, until she thought she would explode.

"Jefferson," she sighed. "Dear God, Jefferson, love me."

Her plea reached him. With a moan of pleasure, he pushed upward and spun her over onto her back. He moved against her and felt the dewy softness of her sweat mingling with his own. He was hot and fueled with desire. The ache in his loins was throbbing with need as a result of her gentle lovemaking. Nothing pleased him more than to hear the urgent, passionate cry that burst from her lips as he rolled over and felt her stretched out beneath him. His knee pressed her legs open insistently, and he lay upon her, touching each of her feminine muscles with their male counterparts. Knowing that she was as inflamed as he was, Jefferson let loose his passion and entered her with a wild, thrusting desire that was only equaled by the stormy lightning in Andrea's green eyes as she gazed up at him. Together they moved and blended in thunderous union, each igniting the other until the dam that had been holding them apart burst open and the shower of their love cascaded over them, sending them rolling in the afterwashes of their combined passion.

"Andrea, I love you," Jefferson whispered as he tumbled beside her and kissed her quietly on the top of her forehead. "I always have." He held her tightly against him and snuggled with her on the carpet. "Let's go to bed," he suggested after a few minutes. "I want to show you how much you mean to me."

She sighed contentedly as he lifted her from the floor and carried her to the bedroom. Tonight, she thought to herself. At least we have tonight. I'll worry about tomorrow later.

CHAPTER NINE

"I COULD GET VERY USED to this," Jefferson declared with a smile as he sat at the breakfast table in Andrea's apartment and finished his plate of French toast and sausage. He took a swallow of his coffee and leaned back in his chair. "You're as good in the kitchen as you are in the bedroom," he mused teasingly.

She smiled over her coffee cup and arched a doubting black eyebrow. "Am I?"

"Well, almost."

"Then why don't you get used to it?"

Jefferson suddenly sobered. "What do you mean? Do you want me to move in?"

"Why not?"

"It sounds great, but there's a hitch."

"An excuse, you mean."

Jefferson's eyes darkened. "Call it what you want, but it doesn't alter anything. I can't make any commitments to you until I find out about Megan."

"Her custody?"

Jefferson nodded and drained his cup. He rose from the table and put the empty cup in the sink. "Lara's very unpredictable. I can't do anything to rock the boat." Jefferson thought fleetingly about the negotiations with Lara. Could he explain to Andrea about the problems he was suffering at Lara's hand? Could he begin to explain to what lengths he would go to get back his child? Would Andrea possibly be able to understand? He looked into her eyes—wide, green and pleading to be a part of his life—and he denied himself. Until Megan was securely in his home, he couldn't trust anyone, including Andrea, with the knowledge of how he intended to get his child.

"I'd rather not talk about Megan or Lara right now," he said.

"Or us?" All the fears that Andrea had hidden in the night began to resurface in her mind.

"What do you mean?"

"I mean that I don't like the idea that I'm supposed to sit here and wait until you decide to see me again."

"What are you talking about? Did I say anything like that?"

She felt thankful that her fears were giving way to anger. "You didn't have to. I read between the lines."

His jaw hardened. "Well, once again you're reading more into this than there is."

"Am I?"

"Why do you insist on fighting with me?"

"And why do you lie to me and hide things from me, only to keep dropping back in my life?" She was trembling and tears began to collect in her eyes. "I didn't invite you here, you know."

"Just as I didn't invite you to the island! But you came, didn't you, for that damned interview! Don't accuse me of hiding things from you when you were the one that wanted to expose my life to the viewing public of America."

"Do we have to go through all of this again?" she asked.

His anger seemed to have simmered a little. "I hope not," he replied.

"Good."

There was an uncomfortable, weighty silence in the room. Jefferson leaned against the sink and stared at Andrea, who feigned interest in her coffee. "I've got to go now," he said softly as he picked up his jacket from the back of the chair.

She didn't respond. She still heard the damning quality of his words as they rang in her ears. He still didn't trust her. That much was evident. She listened while he opened the front door, and mentally she counted his steps as he hurried down the stairs of the apartment complex. In a minute she heard a car engine sputter to life and then roar out of the parking lot. *He's gone,* she thought wearily, and the tears that had been burning at the back of her eyes began to slide down her cheeks.

THE WEEKEND WITHOUT Jefferson loomed before her, and Andrea actually found herself looking forward to going back to work at Coral Productions on Monday. She told herself that all of her fears about Bryce and the interview were only ghosts. Bryce had probably come up with a dozen other names to headline the first interview of the ITV series.

The following week at work was tense but smooth. It was several days before Andrea realized just how desperate her boss had become. Just as she was beginning to relax and get back into the hectic routine of her job, the trouble began.

Bryce hadn't mentioned the Harmon interview, and Andrea assumed that her boss had finally admitted defeat. Jefferson had obviously convinced Bryce that he had no intention of making his personal life public, and the memo Andrea had received earlier in the week confirmed her thoughts. Bryce had requested that each member of the scriptwriting team come up with some alternate personalities for the ITV interviews, should any of the scheduled celebrities cancel at the last minute.

Most of the first five programs had confirmed guests, and Bryce was working on a list of celebrities for the additional ten shows. Andrea had researched the assignment and had come up with an idea for the show. In case Bryce didn't like her first choice, she also had a backup. She was grateful that the pressure was off about Jefferson Harmon. Sondra Wickfield, the imprisoned philanthropist, was slated for the first interview of the series, and for the first time since Jack had suggested Jefferson Harmon as a personality worthy of a television interview, Andrea breathed freely.

The door to Bryce's office was open, and Andrea hesitated slightly. Bryce had requested the meeting, but at the moment he was sitting back in his chair, looking out the window and listening raptly to someone on the other end of the telephone line. His balding head was bent to the side, and he cradled the phone between his ear and shoulder, leaving his hands free. He was busily scratching notes on a yellow legal pad as he listened. Apparently the person on the other end of the conversation was important. The words of encouragement that Bryce interjected into the one-sided conversation sounded reassuring, but the nervous twitch over his eye and the tightness of his skin, drawn over tense facial muscles, belied his calm.

"It will be no problem…just a few minor details to iron out. You know how it is with politicians, never able to pin them down. Don't worry about it. I'll take care of everything this afternoon." Sweat was beading on Bryce's head as he laughed hollowly at something that was uttered to him via the telephone. "Yeah, well, I'll talk to you later. *Ciao.*"

Bryce slammed the receiver back into the cradle of the telephone, wiped his palm over his forehead and let his rigid shoulders slump. "Damn," he muttered to himself before raising his eyes to look into Andrea's questioning gaze.

A sad smile played on his lips as he waved her into his office. "Andrea…come in, come in. Sorry that I was tied up on the phone so long. I promise you that I haven't forgotten about our meeting."

Something in Bryce's gaze troubled Andrea, but she tried to ignore it. "How's the interview series coming?" she asked, hoping to shake off the feeling of uneasiness that settled heavily upon her.

"Fine…fine," Bryce muttered as he scanned the notes he had written to himself on the legal pad and adjusted his glasses. "Sit down, Andrea. Now, tell me, have you come up with any ideas for the additional ten shows?" He held a pencil in his two hands and let his elbows rest on the table as he looked at her.

"I think so," she began. Why did she feel as if Bryce were scrutinizing her? Where was the easiness she usually felt in Bryce's modern office, filled with memorabilia from his successful television career? Everything looked the same—the tweed couch, plush charcoal carpet, cluttered desk—but nothing felt the same.

"So who have you come up with?" he asked with a smile that didn't quite make it to his probing brown eyes.

"I have a couple of suggestions, and I think that they would give a little meat to the series. I know that most of the guests we have slated are either television or movie people, stars with a flamboyant lifestyle."

Bryce nodded thoughtfully as he gazed over the pencil, encouraging her to continue. She did, although somehow she felt as if she was stepping onto shaky ground.

"A guy who has been getting a considerable amount of local press is Tom Reeves." Bryce's brows drew together, and Andrea continued to explain. "You know the man I'm talking about. He's a marine biologist who lives near Marina Del Ray. Lately he's been getting a lot of publicity due to his stand on preserving marine life, especially his concern about the whales."

"I know the man you mean," Bryce interrupted cuttingly. "But he's only a local hero for some of the residents of the coast. He has no *national appeal.*"

"But—"

"Forget him, Andrea," Bryce retorted. "Who else do you have in mind?" Bryce began to tap the pencil nervously on the desk. He was angry and agitated.

"I thought you might be interested in my brother, Martin."

"The ex-CO? Why do you think he would be interesting?"

"Certainly you've read of him," Andrea began. "He's California's spokesman for the rights of the Vietnam veterans. Because of him, and a few others like him, national attention has been given to the veterans: their disabilities, the social problems…"

"Who gives a damn!" Bryce asked, pulling a cigar from out of the box on his desk. He bit off the end and lit it.

"What?" Andrea asked, incredulous.

Bryce puffed furiously on the cigar until a cloud of blue smoke wafted over his head. "I said, who gives a damn about those crybabies? For Christ's sake, Andrea, men have been marching off to war since the beginning of time. Who the hell do these guys think they are to ask for special privileges? Their country called, and they answered. End of story."

"You can't be serious!"

Bryce rotated the cigar from one side of his mouth to the other. "Who the hell cares, Andrea? Certainly not *our* viewers! Do you think the same couple who watched an in-depth interview with Sondra Wickfield…or the pop singer, what's-his-name, Ricky Faith—the one who married the fifteen-year-old groupie—would be interested in watching a blind guy complaining about the way his country wronged him? Or some hillbilly of a marine biologist who spends his time worrying about whales and dolphins?" Bryce asked, brusquely. "No! Our markets center around the people between the ages of eighteen and twenty-eight who are either too young to remember the war, or had enough of it thrown at them ten years ago. What we need are topical, newsworthy personalities, stars that intrigue the public."

Andrea listened in silence, watching Bryce as he warmed to his subject. He got up from his chair and paced restlessly beside the desk, puffing angrily on the cigar.

"What you're saying is that you want only the most flamboyant, eye-catching celebrity willing to tell all, is that it?"

"Not quite." Bryce's eyes never wavered as he held Andrea's astonished gaze. "I'd settle for a respectable has-been politician with an active ex-wife and a scandal haunting him from the past!"

"You're still seriously considering Harmon?" she asked, and her stomach lurched uncontrollably.

"I'm not considering him, we're past that point. It's now just a matter of convincing him."

"I thought you already tried that."

"*I* did, but *you* haven't."

Andrea gasped, although she was trying desperately not to show her amazement. "You know I can't ask him."

"Why not?" Bryce sat down in his chair moodily. Once again he toyed with the pencil as he challenged Andrea with his blazing brown eyes.

"First, it wouldn't do any good. He's not going to listen to me any more than he listened to you."

"I wouldn't be so sure of that."

"But it's true! How could I convince him otherwise, even if I wanted to?"

"I'm sure you can be very persuasive when you have to be," Bryce intoned suggestively. "Use your imagination."

Andrea's eyes turned to green chips of ice. "What are you implying?"

"Look, Andrea," Bryce began, using a slightly more professional approach. He took the cigar from his mouth and let it burn, neglected, in the ashtray. "We're both adults. I know that you had an affair with Harmon ten years ago, and I'd be willing to bet that while you were on vacation, the two of you took up where you left off."

Andrea's back stiffened, and she swallowed with difficulty. She was silent as she listened to the end of Bryce's tirade.

"I don't expect much from you, just that you convince Harmon to talk to the public. That's not asking much. After all, they elected him. It's his duty to explain himself to them."

"I don't think so."

"What would it hurt?"

"I can't, Bryce, you know that."

Bryce pursed his lips firmly together, and his next words came out quickly and angrily. "Consider it part of your job."

Andrea felt sick to her stomach, but she wanted to be

certain that she understood Bryce before leaving the room. "Are you suggesting that I sleep with Jefferson Harmon in return for his agreement to do the interview?"

Bryce frowned. "That's a callous way of putting it."

"But precise."

"Andrea, we're desperate. The bigwigs at ITV insist that Harmon be the leadoff story."

"Because you promised that he would," she guessed.

"It doesn't matter. The bottom line is that if we want to save the production company, we've got to get Harmon." Bryce's voice softened, and the hardness left his eyes. "I haven't asked much from you in the past, Andrea."

"What you're suggesting is illegal, Bryce."

The angry knot at the base of Bryce's jaw tightened, and the smile that covered his face was ruthlessly grim. "I don't think that you're willing to go to the Civil Liberties Union and tell them that I suggested that you sleep with Jefferson Harmon in order to keep your job. What would that accomplish? Exactly what you and Harmon are hoping to avoid—publicity. The scandal in the past, the divorce, your affair—everything that you and Harmon have worked so hard to keep private would be out in the open again."

Andrea felt backed into a corner, and a desperate feeling of defeat encircled her. Bryce saw her vulnerability, and he pushed his point home.

"Come on, Andrea. We really need Jefferson Harmon for the interview. And maybe his ex-wife would be willing to be a guest at the same time. Just think of the public appeal that would hold, especially with all of the noise about her recent accident, and the fact that Harmon has agreed to defend her."

Andrea's lowered head snapped upward. "Jefferson is going to defend his ex-wife?"

"How about that!" Bryce smiled. "This is the kind of thing that will help our ratings rocket to the top."

Andrea's voice was calm when she found it. "I can't do anything that you're suggesting, Bryce."

"What?"

"I'm quitting. You'll have my official resignation within the hour."

"You're not serious."

"I am. I don't want to be a part of this."

Bryce's smirk became ragged. "Of course not, Andrea. You're a prima donna. I should have known I couldn't count on you when the chips were down."

Andrea left Bryce's office feeling suffocated from his taunts and the stale cigar smoke that had clouded her vision. Her chin was set in rigid determination as she cleaned out her desk and quickly typed her simple resignation.

"Andrea," Bryce called to her pleadingly. She felt all of her muscles tense at the sound. As her eyes moved up from the typewriter to the doorway where he was standing, she took in the beseeching look of pain in his eyes and the weary droop of his shoulders. She was still angry with him, but something in his dejected carriage made her anger slowly dissipate. "I'm sorry," Bryce apologized. "I shouldn't have jumped down your throat just because I'm having a bad day."

Andrea didn't move, but the challenge in her pale green eyes faded.

"I didn't mean half of the things I said."

"It's all right."

"No…no, it's not, and I hope that you'll reconsider resigning." He shrugged his shoulders awkwardly and pushed his hands into the tight pockets of his jeans. His eyebrows quirked nervously. "You and I, we've worked together a long time. I don't want to end it this way, when you're angry." He pulled the glasses from his face, folded them and tapped them against his chin.

"I think it would be best if I did leave," she sighed.

"We've had arguments before."

"Not like this. This is different, Bryce." Her voice was low and well modulated, her opinion resolute.

"Things are different around here," Bryce explained.

"I know. That's why I think it would be best for me to leave."

"You don't approve of the changes I've made, do you?"

Andrea pursed her lips together thoughtfully. "No, I guess I don't."

"I had no choice. We had to go commercial in order to survive. This is a cutthroat business. You know that."

Andrea nodded and ripped the resignation from the typewriter. It was shaking in her hands when she gave it to Bryce. "I still think it would be best for all of us if I left now, today. The only thing I expect from you is a letter of recommendation."

"You won't reconsider?" Bryce asked tonelessly.

"No."

"All right. If it's what you want. But let me be the first to tell you, jobs aren't exactly plentiful these days."

"I realize that," was her clipped reply. The longer the conversation continued, the more uncertain she felt. For the first time in eight years she was giving up the security of a job, a good job.

Bryce turned on his heel and left her without so much as a goodbye. She wavered for an instant, but his taunts and mocking manner of only an hour before rang loudly in her ears. With quiet determination she slung her purse over her shoulder, picked up a small box of her personal belongings and headed out the door of Coral Productions for the last time.

CHAPTER TEN

THE DAYS SLID INTO WEEKS for Andrea. Though Southern California should have been abundant with employment for out-of-work scriptwriters, Andrea had no luck in finding a job. She hurried out of her apartment at eight-thirty every morning, anxious to get to the next interview, and came home every evening discouraged and tired.

Every time the telephone rang, Andrea's heart stopped. Could it be Jefferson? Or could it possibly be a positive response to her most recent employment interview? Or, on the other side of the coin, might it be her parents asking about her life? So far she had been lucky. How could she explain to her soft-hearted mother and self-disciplined father that she had left a decent, well-paying job because of her involvement with Jefferson Harmon—the man they had openly denounced ten years ago?

Andrea was soaking in a warm bath when the telephone rang. Hurriedly she jumped out of the tub, wrapped a towel around her body and sprinted to the phone, leaving a wake of watery footsteps behind her.

"Hello," she called breathlessly into the phone.

"Andrea! God, I'm glad I caught you at home." Gayla's voice was a pleasant balm to Andrea's raw nerves. It had been ages since she had talked to her younger sister.

"You should talk," Andrea laughed back kiddingly as

she adjusted the towel on her body and sank back onto the bed. "I've been trying to reach you for over a month and never gotten through."

Gayla's gaiety immediately subdued. "Yeah. Well, I haven't been around much."

"Not at all."

There was a long sigh on the other end of the wire. "I guess you're right. Doug and I were separated for a while…."

"*What?*" Andrea's heart threatened to stop beating.

"It's a long story," Gayla admitted.

"I've got all night, if you want to talk about it."

"There's not much to talk about," Gayla sighed. "It's all so involved…a lot of emotions. I suppose I'm a lot to blame."

"I can't believe that!"

"Well, it's true. After Joey was born, things began to change for me. I didn't have my job anymore, finances were tight, and Joey hasn't been an easy child. Quite frankly, Andrea, I wasn't sure if I was cut out to be a mother."

"Of course you were."

"It's not that I don't love Joey," Gayla hastened to explain. "I love him more than I ever thought possible. It's just that it's hard, you know, being a wife to Doug, as well as a mother to Joey. I just didn't feel that I had any time left for *me!*"

"So you left Doug?"

"Only for a little while. Until I could sort things out," Gayla offered, and even over the long-distance wires, which spanned thousands of miles, Andrea knew that Gayla was crying.

"What about now? Are you happy now?"

For a moment there was a pensive silence as Gayla pulled herself together. "Things are better," she admitted. "Doug understands that I need more in my life than cleaning house and rinsing diapers. Recently I've been able to get out of the house a little more. I've found a relatively inexpensive exercise club that has a nice nursery for Joey, so I can go to exercise classes. I'm looking for a part-time job."

"That sounds encouraging," Andrea said, thinking aloud.

"It really is." There was more enthusiasm in Gayla's voice. "I guess my problem is that I want it all, Andrea—all life has to offer. I want to be a perfect mother, an understanding, caring, intelligent, sexy wife, *and* I want an interesting career. I don't want to miss out on anything—and that's impossible."

"How does Doug feel about all of this?"

"He's a very special man," Gayla admitted, and Andrea felt a little more at ease. "I think I really pushed him to the limit a couple of weeks ago, but I didn't understand all of the pressures he was coping with at his job." Her voice lowered slightly. "I'm surprised that he put up with me."

"Then you're telling me that I shouldn't worry about the two of you anymore, is that it?" Andrea asked.

"I think the worst is over. But, anyway, how about you? What have you been up to? I tried to reach you at the office today, but that flaky receptionist wouldn't give me any information other than the fact that you were, quote, 'no longer employed with Coral Productions.' What's it all about? Did you get another job? I never expected that you would leave Coral Productions or Bryce Cawthorne. The guy's practically a legend in TV land, isn't he?" Gayla's disconsolate tone had changed to one of enthusiasm.

"It wasn't an easy decision," Andrea hedged, sidestepping the real issue.

"But someone came along and offered you more money and a more prestigious position, right? You just couldn't refuse," Gayla surmised. Before Andrea could deny her sister's rosy-colored evaluation of her employment, Gayla continued. "You know that you've got a great career, don't you? I would give my eyeteeth to do the interesting things that you get to do. I saw *Pride's Power* a couple of weeks ago, and I thought it was great! I can't believe that it's being cancelled."

Andrea winced at her sister's opinion of her life, but then, even when she was younger, Gayla had always been a dreamer.

"Actually, *Pride's Power* never did all that well in the ratings," Andrea said, sighing.

"Who cares, now that you've got a better job? Who's it with? Some big-name production company?"

Andrea closed her eyes and tried to imagine Gayla's expectant face some two thousand miles away. "No, Gayla," she admitted hesitantly. "The fact is that right now I'm unemployed."

"*What?* But I thought—"

"I know what you thought, and I wish it were true, but the fact is that I quit Coral Productions a little over two weeks ago."

"*Why?*" Disbelief and concern rang in Gayla's question.

Andrea sucked in her breath. "I had become disenchanted with Coral, I guess, and then Bryce and I got into an argument."

"An *argument?*" Gayla echoed in disbelief. "You quit because of an *argument?*"

"It wasn't just an argument," Andrea conceded, aware that her sister thought she was covering something up. "It was an argument about Jefferson Harmon."

Andrea heard Gayla's sharp intake of breath. "Oh." There was a weighty pause before the younger woman continued. "What about Harmon? Have you seen him recently?"

"Yes."

"Oh God, Andrea, *why?* After the last time I thought you would never see that man again. Just because he divorced his wife—"

"The divorce had nothing to do with it. I went to see him because Bryce wanted him to do an interview for television. He refused, and Bryce got angry. I didn't want to be caught in the middle, so I quit."

"And what about Jefferson? Do you still see him?"

"He dropped by once, but it didn't work out," Andrea stated, but there was a trace of despair in her voice that Gayla detected.

"Have you talked to him since then?"

"A couple of times."

"And?"

"And nothing. We talked, that's all."

"But you would like there to be more between you, wouldn't you?" Gayla could always see right through her, Andrea mused to herself. She shifted restlessly on the bed.

"I guess so. I'm really not sure."

"That's your problem," Gayla stated flatly.

"What do you mean?" Andrea asked, almost fearful of her younger sister's candid response.

There was a resigned sigh on the other end of the wire. "If I've learned anything at all about myself during these past weeks when Doug and I were separated, I realized that

I had to take charge of my life myself. No one else was going to do it for me. I had to let Doug know how I felt about him, and Joey, and, I guess, even myself. I couldn't hide inside myself and brood about my problems. And, Andrea, the same goes for you. If you really want Jefferson Harmon, then you have to let him know how you feel about him. Find out if he wants the same things in life that you want."

"It's a little more complicated than that."

"It's as simple as you want it to be," Gayla argued staunchly.

Andrea toyed with the edge of the pillowcase. "I thought you considered it a mistake for me to see Jefferson again," she accused.

"It doesn't matter what I think. I was only afraid that you might get hurt again," Gayla admitted. "*But,* you only have one life, Andrea, and you're the one who has to make the decisions about it. You can't hope to keep everyone happy. It just won't work!" Andrea could almost see her younger sister shaking her auburn head in frustration. "You can't sit around hoping that Jefferson will call you. If you want him, take the initiative for Pete's sake. This isn't the seventeenth century, you know."

Just as Gayla was about to continue, Andrea could hear a childish wail on the other end of the line. Suddenly Gayla's thoughts turned elsewhere.

"Look, Andrea," Gayla hurriedly added. "I've really got to go. Joey just tripped over the edge of the coffee table. I'll call you later."

"Sure," Andrea agreed with a smile. Gayla's motherly concern suggested that although she might have doubts about herself as a mother, she was indeed well suited for the role. If nothing else, things seemed to be working themselves out in Seattle.

After replacing the receiver of the telephone, Andrea decided against renewing her now tepid bathwater. Shivering slightly, she stepped into her favorite jeans and an orchid-colored cowl-necked pullover. As she tucked the light sweater into the waistband of her jeans, Gayla's well-meant advice echoed in Andrea's mind. *Take the initiative, Andrea. It's your life; you're the one that has to make the decisions concerning it.*

In some respects, Andrea begrudgingly admitted to herself, Gayla was probably right. But how could her younger sister, so far off and wrapped up in her own problems, analyze or even begin to understand the depth of Andrea's feelings for Jefferson, or the confusion that she experienced whenever she was near him. Sure, Andrea knew that Jefferson wanted her, at least physically, and she wasn't foolish enough not to realize that he cared for her. It was just that all of the misunderstandings of the past prevented him from allowing himself to *love* her. Even though he was divorced now, Andrea doubted that he could ever truly be free of his ex-wife, the mother of his child. Megan was the fragile link that would always bind Jefferson to Lara, regardless of any divorce-court agreement.

Andrea had begun to brush her long, onyx hair as her thoughts took hold of her, and though she stared into the mirror, her eyes didn't catch her reflection as she tugged the brush through her hair in furious strokes. She thought only of Jefferson—his dark, knowing eyes and familiar smile. Gayla had pierced to the heart of the matter in one respect, at least. Andrea wanted to be with him, *needed* to see him again.

It was true that Jefferson had called her twice in the past few weeks, and though the conversation had been stilted and uncomfortable, Andrea had known that, in a small way, Jefferson was attempting to reach out to her. It was true, also, that since that last night in Victoria, Andrea had willfully resisted any deep, feminine urge to contact him. Pursing her lips at the thought, Andrea mentally allowed that perhaps Jefferson's feelings of ambivalence toward her might have stemmed from the fact that she had not recently admitted her feelings for him. Perhaps he was as unsure of her as she was of him.

Andrea tossed the hairbrush onto the bureau with a sigh of disapproval. Then why hadn't he asked to see her? Why did she always imagine a rigid edge of wariness in his voice when he called? Why did she think that he was purposely holding something back from her—against her? *Why, damn it, hadn't he attempted to see her again?*

Angrily she pulled on her boots and sat for only a second on the edge of the bed, wondering if she was about to make a mistake that she would regret for the rest of her life. Preferring action to any further soul-searching, she marched out of the bedroom, snatched her purse from the couch and, with a jerk, pulled her leather jacket from the hall tree. She had decided to visit Jefferson, unannounced. He might not be at the address she had kept in her memory, there was always that chance, but Andrea didn't want to risk the confusion and disappointment of another tense, gut-wrenching telephone conversation. This time she wanted to look into the hazel depths of his eyes when she spoke to him.

The drive to the apartment building was a strain on her. As she wound her way in the clogged streets of the Southern California highway system, doubts crowded her mind. She gripped the steering wheel until her knuckles blanched. The music that blared from the radio didn't distract her, and she could feel her stomach beginning to churn at the thought of walking in on Jefferson Harmon unannounced. Would he be alone? Would he see her? What if he had company, perhaps his daughter, or worse yet, his ex-wife?

Quickly dousing any further conjecture about him, Andrea cranked the wheel of the car and ground to a halt in the parking lot of the high-rise modern apartment complex where Jefferson made his home. The antithesis of the grand old house on Harmon Island, the building was an imposing structure, composed of sand-colored stucco and splashes of rust-hued brick. To blend with the sunny, palm-lined surroundings, the architecture of the building was a modern blend of Spanish design. A large rock garden, nestled in a well-kept courtyard complete with wrought iron gates, guarded the entrance to the building.

Ignoring her rapidly pounding pulse and the butterflies that were fluttering in her stomach, Andrea hurried through the courtyard and pushed open the hand-carved wooden doors of the building. Once inside she was given one last opportunity to retreat. A liveried security guard, wearing a smile that seemed as well-groomed as his clipped moustache, asked her politely to state her business.

Her voice faltered a little as she responded, "I'd like to see Jefferson Harmon. Is he in?"

The guard cocked a graying eyebrow condescendingly, and his smile became routinely bored. "Are you expected?"

"No…no, I'm not," Andrea admitted reluctantly.

"I see."

Andrea squared her shoulders and tipped her chin upward in order to meet the security guard's assessing stare. "Would you please call Mr. Harmon and tell him that Andrea Monroe would like to see him?" she asked firmly.

While the corners of his mouth turned peevishly

downward, the security guard did as he was bid, dialing Jefferson Harmon's floor from memory. As he relayed Andrea's message his sobered expression changed into surprise. Jefferson's response was not what he had expected.

"She'll be up right away, sir," the guard stated into the phone. With a face that had altered from bored indifference to genuine charm, the guard escorted Andrea to the elevator, instructing her to disembark on the eighth and uppermost floor of the building. As Andrea pushed the correct button, she wondered how often in the past the security guard had turned away inquisitive reporters who had hoped to get in to see Jefferson Harmon.

The elevator climbed smoothly upward to settle with a groan at the eighth floor. Andrea tried vainly to curb her growing anxiety and nervousness. Waiting for the unyielding doors to open, she unconsciously tapped her fingers against the brass rail that surrounded the interior of the elevator car. She tried to pull herself together, but found it impossible to appear outwardly calm when her nerves were twisted so tightly in apprehension.

The elevator doors parted silently, and after taking a deep breath, Andrea stepped onto the plush carpet of a short hallway. Before she reached the oaken door to his apartment, Jefferson unlocked the dead bolt. The door swung silently inward, inviting Andrea to enter Jefferson's private hideaway in the dusky California sky.

Jefferson stood near the door, and his demeanor was anything but warm. His dark, questioning hazel eyes studied Andrea with uncompromising intensity. Though he struggled to appear affable, Andrea could tell that he was as tense as she. His lips were pulled into a tight, unpleasant smile, and his hands were pushed deep into the pockets of his gray slacks. His torso was bare and rigid, all of the muscles straining in taut control. A pin-striped shirt was tossed carelessly over the back of a navy-blue sectional sofa, and Andrea guessed that Jefferson had just gotten home and was about to change his clothes before the security guard's untimely call had altered his plans.

"Come in," Jefferson invited tightly.

For a moment all of her determination fled Andrea. The look of foreboding in his eyes, the electricity that sparked in the air and his distracting, well-muscled chest, warned Andrea against entering Jefferson's apartment. "I…I didn't mean to disturb you. Are you busy?"

"If I had been busy, I wouldn't have let you in," he replied callously, and his unpleasant smile turned almost wicked as he recognized her discomfort.

Hesitantly Andrea stepped into the expansive living room of the apartment. The light that filtered into the room was from a long window that faced the western skyline and from skylights strategically placed over the sofa. Andrea's eyes roved anxiously over the dim interior and the furnishings. She noted a staid elegance in the blend of contemporary and antique chattels. Leather editions of law encyclopedias, original surrealistic paintings, elegant brass lamps and modern sectional and period pieces that included leather wing chairs graced the room.

"Would you like a drink?" Jefferson asked smoothly as if to help ease the nervousness that she tried to hide. He stretched to put on his shirt and flicked on one of the lamps, intending to reduce the intimacy of the surroundings.

"Please," she responded, and crossed her arms involuntarily across her chest, as if to ward off a sudden chill in the air.

After casting a disdainful look in her direction, Jefferson strode over to the bar, pulled out an opened bottle of brandy and poured a drink into an empty snifter. Another drink, already half-consumed, was on the liquor cabinet. Andrea realized that Jefferson must have been drinking alone in the darkness, half-dressed, before she had arrived on his doorstep. The gnawing anxiety in her stomach began to grow.

As Jefferson offered her the drink, he spoke. "Well, to what, or *whom,* do I owe the honor of your presence?" he asked, hoisting his snifter into the air in a mock toast.

Andrea accepted the offered glass of brandy and took an experimental sip. "I came here on impulse," she replied, letting her eyes drift upward to meet his. Almost imperceptibly his jaw tightened.

"Is that right?" he mocked. Dark hazel eyes drove deeply into hers, challenging her.

Although she couldn't ignore the sarcasm in his words, she held her temper in check. "I just wanted to see you," she explained honestly.

The sincerity in her eyes reached out to him, and he had to caution himself against trusting her too completely. This time, whether she knew it or not, he was on to her game, and way ahead of her. Rather than feel rewarded in the knowledge, the thought gave him a sickly sensation. Undaunted, he continued. If she wanted to play out the charade for all it was worth, he would comply. "Just like you wanted to see me back on the island?" he asked. "About four weeks ago, right?" His eyes narrowed as he studied her response.

Andrea could feel his coiled tension. She knew he was baiting her, but she didn't understand why. "That was different."

"How?" His question stung the air with disbelief. The

anger that he had tried to conceal became unmasked in the starkness of his probing gaze. "Why was that any different? I thought that you came to see me on the island because you wanted to. Isn't that what you said?"

The sarcasm that tainted his words and the contempt in his disbelieving stare sparked Andrea's barely controlled temper. "You're twisting my words again, Jefferson," she accused. "Of course I wanted to see you on the island, you *know* that I wanted to be with you."

"But…?" he coaxed, settling into the deep midnight blue cushions of the couch and eyeing her speculatively. His shirt, still unbuttoned, opened slightly to reveal his tanned chest and rigid muscles.

"But," she began, picking up his cue, "it was more than just my curiosity to see you again, more than my need to be with you. I also came to the island as a favor to my boss. Is that what you're driving at?"

Jefferson ignored her question. "And this time is different, or so you claim. Do you honestly expect me to believe it?"

"Of course." Andrea was still standing as she looked down at Jefferson. Her eyes locked with his doubting gaze. "You obviously don't believe me. Why not?"

"Your boss tipped me off." He took a drink and emptied his snifter.

"What?" she demanded.

The edge of confusion and dismay in her voice caught Jefferson's attention. He could see that she was clearly perplexed and angry—angry enough to have been telling the truth. Jefferson could almost feel her confusion at his abrupt attitude toward her. He wondered fleetingly if he had been wrong about her, but discarded the traitorous idea. It would be too easy to trust Andrea again. Rather than look into the bewildered, misty eyes, he frowned in concentration at his empty glass.

"Look, Andrea," he sighed as he set the glass aside. "I understand the reasons that you came here…." His gaze lifted to meet the innocence of her eyes.

"You do?"

"Sure." His charming off-center smile, which had been a trademark during his successful political campaigns, fell neatly into place.

Andrea felt some of her anxiety ebb, just as he had anticipated. A small light of satisfaction entered his eyes, and Andrea knew that she should be wary. She waited, hoping that, given a little time, Jefferson would get to the point.

"Good. I'm glad you understand me." She forced herself to smile enigmatically as she took a seat opposite him. The stiff wing chair wasn't comfortable, but she attempted to appear casual as she sipped her drink.

Jefferson eyed her steadily. His pectoral flexed, belying his outward calm. "You can explain to your boss that my position hasn't changed," he announced evenly. His smile seemed tighter, his gaze more severe.

"What?" Andrea nearly spilled her drink at Jefferson's announcement. "What are you talking about?" Her glittering green eyes, filled with anger and confusion, dared him to continue.

"The interview," he snapped impatiently. "Don't bother to play dumb with me, Andrea. It belittles you. Cawthorne hasn't given me a minute's peace since I left the island!" Jefferson's voice lowered dangerously. "He threatened that he would send you—as some sort of sacrificial lamb, I suppose—but I didn't think that he—and least of all *you*—would go through with it! How could you stoop so low, Andrea?" His hazel eyes blazed in fury and disgust.

"Oh, my God," Andrea moaned, finally understanding Jefferson's uncompromising attitude. "You still don't trust me, do you? You honestly think that I'm involved in some sort of seduction that Bryce engineered! For God's sake, Jefferson, give me some credit, will you?" The anger that had been rising in her throat quickly melted into bitter frustration and disappointment as her face drained of color. With hands that shook uncontrollably, she set her drink on the table near the chair. "I'm sorry," she apologized, whispering hoarsely. "I should never have come here. It was an unforgivable mistake."

She rose to leave but found that her knees seemed intent on buckling. Although she started for the door, Jefferson moved more quickly than she had anticipated. "There's no reason to play out this scene," he stated, capturing her upper arm in the strength of his insistent fingers. "Why can't you admit that Cawthorne sent you?" he demanded, giving her upper arm a painful squeeze.

"Don't touch me," she warned. "If you don't realize, if you don't *know,* that I wouldn't have anything to do with something as sordid as the scenario you're suggesting, I never want you to touch me again!"

Proudly she jerked away from him, unashamed of the tears that were building in the wide depths of her pale green eyes.

Jefferson wavered. Andrea's disdainful indignation and the pain in the shadows of her eyes were convincing, and there was more in her gaze as well. Disgust and contempt were thrust angrily in his direction through the sheen of unshed tears. Suddenly Jefferson realized that he had made a terrible mistake.

"Andrea, wait!" Again his arm reached for her, but she was already at the door. She grabbed for the handle and had opened the door a crack when he reached her and roughly slammed the door closed. "Don't go," he pleaded, pinning her against the polished oaken panels.

"I'm leaving, Jefferson," she hissed in response. "I didn't come here to listen to your insults and your lewd, imaginative fantasies." Her small fist clenched and pounded the door in frustration.

"Why did you come?"

"Oh, God," she cried, unable to hide the anguish in her voice. "I came here because I thought, or at least I hoped, that you and I had something worthwhile, something worth saving." Her voice lowered to a raw whisper. "I was wrong!"

"No…no! Don't ever say that." Jefferson's face twisted in a tormented display of the emotions that had ravaged him to the bone in the last four weeks. "You've got to believe that we do have something special, Andrea. We both know it." His hand, gently persuasive, moved upward to brush a tear off her cheek. She turned her head away from his touch and let the tears slide unrestrained from her eyes. "Andrea," Jefferson whispered, his fingers entwining in the soft strands of her ebony hair. "I love you."

She stiffened against the door, and a sob that had been building within her broke free. How long had she waited to hear just such a confession from him? Four weeks? Ten years? A lifetime? His thumb moved over the hill of her cheek, and she felt her body sag wearily against the door. "How can you say you love me," she asked, her voice and body trembling with savage emotion, "when you just accused me of trying to seduce you in order to please my boss?"

"I've always loved you, Andrea," he moaned. "Surely you must know that. Why else would you come back to me?"

"I think you already answered that a little earlier in the conversation. I can't understand how you expect me to believe that you could *love* a woman whom you thought capable of…of prostitution. Because that's what it all boils down to, you know. You just accused me of attempting to make love to you for personal gain. You were only one step away from calling me a *whore!*"

"Damn it, Andrea," Jefferson muttered, letting his head fall forward to rest next to hers against the door. His breath whispered raggedly against her hair as he spoke, and she smelled the sweet brandy mingled with his own woodsy-masculine cologne. His shirt draped open, and his firmly muscled chest pushed tightly against her body. He was too close…too near. His voice, hoarse and raw, seemed to touch the very soul of her being. "I never meant to hurt you. You've got to believe that much. I love you more than any man should love a woman. I always have."

"To the point of believing that I would actually seduce you, and *use* you for personal profit?" she hurled back at him. She tried to slide away from him, but his hands restrained her, pushing her against the door. She longed to believe him, yearned to fall victim to his touch once again, but the open wounds, still stinging from his earlier remarks, were too fresh.

"I didn't mean—"

"I know what you meant," she interrupted, aware that the rising and falling of her chest made her breasts touch his naked torso. "But I don't understand how you could believe it of me!"

Jefferson looked skyward for a moment. "I'm sorry. I know that an apology won't erase the words or the pain, but please accept it. It's just that your boss seems so adamant about that damned interview. He intimated that you felt the same."

"*What?* You talked to Bryce?"

"You know that I did," Jefferson snapped back. "You were in his office when he called yesterday." Jefferson's eyes searched Andrea's. "At least that's what he said."

"I wasn't there."

Jefferson tensed. His whole body became rigid. "You weren't in the room when Cawthorne called me?"

"No."

"But he said that you and he agreed that it would be best for everyone—you, me, the public, even Megan—if all the truth were out, all the skeletons hidden away in the closet were set free."

"And you believed him?" Andrea asked incredulously.

"Why wouldn't I? He asked you to come and see me in Victoria, and you agreed."

"I don't understand any of this, Jefferson. Bryce did ask me to do anything I could to make you do the interview. He even suggested that I…sleep with you," she admitted, and closed her eyes against the repulsive memory.

Jefferson's jaw squared. "And?"

"And I quit. I haven't worked for Coral Productions for over two weeks."

Jefferson took a step backward, putting distance between their bodies. His eyes held hers captive, and his hands were planted firmly on either side of her, preventing her escape.

"All right, I believe you. If you're not here because of the interview, why did you come?"

"I thought I explained that. I thought we had something to salvage."

"But why now—tonight?"

Andrea smiled in spite of herself. "Because I was tired of sitting around my apartment waiting for the phone to ring. I've been looking for a job, and it seems that I'm forever hoping that the phone will ring and that it will either be someone with a fantastic job offer, or..."

He nodded, encouraging her to go on.

"...or that it would be you." Her eyes seemed to glaze with the mist from the sea. "I just wanted to be with you again." Slowly her hands moved upward and tentatively touched the exposed skin that covered his ribs. His eyes closed at the warmth of her touch, and he groaned.

For a moment he stood arrow straight, not moving, just letting himself enjoy the gentle persuasion of her soft hands. But when she pushed her body close to his, he could stand the bittersweet agony no longer. His arms wrapped possessively around her, and his fingers entwined in the rich thick curls of her hair. His lips, when they found hers, were insistent and full of promise. They parted willingly, and his supple tongue sought out and touched hers in flickering bursts of desire.

Andrea's pulse quickened, and her blood heated as it coursed through her veins. Her fingers kneaded the hard, inflexible flesh of his chest and a warm, growing ache spiraled within her body.

"You're a witch," he growled. "You know that, don't you?" Before she could answer, one arm curved under her knees and the other tightened around her back. Effortlessly he lifted her off the floor and, while hugging her close to him, carried her through a hallway toward the bedroom. She nestled against him and could hear his heart hammering heavily in his chest, echoing in the silence against the erratic thudding of her own heartbeat.

She ignored all thought of protest. For the moment she

only wanted to be more intimate with him, to feel one with him. Her body ached for his touch. She closed her eyes and felt her eyelashes brush against the hard muscles of his chest. The love she felt for him was a desperate, passionate ache that controlled her thoughts and her body. His own words of love, whispered with such agony against the door, tore at her heart, but she tried not to think of them. Even in the warm embrace of his arms, she realized that too many years of treacherous misunderstanding had paled the meaning of his confession. But, despite all of the doubts that still plagued her, just as she had in the past, she would let her body rule her mind. Once again she would give in to the joy of expressing her love for him.

The bedroom was in shadows. Only a very dim moon glow and the frosted lights of the city entered the room to disturb the darkness. Andrea's eyes adjusted to the darkened interior and noticed that the pale stream of light from the moon entered through skylights positioned over the bed. The other furnishings in the room blended into the night, and Andrea was too caught up with Jefferson's commanding virile presence to notice anything other than the soft feel of the bed on her back and the warm possession of the man lowering himself near her. His touch seemed electric, even through her clothes. His kisses were warm and erotic, seeming to explode with a passion that had been kept at bay for ten lost, lonely years.

His tongue rimmed her lips as if, by its touch, Jefferson could memorize the feel of the wet, supple softness of her mouth and the urgency of her desire. His hands caressed her lightly, stroking the soft fabric of her clothes to make her want more…all of him. Andrea closed her eyes against the dizzying, heady sensations that he evoked from her willing body, and her fingers massaged the firm, flat muscles of his chest and abdomen, eliciting the same pleasure in him that his fingers were arousing within her.

"You don't know how many nights I've dreamed of this," he whispered against the shell of her ear. "I thought I would go mad with the need of you."

"You should have told me."

"I couldn't," he groaned, and his lips captured hers once again. This time the gentle persuasion of his kisses had deepened into hungry demands. His hands pulled the hem of her sweater from her jeans and found the sensitive skin over her stomach. Involuntarily Andrea sucked in her breath, and Jefferson's fingers lightly skimmed the waistband of her jeans, softly brushing her hips.

Andrea sighed in contentment and wound her fingers in the thick, near-black waves of his hair. Urgently she pulled him against her, and with a groan he pulled her sweater over her head.

For a moment he stopped and stared down at her. Her raven-black hair was splayed in tousled curls against the light color of the bedspread, and her eyes, partially closed, reflected the silver moon glow in their misty green depths. Pupils, dilated from the darkness and the heat of passion, seemed almost iridescent as Andrea looked up at him. Her breasts, swollen in her need of him, strained against the lacy fabric of her bra, and the dark nipples waited expectantly for his expert touch.

Andrea felt drugged, and her eyelids half-closed as Jefferson took one supple breast in his warm hand and feathered his fingers across the taut, straining nipple. Andrea moaned with pleasure and arched upward against him. His fingers dipped beneath the flimsy barrier of the white silk, only to retreat and leave her aching for more of his sensitive touch. Slowly, as if with deliberate leisure to prolong her inflamed agony, his head descended, and in gentle strokes he licked her breast over the filmy bra, sending lightning bolts of passion through her blood and heating the molten desire in her body until she could stand no more of the sweet torture.

"Love me," she pleaded desperately, longingly. Her prayerful request made him groan in satisfaction. "Jefferson, please, make love to me as you never have before." In response he lifted his head and let his tongue rim the nipple before it slid over her breast to her collarbone. There he lingered, rimming the delicate bones in moist, sweet circles of desire that sent Andrea soaring to new heights of need and burning want. His tongue slowly climbed her throat until it found her parted lips. Slowly, lazily, he rimmed her mouth, deliberately ignoring the open invitation as she sighed.

He teased her, darting in and out of her mouth seeking a response. When at last he probed the furthest reaches of the dark, sweet cavern of her mouth, he let his tongue dance and mate with hers until she felt shudders of smoldering passion ripple through her.

His fingers toyed with the fragile, wispy bra until at last Andrea felt it part and her anxious, full breasts fall into Jefferson's waiting hands. With a groan of pleasure he pushed his fingers into the soft flesh and then lowered his head to take one nipple gently between his teeth. He tugged softly, and Andrea, overcome with the need of him, pushed his head into her so he could take all of the nipple in his mouth and end her torment. As he kissed and sucked at her breast, his hands found the waistband of her jeans and began to explore beneath the denim material. His hands touched her, stroking the most intimate parts of her until she felt as if she would be consumed in the fire of torment that was building.

When he pulled away from her, disappointment welled in her eyes, but he ignored it, and instead sat at the foot of the bed. Carefully he pulled off one of her boots, and then the other before sliding his hands caressingly up her calves under the legs of her jeans. His fingers reached upward, and she arched to meet him, frustrated that she was unable to feel the hardness of his muscles against her.

He inched the jeans downward, past her hips, and smiled wickedly when she lay on the bed waiting for him, wearing nothing but soft, lacy panties. His fingers played with the final barrier that stopped him from entering her. He seemed to delight in the hot whirlpool that was swirling inside her, running up her veins, giving her skin a rosy glow. "You are a sea witch, Andrea, but you're mine. My own."

With measured time he tugged at her panties, pulling them slowly over her hips and legs, letting his fingers touch each part of her leg as he removed the unwanted garment. His kisses started at her toes and moved upward, retracing the path that his fingers had blazed. Andrea felt the weight of his body as he lay on her, and she sighed in contentment.

"Undress me," he called into her sensitive ear. Quickly she responded, trying to restrain herself and bring as much pleasure to him as he had given her. She lowered his shirt from his shoulders and let her fingers graze the contour of his muscled arms. Before touching his pants she let her hands massage the flat muscles of his chest and abdomen, moving her fingers in loving circular patterns against the taut male nipples. Teasingly she put one in her mouth and felt Jefferson's groan of pleasure and satisfaction. The salty male flavor of his skin stayed upon her tongue and lips, and when he bent to kiss her, she felt as if she were drowning in the taste of him.

Her fingers touched the muscles of his back, his buttocks and his thighs as she pushed his slacks off his legs. When he was nude, lying near her, she touched his hot, naked skin in featherlight strokes until a thin layer of sweat gilded his body. His breathing became as labored and shallow as her own.

She continued to stroke him until with a groan of frustration he rolled over and lay upon her. His hands clasped over her forearms as he held her against the sheets. “You’re a tease,” he whispered, dipping his head to kiss her just beneath the ear.

“And so are you,” she countered breathlessly, not listening to the conversation, concentrating instead on the small spot below her ear where Jefferson’s tongue melted against her skin.

Slowly his arms folded and his weight settled firmly against the soft bed of her skin. Everywhere they touched Andrea felt warm needles of electricity piercing her skin, forcing her heart to beat more rapidly. He kissed all of her, leaving wet trails of fevered desire across her body. No part of her was unknown to him, and no part of her wanted for fulfillment. He loved her with the same desperate, driving need that was only matched by her own rapturous desires.

She lost herself to him and experienced the satisfaction and pleasure that only he could give. His hands molded her, teased her, and his lips and tongue pressed against her warm, salt-sweet skin. Her breasts were kneaded and kissed until they seemed engorged, and when he entered her, she willingly gave all of herself to him, melting against him with a gasp of surrender as she felt him join in ecstatic union with her. In her love-drugged mind, it seemed as if there had never been a time when they had been apart. His flesh, her flesh, belonged together until the end of time.

She moved with him, found his rhythm and felt the hot throbbing force of his desire inside her. His hands and fingers guided her, touching her in all of the intimate places that pushed her to higher planes of sexual delight. The tension in her body began to coil and tighten until she finally burst in satiation. She felt shock waves of rapture race through her blood as his body pushed her into the final, shuddering explosion of long-denied passion, and the two of them blended together in a breathless union of flesh and spirit. Never had she felt so wanted. Never had she felt so free. Never had she loved him more than she did in those first few moments of afterglow.

His fingers caressed her skin, and his kisses continued until Andrea drifted off to a trouble-free sleep as she snuggled in the strong comfort of Jefferson's arms. How long had she dreamed of such blissful surrender? How many years had she waited to share just such a night with him?

Jefferson's passion seemed to feed upon itself. Later in the night, when both she and Jefferson had been sleeping, Andrea awoke to find Jefferson kissing her body. Her breasts were once again straining against him, asking for the sweet assuagement that only he could give. He suckled and held her close, as if he were drawing as much pleasure from her body as he were giving. Andrea held on to him, content to feel the gentle pressure of his mouth around her nipple, thrilled by the feel of his hands as they touched and petted her inner thigh, warmed by the feel of his kisses as they caressed her neck and shoulders. Once again they found each other, and warmth cascaded over Andrea when Jefferson lifted her on top of him, and encouraged her to move above him. Her black hair fell forward, and Jefferson ran his hands through the silken, raven tresses. Her breasts swayed above him as she moved her hips in rhythmic strokes, and Jefferson lifted his head to capture a dancing nipple in his mouth. The pressure of his lips pushed Andrea upward, higher and higher until with a shudder of rapture, she collapsed upon him in radiant pleasure.

The pleasure didn't stop. Once more before morning Jefferson awakened Andrea. She found herself dragged into consciousness by the erotic teasing of his lips brushing provocatively against the tip of her breast. His fingers touched her in featherlight caresses and aroused her until all desire for sleep left her and she longed for more intimate seduction and satisfaction from him.

It was near dawn when he finally wrapped his arms around her and settled into a deep, worry-free sleep. Andrea had never felt such utter contentment, not since the day she had first given herself to him ten years ago.

CHAPTER ELEVEN

ANDREA SQUINTED AGAINST the obtrusive, bright sun, and she tried to snuggle back into the peaceful slumber that slipped away as the sunlight settled boldly against her eyelids. It seemed that no matter how she turned on the large bed, the piercing light insisted upon disturbing her. Where was she, and why was the light so unyielding and bright?

The sudden realization that she had spent the night in the arms of Jefferson ran like ice water through her cloudy mind, and immediately she awakened. It was difficult to get her bearings in the strange room. The brilliant California sun impaled her from the skylight and didn't help clear the last remaining cobwebs in her groggy mind.

"So you decided to wake up after all." Jefferson was standing near an open window several feet from the bed and had turned to face her at the sound of her awakening.

Andrea pushed her hair away from her face and attempted to straighten the long ebony strands with her fingers. Her eyes became accustomed to the sunny interior of the room, and she stretched. "What time is it?"

Jefferson watched her unguardedly as the satin sheets slipped against her body and outlined the perfection of her slim figure. A smile crept onto his face for a moment. "Be careful," he warned as his hazel gaze drifted seductively over her body. "If you don't stop looking so damned provocative, I'll be tempted to climb back into bed with you and make last night look tame compared to what I intend to do to you."

She couldn't avoid the challenge. Seductively one of her black brows cocked over her heavy-lidded green eyes, and as she moved on the bed the sheet that had been draped over her breasts slipped just a fraction of an inch.

Jefferson's smile curved in wicked satisfaction. "I was right last night when I called you a witch. I'd like to—"

"What?" she asked in feigned innocence.

He hesitated for a moment, and then he shook his head in stiff determination. "You know damned well what I'd like to do to you, but it will have to wait. I'm late as it is."

"Late?"

"For work." He buttoned his shirt and slung a necktie under the collar. "Even ex-governors have to earn a living, you know," he stated as he knotted his tie and tucked the hem of his shirt into his pants.

"The law firm?" she asked.

"Yes." He nodded and straightened his tie. He hesitated for a moment, as if he wasn't sure how much he wanted to tell her about his work. His explanation was short and simple. "After a few months of restlessness, just after the resignation, I decided to reestablish my practice."

"Corporate law?" she asked, sensing that he was deliberately holding something back from her. She couldn't help but pursue the conversation. When he didn't immediately respond, she sat up in the bed and drew her knees to her chin, letting the sheet drape over her as she huddled on the bed and watched him. "That was your specialty, wasn't it?"

"Right."

He picked up his suit jacket and slung it over his

shoulder. Although his stance appeared casual, Andrea felt an underlying chill to his curt replies. After the passion of the night before, she refused to be shut out. He must have guessed her thoughts, and with a sigh he dropped the jacket and came over to sit on the edge of the bed.

Jefferson's eyebrows drew together to form one dark, angry line, and his lips pulled into a tight, grim frown. Restlessly he raked his fingers through his dark hair. "For the most part, I work in corporate law," he conceded. Then, as if to change the course of the conversation, he picked up his watch from the nightstand and slipped it on to his wrist. "It's nearly noon," he announced, almost as if talking to himself.

"No!" Andrea jumped out of bed and began gathering her clothes. "I've got an interview across town at one thirty. I'll never make it!" She tugged on her jeans and as hurriedly as possible pulled her sweater over her head. Jefferson stood and watched her as she got dressed, bending down to pick up her boots and hand them to her as she needed them. He wrestled with a decision in his mind and wondered just how much of his life he wanted to share with Andrea. One part of him wanted all of her, every bit of her life, to blend with his, but another, more wary side of his being reminded him of the pain he had borne in the past at her hand, and noted that any further involvement with her might cause more agony to not only him and Megan, but Andrea as well.

Andrea eyed Jefferson curiously as she slipped into one boot. It was obvious he was wrestling with a weighty decision.

"Well, are you going to tell me what's going on in your mind?" she asked. His eyes asked an unspoken question. "It's obvious that you want to tell me something, but feel, for God only knows what reason, that you can't." She crossed her legs and looked upward at him. "Don't you think it's time we stopped playing games with each other? If you have something to say to me, say it."

"You're not the only one who's late," he admitted. He came nearer to her, and his hand reached out to cup her chin and force her eyes to hold his. "I have a client who, no doubt at this very moment, is pacing the reception area of my office." His voice was low and somber, and his eyes darkened as he searched Andrea's face. A scene from the night before flashed in her memory—Jefferson drinking alone in the dark.

"Someone important, I gather," she said lightly as she pushed a clinging strand of hair out of the neck of her sweater.

"You might say that," he agreed vaguely, teetering between holding his silence and confiding all of the secrets of his life to the petite woman he couldn't drive from his mind.

"Who?" she asked. Her voice was offhand and casual, but she felt a tension beginning to contract within her. She reached for her other boot and began to pull it on.

"Lara."

Andrea let the boot fall to the floor, and her green eyes swept upward to study Jefferson's grim face. She let her teeth sink painfully into her lower lip before she could trust herself to speak. "So it's true. I had heard that you were going to defend her."

Jefferson's fists clenched, and he ground his teeth together in frustration. "It's true, but it wasn't by choice!"

Suddenly she didn't want to see any more clearly into what had been his marriage. She felt herself an unwanted intruder in a life she hadn't shared with him. Another woman had first claim on him. Her voice was surprisingly even when she responded. "It doesn't matter. It's really none of my business...."

"It is your business, damn it!" He sat beside her on the edge of the bed and rubbed his hand over his forehead. His shoulders sagged wearily. "I know that this is probably hard for you to understand, but right now, with things as they are, I can't make a commitment to you."

She felt as if a cold, sharp knife had been thrust in her back. "I haven't asked you for one," she reminded him.

"But you deserve one, don't you see," he hurled back at her. "Look." He stood up and began pacing at the foot of the bed, his hands pushed into his pockets. "You know how important it is that I gain custody of Megan?"

She nodded silently, never letting her eyes off his worried, strained face. Thoughts raced through her head. He was going to reject her again; she could almost feel the cruel sting of his words before they were uttered. Holding her emotions at bay, she dug her fingers into the bed and listened while silent dread overcame her.

He continued, and his pacing never slackened. "Then you understand that I would prefer not to drag her through the torture of a messy custody hearing? I don't want her to ever feel that she's a possession that Lara and I have to fight over. I hope that somehow we'll be able to avoid hurting Megan any further. A custody battle made public by the press is something I want to avoid. However, I am willing to take my chances with the court if nothing else works."

"I know," she whispered, almost inaudibly.

He paused for a moment and cast a stern look in her direction. "Lara seemed determined to fight me for Megan," he began, his hazel eyes darkening. "And I accepted the fact that without a doubt we would have our day before the judge." His eyes narrowed thoughtfully, and a sinister smile twisted on his lips. "But that was before my ex-wife broadsided a car while intoxicated. Now one of the passengers is suing her, and she's in serious trouble. Fortunately Lara realizes what kind of trouble she's facing."

"So she asked you to defend her?" Andrea guessed.

"And I refused." The pacing stopped.

"But I thought you just said—"

"I know what I said. Just listen for a moment. I told Lara no flat out, and she became desperate. It seems that no other attorney worth his salt would risk his reputation on her case. She had no choice but to ask me."

"But I thought you weren't available."

"I wasn't. Not until Lara made an offer."

"An offer?"

"Think of it as a deal. We struck a bargain." His jaw tensed with the disgust that he so obviously felt.

Andrea's green eyes widened in horror as the meaning of Jefferson's words became clear to her. "You bargained for your daughter?"

"Sounds a little callous, doesn't it?"

"Jefferson, how could you *bargain* over an innocent child? You said you didn't want her thought of as a possession, but it seems to me you treated her as if she was some sort of commodity. You used your wife's misfortune to get her to agree to give up her daughter. Good God, Jefferson, that's right out of 'Rumpelstiltskin'!" Andrea blanched, shock and disbelief cascading over her.

Jefferson's eyes glittered mercilessly as he disagreed. "Not quite. You're forgetting that I'm Megan's father, and that her mother is a neglectful alcoholic. Megan has to get away from Lara!" His features softened slightly. "You know that I would be willing to let Lara retain partial custody if and when she successfully wins her battle with alcohol. But until that time I'll stop at nothing to see that my daughter is safe and cared for!"

"I still think it's cruel," Andrea said, sighing.

"To whom?"

"Megan, for one."

"How? She's too young to understand right now. And when she's older, she'll respect my point of view."

"You're sure?"

"Nothing's certain except that I have to do what I think is best. And just think about the scandal and problems a custody hearing will cause." Jefferson shook his head thoughtfully. "No, I've considered all of the alternatives, and as far as I'm concerned, I've come up with the best solution for Megan's welfare, and that's really what custody is all about, isn't it? If I honestly thought that Megan would be better off with Lara, I would let her stay with her mother. But it's obvious that my child is being neglected, and I won't stand for it! Nothing…no one…will stop me from doing what I feel is best for Megan. *No one!*" The severity of his gaze and the brittle harsh sound of his voice startled Andrea. His words could only be construed as a warning to her.

Andrea wet her lips anxiously. "Jefferson, are you suggesting that I'm a threat to your relationship with Megan?" she asked, puzzling over the dark shift in his attitude.

His face softened slightly, and he put a comforting hand on her shoulder. "Of course not," he murmured earnestly, and bent down to place a kiss on her forehead. Andrea thought she would melt with relief.

"But you were including me when you said that no one would stop you from doing what's best for Megan, weren't you?"

His eyes clouded, and the corners of his mouth lifted into a grim smile of self-defeat. "I know that you wouldn't consciously do anything that might jeopardize my chances for custody of Megan."

"Of course not!"

"But I don't trust Lara. Just because she's agreed tentatively to give me guardianship of Megan doesn't mean a damned thing. It's not as if I can draw up a legal document stating that in exchange for my legal fees I expect to become Megan's guardian. The law doesn't work that way."

"Thank goodness!"

"Touché." His smile became wistful. "But the point is that Lara hasn't signed the change of guardianship papers I gave her, as yet, and I'm only giving her till the end of next week to do it."

"Why?"

"What if she doesn't sign?" Jefferson countered. "How would it look if, on the one hand, I'm in a custody battle with my ex-wife, claiming that I'm more fit than she to take care of my daughter, and on the other hand, I'm defending her against someone who might well have a legitimate claim against her?" Once again Jefferson raked his fingers through his hair. "I think the term most commonly used in a case such as this is conflict of interest."

"Then you may not be able to defend her anyway."

"Right. If the prosecuting attorney for the victims of the automobile accident cries 'foul,' then I'll have to drop the case. And," he admitted raggedly, "I'll be back to square one."

"A custody hearing?"

"And fight."

"Then what have you gained?" Andrea asked. "And what does all of this have to do with me?"

"You're one of the reasons I'd rather not wind up in a custody battle. If Lara decides to fight me for Megan, she'll try to paint a very black image of me to the judge. It could get very ugly."

"And she could dredge up all of the scandal about us from the past?"

Jefferson's repressed anger flashed in his eyes. "For starters, yes. And then she'll claim that I never got over you, and that I failed her, and probably that we—you and I—were having an affair during the entire duration of my marriage to her."

"But that's a lie!" Andrea nearly shouted.

"You know it, and I know it, but the judge doesn't," Jefferson conceded.

Suddenly everything that Jefferson was saying made sense, and she finally understood his point. "Oh, dear God," Andrea whispered desperately. An invisible leaden weight settled on her slim shoulders. "I shouldn't have come here," she thought aloud.

"Don't be ridiculous."

"I'm not!" Don't you see? If she finds out, Lara will crucify you. If she knows that we're seeing each other, she'll use it against you!" A new horror, deep and filled with pangs of twisted guilt and anguish, buried itself in her heart. "We can't see each other again…not until you have your daughter." Tears threatened her eyes and burned in her throat, but she refused to break down and cry.

"That may be a long time. I don't want to lose you, not again." Jefferson thought for a moment, and sat down on the bed next to Andrea. "If Lara signs over the guardianship papers, everything will work out. A custody battle won't be necessary, nor will a hearing. No judge will argue with the parents' mutual consent. If that's the case—" he placed a comforting arm over her shoulders "—we could be married."

"Married?" Andrea repeated, stunned.

"Of course. Andrea, we should have been married ten years ago."

Andrea shook her head, and her black hair swept across her shoulders. "And what if Lara doesn't agree?" she asked, thinking about the future. Dread steadily inched up her spine and her green eyes, filled with both love and regret, drove into Jefferson's, demanding an answer.

He frowned. "Then we'll just have to be discreet until everything is settled. Once it is, we'll get married."

The silence and tension that were building between them was heavy and oppressive. The joy that should have erupted in Andrea at the prospect of marrying Jefferson was killed by the knowledge that the future with him was only a dim hope, an elusive quest. Too many obstacles stood in the way of their happiness.

Jefferson looked at his watch, shook his head and reached for the jacket. "What's wrong?" he asked, touching her lightly on the knee.

"You make it sound so simple."

"It's not simple," he admitted, "but we can work it out." He helped her to her feet and guided her by the elbow out of the bedroom.

Her mind was whirling with vague thoughts of the past blending unevenly with hopes of the future. As she reached for her purse and jacket, Jefferson took hold of her shoulder and gently turned her around to face him. "All I want from this life is to have you as my wife and to live with both you and Megan. That's not really so much to ask, is it?" His head lowered, and his lips found hers before she could answer. His kiss was warm and enticing, touching the very core of Andrea's soul. Jefferson's hands, broad and strong, pushed against the small of her back, forcing her body to mold uniquely to his. A sob broke in her throat, and tears pooled in her eyes.

When he pulled himself from her embrace, it was to look down upon her with eyes firm with resolve. "We just have to be patient a little while longer. That's all we need…a little time."

Andrea shook her head in despair. "I don't know if I can wait any longer, Jefferson. It's been over ten years."

"I know." He kissed her lightly on the forehead, and his lips lingered on the smooth surface of her brow. "A little longer won't hurt."

Why was the pain twisting inside her like a cold, silver dagger? Andrea didn't think she could bear any more of the agony. "I think it would be best for everyone concerned if we, you and I, didn't see each other again. At least not for a while," she stated in a voice that trembled from her emotions.

"No!" Jefferson's denial was vehement, and his eyes began to blaze dangerously.

"I don't see how it can be any other way. At least not until you have custody of Megan."

"Don't worry about the custody, or anything else. I can handle all that. As I said before, by the end of next week I should know where I stand with Lara and whether she'll grant me custody without a battle." He unlocked the door of the apartment and propelled her by the elbow toward the elevator. They stepped inside, and as the elevator car groaned into motion, Jefferson continued. "The only reason that you and I have to be discreet is because of the past. Since I knew you before I met Lara, and because of all of the publicity and scandal that was involved ten years ago, we have to be careful. Although Lara and I have been separated for several years, the divorce was final only a couple of months ago. I can't do anything that might look bad before the court."

"You're saying that we'll have to act as if we're ashamed." She pulled her arm away from him gently and continued. "I don't think I can do that. I don't think I can continue seeing you in the dark, always looking over my shoulder, afraid of who might be watching, on the lookout for the press or your ex-wife." She shook her head firmly, and her eyes glittered with determination. "I can't hide in the shadows, Jefferson, while you put on a public facade."

"That's not what I'm asking."

"Think about it! You expect me to hide my love for you, don't you? Well, I've hidden it for ten years, and I don't think I have the strength to do it any longer! Besides which, I don't care to be put in the middle, between your daughter and your ex-wife.

"I want what's best for you, Jefferson, and right now, things being what they are, the best thing for you is to find a way to get control of Megan. Everything else, including me, has to be secondary, which I'm willing to accept, but I can't hide, damn it! I won't!" The tears that had been threatening to spill began to slide down her cheeks. Her voice, rough with emotion, failed her, and she whirled away from him to stride through the elevator doors as they parted.

Jefferson was on her heels, and when she reached the parking lot he caught her arm and whirled her around to face him. She began to lose her balance and fell against the hood of her car. "I'm not letting you go, damn it!" he bellowed, emotion ravaging his face. So loud was his proclamation that an elderly couple turned to see who was making the commotion.

"You're not giving me much of a choice," she countered, and added with a hissing whisper, "Don't you see that?" She struggled to break free of his uncompromising grasp.

"What I see is a ten-year-old scene being replayed by a woman who hasn't really grown up!"

"What?" she gasped, her eyes brilliant with indignation.

"Isn't this exactly what happened ten years ago, Andrea?" His voice was as raw and savage as the fury that flamed in his eyes. "Things got a little rough for you then—the water too deep—and you ran away!"

"No!" She raised her arm as if to strike him, but his furious gaze restrained her.

His grip on her arm tightened. "You ran out on me ten years ago, when the press and your family were ready to nail me to the wall, and you're doing it again! Your excuses might have changed, but the result is the same. Well, this time I'm not going to let you have the privilege of hiding from the truth!"

"Don't use your courtroom tactics on me, Jefferson. I know you too well, and I won't let you twist my words with your convoluted logic!" Haughtily she raised her head and her eyes over the sarcasm and mockery in his words.

"I don't have to twist your words, Andrea. What you're attempting to say is coming out loud and clear. Why don't you, with your straightforward, common sense approach, explain to me why it is that each time we get close together, each time I think we're falling in love, you run out on me like a frightened animal. Is it me you're afraid of? Yourself? Or the commitment of love that terrifies you?" The sarcasm in his words was reflected in his eyes, which were as cold and hard as stones as they pinned her against the car.

"You seem to forget that I was the one who came to you last night. Just as I was the one who visited you on the island." Her trembling lips pulled into a grimace as she jeered, "I don't recall that you made much of an effort to see me!"

He twisted her arm slightly in his anger. "I searched everywhere I could to find you ten years ago! And as for recently, I only wanted to wait until I had everything straightened out with Lara concerning Megan before I saw you again!" He released her arm and shook his open palms skyward in exasperation. "I was only trying to avoid another misunderstanding with you, Andrea."

"And you did a great job, didn't you," she taunted, sarcastically.

"Damn it, woman! Can't you understand? Don't you know what torture I've put myself through because of all of this?"

"Torture? Torture? Don't use your courtroom theatrics to gain my sympathy. The reason you never came to see me in L.A. is much easier to explain. You told me so yourself last night. You thought that I was working with Bryce Cawthorne in order to get an interview for the television program, remember? Last night you accused me of offering my body to you in order to get a story!"

Jefferson stepped backward as if he had been struck. "There's no reasoning with you!"

"That works two ways, Jefferson," she replied hotly, fumbling in her purse for her keys. Her heart wrenched at the painful words they had thrown at each other, and her fingers quivered as she unlocked the car door and settled inside. Tears were streaming down her face, and quiet sobs escaped from her throat as she started the car, put it into gear and roared out of the parking lot. She didn't look backward and avoided the image in the rearview mirror. She didn't have the strength to cope with even one last fleeting glimpse of the man she loved.

CHAPTER TWELVE

AS THE 747 JET INCREASED in speed to take flight Andrea's anxiety increased. The huge jet lifted upward, but Andrea's stomach seemed to stay on the ground. Only after the jet had leveled did Andrea's tense fingers release their white-knuckled hold on the armrests. She watched the earth below her, studying the countryside until a thick bank of clouds obstructed her view and the only image visible in the small window of the plane was the reflection of her own pale face.

Even though earlier in the day she had taken pains with her makeup, the strain in her weary eyes was beginning to surface, and the color of her skin, usually rosy and slightly tanned, was now morbidly white. Dark circles were evident under her eyes, and her full cheeks had hollowed. Her appetite had become minimal, and even the expensive weave of her heather-colored wool suit couldn't hide the fact that she had lost nearly five pounds in the past six weeks. She recognized the symptoms for what they were. Hadn't the same malady ailed her ten years ago? But knowing what the cause of her problem was couldn't give her back her usual zest for life. No, once again she would have to rely on time to heal her wounds.

As if to dislodge the thoughts beginning to take hold of her, she reached under her seat and pulled out her leather briefcase. Quickly she pulled out a neat stack of typed correspondence. Though she had read the letters from Carolyn Benedict at least a dozen times in the past week, she once again studied the request that had prompted her sudden trip to New York.

Carolyn Benedict was the producer of *Days of Promise,* a New York based, mediocre daytime soap opera. The ratings for the show had been slipping, and Ms. Benedict was looking for several fresh writers. She had learned of Andrea from some discreet checking concerning the writing staff of *Pride's Power,* cagily deducing that with the cancellation of the night soap, possibly a few writers would lose their jobs. Carolyn was a cunning woman and realized that what couldn't hold a viewer's attention during prime time, might well be a success during the early afternoons. Hence the letter to Andrea.

After nearly two months of job hunting, it looked as if Andrea might be offered decent employment. Thoughtfully Andrea tapped the letters from Ms. Benedict against her skirt. When she had first received them, Andrea had been hesitant to accept the invitation to New York. But the other job offers she had received had been poor and few. After her initial ambivalence about moving to New York had subsided, Andrea reasoned that a move might be the best thing for her at this point in her life. A change of scenery might be the only thing that could snap her out of her recent depression.

After all, Andrea had asked herself, what held her so passionately to California? Without a job and without Jefferson there was nothing in California that couldn't be found elsewhere. She bit her lip at the thought and continued tapping the letters against her knees.

Since her last quarrel with Jefferson, Andrea had

replayed the damning scene over in her mind so often that it haunted her nights and nagged at her during the day. Pieces of the heated argument lodged themselves in her mind, and she had trouble ignoring them. The hot words, Jefferson's savagely angry face, her own unfair and cruel words, wouldn't leave her a minute's peace. To make matters worse, a day hadn't passed without seeing something to remind her of Jefferson and what he must be going through. Stories about him, some true and some outrageously false, occupied the headlines of all the local scandal sheets. Even the more reputable tabloids had tidbits of his life to fill leftover space on the social pages.

The news that Jefferson Harmon, California's ex-governor, had agreed to defend his wife in a scandalous lawsuit had hit the newsstands full force. And then, when two weeks later it was rumored that Harmon had resigned as Lara's attorney, the fires of gossip flamed to new heights. Rumors concerning the once-popular politician and his socialite wife spread, and all of the interest in Jefferson Harmon's stormy marriage rekindled.

The custody battle over Megan, once discreetly avoided by the press, was now the subject on the cover of most of the weekly gossip tabloids. Even Andrea's name had crept into the copy of some of the stories, and the anonymity of an unlisted telephone number hadn't deterred a few persistent reporters. More than once in the last two weeks Andrea had slammed the receiver of the phone down in anger when an inquisitive reporter had called and asked her galling questions about Jefferson, if she was, indeed, the Andrea Monroe who had once been involved with the man.

Dinner was served by an efficient stewardess, and for a short time Andrea was distracted by the meal. Just as she had for the last six long weeks, she attempted vainly to push thoughts of Jefferson from her mind.

The flight was long and tedious. When at last the plane touched down and sped along the lighted runway of JFK International, Andrea let out a sigh of relief. Though only seven o'clock in L.A., the three-hour time difference took hold of Andrea, and she felt as if it were, indeed, ten. Andrea disembarked as quickly as possible, waited for her luggage and hailed a cab. It had been several years since she had last visited Manhattan, but tonight the excitement and electricity of New York held no fascination for her.

The hotel was located not far from the studio, and the room assigned to her was clean, if not inviting. After a long, hot bath, she pulled on her robe and turned on the late news to take her mind off her worries concerning the interview that was scheduled for early the next morning. Though she was tired, the night stretched before her, and she wanted to fill as many hours as she could so she would be tired enough to fall into a deep sleep.

The anchorman was discussing the President's most recent peace keeping trip to the Middle East when the picture on the television became clear. Andrea listened to the story with interest, and when the commercial break came, she began leafing through a magazine that had been left on the nightstand.

Perhaps it was the brawny anchorman's lead-in line or the more personal tone his well-modulated voice assumed, but whatever the reason, Andrea dropped the magazine to stare at the television.

"Unfortunately, today a glamorous life, once the envy of most Californians, has ended in tragedy." Andrea's eyes widened in horror and her throat became raw when a recent still photograph of a beautiful, slightly wistful Lara Harmon flashed on to the screen.

"This afternoon Lara Whitney Harmon was pronounced dead on arrival at Mercy Hospital in suburban Los Angeles. Cause of death is uncertain at this time, although there is speculation that Mrs. Harmon's death might be alcohol-related." The picture on the television changed to show an older photograph of Lara standing beside Jefferson during the inauguration ceremony while he took the oath of office as governor of California. Jefferson looked younger and less haggard than he did now, but even then, some five years ago, there was a haunting, savage cast to the clean, even lines of his face. The newscaster continued with the story.

"Mrs. Harmon, considered at one time to be San Francisco's most eligible banking heiress, was married for eight years to California's ex-governor, Jefferson Harmon. Governor Harmon resigned his position before completing his term, citing 'personal reasons' as explanation for his hasty retreat from public office. At the time there was speculation that the cause of the governor's resignation was related to Mrs. Harmon's rumored alcoholism. That rumor was firmly denied by Mr. Harmon's press agent."

The photograph of Jefferson and Lara was replaced by live coverage of the apartment building that Andrea recognized as Jefferson's California residence. Jefferson, appearing haggard, lean and worried was clutching a frail-looking child to his chest and pushing through an insistent throng of reporters who had gathered near the entrance to the building. Questions were shouted at his retreating figure, but he ignored them all, only pausing once to hurl a look of frustration and annoyance toward an intruding camera. Then he disappeared into the guarded building, and the reporter began to speculate further into the personal, mysterious life of Jefferson Harmon.

"Oh, dear God," Andrea moaned as she lay on the bed and clasped her hands over her mouth. She closed her eyes and listened while once again Jefferson's life was rehashed by the local reporter and the anchorman summed up the events leading to Lara Harmon's untimely death.

Andrea felt as if she should run from the room, scream the anger and confusion boiling within her out of her lungs and attempt to find a way to comfort Jefferson and his daughter. Jefferson's agonized face, captured by the television camera, vividly burned in Andrea's mind. And the image of the child, small and distraught, clinging to Jefferson in a death grip, tore at Andrea's heart. She wanted to cry, she wanted to shout, she wanted to ease the pain of both Jefferson and his young child.

Instead, still holding her hand against her mouth, she got up, snapped off the television and went into the small bathroom. She stood over the sink to douse cold water on her skin and after the first icy splash looked dubiously into the mirror at her ashen image. Lara was dead! The thought drove thin needles of disbelief into her mind. Dead! How could it be? Andrea sat down heavily on the edge of the bathtub and rolled her head in her hands. "No," she whispered to herself. "No…no…."

A half an hour must have passed before Andrea found the strength to make her way back to the bed and collapse heavily upon it. She was surprised at her reaction to Lara's death and tried to think rationally about it. Although she had never met Jefferson's ex-wife, she felt as if she had known her, at least vaguely. Lara Whitney Harmon had always graced the headlines of the social pages, and there was something elusively beautiful about her that had made her the darling of the press. Even when her alcoholism was suspected, the press, and therefore the rest of the world, considered it more Jefferson's failing than Lara's problem. Even Jefferson himself admitted as much.

Andrea slipped under the covers and felt a chill pass through her body. How was Jefferson handling Lara's death? Was he able to cope with Megan? Was the child old enough to understand what was happening? Tears welled in Andrea's eyes and slid backward toward the pillow as Andrea wondered dismally about Jefferson, thousands of miles away from her.

The telephone sat invitingly close to the bed. Jefferson's telephone number blazed in Andrea's mind, and after a moment's hesitation she picked up the receiver. She started to dial, but quickly changed her mind and hung up vehemently. What could she say? It probably would be impossible to get through to him anyway. Dear God, was he all right?

Andrea flipped off the light near the bed and shut her eyes. She tried to concentrate on anything other than Jefferson or Lara, but no matter how sincerely she tried to erase the painful picture from her mind, the haunting image of Jefferson, his dark hair disheveled and his suit wrinkled, remained as if frozen in her mind's eye. She tossed and turned in the bed as she replayed the scene of Jefferson shoving his way through the unyielding crowd of reporters. And then there was Megan, so small and frail looking, clinging to Jefferson.

Sleep remained elusive for the rest of the night. It was just as well, because any moment that Andrea did doze, bizarre nightmares of Jefferson and Megan would permeate her thoughts and awaken her. Each time she awoke, Andrea found relief in the knowledge that she had only been dreaming, until she realized that Lara Harmon was, in fact, dead. Jefferson's ex-wife, the mother of his little girl, was gone forever.

An intense, dull, throbbing headache pounded relentlessly in Andrea's mind throughout the night, and by the time that the first slanting rays of dawn crept through the crack in the drapes, Andrea was glad for the excuse to get out of bed and away from her miserable thoughts.

She dressed more hurriedly than she normally would have, but suddenly her appearance didn't seem important. The smart, ebony suit appeared professional. Its tailored lines accentuated the turquoise silk blouse and its bow, which tied around Andrea's throat. She took some care with her hair, pinning it carefully to the back of her head into a loose coil, and she used more color on her cheeks than she normally did. It wasn't a very good disguise. The ashen color of her face and the dark circles under her eyes were still evident.

Andrea still had over an hour before the interview. She hurried to the lobby of the hotel and located a small restaurant near the entrance of the building. She didn't feel like eating, but she knew that it might be hours before the opportunity for a meal arose again, and somehow she had to try and calm her queasy, churning stomach.

The cup of tea didn't calm her nerves, nor did the toast and jam settle her stomach. She found herself ignoring the hasty breakfast to stare at the clock or a copy of a newspaper that some patron had left on a nearby table.

Telling herself that it was a mistake, she reached for the paper lying open to the sports section. She refolded the paper and found the front page. In the lower corner of the front page was a picture of Lara Harmon—the same wistful portrait that had flashed on the television screen only hours before. Steadying herself with a swallow of tepid tea, Andrea read the article. A picture of Jefferson and his daughter accompanied the article located in the midsection of the paper.

The story was essentially the same as had been reported the night before, but speculation had apparently grown that Lara Harmon's death was suicide. Whether intentional or not, authorities had determined that a lethal combination of alcohol and sleeping pills had cost Lara her life.

The picture of Jefferson and his child wasn't clear, and yet Andrea saw through the anger in his eyes as the photographer had caught his attention. There was more than fury on his glowering face—it seemed to Andrea that there was desperation in his eyes. Once again Andrea thought of calling him, but she didn't. No doubt he'd had a restless night himself, and there was a three-hour time difference to consider. It wasn't even five o'clock in L.A.

After tossing the paper aside, Andrea stared into her teacup. What was she going to do? Should she call Jefferson, give him words of sympathy and comfort, or would he think she was once again intruding into his private life? What was he doing? What was he thinking? How was he coping with his child? The questions came so quickly into her mind, and she couldn't find answers to any of them.

Disgusted with herself for dwelling on something she couldn't alter, she decided to walk the seven blocks to the studio and wait there until the time of her appointment. Perhaps the bustle of activity on the set of *Days of Promise* would take her mind off Jefferson and his child.

TO SAY THAT THE STUDIO WAS busy would have been a gross understatement. Although Andrea had spent the last eight years writing for Coral Productions, nothing that

Coral had done could come close to the level of activity that accompanied the rehearsal in progress on the set of *Days of Promise.* It seemed as if the entire thirty-person cast was scrambling around the studio rehearsing lines or waiting for the sets to be complete or studying last-minute changes to the script. The cameramen, lighting technicians and production crew added to the confusion.

A secretary led Andrea to another area of the building to wait in Carolyn Benedict's office.

"Ms. Benedict will be here shortly," the redhead explained apologetically. "Could I get you a cup of coffee while you wait?"

"Yes, thank you," Andrea murmured, and the secretary hurried out of the office. Andrea was still standing in the middle of the room, looking at the various pictures adorning the walls. She recognized several movie and prime-time actresses that at one time or another had played a role on the twenty-year-old *Days of Promise.* Andrea couldn't help but smile when she recognized a much younger Nicole Jamison in one of the photos.

"Here you go," the secretary said as she entered the room with two steaming cups. "Do you take anything in your coffee?"

"No, black is fine."

A smile spread on the secretary's impish face. "Good. I just saw Carolyn. She's on her way."

"Thanks." Andrea took an experimental sip and continued to peruse the old photographs. At the sound of Carolyn Benedict's entrance Andrea turned to face the door.

"See anyone you recognize?" the smiling, gray-haired woman asked.

"A few." Andrea returned the smile.

"Did you notice Bryce Cawthorne?" At the surprised

look on Andrea's face Carolyn continued. "Down there on the left…in the black and white. Bryce was in the original cast, twenty years ago."

Andrea had to bend over to look at the slightly faded photograph. There were several members of the cast assembled, and one was indeed Bryce Cawthorne. "I didn't know he worked on *Days of Promise,*" Andrea explained, lifting her eyes from the photograph to study Carolyn's face.

Carolyn waved in the air as if to brush Andrea's statement aside. "Most of the actors in the business have been on a soap at one time in their lives. Of course I wasn't here at the time, but Bryce Cawthorne was the original Andre Van Cleave," Carolyn explained. "But enough of that. I guess by now you know that I'm Carolyn Benedict."

Andrea's smile widened. There was something forthright and personable about the middle-aged woman. "I guessed as much."

"You got my letters, obviously, or you wouldn't be here." Carolyn sat behind a desk and pulled out a file from her drawer. "Sit down, sit down," she said with a wave of her plump hands.

Andrea took a sip of her coffee while Carolyn adjusted her reading glasses and studied the papers in the file. "By the way, I talked with Bryce Cawthorne about you."

Andrea swallowed with difficulty.

"He seems to have the highest regard for you." Carolyn's deep brown eyes looked over the top of her glasses and found Andrea's expression to have changed from pleasant to shocked. It took Andrea a minute to recover her professional poise. The last thing she expected was praise from Bryce.

"I worked with Mr. Cawthorne for eight years," Andrea said weakly.

"And you quit because of the cancellation of *Pride's Power?*"

"It was time for a change."

Carolyn's eyes narrowed speculatively. "Yes, well, I guess it was." She lit a cigarette and blew a blue stream of smoke upward in the air. "Let's get right to the point, shall we?"

"Fine with me."

"*Days of Promise* is having problems of its own, and our ratings have begun to slip. Part of the problem lies with the fact that ABS has rescheduled their afternoon lineup, and the show playing opposite *Days of Promise* has a lot of viewer appeal. What we've decided to do is change the direction of our story line and beef up the script. We're going to add three new writers and introduce several new, young characters. By summer, when the teen viewing audience peaks, we hope to have story lines centering around the new, younger characters."

Carolyn had stopped, as if she expected Andrea to comment, and Andrea quickly nodded her agreement.

"You realize that this is quite a bit different from writing for prime time?"

"Yes."

"Then you know that we churn out four times the scripts that you're used to. And that's on a daily basis, and doesn't include the rewrites." She stubbed out her cigarette as she eyed Andrea. "Do you think that you can handle that?"

"I'm sure of it," Andrea said.

"And you wouldn't mind moving to New York?"

"Not at all." Andrea felt her heart twist at the false words, but she attempted to maintain her composure.

"All right, let's go down to the set and I'll show you around.... You can meet a couple of the other writers and the director, and we'll discuss the salary we're offering." Carolyn got up from the desk, tucked the file folder neatly away and led Andrea out of the office. "And before any decisions are made, I think you'll be interested in seeing how we get through each tear-jerking episode of *Days of Promise.*" The short producer gave Andrea an exaggerated wink as they walked down the hallway toward the studio.

CHAPTER THIRTEEN

WHEN ANDREA ARRIVED HOME the next day all she wanted to do was hide in her bed. She knew that the interview had gone worse than it should have, due largely to the fact that she couldn't take her mind off Jefferson. Wherever she went it seemed that his name appeared. On television, in the papers, or as the subject of idle conversation, Lara Harmon's death was *news.*

For the next few days she kept herself busy by visiting friends and relatives. She went shopping, had lunch with Katie, walked in the park and still hunted down jobs. She avoided staying home alone in her apartment, and installed a tape-recording machine to answer her calls. She didn't want to miss any job offers that might come over the phone, and yet she couldn't stick around her apartment. If she had experienced phone calls from nosy reporters before Lara Harmon's death, they had doubled since the tragedy. She felt visible and vulnerable. There was no place to escape.

She had tried to get through to Jefferson, but it was useless. The recorded message left on his telephone indicated that he was indisposed for several days. Feeling as if she had to let him know how she felt, she had written him a quick note of sympathy and then mailed it before she could tear it to shreds. There was nothing she could say that would even hint at her true feelings. How could she explain that she loved him, desperately, passionately, and yet felt a deep, welling sense of remorse—or was it guilt—at his ex-wife's untimely death. How could she say that she wanted to be with him every moment of his life, and yet felt that she couldn't?

It was late Friday evening by the time that she returned home from the shopping mall. She was empty-handed but weary, and she hoped that she would be able to fall into a deep and dreamless sleep. Lara's funeral, a private ceremony, had been held on the previous day, and since then much of the publicity concerning her death had quieted.

After kicking off her shoes Andrea absently flipped on the recording machine, intending to listen to the messages as she got ready for a long hot bath. For the first time in a week there were only a few messages, and only one from one of the more persistent reporters.

The call that surprised Andrea was from Carolyn Benedict. It was simple and to the point. The producer of *Days of Promise* wanted to offer Andrea a job as a script-writer for the soap opera. She left the number of the studio on the machine, with instructions for Andrea to call her to work out the terms of employment.

Andrea glanced at her watch. It was eight o'clock in the evening, eleven in New York. She hesitated a moment, bit her lower lip and dialed the number. It was unlikely, but perhaps someone might be working late. Andrea's throat went dry when her call was answered, but her expectations were short-lived as she listened to a recorded message explaining about the studio's regular hours of business. Somehow Andrea was relieved. Although she had tried to convince herself that the best thing for her would be moving to Manhattan, thousands of miles away from Jefferson, a small part of her had argued against her logic. As a sigh of relief passed over her lips she placed the receiver back on the telephone and turned the recorder off for the night.

She had just gotten out of the bath and settled into bed with a bestseller when the phone rang. She waited for the machine to answer the call before realizing that she had turned it off. Her stomach knotted as she reached for the phone near the bed. What if it was another reporter?

With false confidence and a slightly irritated tone she answered the phone on the fourth ring. "Hello?"

"Andrea?" Jefferson's voice asked. Andrea felt herself tremble at the familiar sound of his voice. In her mind she pictured him, and saw his dark eyes and noble face.

"Hello, Jefferson," she whispered. All of the emotion that she should have hidden from him surfaced in her words. Her throat became constricted, and she found it difficult to speak. For no reason other than that he was on the other end of the line, tears began to well in her eyes. "I…I want you to know how sorry I am about Lara," Andrea managed to say, though choking.

"I know…. I got your card."

"Oh, Jefferson…why? What happened?" she asked, her voice ragged and raw.

"I don't know, no one does, not even her latest boyfriend. Or if he does, he's not saying."

"Are you all right?"

"Fine."

"And Megan?" Andrea asked, hardly daring to breathe, afraid that the sobs building in her throat might surface. Slowly she attempted to regain a modicum of her composure.

"It's been difficult," he admitted. His voice sounded

strained and tired. "But I think it will get better," he added flatly.

Though tears were spilling from Andrea's eyes, she kept her voice steady. "I'm sure it will." *Oh, God, Jefferson,* Andrea thought to herself as she clutched the receiver, afraid to lose him, afraid of breaking the frail connection that held them so fragilely together. *What can I do for you…for your child? If you only loved me the way I love you, I would touch you, caress you, make love to you, until the pain went away. If you only knew how much I need you, how much I want to take care of you and Megan.*

There was an unsteady silence, but Andrea couldn't bring herself to end the conversation. Finally, in a tight voice, Jefferson attempted to ring off. "I just wanted to thank you…for the card. Good night."

"No!" Andrea blurted, and a sob erupted in her throat. "Don't hang up!"

Again the silence.

Andrea pulled in a ragged breath and wished that she could control her emotions.

"What?" he asked severely.

"I…I just want you to know that I care," she breathed.

"Oh, Andrea," he sighed, and hesitated. "I wish that I could believe you."

"But I do. I always have."

"There are so many things…" His voice lowered and became distant. "I would like you to meet Megan," he said at last.

"I want to."

"She's still up…." Was it an invitation?

"Now?" Andrea asked. "You want me to meet her now?"

"If you would." His voice seemed empty.

"But don't you think it's too soon after…"

"Life goes on, Andrea."

"But…"

His voice had become severe, the edge of his words bitter. "But what? What kind of an excuse can you come up with this time, Andrea? You always have a reason to push me away, each time that I try to touch you!"

"No!" she cried, attempting to defend herself. The sound of a receiver being shoved back into its cradle echoed in Andrea's mind, and the flat buzzing to remind her to hang up filled the silence of the room before Andrea could find the strength to disconnect her end of the conversation.

Was he right? Was she running from him again? That was ridiculous! She loved him with such passion that it sometimes scared her. She talked angrily to herself; she told herself that it was all his fault. He was the one who continued to distort everything she said.

When the phone rang again, Andrea jumped to answer it. It had to be Jefferson, repentant over his hasty harsh words. Andrea was ready to forgive him, to be with him, to somehow make things right between them.

"Hello," she answered breathlessly.

"Hi," Martin called back to her. "You must have been sitting on the phone! How are you?"

"Fine," Andrea responded weakly.

"Well, aren't you going to fill me in on the job in New York? Gayla just called me last night and told me about it. The least you could do is keep me informed. I'm still your brother, you know."

Her spirits lifted slightly at the sound of Martin's warm voice. "All right, all right. It wasn't that I was hiding anything from you, it's just that until a few minutes ago I really didn't know anything."

"But you do now?"

"Yeah. Carolyn Benedict, producer of *Days of Promise,* left a message for me on my answering machine just tonight."

"And...?" he asked expectantly.

"She offered me the job."

"How about that! Are you really going to move to New York? I can't believe it!" He sounded oddly relieved.

"I...I don't know," she admitted.

"Why not? Something wrong with the pay or the hours?"

"No, it's not that," she tried to explain, feeling suddenly caged. "It's just that I haven't had a lot of time to think about it."

"What do you mean? Wasn't your interview with that producer over a week ago?"

"Yes, but..."

"But what? You have a better offer in L.A.?"

Andrea let out her breath. "Don't I wish," she sighed.

Martin's voice turned frigid. "I bet this has something to do with Jefferson Harmon, doesn't it?"

"Why?"

Martin snorted. "Gayla told me you were seeing him again, and I really couldn't believe it. Not after the way he ran out on you the last time."

"He didn't run out on me."

"No? Then why was it that you moped around for him for a couple of years? Why did he marry that other woman? Hmm?"

Andrea's nerves had already been stretched by Jefferson's call. Now, with Martin's needling, she felt even worse. It was with difficulty that she held on to her composure. "That was a long time ago. We all did things, said things, that we didn't really mean."

"Come off it, Andrea. Harmon dumped on you. He'll do it again."

Andrea's temper snapped. "You had a little to do with it, as I recall. All those horrid stories you told your friend at the campus paper…and he printed them all!"

"We've been through this before," Martin muttered.

"I know."

"But if Harmon had really wanted to find you and keep in touch with you, he could have. He didn't have to wait for ten years."

"Drop it, Martin," Andrea said.

"Don't you like being reminded of the way Harmon treated you ten years ago?" he taunted.

"I don't like being reminded of the way that you treated me!" she bit out.

"I've paid my dues, Andrea, and then some," he retorted hotly. Once again Andrea was reminded of the agony that Martin had suffered—the physical torture of his wounds and sightlessness and the mental pain of a sister who couldn't find the forgiveness in her heart to write him one letter while he was fighting for his country. Pain, anger and humiliation washed over Andrea.

"Let's not fight," she whispered. "It's so pointless."

Martin sighed. "You're right," he admitted. "I'm sorry I got so mad. It's just that I can't stand Jefferson Harmon. Maybe it wasn't his fault, but I can't forget about the way he turned his back on me, and the pain he caused you."

A protesting noise began in Andrea's throat, but Martin ignored it as he continued. "I know I hurt you, too, sis, and you know that I didn't mean to, but—oh, hell! Let's not go into all of that, not now. I just called to check up on you, to see if you were serious about moving to New York."

"I'm considering it."

"Good."

"Sounds like you're trying to get rid of me," she joked, but the humor fell flat.

"You know that's not it. I've just been worried about you, ever since Gayla told me that you were seeing Harmon again. That man's trouble, Andrea, you've got to realize that. Look what happened to that ex-wife of his. There's talk that she committed suicide, for God's sake. You can't tell me that her problems didn't stem from being married to Jefferson Harmon."

"You don't know that."

"It's a good guess."

"I don't think so!" Once again Andrea's voice had a razor sharp edge to it.

"Okay, okay," Martin said reluctantly. "I'm sorry I brought the subject up. Just be careful, okay?"

"I will." Some of her temper ebbed.

"I wish I could talk some sense into you, but then I never have been able to," he muttered.

"Don't worry," she pleaded.

Martin hung up, and Andrea set the receiver back down gently. Martin's worries haunted her; they were the same doubts that she had felt but hadn't admitted. Could he possibly be right about Jefferson? Or was he still holding a grudge that he couldn't dismiss because of the bitterness of the war in Vietnam?

Jefferson's words came into her mind: "I would like you to meet Megan. She's still up."

Silently she began to get dressed, never actually making the mental decision to visit him. How many times must I go to him? she asked herself. Why is it always me that is knocking on his door?

Not fair. He had called several times and visited her

after her return from Victoria, and every time they had separated, it was because she walked away from him, or his proposals for their future. This is the last time, she swore to herself. I will never go crawling to him again.

It was raining and dark as she headed her car out of the parking lot and onto the busy freeway. With her visibility curbed and the hazard of slick streets after a long dry spell, Andrea felt as if she were indeed crawling—at a snail's pace—to find Jefferson.

Jefferson's apartment house was well lit. The wind whistled through the giant palms, and the tall, spindly trees moved in the night to make dark, eerie shadows on the tall apartment building. The rain that had only been a drizzle when Andrea had left her apartment had increased in volume, and by the time Andrea parked the car, the wind was carrying sheets of rain to the earth.

Andrea steadied herself for a moment in the parked car. In the solitude and darkness of the small automobile she looked up toward Jefferson's apartment on the top floor of the building. It was dark except for a feeble light coming from the window that she guessed to be the living room. *What am I doing here?* she asked herself, and a cold tingle of apprehension spread across her shoulders and skittered down her spine.

Her determination faltered only slightly, and with a mumbled oath at herself for being such a fool where Jefferson was concerned, she slid out of the car, slammed the door shut and ran toward the building. The tempo of the wind increased, and she was reminded of another stormy night—which seemed to be years ago—on the island.

Andrea shook the raindrops from her hair as she entered the lobby. The guard at the desk was the same man she had encountered on her visit several weeks in the past. His unyielding and stern smile at her entrance softened in recognition as she walked toward the desk.

"You're here to see Mr. Harmon," he guessed.

"That's right," she agreed, forcing a smile.

"You're expected?"

Her mouth twisted into a thoughtful smile. "I don't think so, no." She shook her head with her admission, and her black hair brushed against the light fabric of her coat.

"Then I'll have to call Mr. Harmon," the guard said apologetically.

"That's fine. I'll wait."

It took only a few minutes before the guard hung up and escorted Andrea to the elevator. "I'm sorry you had to wait."

"No problem." She smiled at the kindly old man until the elevator doors closed and she was once again alone.

JEFFERSON HUNG UP THE phone and flung himself down on the couch. Andrea had decided to come after all. He slammed his fist against the edge of the navy-blue sectional and whispered a stream of invectives, largely aimed at himself.

After she had refused to come to see him earlier, he had put Megan to bed and decided that no matter what, he would shove Andrea Monroe out of his life forever. And now all she had to do was waltz back into the building, have the security guard announce she had come to visit him and all of his resolve had melted. Damn him! Damn her! Damn the whole ridiculous situation that pulled them apart and thrust them together. He cursed the day that he had ever laid eyes upon Andrea Monroe, but even now, as he conjured in his mind the first time he had seen her, innocent and wise, beautiful and young, trusting and independent, he knew that he was lost to her forever. He had never loved a woman so fervently, never felt the pain of loss or anguish that she could instill in him with only the disdainful arch of an exquisite black eyebrow. Damn it all! Damn it all to hell!

Jefferson poured himself a quick jigger of Scotch and downed it quickly. He was about to pour another when the knock at his door stopped him. He held the liquor bottle in midair for a moment, hesitating. *Let her wait,* he thought to himself. His mouth twisted into a mirthless smile as he poured the second drink and took his time savoring it.

The second time she knocked, more sharply, it seemed, the sound was louder, more insistent. His angry smile pulled more tightly at the corners of his mouth. Still, he lingered at the bar. *It served her right. Let her find out what it feels like to always be begging and never receiving. Let her see for herself how it is to be on the other side of the door.*

The knocking subsided. Her voice, full, rich and obviously concerned, finally compelled him to answer the door. It was as clear and sweet as he remembered, the same voice that called to him in the middle of the night when he was alone in his bed. His smile faded as he strode across the dimly lit room.

"Jefferson," Andrea called anxiously against the hard wood of the door. "Jefferson, are you all right? Jefferson?"

Just as Andrea was about to knock again, the oaken door swung silently inward. Andrea held her breath for a moment as she came face to face with Jefferson and his condemning stare. His eyes were as cold as stones, and as she lifted her face to meet his hardened gaze, she involuntarily trembled. He looked tired and angry.

"Thank God you're all right," she breathed, stiffening her shoulders for the impending attack she could see developing in Jefferson's savage eyes. "I was beginning to worry about you." Her voice echoed the relief she felt at the sight of him.

"You don't have to worry about me, Andrea," he replied, his mouth set in a grim, hard line. "I can take care of myself." He shifted to lean against the door. "So you changed your mind and decided to come over here after all," he said tonelessly. "How nice. Come in," he invited in the same cold, flat voice.

Andrea moved from the security of the brightly lit hallway into the darkened interior of Jefferson's apartment. Only one small reading lamp in a far corner of the room was lit, but even in the shadows Andrea could see that the room had become cluttered. All of the tidiness of the roomy apartment was gone, and it appeared disorganized and unkempt. If Jefferson noticed Andrea's quiet appraisal of the room, he didn't show it. Instead, he looked steadily at her, adding to the uneasy feeling that was growing within her.

"How about a drink?" he asked suddenly, but his severe expression didn't change.

"I don't think so." His barely restrained hostility and the scathing mockery in his voice shocked her. She realized that his anger was directed at her, and she didn't understand why. He was the one who had invited her over to meet his daughter, and once she had come he was barely civil to her. Had she unwittingly intruded into a crisis with his daughter? Where was Megan?

Jefferson ignored Andrea's wishes and poured her a stiff drink, along with another for himself. It was unlike him to rely on alcohol for any source of comfort or strength, but Andrea's unexpected presence unnerved him. Part of him wanted to toss her out of the apartment and tell her in no uncertain terms that he had no use for a woman who couldn't make an honest decision and stick by it. She had spurned his proposal the last time she'd been alone with him, and now she was back—just to taunt him. He was angry with himself and his weakness for her. He should never have let her back into his home, and yet a traitorous male part of him still wanted her, both physically and mentally. Just the sight of her made vivid pictures of her naked body and pleading eyes flash into his mind's eye. He felt a need to hold her, caress her, protect her forever. The thought of his weakness and need for her made him tighten his jaw in determination. With effort he willed his trembling hands to still as he poured the stiff, amber-colored Scotch.

Andrea watched Jefferson in silence as she stood in the middle of the room still wearing her coat. She didn't know if she should stay or flee. She could feel the tension in the room as sure as if it had been a visible barrier between them. She was both afraid and angry, confused and determined, torn and whole. She wanted Jefferson, needed him, but she couldn't understand him. Suddenly she wondered if she ever had.

It was obvious that Jefferson, too, was torn with conflicting emotions. He was dressed more carelessly than she had ever seen him. His dress shirt was rolled up at the sleeves and pulled out of the waistband of his jeans. His hair was so rough and disheveled, he would have appeared boyish, had it not been for the savage look to his eyes. Though years had passed, Andrea was reminded of the dashing young California senator who had stolen her heart ten years ago. Even with the angles of his face hardened in anger, Andrea could see in him the air of charm and warmth that had captivated the Californian voters. He was enigmatic, frightening, mysterious and yet loving. If only she could get past his cold, biting words. If only he would love her again.

When he crossed the darkened room and walked to within inches of her, Andrea held his cold, arrogant gaze. His eyes swept her body, and for a fleeting moment Andrea recognized the raw and persistent passion that still burned silently, hungrily, beneath the facade of ice.

"So why are you here?" he asked, with only the merest trace of interest. He handed her the drink and took a long swallow of his as he sat back on the couch to study her.

"I came to meet Megan, as you suggested," she replied. Wasn't it obvious?

"Megan's been asleep for over an hour."

"You told me she was awake."

"She was *then,* but when you said you weren't coming, I put her to bed."

"I guess I should have called," she said, testing the water. Why was he so angry?

"That would have been nice."

"But I got tied up. Martin called."

Jefferson stiffened at the mention of Andrea's brother. He set his drink aside and smiled wryly to himself. "Your brother, Martin? He called you?" His bitter sense of humor surfaced. "Oh, I get it, Martin talked you into coming and seeing me, right?"

Andrea felt the deep pang of pain at the mockery in his words as surely as if Jefferson had stabbed her. She shook her head and pursed her lips. "No, as a matter of fact he thought it was a bad idea."

"Wonderful guy."

"You don't even know him."

"I don't want to!" Jefferson reached for his drink and

finished it in one deep swallow. "I had enough of your brother to last me a lifetime."

"He's changed!"

"Just like you have?"

Andrea's eyes blazed. "Damn you, Jefferson, I came over here willing to apologize for the last time we were together." Her voice began to quiver, and she could feel her body beginning to tremble. "I came here because I thought you wanted me to."

"So you could meet Megan?"

"Yes!" she cried desperately. Tentatively Andrea sat on the couch next to him. "Jefferson, I do want to meet your daughter." Her green eyes were pleading with honesty, and her hand came out to rest upon his knee.

Jefferson closed his eyes at her touch. He tried not to think of the warm, enticing pressure of Andrea's fingers against the light fabric that covered his thighs. "Megan has been through a helluva lot," he said, rubbing his forehead with his hand. Good God, would the heat that Andrea was causing in his legs stop before it traveled upward and he was lost to her and his own blinding passion?

"I know it must be hard on her," Andrea whispered.

With a groan Jefferson slid away from her, and his eyes narrowed skeptically. "You can't even begin to imagine," he snapped. He moved over, hoping to put some distance between them and cool his heated blood. She leaned seductively closer to him, hoping to catch hold of that part of him that wanted her so desperately.

"I thought you wanted me to come here."

Jefferson made a deprecating sound. "And I thought you were too busy."

"That's not what I said."

He crossed his arms over his chest, causing the muscles

to bulge on his shoulders and upper arms. "Then what exactly is it that you did say?" he asked rhetorically before answering himself. "Something to the effect that you needed a little more time?"

"Not me, Jefferson—Megan. She's only five and probably doesn't understand death, especially not her mother's. I thought she might need a little more time to adjust to the change and emptiness in her life. She just lost her mother, for God's sake, and now she's living alone with you. The poor thing must be confused and lonely."

"Don't preach to me, Andrea. I live here, remember? I see every day what my daughter is going through. I'm here at night to witness the nightmares!" His words were hot and venomous, but something in his face changed, and he raked an impatient hand through his thick, near-black hair.

"Look, Jefferson," Andrea began, not knowing exactly how to deal with him. He didn't want her, at least he didn't want to want her. That much was clearly evident, and maybe he was right. Maybe there never could be another time for the two of them. What they had in the past might never again be relived. "I just came over to see you and to meet Megan. Obviously you don't want me here... and...and I can deal with that." Contrary to her bold words, the rejection began to burn in her throat, and she knew that if she didn't leave soon, all of her pride and dignity would crumble. She would break down in front of him. She couldn't allow that to happen, not now, when he had almost cringed when she touched him. Jefferson's head snapped up at the catch in her voice. Confusion paled his eyes. Her voice sounded nearly dead when she continued. "I've been offered a job in New York." A small, betraying smile played upon her white lips.

"What?" he asked hoarsely.

"And I've decided to take it." Her last words had spilled from her lips in an unconscious tumble of feelings. She stood up and walked hurriedly toward the door. She wanted to leave as quickly as she could, before her ragged emotions got the better of her. She didn't look at him, couldn't bear to see his condemning face another moment, as she reached for the doorknob. The small, frail, frightened voice of a child stopped her.

"Daddy! Daddy!" The high-pitched voice grew louder and more fearful. "Daddy?"

"Andrea, wait. Please stay," Jefferson said as he dashed from the room. There was an urgency to his words that compelled her to hesitate. *Go. Leave while you have the chance,* a voice inside her mind commanded. *Don't stay!* She sagged heavily against the door, her hand still clutching the knob. Her ears heard, over the wind that whistled outside, the sound of a door opening just as the child began to scream frantically at the top of her lungs.

"Daddy…Mommy…Mommy, where are you? Mommy, I want Mommy!" Sobs erupted in the small, frightened voice.

Andrea felt her knees buckle in compassion for the child she had never met, and tears began to slide down her cheeks. The sobbing grew quieter, and Jefferson's voice, soft and reassuring, whispered words of comfort to his child. Not taking the time to understand her own motive, Andrea moved and followed the direction of the sound. It was dark in the hallway, but a shadowy light from a bedroom guided her. In the small room, on the single canopy bed, Jefferson sat rocking his daughter. He was holding her as tightly as she was clutching him, and softly intoning comforting words.

The child had her arms draped around his neck. Her

thin, pale skin contrasted to the dark, curling hairs on the back of Jefferson's head.

"It's all right, sweetheart. Daddy's here, and I'll never leave you. Everything is all right."

"But Mommy…where's Mommy?" the little girl asked more quietly, and Andrea's heart wrenched in sympathy with the pain the small child must be suffering.

She didn't hear Jefferson's quiet response, but when he shifted his position on the bed, Andrea saw Megan's face for the first time. Her large, luminous eyes, lighter than Jefferson's, were shimmering with pooled tears. Her blond hair cascaded to her slim shoulders, which tightened as Megan attempted to stifle her remaining sobs against her father's chest. The comforting words continued as Jefferson tucked the child snugly into her bed.

Andrea backed down the hall, letting her hands guide her in the darkness. She was afraid to take her eyes off the intimate scene of father and child and yet fearful of being caught intruding on a private moment.

Once she was back in the living room, Andrea waited, pacing the room, while Jefferson continued to calm Megan. Images reeled mercilessly in her head as she paced: Jefferson comforting his daughter; Jefferson as a young, captivating senator; Jefferson lying over her, naked in the bright Pacific sun; Jefferson holding her hand while they walked barefoot in the tide.

The images flashed faster and faster with the increased tempo of her pacing. The tears that she had attempted to keep at bay were cascading freely down from her eyes to stream down her face. So caught up was she in her vivid, heart-wrenching memories that she didn't notice when Jefferson's voice had stopped soothing his child, nor when he had entered the room to stand and watch her.

Suddenly Andrea realized that she wasn't alone. A small tingling sensation in the small of her back made her whirl about to face the hallway where Jefferson was standing. She blinked back her tears and looked into Jefferson's confused face. The questions in his eyes demanded answers.

"I came to the bedroom.... I saw you with Megan," Andrea stammered, hoping somehow to explain herself. "Oh, Jefferson, I didn't mean to intrude."

"You didn't."

"I'm just so sorry about all of this," she whispered.

"It's not your fault," he assured her, walking over to her.

"But I wish there was something I could do." She turned her eyes upward to seek his.

He closed his eyes as if afraid of his own suggestion. "There is something you could do."

"What?"

His fingers reached out and touched the edge of her jaw. They stroked her skin for a second as hesitation wavered in his eyes. "I've asked you before, and I want you to think about it again. Marry me, Andrea."

"Oh, Jefferson, why?" she asked, letting herself fall against him. "You can't expect me to fill Megan's empty heart. She needs Lara, not me."

"I'm not asking you for Megan," he whispered into her hair. His warm breath seemed to caress her skin. "I'm asking you for me...for *us*. Damn it, woman, I'm trying to tell you I love you!"

His arms encircled her and pulled her tightly against him. "I'm not setting down any rules this time. We can get married immediately or we can wait, but for God's sake woman, let's do it!"

Andrea pulled herself away from him, but he drew her

closer. "When I came into this room," she stated, "I knew that you wished you had never laid eyes upon me."

"That's because I thought you would come into my life fleetingly and then be off. I can't stand being toyed with."

"I never intended to play games with you."

"Just drive me insane!"

"Never."

"But you did…for ten years. And I can't stand it any longer. I want you to marry me, and I want to go back to Victoria. Let's leave California."

"But my work…."

"And forget about New York, too! If they want you so desperately, you can freelance."

"Oh, Jefferson," she sighed, resting her head against his broad chest. She could hear his thundering heart, and she felt nearly weak at his touch. "What about Martin…and my family?"

"Let's not worry about them. For once let's think about ourselves."

"And Megan?"

"Of course Megan. What is it, Andrea? Don't you want to marry me?"

She was compelled to honesty. "I've wanted to marry you for over ten years."

A smile, radiant and warm, spread over his lips. It was off center and boyish, the smile she remembered from his youth. "Well, ma'am," he drawled, "looks like this is your lucky day."

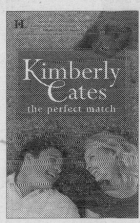

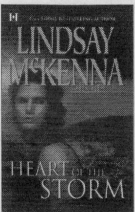